After Life

After Life

a novel

By Rhian Ellis

Introduction by Nancy Pearl

Text copyright © 2000 by Rhian Ellis
Introduction and Readers' Guide copyright © 2012 by Nancy Pearl
All rights reserved.

A Book Lust Rediscovery
Published by AmazonEncore
P.O. Box 400818
Las Vegas, NV 89140

ISBN-13: 9781612182988
ISBN-10: 1612182984

Introduction

Rhian Ellis's debut novel, *After Life*, is one of the books that always comes to mind when I tell my students at the University of Washington's Information School that no two people ever read the same novel (and, moreover, that no one ever reads the same novel twice). What I mean by this is, of course, that a novel, as a work of art, is not something that should be simply and passively received, or absorbed, by a reader. (Is this perhaps an essential part of what it *means* to be a work of art? I think so.) When we read a novel, we all bring ourselves—our thoughts, our feelings, and our experiences—to the pages of the book. And those thoughts, feelings, and experiences are, of course, different from one reader to the next. In a very real sense, then, we collaborate with the novelist in writing the book we're reading. (Novelist Paul Auster expressed the essence of what I have in mind here with admirable conciseness in his book *The Art of Hunger: Essays, Prefaces, Interviews* when he wrote: "The one thing I try to do in all my books is to leave enough room in the prose for the reader to inhabit it. Because I finally believe it's the reader who writes the book and not the writer.")

After Life is a strange and wonderful novel that I found myself inhabiting. The "roominess" in its prose is reflected in how difficult it is to categorize. When I first read it in 2000, shortly after it was first published, I remember wondering if there was any other contemporary novel that could be read in such a myriad of ways. I couldn't come up with one. Is *After Life* psychological suspense, like the novels of Barbara Vine or Shirley Jackson? Is it a tale about the often fraught relationship between mothers and daughters, like Carol Shields's *Unless* or Gail Godwin's *A Mother and Two Daughters*? Or is it a coming-of-age novel, such as *The Little Friend* by Donna Tartt or *Ellen Foster* by Kaye Gibbons? Or might it be a "whydunit" sort of mystery, in the manner of Elizabeth George's *What Came Before He Shot Her* or Ruth Rendell's *A Judgement in Stone*? (It's certainly not a "whodunit," since we know from Ellis's wonderful opening line, "First I had to get his body into the boat," that a killing has occurred, and there's no doubt about who committed it—the title of the first chapter is, after all, "what I did.")

You might think that the strangeness of *After Life* is due simply to the strangeness of many of its characters, who are mostly involved with the spirit world in one way or another as clairvoyants, mediums, fortune-tellers, psychics, and such. But for me it was mostly the ambiguity, the slipperiness, of the novel's narrator, Naomi Ash. (Ah, Naomi! I simply didn't know what to make of you.) Normally, I must confess, I don't do well with ambiguity. I would really rather know how a book ends before I begin it, and I all too often feel the urge—not always resisted successfully, alas—to peek at the last chapter immediately upon finishing the first, simply to relieve the tension. That's why I tend not to enjoy novels with unreliable narrators. The uncertainty makes me too nervous. In order to allow myself to be absorbed into the voice of the narrator (or to have the narrator's voice absorbed into me)—which for me is at the heart of the pleasure of reading—I need to believe that he or she is telling me the truth, or at least attempting, in good faith, to do so. (Thus my fascination, and love/hate relationship, with memoirs, where this is always an issue.) So Naomi both fascinated me and made me extremely uncomfortable, because I just couldn't tell how reliable she really was as a narrator.

Everything she related, from the disposal of the body in the first chapter to the resolutions of the last, sounded so plausible. Perhaps too plausible? I just couldn't shake off the niggling questions that arose: Has Naomi really told us everything that she could have about her childhood? And her relationship to Peter (the body she's trying to get into the boat)—has she told us all that we need to know about his death? And if not, might the book mean something entirely different than what I thought? And then I realized that that uncertainty—what kind of book am I reading? what is Naomi really like?—despite my discomfort with it, is a major reason why I fell under the spell of *After Life* and why I knew I had to include it in the Book Lust Rediscoveries series.

After Life held other delights for me as well. The way an author uses language is always important to me in the books I choose to read. I realized a long time ago that, of all the books I've most enjoyed, the vast majority are characterized by their authors' ability to put words together in ways that surprise and enchant me, ways that cause me to look at the world as I never had before. Invariably, there are sentences and paragraphs in these books that I am compelled to read aloud to my husband (or whomever happens to be close by), post on the bulletin board in my office, and copy into the by now multi-volumed set of notebooks I have kept for years and years, which contain my favorite poems and lines from the books I've loved, to be read to myself when I need comforting or aloud, by my husband, to help me fall asleep.

Here are two of the lines from *After Life* I wrote down in 2000 in my notebook. One is, I think, central to understanding Naomi, while the other I am drawn to simply because it puts into words an inchoate feeling I've often had.

The first: "My mother began in honesty and ended in fraud; I began in fraud and ended in something at least close to truthfulness."

And the second: "…and I felt a small but swelling happiness, the kind that comes from a smooth carrying-out of an errand."

Perfection.

Finally there is Ellis's evocation of the setting of *After Life*. Although I am a novel reader who, as might be apparent by now, tends to pay more attention to character development and agility with language than a novel's setting (unless I'm reading historical fiction), I found it impossible not to be wowed by the way Ellis brought the upstate New York town of Train Line to life. Train Line is based on the real community of Lily Dale, New York, which I felt I had heard of before I read Ellis's novel. But maybe not. I'd certainly never felt any particular urge to visit there until after my first reading of *After Life*. When I finished the novel, I actually sat down at my computer and tried to figure out how many planes, trains, and buses it might take for me to get there from Seattle. (And believe me, it was much harder to get that kind of information in 2000 than it is today.) I still Google Lily Dale occasionally, noting with a skeptic's delight that I could obtain a list of all the registered mediums in town, should I ever feel the need to consult with one. I have yet to make the trip, in part, I think, for fear that the possibly mundane reality of Lily Dale would mar the wonder of Train Line and of the young woman at the center of this unforgettable tale (written by Rhian Ellis—and me).

I hope you enjoy *After Life* as much as I did.

Nancy Pearl

for Diane Vreuls and Stuart Friebert
and my parents, Sally and Robert Ellis,
with love

Notes and Acknowledgments

Spiritualism is a philosophy, science, and religion founded in the nineteenth century and still practiced by many thousands of people across the world. This book, however, is a work of fiction, and the specific principles and beliefs set forth here are not meant to represent those of any particular group, sect, church, or person.

Among the books I consulted while writing this novel are *Thirty Years of Psychical Research* by Charles Richet; *Zolar's Book of the Spirits* by Zolar; *The Science of Seership* by Geoffrey Hodson; *The Law of Psychic Phenomena* by Thomson Jay Hudson; *Beware Familiar Spirits* by John Mulholland; and *The "I AM" Discourses*, volume 3, by the Ascended Master Saint Germain.

For help with research into Spiritualism, thanks to my sister and brother-in-law, Laura and David Goodworth. For New Orleans info, thanks to Mary Bosworth.

And for other kinds of help, thanks to: Julie Grau, Lisa Bankoff, Mary Evans, Lisa Dicker, Alex Babanskyj, Rebecca James, Ed Skoog, Jill Marquis, and Leslie Van Stavern Millar II of the Brunswick Building in Missoula, where this was written.

Deepest thanks to Betsy Lerner, to Carole DeSanti, and to John.

After Life

1

what I did

First I had to get his body into the boat. This was more than ten years ago, and I've forgotten some of what came before and after, but that night and the following day I remember in extravagant detail. I had lain awake all night, trying to imagine how I might get him off the bed and down the stairs and into the rowboat, since he weighed at least a hundred and fifty pounds and might have gone stiff. My bed, I remember, felt absurdly uncomfortable, as if someone had slipped walnuts and bolts into the layer just beneath the ticking, and there was something sharp and prickly, like hay, poking out of my pillow into my face and neck, yet I hardly moved all night. Every noise paralyzed me with fear. I had to force my eyes shut to think, literally hold them shut with my fingers, and in this way I worked through the problem—getting him into the boat—over and over again, allowing for variations, so that by morning I was pretty sure I had it down. Once he was in the boat it would be easy.

When it was light I sat up and put my feet on the floor. The room rocked and tilted slightly, like a room in a fun house or a ship. Lack of sleep made me dizzy, which caused a sense of unreality that I found comforting, as if now I was finally asleep, and only dreaming. But the feeling did not last, and after a minute or two I found some clothes on the floor and got dressed. I had worn these same clothes the day before, and perhaps the day before that, and as a consequence they were limp and smelled a little like onions. I washed my face in the bathroom sink, used the toilet, and went downstairs.

In the kitchen I made myself a sandwich and put it in a plastic grocery bag, then got a small shovel from the back porch. It was the trowel I used in the garden, still caked with hard lumps of dirt. I cleaned it off as well as I could with my fingers, then gathered myself together and walked over to my mother's house.

Though it was still August it was getting cold in the mornings, and the grass was dewy, and a mist hung over the lake at the end of Fox Street. The air, when I breathed it, had a taste like cold lake water. Later, I knew, it would get hot and the wind would carry the smell of the ketchup factory from across the lake in Wallamee. That smell had always been a signal for me to dig out my leather shoes and wool skirts, that summer was ending and school was about to begin. Though I had been out of school for four years by that time, the smell still had the power to excite me, or more exactly, stimulate me. I had a tendency to be lazy in summers. It was a delicious feeling at first, but it cloyed. Fall aroused me to action, though I don't mean this as an excuse for what happened.

The boat—a battered metal rowboat with peeling green paint that had washed ashore on Train Line's little beach one day, and that no one else had wanted to claim—was in the garage behind my mother's house. The garage was rickety and packed with junk, but I kept my boat there because I had no storage space at my apartment. I took it out on the lake quite often, so I was pretty sure that anyone seeing me drag it down to the dock would not find it odd. I lugged the boat up to the back door, attached the hose to the outdoor faucet, and pretended to wash the hull. Water tributaried across the small dead lawn and puddled around the laundry pole. The sun, though it was barely up, burned the top of my head and made me feel spotlit and uncomfortable, as if I was being watched. Just in case, I continued my charade: giving the hull another good rinse, winding the hose back up, smiling slightly. Then I got a blue tarpaulin and some nylon rope out of the garage and went inside to get Peter.

He was where I'd left him, of course, in the upstairs bedroom that had once been mine. When I was a little girl, I'd demanded red gingham wallpaper. It was still there. So were the shelf of paperbacks, the failed ant farm, the blue-flowered linoleum, and the rag rug made from my old dresses. It smelled of dust and dead wasps, the closed-in odor it always got in summer when I'd left the window shut. And another smell, a hot, difficult one I didn't want to acknowledge: Peter's smell. He smelled more powerfully like himself now that he was dead than he had when he was alive. It made me angry—suddenly and obscurely—that this had been done to my room, where I had once been so happy.

Peter was in bed. One of his feet, still in its worn brown shoe, stuck out from the blankets. I recalled closing his eyes when it happened—I was sure I had done it—I remembered that I couldn't look while I was doing it and that I had to turn away and find them by touch. But now one had opened up again. It stared milkily at the lightbulb on the ceiling. With my thumb I pushed the lid down again; this time it would stay only halfway shut. His mouth hung open, too, but there was nothing I could do about that except not look at it. It occurred to me then that I had not lost my mind, but had instead put it somewhere so far away and hard to reach that I had little hope of ever retrieving it.

Dragging him from the bed onto the tarpaulin, which I'd spread on the floor, was like pulling a long root from damp soil. I couldn't lift him, so I tugged him by his arm, then by his leg, and little by little extracted him from the bed. He hit the floor and the whole house shook. Again without looking at his face, I got him wrapped in the tarpaulin. By this time I was sweating and having trouble catching my breath. I sat down to rest at the top of the narrow staircase and looked down into the living room below. Hardly any light made it past the drapes, but I could see the glint of the clock pendulum and the long-legged shape of the oscillating fan. *Good-bye,* I said to it. *So long.* I wasn't really going anywhere; I'd be coming back and this room would be exactly the same, but this ordinary fact was impossible to believe.

I had to push Peter down the stairs. He slid, like a large fish, about halfway, then I pushed him again.

⚮

I dragged him to the boat, tipped it onto its side, and rolled Peter into it, then hauled the boat the block and a half to the lake. Anyone looking might have noticed I had something bulky and heavy in it, but I was right to think no one would be out. Summer was almost over.

On the lake, I rowed hard, my feet braced somewhat awkwardly on either side of Peter. Mist still hung over the surface, and droplets clung to my eyelashes and hair. The lake had been carved by glaciers; it was long and slender as a crooked finger. I rowed the length for half an hour, then navigated my way through a narrow inlet. There were cattails here, and the wreck of an old beaver dam, but my boat was steady in the water and nimble, and I slipped right by.

I was going to a place I'd visited a few times as a teenager, at the end of the lake and up the shore a bit. In fact, once I'd brought Peter there for a picnic. It was a grassy clearing, hidden from boaters on the lake by a tree-covered spit of land. A little farther inland there was a dilapidated barn: the only sign of people anywhere around. At the edge of this clearing, about fifteen feet from shore, was where I planned to dig the hole.

I left Peter in the boat while I dug. I didn't care if the hole was very deep, just that it was long enough. Once when I was a child I tried burying a dead cat in a hole not big enough for it, and I still cannot forget pushing down on it to make it fit, pressing its head with my trowel. Its ears filled horribly with dirt.

⚮

It took all day. Though it was a clearing there were lots of rocks and roots I had to dig out, but I'd told myself all night that I would be patient, that I wouldn't do a rush job under any circumstances. At one point, a pair of fishermen floated around the spit. I lay in the weeds, looking at my dirty hands and praying they wouldn't find my boat, which was hidden in a stand of cattails. I could hear them talking.

"Too shady back here, man."

"You think?"

"Like the underside of my ass."

"Well. All right."

"I know this other place, back where we were."

"Whatever you say, man."

They floated off again.

The dirt, which was soft and wet, had a fetid odor. It was the smell the lake acquired in summer, sometimes, when the water fell and exposed the rank mud. It was an odor of such active decay that I felt reassured—the earth would absorb Peter in no time.

I couldn't eat the lunch I'd brought.

By mid-afternoon the hole was about four feet deep and five and a half feet long: the length of Peter Morton. I pulled the boat to shore—I was quite tired by this time, and shaking—tipped Peter onto the ground, then rowed out around the spit to make sure no one was coming. There was one boat on the lake, a speedboat, but it was far off and didn't appear to be headed in my direction, so I rowed the boat to shore again.

I realized, after I'd dragged Peter over to the hole and opened up the tarpaulin, that I should probably take his clothes off. People can be identified by their clothes; I had read this somewhere, or maybe seen it on a television mystery. The thought hit me with a wave of sickness, of almost incapacitating regret. I took his wallet from his pocket, put it in my lunch bag, then unbuttoned his shirt. I had to tear it to get it off over his arms. His pants were easier. I unzipped the fly and pulled them down, an action so familiar I could close my eyes and pretend for a moment that we were somewhere else, in any of the dozens of places we had made love. I quickly tugged off his briefs and rolled him into the hole.

Oh, Peter!

He lay facedown. He had pretty hair, black and wavy and shiny as an otter's. I couldn't bring myself to throw dirt on it. I couldn't do it to his narrow back, either, with its delicate, knobby spine and shadowed ribs. I was almost knocked over by an urge, then, to pull his face out of the muck and blow into his mouth, to clear the mud from his eyes and his nose and save him.

I turned and ran into the woods. I despaired that I would never get lost in them, that I would always be with myself, that the world was not big enough to swallow me whole. I wanted him to get up and be alive again; I wanted to fly apart. My forehead slammed and tore against the rough bark of a hickory tree, and the pain calmed me.

Wiping blood from my eyes, I filled the hole.

When it was all done, I threw my shovel and his clothes, weighted with stones, into the lake and walked up the rise to the old barn. Inside I found a wooden trough full of rainwater. I washed my hands and face as well as I could, then I lay down on a fallen beam, looking upward. Through the gapped boards of the roof, the sky was blue. I watched clouds slide by.

It was a ruined world.

2

intercom

When I was a child we lived in a house with an intercom. It looked like a telephone but it was made of a tortoiseshell kind of plastic, and instead of a dial it had a set of buttons, numbered one to eleven for all the rooms of the house. You could speak into the handset and your voice would come out of a speaker in whichever room you chose. This house also had a complicated and thorough system of dumbwaiters. Someone small enough—me, at the time—could climb inside and show up in any one of several rooms or corridors, or simply sit there inside the walls, listening.

Since my mother was a medium, and held séances and gave readings at home, she found these features handy. Sometimes she let me work as her accomplice. I'd rap out ghostly messages from my place behind paintings, I'd fling objects across the room, I'd whisper through the intercom's cracked wiring. Sometimes I'd hold the handset on the other side of a box fan, and speak through that, which gave my voice an interesting, otherworldly sound. Once my mother dressed me up in a lace tablecloth, doused me with talcum powder, and had me stumble around the séance room, posing as somebody's dead child.

My mother was not, however, entirely a fraud. The floating trumpets, the ectoplasm, the spirit rappings: all this, she said, was Theater. Every profession has its necessary theater—teachers with their apples and rulers, doctors with their tongue depressors and white coats. People demand a show. This was especially true in New Orleans, where we lived at the time. In that city you couldn't go to a parade without having candy and beads hurled at you, or being flashed by somebody in a fright wig, even on the

Fourth of July. My mother's theatrics, she said, were a kind of misdirection. If she could shock and astound, she'd crack open a tiny hole in people's skeptical armor—only briefly, perhaps, but long enough to sneak some truth in. People believe first, disbelieve later. Or anyway, that's what she said.

But I, for one, couldn't always disentangle the real from the fraudulent, the truth from its trappings. Sometimes it seemed as if my mother's fakery was just a more interesting and beautiful version of what was real. Sometimes it seemed that the truth *needed* the lies, as if there wouldn't be any truth without them. At any rate, whatever my mother was doing, it was a rare and powerful thing, perhaps even a form of magic. It enthralled me.

❧

We lived in New Orleans until I was ten. My memories of that time are scattered and odd but mostly good: taking baths in the kitchen sink while my family sat around the table, playing backgammon; a sugar skull given to me by a customer of my mother, which I left under my bed until one day when I found it half-dissolved and swarmed over with ants; the green velvet walls of the séance room; and helping my mother, when I was three or four, to attach the fabric to the walls with a staple gun. Our house didn't have air-conditioning, so every room had a collection of fans—ceiling, box, oscillating, paper—each with its own prevailing winds. Summers, we'd stagger from room to room and fan to fan, windblown and exhausted. To escape the heat, my grandfather and I went to the movies. I remember buying pickles in brown paper and eating them in the chilly dark. When the movie was over and we stepped back outside, the heat would feel intensely good for a while, damp and intimate but slightly threatening, like the breath of someone leaning in too close. Later, when my mother and I left for good, I would miss this heat more than I missed the house, or the city, or even what was left of my family by then.

This was my family: my mother and her parents. My grandparents were kind, shy people; my grandmother was a librarian at my school, Saint Ann's, while my grandfather—a gentle old man with a fringe of white hair on his forehead—kept house. He'd sold his stationery store around the time I was born and now puttered around in his tennis shoes, always sweeping and pulling weeds. The house belonged to my grandfather. It even looked a little like him: tall, hunched, dapper.

The man who was my father did not live with us. He was my mother's dentist and a good friend of hers, but no one, she said, she could marry. Anyway, he was already married. He visited us now and then, and would sometimes hang around during his lunch hour, wearing a white dentist coat covered with little blood spatters. My mother fixed him sandwiches and he made polite conversation with me. He called me "Squirt." I was not supposed to let on to him that I knew he was my father.

It was an awkward situation. My mother loved him. I could tell by the way she pretended not to: she avoided his eyes if anyone else was looking, and made a big deal about "forgetting" her dental appointments, as if they meant nothing to her, but she always called to reschedule. He might have loved her, too, though my mother didn't think so. "Two people never love each other at the same time," she told me once. She had just returned from a dental appointment and was sitting in the kitchen holding a teabag to a tooth, and frowning. "One loves, and the other is in love with *being* loved. The fun is in guessing which one's you."

Bottles of perfume and silk scarves had a way of appearing around the house, and we were never short of toothbrushes. But if they ever planned to get together, if he ever thought about leaving his wife, I knew nothing about it. I would be surprised if he did. Run off with my mother? She did not seem to be the running-off-with kind. She was tall and bossy and had a big nose; I couldn't picture her collapsing in someone's arms, or galloping away on horseback. In any case, by the time I was seven or eight he was gone, to an army base in the western part of the state. And that was that. I never saw him again, though before he left he gave me a checkup and a set of windup choppers. To tell the truth, though, I was relieved. I didn't like what he did to my mother. He made her moony and wistful, made her want something she could not have.

It would have been easier for her, I think, if he had died. She had special access to the dead. Living, but disappeared, he was completely out of the picture. If he'd died she'd at least have bits of him, now and then: his voice, flattened and tinny and small, floating from her trumpet, or a whiff of his aftershave in a darkened room, or—best of all—his ghostly fingers, probing her mouth for signs of decay.

⁓⊹⁓

Those years, the years we lived in my grandfather's house, my mother practiced a particularly outdated and quaint brand of spiritualism. She didn't know. This was the seventies, and by then most mediums had turned into "psychics" or "tarot card readers," and spent more time developing their ESP than communing with the departed. The few remaining spirit trumpets—the big tin cones that amplify the voices of the dead during séances—were preserved in museums or stashed in attics, but my mother had one, and sometimes it even levitated for her. I think she suspended it from a horsehair; it was lighter than you'd think. Modern psychics have no use for the dead at all. The living is what they care about, and lottery numbers, and horoscopes. My mother wasn't aware of this trend. She learned what she knew from books. She ordered her equipment out of an obscure catalog from somewhere up north. I remember it—the pages were rough newsprint; the printing type, minuscule.

But her work had a large following, especially among the old and morbid. One of these people was a woman named Beryl Kemper, who was obsessed with the thought of her own death. When she and my mother got together for one-on-one sessions, which they did every other week or so for several years, she'd often whip out her left hand and display the break in her lifeline. "What do you think?" she'd ask my mother, breathless. "Do you think I have three more years? It looks to me like I have at least two. Look at that crossline there."

My mother, neither fortune-teller nor palmist, would politely push Miss Beryl's doomed hand back into her lap. "You know that stuff's bunk. Besides, your left hand's what you were born with, and the right is what you do with it. You can guess my advice, Beryl."

They'd drink coffee and gossip for several minutes, then my mother would take both Beryl's hands into her own, as if to warm them. "Your mother's here, dear," she might say, looking right into Miss Beryl's eyes. "She wants you to take better care of yourself. There's an empty pot on the stove, she says. Does that makes sense to you?" Beryl ate it up. She didn't need evidence—a floating guitar or a tipping table—as some people did. The session would always end with a long chat with Miss Beryl's dead daughter, via the intercom. I would put on a gaspy, choked voice, because Irene had died of the croup when she was a little girl. For a baby, Irene could impart a great deal of wisdom. I would sometimes read from *The "I AM" Discourses*:

> Out of the heart of that Great Silence comes the
> Ceaseless, Pouring Stream of Life, of which each one
> is an individuized part. That Life is you, Eternally,
> Perfectly, Self-sustained…

Beryl knew it was me. How could she not? But she'd always cry to hear "Irene's" voice, and she seemed comforted by my mother's prayer, which ended, "And there is no Death, and there are no Dead. Amen." If I met her in the kitchen as she was leaving, she'd squeeze my shoulder and tell me to come by her house on my way home from school, so she could give me a Mallow Cup. Whether what had happened was "real" or not didn't matter a bit to Miss Beryl. She—and really, all of my mother's customers—swallowed it whole, and why not? My mother made their lives more interesting and more meaningful. From these old women I learned that belief didn't have to be something you got after weighing the evidence; you could just have it. Belief was a decision you could make.

Miss Beryl lived on Carondelet Street, which wasn't on my way home from anywhere. But sometimes I wandered around after school, chasing cats and looking for money on the sidewalk, and one day I decided I would stop by and say Hello to Miss Beryl, and maybe get my candy. Mostly, I wanted to see the house where a dead girl had lived. I had never known any real dead people, let alone dead children.

I knocked on the door, and after a long wait Miss Beryl answered, surprised to see me and without any makeup on. She let me in, though, and I stood in her front room while she burrowed through mounds of things, looking for her Mallow Cups. On the wall, over the piano, there was a blown-up picture of a child's face, a girl's. There was something odd about the eyes.

"That's Irene in her casket," said Miss Beryl. "I had a man paint her eyes in."

It was chilling. I stared and stared at the photograph, unable to get enough of it. Her pale hair was clasped with two silver clips, and the fingers of one hand curled along the bottom of the picture, the nails dark. Her painted eyes could have shot bullets.

When I said good-bye and was back on the sidewalk again, I noticed the Mallow Cup Miss Beryl had given me was so old—its yellow wrapper faded to white—it might have once belonged to Irene. The chocolate gave way under my fingers into a sticky, powdery mass, and the marshmallow in the middle was tough as cartilage. It smelled like an old book. I ate the thing anyway.

For a long time after that I could not think about death without remembering the photograph of Irene Kemper in her casket. That picture became death to me: to be dead meant being suspended over someone's cluttered piano, twice life-size, eyes forced open in an unnatural, unblinking gaze, forever.

ର୍ଧ

If I were to die, I often wondered, what would my mother do? How would she feel? These questions haunted me. Until I was eleven or twelve, I was sick a lot—so sick that I sometimes thought I *would* die, though I never mentioned this to anyone. My illness was mysterious: every couple of months I'd begin throwing up everything I ate or drank, and couldn't even brush my teeth without vomiting. This would go on for a week or more. I'd lie in bed almost unable to move, falling in and out of sleep, under the *flick flick flick* of the ceiling fan. If I touched my fingers to my lips they felt like something else, not like lips at all, but like a bit of carved ivory or bone. I'd listen to the voices of people in the street outside and not remember what it was like to be well.

The doctor didn't know what it was. Except for the throwing up, I was fine. He gave me a bottle of pink stuff I couldn't keep down and some advice: *Don't be so nervous! Take some deep breaths if you feel like you're going to heave-ho. Lots of fresh air can't hurt.*

Before he left, the doctor would pat my hand and tell me it would pass, and it would. After a week or so I'd wake up and see a glass of water by my bed, and it would look good. I'd sit up on my elbow and drink a little, then a little more. Later, when I woke up again, I'd notice the sunlight in the leaves by the window, and the shadows on the wall, and the bright blues and reds of the books on my shelves. Once, I smelled my grandfather cooking chicken downstairs, so I crept down to the kitchen, joined my family at the table, and began to eat without saying a word. My mother and grandmother glanced at each other, then at me.

"I had a little chat with the doctor," said my mother. "He said it's all in your head." She gave me an accusatory look.

"My *head*?"

"What's that supposed to mean?" asked my grandfather. He frowned, brandishing his silverware.

What she meant was, I was doing it for attention, though not necessarily on purpose. The very thought made my heart pound with shame.

"Utter baloney," said my grandfather.

"She knows," said my mother, still giving me a look.

I swallowed my chicken. Could it be true?

The next time I was sick, my mother's manner was brusque and distracted. She set a glass of water on my night table and squinted out the window. It was raining.

"I'm *not* doing it on purpose," I whispered. My mouth was parched, dry as paper.

"Oh, I know," she said, still watching the rain. "But you don't see me or your grandmother getting sick, do you? We have work to do. We couldn't possibly lie around in bed."

I closed my eyes, trying to cry, but no tears came.

"You're not much of a trooper, are you?" said my mother.

∾⚬∾

I didn't die, of course. Instead, my grandmother did. It was a shock to all of us; she seemed immortal, not old at all, though she must have been seventy then. One spring afternoon she did not come home from work at Saint Ann's. That night my mother called the police, who found her bicycle the next day, propped up against a fire hydrant in a not-very-nice part of town. Foul play was suspected. And though they found her a few hours later, alive but incoherent, wandering along the riverfront, she died in the hospital before we could get there. She'd had several strokes.

My mother screamed in the hospital waiting room. *How could this happen?* she wanted to know. How could a sick old lady walk around town for an entire day, without anyone helping her?

Unfortunately, they said, there's no shortage of sick old ladies in this town. And anyway, somebody did help her. When the police found her, she was clutching a sack lunch some kind person had given her: an egg salad sandwich, a nectarine, and three sugar cookies.

They handed the sack lunch over to my mother, who pressed it to her face and wept.

But that was all the grief she allowed herself. By the time we got home that afternoon, she was, to all appearances, over it: she threw herself into housecleaning and funeral preparations with the energy of someone organizing a carnival ball. My grandfather, shrunken and pale, climbed the stairs slowly and shut himself in his bedroom. I wandered from room to room, crying and hiccuping. In the parlor my mother swept past me, smelling of lavender furniture polish. She turned and put her large hand on my head.

"Poor Naomi. Silly Naomi. You're crying for yourself, you know. Your grandmother hasn't gone anywhere. She's right here watching you." She pointed to the corner, where there was a large vase of peacock feathers. "You're making her sad."

I wiped my tears with my fingers. There was nothing in the corner, as far as I could tell, except for the feathers, which drooped and were clumpy with dust. I tried hard to see something else, a shimmer or a quiver or a glow, but there was nothing.

"It's your grandfather you should be crying over. Stubborn fool has no faith. I don't know how he gets through the day, I really don't."

She squatted on the floor with her cleaning rags, her cotton dress pulling across her muscular back. A bead of sweat slid down her neck.

"Come, help," she said, and tossed me a rag. "In a couple of days this place will be full of weeping librarians. And don't think for a minute they won't notice the housekeeping—that's all they'll notice. That and the finger sandwiches. Right, Mother?"

It was a bit eerie. A few hours before, I had seen my grandmother lying dead on a hospital bed, looking not at all like herself—gray-faced, her hair tied on the top of her head with a rubber band—and now my mother was chatting with her as if nothing had happened, as if my grandmother had simply misplaced her body but might find it again at any time, under a sofa cushion or in the back of the fridge. Until that moment, spiritualism had been a fun sort of game to me, but suddenly the momentousness of it unfolded darkly in front of me: it could allow you to raise the dead.

I rubbed hard at a table leg, watching my mother. A dark lock of her hair slipped down over her forehead; she left it there. She was beautiful, in spite of her big nose and broad, mannish shoulders. I wanted to put my arms around her and bury my face in her bosom, but I knew if I tried anything like that she'd give me a shove and tell me to act my age, so I didn't. Instead, I knelt alongside her and worked hard at polishing the table leg.

She glanced over at me and nodded approvingly. "Good girl."

I rubbed harder. I loved her so much.

ço

Over the next few months, my mother's mediumship acquired a new intensity. All sorts of exceptionally peculiar people—and not just old ones, either—began hanging around the house: a young man with hoop earrings, a woman who scolded me for my "prickly aura." And others: hippies and transvestites and young women in torn vintage dresses. They would start in the kitchen, eating crackers and cheese and drinking tea with my mother, then move into the living room and begin rummaging through the liquor cabinet. They'd lie on the sofa with their feet hanging over the armrest, drinking and shedding crumbs and giggling at nothing. By dark they'd be in the séance room, alternately silent and roaring with laughter. This is when my mother took on her new name: no longer Patsy Ash, she was now Madame Galina Ash, or sometimes just Mother Galina. She began to wear tight sweaters and slacks and eye makeup, and she was voluptuous and dark: sexy. She painted her nails fire-engine red, toes as well as fingers.

I found myself feeling nervous and vaguely jealous. My mother needed less and less help that summer, so I was left to moon around the house alone, or play board games with my grandfather. He wasn't taking the constant parade of visitors well. "Lowlifes," he called them, ungenerously. "Parasite weirdo circus freaks." We hid out in his room.

It was the spirit of my grandmother, I discovered one day, that was causing all this uproar. I found this out by climbing into the dumbwaiter and squeaking up behind the wall of the séance room. I was getting too big for it, for sure: I had to press my face into my knees, which made it hard to breathe. But I was certain about what I heard.

"Dora?" said someone, possibly the young man with the earrings. "How are you feeling today? Are you ready to help us?" This was said in the too-loud, condescending tone people use when speaking to the very old, the very young, or spirits.

There was a groan. It sounded like my mother, but I couldn't tell for sure.

"That's all right, Dora, take your time."

Dora Ash was my grandmother's name. The woman had no use for spiritualism; she, like my grandfather, was a lapsed Catholic, an ardent materialist until the day she died. To think of her on the other side of the wall, talking to these people, shocked me.

I listened for a while. Most of what "Dora" said was mumbled, and I couldn't make it out. She said something about "Paradise," something about "The River." The voice came from different places in the room, and I heard what sounded like footsteps. It took a while for me to figure it out: my grandmother was controlling my mother's body, speaking through her, and walking around the room. I imagined my mother's eyes closed, her head lolling on her shoulder, her feet doing a slow shuffle, and for a moment I was sickened with embarrassment for her. But then I was struck with another thought: what if it *was* my grandmother in there? Could the soul of my grandmother—who was a small person, and fragile, like a shorebird—have put on her daughter's body like a huge and heavy dress? And if so, where, then, was my mother?

The dumbwaiter was hot and had a sour, dusty smell. Claustrophobia wrapped me in its panicky arms. I wanted to push the walls away from me, explode out of there and drink up the fresh air like water, but for the moment I was trapped, like the house's own soul.

Breathing slowly, I felt for the ropes, then inched the dumbwaiter upward. I stopped outside my grandfather's room and risked opening the door a crack, then pressed my eye to the opening. He was absorbed in a jigsaw puzzle and didn't hear me. The back of the old man's neck was red and creased and prickled with short white hairs, and a plate with a cheese sandwich, half-eaten, sat on the card table by his elbow. He was hunched in a pool of yellow light. When he picked up the puzzle box to examine it, I saw what it was: the Taj Mahal in front of a greenish, faded sky. Over the months he had done dozens of puzzles, always buildings, always beautiful: monument after monument to his tireless, bottomless, glorious loneliness.

☙

The heat that summer was an aberration—a torment. For months the city was delirious with fever, but no rains came. Giant purple clouds rolled in every afternoon, glared down at us, and moved on. The heat itself seemed to originate not from the sun, but from the things around us: the buildings and the cars and the trees, and in particular, the people. The furniture in our house seemed too hot to touch. Eating was difficult; wearing clothes oppressive. Small things began to go to pieces. Plaster walls softened; clothes soured in their drawers. A peculiar odor filled the house—it was like a wet animal at first, and then like a dead one—and finally my grandfather discovered a plastic sack of potatoes in the back of a cupboard, deliquesced.

In spite of this strange weather, or perhaps because of it, my grandmother continued her visits. She had things to say about it, and about politics and the stock market, and Indian ancestors, and impending illnesses. Once, she made a flashlight gallop across the room. A perfume pervaded the room when she appeared—a minty, lily-of-the-valley-type scent, according to the rumors. People you'd never expect to see at a séance showed up at the ones my mother held. The wrong types, my grandfather said: gangsters and buffoons. But it was as if the weather had persuaded people that anything was possible, that everything they thought they knew about the world had come unfixed.

One night I overheard an argument between my mother and grandfather. Before his wife died, my grandfather never expressed much of an opinion about spiritualism. He tolerated everything, and would nod and say, "Interesting," or "What do you know!" when shown spirit photographs, spirit fingerprints in wax, flowers that appeared from nowhere. But things had gone too far.

"My wife is dead," he told my mother. *"Dead!"*

"Not to me, she isn't," she said. They were in the kitchen, leaning over the table at each other. "To me she's still here. To me! And that's what a spirit *is*. I feel sorry for you, if she really is dead to you."

My grandfather's face darkened. He began to shake. "You have the wrong woman!" he roared.

~❧~

Though my mother enjoyed her sudden popularity, it had its problems. The least of them was the friction with my grandfather. He was, above all, a quiet man, and would usually rather ignore what was happening in his house than make a scene. More problematic were the police. There were rumors that my mother was running some kind of drug den. This they couldn't prove, so then they told her that fortune-telling for money was illegal in

New Orleans. My mother spent a lot of energy trying to convince them that what she was doing was religion. They wanted to know what church. She actually found one—the Church of Spiritualist Studies, headquartered in upstate New York. She joined a local branch. It met every Monday in a tiny storefront on Terpsichore Street. I went with her often. There were folding chairs and plates of snacks and a podium draped in white velvet. Most of the spiritualists were quite old, but I was used to that. They took turns giving lectures: "The Rainbow as Spirit Matter" was one, "Was Eisenhower a Spiritualist?" another. Dull as it was, I was relieved to be going to church at last. I had never gotten over feeling that I could die at any time, and, in that Catholic city, I couldn't help but feel that not going to church was a very bad idea. And I liked this kind of spiritualism: predictable, bookish, reverent.

Most of all, I enjoyed the message service at the end of every lecture. Each week a different medium was scheduled to serve. She or he stood in front of the podium and gave out spirit messages to the audience—*I have an Emma here. Does anyone here know an Emma? It might be her middle name. A small woman, white hair…that's right, she's yours, Barnard…*—prosaic things, for the most part. The recipient of the message would smile and respond loudly and happily, though they must have all gotten ten thousand such messages during their spiritualist careers. I got very few, myself. Once a tiny fat woman told me, in no uncertain terms, that my father was there. She said that he wanted me to know that he loved me very, very much, and that he was happy in the afterlife, and that he didn't miss me because he visited me every single night while I was asleep.

I leaned over to my mother and whispered, "But he's not dead, is he?"

She rolled her eyes. "Sloppy work," she whispered back.

Another time, I was told that I had to take better care of my eyes, because this life would have a lot to show me. I touched my eyes through their lids. They felt hot, tender, ready to explode.

We left New Orleans suddenly, one November morning. That is, my mother and I left. My grandfather remained, alone, in the tall, narrow house full of contraptions he had no use for. While we stood on the curb, waiting for the taxicab that would take us to the bus station, he stayed inside. He was too softhearted to even say, So long. From the back window of the taxi I caught a glimpse of him, watching us leave from my old bedroom then letting the curtain fall shut. He was my pal, my staunchest ally, but by leaving I had betrayed him. I hadn't had a choice, of course. But in my love for my mother I knew I was complicit, and when he died, a few years later, I believed that in the subtlest way I had helped kill him.

The Church of Spiritualist Studies owned a whole town in the middle of New York State, and that's where we were headed. My mother showed me the pamphlet on the bus. Originally, the town—it was called Train Line—had been planned as a spiritualist summer camp, though people now lived there year round. There was a lake with swans, many tall trees, tiny gingerbread cottages. We'd stay there a few months, maybe, at least until the police forgot about her. She thought they might have had our house under surveillance: she found some tramped-down grass and a pile of candy bar wrappers under a bush in our side yard. These, I knew, were my grandfather's. He'd taken to lurking out there, sick of the constant comings and goings in our house. For months my mother had been growing increasingly nervous and paranoid, overwhelmed by the new life she'd created for herself, and our leaving had the character of flight: things forgotten and left undone, mail unforwarded.

We got on the bus and trundled northward. Outside, the landscape stiffened and cracked. One morning we were wakened by the idling bus to find ourselves surrounded by snow. I'd never seen it before, or at least, so much of it—occasionally a few damp flakes fell in New Orleans, melting before they hit the ground—and at first I thought we'd parked in a field of concrete. My mother took my arm and we ran out to the gas station to buy a box of crackers before the bus left again, our impractical shoes slipping on the asphalt. The air smelled different, like water in a tin bucket, and crows flapped in circles over our heads. When I spoke, my voice fell straight out of my mouth, completely swallowed up by snow.

Somewhere in Pennsylvania we had to switch bus lines, and there was a long layover. It was eight o'clock in the morning. We tried to sleep in the molded plastic bus station chairs, acrobating ourselves into complicated positions, but failing that we went outside and took a walk along the highway. The sun was just up. It was watery pale and much farther away than it usually seemed. A cornfield stretched along one side of the road, its dead, broken stalks poking through a crust of snow. My mother walked briskly. Her pantsuit flapped against her legs, and her hair, sprayed into a stiff globe, bobbed along with her gait. I had to skip to keep up.

Not far from the road there was a house. It was long abandoned; we could tell because none of the windows had glass in them and the front door hung open like a mouth. The clapboard siding was silver in the morning light, as if it had never been painted, and there seemed to be no way to get to the house other than cutting across the field. We waded through the ditch, my mother taking my hand, and tromped toward it.

The front steps of the house had been taken away, so we clambered up some broken cinder blocks to get in through the doorway. We walked the house carefully, watching for weak floorboards. There was nothing in it but wallpaper—so faded I couldn't make out the pattern: flowers, maybe, or faces—and a rusted iron stove, and a suitcase. The suitcase lay open on the floor of an upstairs bedroom, as if someone had stayed for a bit, then left without it, arms full of clothes. It had a water-stained, aqua-blue lining.

My mother said she knew all about the people who'd lived there. She could feel it. She walked around, touching window frames and doorjambs.

"Here," she said. "Here's where the young daughter lay, in a bed right here. See how she could look out the window?" Through the glassless panes I could see more cornfield, a stand of trees at the end of it, some hills behind. It was all a dull winter gray. "She died in springtime. She knew she'd never get to walk through the woods again, but she could look at them and imagine it. She died of consumption. Lots of people did, in the old days."

"Really?" I said.

She nodded slowly, her large glasses opaque with reflections. Something about my mother's remarks made me uncomfortable. I had my own feelings—surprisingly powerful ones—about who once lived here. A nasty old woman, hoarding her things, going slowly mad, alone. She would put on a pair of black rubber boots and get her dog and go for walks in the cornfields.

"Honestly!" said my mother, angrily turning to me. "Do you have to stomp when you walk? Be quiet!"

I trailed behind her as she walked slowly through the other rooms. Now and then she stopped to caress the wallpaper, her hand cupped and fingers splayed in a gesture of such forceful intimacy that I found it hard to watch. The old woman— my old woman—would never survive in the bright light of my mother's vision.

The house was so quiet. Sunlight filled the empty rooms.

∽✧∾

We got to Train Line early that evening. The bus dropped us off at the tall iron front gate. We'd rented a house over the phone but had no idea how to find the place, so I waited by our suitcases while my mother went to look for the main office. Alone with our stuff, I realized I had brought all the wrong things: a new stuffed dog that I hadn't even named yet, a dictionary, and a glass jar full of coins I'd collected. It had seemed foolish to leave money behind. The thought that there were so many things that I might never see again—my mother's cauliflower-shaped pot-holders, or my old slippers—struck me with tremendous force. I wanted to cry out. A cold wind blew off Lake Wallamee, biting my lips and ears and chilling my skull. I no longer owned even a hat.

When my mother came back, she brought a short, chubby woman who was wearing a T-shirt and rubber thongs. She had black hair and giant breasts. She noticed I was staring at her.

"I don't need a coat because I don't feel the cold," she said. "My skin gives off heat. Feel my arm."

I felt it. It didn't seem especially hot to me, though it was quite hairy for a woman's.

"Naomi, this is Mrs. Blackthorn," said my mother.

I curtsied—my grandfather had taught me that. "How do you do?"

"Oh, for Christ's sake, call me Robin," said the woman, and grabbed three of our suitcases.

We followed her up a narrow, unpaved street lined with houses. The houses were very small, pushed right close together, with no room in front of them for yards. They had one or two stories and large pointed roofs. Most were dark and closed up, but lights burned in some, and the glow of a television in others. My first impression of the town was of clutter. Cars were parked nearly on the front steps, cats jumped from porch roofs and windowsills, hanging plants and wind chimes and mobiles dan-gled by every door, WINNIE SANDOX—said one painted wooden sign—READER. And another: MRS. LAWRENCE, MEDIUM, IS OUT. I couldn't believe it: a town made just for us. The air was bitter and smoky, something I'd later learn to associate with wood stoves.

We stopped in front of a shabby cottage with a frill of gin-gerbread under its eaves. Robin Blackthorn fumbled with a ring of keys, then bumped the door open with her hip. She said to call the office if we needed anything, and we went inside.

∽✕∾

The next few years were the coldest of my life. We heated with kerosene, which meant we had to keep a window cracked open so we wouldn't suffocate. I'd wake up in the morning with snow in my hair, with ice crusted on the wallpaper. Our windows got so caked with ice I'd have to melt a little hole with my thumb to see out of. Even in the summer, when it was quite warm outside and even hot, I imagined that if I stuck my fingers deep into the soil I'd find ice crystals, a permafrost. I put on weight, maybe because I wasn't getting sick anymore, or maybe my body wanted to stay warm. If so, it didn't work. Every year the cold sank deeper into me.

From the little window in my bedroom I could see Lake Wallamee. In the winter it froze, and people rode snowmobiles and skied across it. For those months it would look like a field, vast and remarkably flat, the crops snowed under. The rest of the year it varied in blueness: sometimes gray, sometimes a deep navy, sometimes an algae-choked green. Train Line was on a spit, so the lake surrounded it on three sides. If I pressed my face to the window glass I could see the lake, its ripples flashing silver behind the trees, in any direction I looked. I imagined it had no bottom. It seemed like that to me: dangerous, enveloping, infinitely secretive.

∽✕∾

I thought of a strange thing, lying in my new bed that first night. Strange shadows moved over the room's slanted ceiling. My ears still roared with the sound of the bus, and when I closed my eyes I could feel the motion of the wheels beneath my body. I managed not to think of my grandparents and our house and my friends from school and my teacher. Instead I thought of Miss Beryl Kemper and the dead Irene. With my mother moved away, Miss Beryl might never speak to her daughter again. Of course, I had been the one speaking to her in the first place. But still. Something had been lost. What was it?

In the dark, I felt Irene Kemper's painted eyes stare down at me, reproaching me for letting her die twice.

3

an empty grave

Peter stayed buried for ten years. When they found him, I had lived in Train Line for more than twenty, almost as long as Peter's whole life, and I was thirty-one.

It happened the day before Labor Day, a bright and windy Sunday afternoon. A rich man who wanted a house on the shore of the lake had hired some men to build it for him. They were digging the foundation, hoping to finish it and put the walls and roof up before snow fell, when they came across the skull in a mound of excavated dirt. At first the men thought it was a joke. The skull was so perfect, with such delicately arching cheekbones and flawless, even teeth, that it looked like a prop from a doctor's office or a play. But a little more probing into the pile of dirt turned up a scapula and a collarbone and a long section of vertebrae, still connected. They stopped their machines and someone called the police.

I didn't hear about it right away. I wasn't there when they unearthed him, of course, and I wasn't there when the police arrived and roped off the area, scribbling notes and kneeling in the soft dirt to take photographs. Still, I could picture it. Over the next several weeks I imagined the scene obsessively, adding details and making corrections: the grass trampled into the mud, the stiff wind, the cops' hairy arms and shaved necks, the bones with something of Peter still clinging to them. Soon I'd almost convinced myself I'd been there, perhaps even helped with the digging. It's the kind of thing you get good at, if you're a medium.

I was at the supermarket in Wallamee when I heard the first rumors. Usually I bought my groceries at the cramped and ill-lit

Groc-n-Stop in Train Line, where they were used to me and I could buy my things in peace if not in private. People often came up to me at the Wallamee Safeway. Sometimes they'd grab me by the arm; sometimes they had tears in their eyes. *You were so important to my mother at the end of her life here.* They always looked at what I had in my basket: what does a medium eat? Sometimes they kept a cautious distance, but I could feel them looking, whispering to each other, pointing covertly.

But there were certain things you couldn't buy at the Groc-n-Stop—the cookies I liked for one thing, and chicory coffee for another—so once every month or so I borrowed my mother's car and drove around the lake to Wallamee. I tried to go early, soon after the store opened, because the Safeway could be crowded by afternoon. That Labor Day morning, the day after they found Peter, the store smelled like a bakery and the floors shone. A stock person said hello to me in a friendly way, and I felt a small but swelling happiness, the kind that comes from the smooth carrying-out of an errand. I found my coffee and my cookies and some other things, and I set them on the conveyor belt at the checkout stand while I dug in my pocket for money. The bag boy, a fifteen-year-old with an unflattering buzz cut, snapped open a paper sack and said to the cashier, "They found a dead lady in the woods."

The cashier picked up my groceries, scanned them, and tossed them down as if they'd gone bad.

"Sick," she said. "Where did you hear that?"

"My dad. His buddy's got a multiband radio."

"Probably your girlfriend."

"Jesus, Crystal. You're the one that's sick." The boy raked my food into the sack and handed it to me. "Here you go, ma'am."

I took my bag. There was something ominous about the exchange, something that made me pause before leaving: a microscopic wind that raised the hairs on my arm. I thought maybe I should say something.

"You know," I said, clearing my throat. "You really shouldn't joke about the dead."

Clearly, they thought I was nuts. They gaped at me. After a long moment, during which I decided that explaining myself would just make it worse, the cashier handed me my receipt.

"Thank you," I said, and gave her a rigid smile. Nervous guffawing followed me out the door.

Back in the parking lot, I sat in the car and tore open my cookies. *A dead woman in the woods.* It was just a rumor, just hillbilly gossip—possibly true, more likely not. There wasn't much crime in Wallamee. Occasionally someone got drunk and shot someone else, and once in a while someone died after a knife fight. Crime, in Wallamee, was a natural but unpredictable derangement, like the blizzard we got every five years or so that collapsed roofs and power lines and froze old people in their beds. A dead woman in the woods would be news for a while, even if it turned out not to be murder. I wondered if the police were thinking of consulting a medium. Any time something interesting happened in Wallamee County, the Train Line mediums had a thing or two to say about it.

I closed my eyes, trying to picture the woman.

White thighs, I said to myself. *Loamy soil.*

Moss, bark, leaves.

Nothing. I tried again.

Trees…trees…

It was no use. Perhaps there was no woman. Each time I tried to picture her, my mind bounced back to myself; all I could see was a big girl in a big Oldsmobile, a bag of cookies in her hands and a lap full of crumbs.

You are a crummy medium, I said to myself, and laughed aloud.

❧

It was a lady, the kid had said, and she was in the woods. But to reassure myself I didn't drive straight home, instead took the long way on Vining Road past the clearing where Peter was. Once in a while I did this. Monitoring the site was a half-conscious accommodation I made to my secret. Usually I didn't even turn my head to look, just checked that the place was as it had always been. And always, until now, it was: a weedy tangle of trees, the clearing down below, then the lake, of which only a brief blue flash was visible. There were a thousand places exactly like it around Lake Wallamee, unremarkable and undisturbed.

I hadn't gone far on Vining Road before I began to feel nervous. Driving was not a natural act for me. In fact, I didn't even have a license—mine had expired a couple of years before, and instead of going through the trouble of getting a new one, I'd thought I'd just drive only once in a while, and as inconspicuously as possible. I probably wouldn't have passed the test again. There was something I lacked when it came to driving, though I was hard put to say what it was. Maybe it was the ability to relinquish awareness of my own body. I've heard other people say that when they drive, it's as if they become the car, that maneuvering the car through traffic is no harder than walking one's own body through a crowd of other bodies. Easier, even, because there are rules. But I became more aware of myself when I drove—of my sweating armpits, a tickling hair—and so my attention habitually strayed from the road. Often I found myself on the shoulder, spraying rocks and dirt, or nosing my bumper into the car ahead. My trips to the Safeway were sometimes harrowing.

But my nervousness on this trip had to do with the big yellow earthmover in front of me, which was going about twenty miles an hour. Bits of dirt flew off it and plinked my windshield. I couldn't pass it, because the road twisted too much for me to see very far, and whenever I moved over to see if the coast was clear, a car came out of nowhere and whizzed by.

Where could it be going, I wondered, on Labor Day?

The tractor slowed down even further, and its round yellow turning signal began to flash. To my horror, it turned into the trees at a place where before there was no road, but where there was now a rutted, muddy track leading down toward the lake. I recognized the place: there was the maple tree with the shattered limb that pointed out over the road, and there, beyond the trees, was the old barn. Not far from the makeshift driveway a bit of yellow police ribbon fluttered from a stake driven into the ground, like the flag of a small doomed country.

I drove a short distance farther and stopped the car. In my rearview mirror the tractor trundled down the slope and disappeared. From here, I couldn't see much of what was going on down below. When I opened my window a little, though, I could hear groaning machinery and shouting voices. I stared hard at the rearview mirror, half-hoping to see something without getting out of the car, half-hoping not to. The trees were just beginning to change color—here and there was a branch of red leaves, or orange—but the foliage was still dense and impenetrable. I couldn't see a thing.

After several minutes I started the car again and continued driving. *They haven't found him,* I told myself.

Outside, the sky was bright blue. Small ragged clouds sped across it. The weather would change soon: the trees on either side of the road tossed their branches in the wind. I took a deep breath, and braced myself.

༚

After dropping the car at my mother's, I took my groceries home and made coffee. There was no one else in the house. I was relieved at this, because I had to think, and it was hard to think with Jenny and Ron around. Until a year ago the house had been owned by an old woman named Welchie Pratt, from whom I rented two of the upstairs rooms. She was a grumpy, unpopular medium—she told people terrible things, which were too often true—and we weren't friends, but we stayed out of each other's way. She kept the shades pulled down and made very little noise. When she died, Ron, a social worker and medium-in-training, bought the house, and suddenly the windows were washed, fresh curtains hung, the old crusty appliances replaced, and Ron's somewhat giddy presence was everywhere: I could hear him laughing through the floor of my séance room, and when he stomped around, the house shook. Jenny Butler, a medium from Canada, moved in a few months later and took the rooms across the hall from me. We worked out a chore schedule for the shared parts of the house, and all in all I was grateful Ron hadn't made me move.

Still, sometimes I missed Welchie Pratt. I used to sit in the living room for hours, just watching the sun slant through the cracked shades, thinking. No one bothered me. No one asked me if I'd mind taking over her mopping this week, since she'd be attending a crystal-healing seminar and didn't want to be distracted, and nobody filled the living room with his men's meditation group. In the old days the place smelled like ointment, the kind Welchie bought in a flat round can and rubbed into her knobby fingers.

I poured my coffee into a mug and found a note, butter-stained, on the kitchen table:

Naomi—
J and I are at the Psychic Faire—waited for you but then had to go. Hope that's a-okay!!!
 Don't forget: trash goes out tonight, so if there's any in your room...
            See ya!—Ron

Ron knew I never went to psychic fairs. They were held at the Rochester Holiday Inn two or three times a year—sordid events, where you had to wear a name tag and sit at a card table and dispense five-dollar dollops of advice—and the Train Line mediums rustled up extra business by attending them. I'd had bad experiences at psychic fairs. People would give me false names or demand I tell them lottery numbers, and one awful time a man tried to get me to reveal my "secrets," as if I was a stage magician, and then he wrote an exposé for the local paper. Anyway, I neither needed nor wanted extra business. I was a very popular medium, even though I rarely left Train Line; I never had to do bridal showers or birthday parties or office bashes. Some of the other mediums in town accused me of being a snob, and perhaps it was true. Still. Some people preferred my mother, who had had her own radio show—*The Mother Galina Psychic Hour*—and some preferred the New-Agey vagueness of mediums like Jenny and Robin Blackthorn, but I, for better or for worse, was the one they told stories about.

For instance: people would sometimes tell how I saved a man's life. The man came to me, the story went, with incurable cancer, and I told him to find another doctor, a city doctor, who could help him. He did, and lived five more years. It's a true story, though it wouldn't be right for me to take all the credit. His wife came to me and I just repeated what she said: *See a specialist, Harry. Don't be a cheapskate.* There was another story about a will, and a lost inheritance, and some people who became millionaires. It showed up every few years. To be honest, I wasn't sure where that story came from, but I suppose it could have been true. And another said that I helped someone finish his master's thesis, and another that I cured someone's addiction to shopping. There were more. The truth of these rumors varied: some were slightly distorted versions of what really happened, others appeared whole and out of nowhere, like moon rocks. I didn't bother to deny them. They were, for the most part, innocuous.

There was another rumor, a stupid one, which I am almost too embarrassed to repeat. But it does shed light on my situation—that is, it sheds light not on me, exactly, but on the part of New York State I found myself in, and on the kind of place it was. The rumor was this: that once I had nearly died, and that in order to continue living I had made a pact with the devil, and promised to do his work here on Earth. That I was the devil's proxy didn't seem to stop anyone from coming to me for readings. Much of Wallamee County was alcoholic, superstitious, and backward—and hypocritical to boot. I was just a good medium, nothing more. And that's what people said most often; I heard it when I walked past them.

See that woman? That's Naomi Ash.

Oh, she's good.

❧

I sat at the kitchen table, drinking my coffee and trying to formulate a plan. What I needed, I decided, was a newspaper. I poked around the house, checked in the recycling box: no dice. Ron and Jenny must have taken it with them to the psychic fair. Jenny would want to do the crossword between customers; Ron would be combing the classifieds for a new waterbed. I sat down again, drummed my fingers on the tabletop. Through the small kitchen window the sun was high: it must be almost noon. The Groc-n-Stop, I knew, didn't carry the morning paper, which was from Rochester, and the *Wallamee Evening Observer* wouldn't be out until three o'clock or so. Hmm.

My mind wandered. I let it. I thought of the coming fall, then the winter, how icicles would grow from roof edges clear to the ground, how snow would pile as high as cottage windows. I thought of it longingly. In the middle of winter I would hate it, but picturing it now, it seemed beautiful and safe, with the lake frozen solid as a table and everything hidden under blankets and blankets of snow.

I closed my eyes and put my head down, forehead to the Formica. It was cool.

I should have buried him deeper.

❧

After Peter died, I thought for a long time I would have to kill myself. I was terrified. I was frightened of being caught, of course, but that was not the only thing. I was frightened of *him*. I had never been afraid of a spirit before. I wasn't afraid of my grandparents, who came to me occasionally with kind if vague words, and I wasn't even afraid of the angry, confused spirits I sometimes came across. But I had never had a spirit who hated me. I was sure Peter hated me. For two or three years I suppressed my mediumship, scared to conjure him up by mistake, or to allow him a way back. But I missed him, too. After all, I had loved him, and once he had loved me. And if I killed myself, I could be with him, and surely he would forgive me. Or would he? I fantasized about it all the time, the various methods: eating poison, walking into the lake, rope, razor, car crash. In the end I didn't do it, of course, and instead chose to live with what had happened.

Those were terrible, dark months. I worked at the Ha-Ha, a convenience store in Wallamee, during the day, and plotted my suicide at night. Every morning I rode my bike the five and a half miles around the north end of the lake, past groups of kids with lunch boxes waiting for the school bus, and past flocks of ducks flapping through cattails, and past gas stations and real estate offices opening for the day. I rode through most of the winters, too, though when there was a lot of snow I got a ride from Teeny Lawrence, my neighbor, who worked similar hours as I did at a doctor's office not far from the convenience store. I preferred to ride my bike, though. I wasn't very good at small talk.

I didn't mind working at the Ha-Ha. In a way I liked it, or at least I took a desperate pleasure in the sameness of it. Every day I wore the same orange smock, rang up the same items—cigarettes and colas and overpriced groceries and lottery tickets—and said the same things to the same people. From my place behind the counter I could see the front door of a biker bar across the street. I watched couples stand in the parking lot arguing, sobbing drunkenly on each other's shoulders, riding off too quickly with no helmets. Often they came into the Ha-Ha to buy a snack or a smoke before roaring away. I remember watching them, filled with incomprehension, completely unable to imagine their lives.

Though Wallamee was not a big town by any means, and I never worked any night shifts, I managed to be on duty twice when the store was held up at gunpoint. Maybe something about me invited it. Or maybe criminals found it appealing to rob a store called Ha-Ha. The first time, the gunman lurked in back by the ice-cream freezer until everyone else was out of the store, then ran up to the cash register and pointed a snub-nosed pistol at me so fast that at first I didn't even recognize the thing as a gun. I just looked at him, trying to figure out what was going on, then slowly backed away and let him take the money from the register himself. When it happened again, there were two of them. One stood by the door and made the other customers lie on the floor—just like in a Western movie—while the other held his gun to the side of my head. The right side of my head, just over my ear. I couldn't move. The man was shouting at me, over and over, *I want the money! I want the goddamn money!* Finally, in slow motion, I punched in the code and the cash drawer shot out, and I gave the man everything that was in it, even the video game tokens and the food stamps and the credit card receipts. *Thanks, you fat bitch,* he said as he left.

This was not as frightening as it sounds. I rode my bicycle home after it happened and tried to figure out how I felt. The answer was *exhilarated.* It was early spring and the air had lost its edge, and the long, bare branches of the willows along the lakeshore had turned yellow. Dirty piles of snow still lined the road. It seemed quite beautiful to me. I could still feel the place on my head that the man pressed the barrel of his gun to. For that moment, I had been able to imagine something besides Peter and what had happened to him. I could imagine my brains flying out the side of my head, obliterating every memory I had. For some reason, this made me feel better.

I quit the Ha-Ha after that, with my boss's blessing.

Sometime during my stint at the convenience store, Vivian was born. I knew her mother. Elaine came in several times a week to buy a huge thirty-two-ounce cup of cola and sometimes a microwave burrito, and I'd chat with her while she dug through her enormous purse for money. She was cheerful in a relentlessly stupid, exasperating way. She dyed her hair bronze and wore floppy pantsuits over her chunky, then pregnant, body, and told me things I didn't really want to know about her personal life. She took a leave of absence from her job a few weeks before the baby was born and didn't come in anymore. Then, of course, the store was held up, and held up again, and I didn't come in anymore, either.

But when I answered an ad in the *Observer* for a babysitter, and it turned out to be Elaine, she gave me a big hug and kiss and said she missed me, and of course I could be her babysitter. We met at her house, a low brick one-story with an array of pillars across the front.

"I'd heard you got shot," she told me as I stepped inside. "I'd heard you almost died."

"No, no. I'm fine."

"Well, good!"

I followed her through the house. It was decorated in a country style—there were wooden ducks and faceless dolls and watering cans painted with American flags, all piled apparently randomly in corners and on shelves. The impression it gave was of madness. Then again, I hadn't gone into many houses other than my own; perhaps this was typical. We went into the kitchen and sat down.

"I don't really like my baby," Elaine told me over a cup of herbal tea. "I hate to say it, but it's true, and I believe in being honest with myself." Elaine had changed since I'd seen her last. The bronze dye was half grown out, and the only jewelry she had on was a lumpy rock on a black cord. *New Age*, I thought to myself. The country decor was probably on its way out.

"I should never have named her after my mother-in-law," she went on, "but I thought, you know, Vivien Leigh, Vivian… aren't there other Vivians? I thought it could be romantic. Huh. Anyway, it seems to suit her."

The baby was about ten months old, large-headed, with a tiny pair of eyeglasses. She had straight, dark eyebrows that shot out each side of her glasses, like pot handles. She was an odd-looking baby. She sat calmly in her high chair, gazing at the tail of the cat clock that swung back and forth on the wall.

Elaine put her chin in her hands and leaned toward her. "My little egghead. Baby professor. Huh? My little professor. Actually," she said, sitting back, "she's not that smart."

"Oh," I said, startled. "Well. She's still a baby."

Elaine looked at me glumly. The wind had been taken out of her. "You know what I mean. I'm terrible, I know."

She told me how she was going back to work and didn't want to put the baby in day care—"all those diseases and pedophiles and who knows what! I mean, I'm not a *bad* mother"—and hoped it would be okay if she brought Vivian to my house, instead of my coming there. Her husband had a home office, she said apologetically, and it had been hard for him these last months, with both her and the baby there. I nodded, said it was fine. I was still imagining, on and off, the feel of the gun barrel on my head—over my ear, at my temple, between my eyes, in my mouth.

"I *need* to get back to work!" she said, gripping her mug. "And with you looking after Vivian, instead of some stranger, well, that'll be a load off my mind."

Funny, I thought, how she could think she knew someone after less than a year of small talk, and most of that small talk having come from her.

When I told her where I lived, her face lit up. "Really! I've been meaning to get over there. Is it true there's a herb shop, and a crystal shop?"

I told her it was.

"Neat!" She wrote down the address and telephone number on a yellow, duck-shaped pad. "Does that mean you're a medium, then?"

I said yes, but that was something of a lie. It had been two years since Peter, and I was still giving very few readings, and mostly faking those.

"That is *so* interesting! You'll have to give me a reading sometime."

"Certainly," I said, smiling.

Elaine shook her head. "I should get into that. Really. I mean, real estate is just a dead end around here." She folded her arms and looked at her baby, who was sucking its fingers and rocking back and forth, back and forth, looking at nothing.

❧

So then I had Vivian. Apparently real estate wasn't such a dead end, because Elaine worked longer and longer hours, and got happier and happier. Vivian and I spent whole days with each other: taking naps together in my apartment, watching ants in the grass. I fed her from little glass jars of puree I bought at the Groc-n-Stop. She said her first word to me: *Mama*. I didn't tell Elaine. There were times when she felt like my child, and I realized why people got married, took jobs, had children. She was a reason to get up in the morning.

One night I dreamed about Peter. As in many of my dreams, I was burying him, but in this one, I was burying lots of people, it was my job or something, and the feeling was one of resignation: *All these dead people, better bury them quick.* They were the victims of a disease, or a natural disaster. Some were not quite dead yet, though. Peter was one of them. But I had to bury him, that's the way it was. I had a white shovel and there were bouquets of roses to put on the graves. I flattened the soil with the back of my shovel and turned to go. As I did so I heard a noise, a faint groan, and a hand reached out of the ground.

What to do? I recognized the hand as a sign of confusion; he didn't know what was going on, didn't know he was just about dead and already buried. So I put down my shovel and knelt down next to the grave. I took his hand in mine. And I held it like that until he died for real.

The dream spooked me, though it was not, really, a bad dream. When I woke up that morning I felt calm. The day was sullen and overcast, a Sunday, and I'd slept too late, but it was *all right*. I tested myself: *Peter's dead because of you, you buried him, you threw dirt on him and left him there in that clearing.* I pictured the grave site, the dull clouds over the clearing, the wind moving the trees beyond it, his body rotting in the soil. And it didn't frighten me. All I felt was calm.

After that, much of the power Peter had over me dissipated. Days went by during which I forgot to think, *Any time now, they'll come and get me.* I gave some readings that felt good, felt right, almost. Vivian learned to say my name, and we went around Train Line piggyback. Peter was not coming back, neither to forgive me or to blame me. He was gone. This was difficult and lonely knowledge. It meant that I had gotten away with it, and that death was for real. This seemed intolerable, impossible, against everything I wanted to believe.

But I managed somehow to live with my imperfect faith, as someone might learn to live with false hands, or blindly.

❧

I spent the rest of that Labor Day afternoon in the library. Since it was a holiday the library was closed, but because I worked there part-time I had a key. It was a small building of imposing design, a tiny Parthenon on a hillock above the lake. Upstairs were the book stacks, all three of them, and downstairs was the museum, a room full of spirit photography and spirit paraphernalia: trumpets, slates, Ouija boards, planchettes. I thought I would get a head start on my project for this winter, which was to catalog the collection. This task required that I read enough of each book to see what it was about, then assign it a Dewey decimal number and type up some cards. I liked working when no one else was in the building, typing at the humming Selectric all day and watching motes of sunlight writhe across the floor. It was always shady and cool in the library, like the inside of a safe.

Around four o'clock I took a break and stretched out in the reading room, using a thick leather-bound book for a pillow. I meant to just rest my eyes, but when I woke up it was nearly six. At six I was supposed to meet my mother; Monday night was Circle Night, and we always met for a drink beforehand. I stood up and shook the crumbs of leather from my hair, then grabbed my sweater and locked the place up. The sun was going down and the air had a chill. I wouldn't have time to get a newspaper.

I walked across Train Line rubbing the sleep from my face. The shadows were long and the setting sun lit up the grass. This is the kind of evening the Victorians had in mind when they designed Train Line, I thought: the twilit fairyland architecture, the fingers of mist creeping up from the lake. Not much had been added since then, just the cars and the telephone wires, and a general ramshackle feeling. Every other house, it seemed, had an orange FOR SALE sign in a window, and many were boarded up, bald of paint, tipping. It was worrying, but people had been predicting the end of Train Line for fifty years, and still it hung on. Inertia is a powerful thing.

I crossed through a stand of trees, then down the hill toward the entrance gates. The gatehouse was closed up for the year, and the window boxes of geraniums were gone. The fountain—a naked golden baby topped with a showerhead—was dry. Labor Day marked the end of the season for Train Line. Many mediums had left already for warmer climates; more would leave before snow fell. There'd be no more daily lectures until June, and no public message services or workshops. Monday night Circles were one of the few regular events we had in the winter, besides Sunday services. A schedule in the main office listed the presiding mediums for the month's Circle Nights. Most mediums tried to get out of it any way they could, but a few liked Circles. Troy Versted, for example, who was from a long line of Australian mediums, worked every week. He had a hook nose, white hair, and pastel-colored slacks with matching shirts. Another person who filled in for less accommodating mediums was Robin Blackthorn. Another was my mother. I went when I was scheduled, no more and no less.

The bar where I was to meet my mother, Maxwell's, was outside the gates of Train Line. Train Line was a dry town. The Victorians saw their summer colony as a place to better one-self; the only pleasures they approved of were the loftier kind. I walked down Line Drive, which curved along the shore of the lake and through arching trees. A breeze off the water got inside my sweater and cotton dress. My mother was on the deck when I got to Maxwell's, sitting slumped in a shiny green outfit, a drink un-drunk in front of her. She didn't appear to see me as I approached, crossing the gravel parking lot past a long row of motorcycles. Inside, I got a plastic cup of white wine from the bar, then took it out to the deck.

"What's wrong?" I asked my mother.

She didn't answer me right away, but stared into her drink. Then, "I've been waiting a long time, you know."

"I'm sorry, Mama."

"It wouldn't have taken much to call. You can be awfully irresponsible."

"I know. I—"

She waved her hand. "I don't want to hear it. I've had a horrible day. You won't believe what happened."

My mother was a physical medium. Most of us are not; we're mental mediums, and we use only our minds in our work. Occasionally my mother still used her spirit trumpet, which she kept wrapped in a long piece of brown velvet on her living room mantel, and once in a while she levitated something.

It embarrassed me to see her do levitations. I knew her tricks: the hidden rods, the threads, the surreptitious flings. The conventions of Train Line had worn her down, though, and she saved her most blatant sleight of hand for sweet-sixteen parties and appearances down at the senior center. As a rule, the only tool she used was her body.

This is what she did. She'd sit across from her customer— "the bereaved," as she liked to put it, though by her definition we're all bereaved—hold his hands, and give him a long, searching look before closing her eyes. If the reading was successful, and it usually was, she'd soon make contact with a spirit who wanted to get through. Then she'd give her body over to the spirit, who would speak in a voice not unlike my mother's—they were her vocal cords, after all—and perhaps even stand up, walk around, gesticulate, dance. This kind of performance could make some people extremely uncomfortable. My mother had, however, a large and loyal following. And I believed in her.

Well, I *mostly* believed in her. A certain percentage of what she did was faked: I knew this, and I knew that it was part of who she was to go just a little too far, to push her material a bit further than it would stretch. Somehow, she carried it off, just as she carried off her flamboyant clothes and her long, unmistakably dyed hair. Though she was fat now, her nose was still her dominant feature; it looked ready to weigh anchor from her face at any moment.

"I'll believe it," I told her. "What happened?"

She gave me a sharp look. "Look, there's no need to get snotty." Then she sighed deeply, shifted in her chair, and took a sip of her drink. "They're going to cancel my show."

Every weekday morning for the last twelve years, from nine to ten a.m., the local talk radio station broadcast *The Mother Galina Psychic Hour*. People called in with questions—"Should I quit my job?" and "Is he the man for me?" and "What color should I paint my house?"—and my mother, working with a team of what she termed "spirit advisers," answered them, often so deftly and probingly the caller would break into tears. "What you need to do," she said several times a week, "is get to the real question." She was very, very good. And she was right: I *couldn't* believe they'd cancel the show.

"Why would they do a thing like that?"

My mother shook her head. Her earrings, fat chunks of amber with ants in them, swung back and forth. They matched her hair, which was an extraordinary brassy color. "They say they want a change, that it's been twelve years and I've answered everyone's questions. They're thinking of putting a shrink in that spot. A shrink! What do they think *I* do?"

"Well, they're making a big mistake."

"Obviously, Naomi." She stared into her drink again, brooding. "I'm the only reason people listen to that godawful *Morning Show*. Do they think anyone wants to hear those two buffoons complain about town council meetings?"

I took a long slug of my wine—it was terrible, like cough medicine—and when I put my cup back down again, I noticed that there was a newspaper sticking out of my mother's tote bag. It was neat, tightly folded. She must have picked it up on her way over and not had time to read it.

"Look, there's Troy," said my mother, waving. "Troy! Over here!"

Troy smiled, waved back, but didn't move. He was talking to a young woman in a blue blouse.

"Lecher," said my mother. "Hold on a minute, I've got to talk to him." She pushed her chair back and struggled up. She'd been having trouble getting around lately: a bunion operation last year, and all that extra weight.

When she was gone I slid out her newspaper and flattened it out on our table. Wind ruffled the pages, and I weighted them with our drinks. This was the headline:

BONES FOUND IN TOWN OF WALLAMEE:
CRIME OR ARCHAEOLOGY?
POLICE INVESTIGATING

And there it was: a full-color picture of the clearing by the lake. A big yellow earthmover, like the one I'd followed that morning, was parked next to a pile of rocks and dirt. Some official-looking men were standing around, not far from the old falling-down barn. I brushed my fingers over it, disbelieving.

"That Troy!" said my mother, back already. "You'd think he…"

I looked up at her, startled.

"What's the matter?" she said quickly.

I looked down again, took the drinks off the newspaper, and began to fold it back up. I hadn't had a chance to see whether the skeleton was a woman, or a man, or what. "Hmm?"

She pulled her chair out, eased herself back into it, and smiled. It was a long, knowing, absolutely devastating smile. My mother had built her career on the effects of this look; it could make you think, *She knows me better than anyone in the world.* It could make you want to give her everything in your wallet. Of course, I was used to it. I had spent my life steeling myself against it.

"You look," she said, still smiling, "exactly like you did that day you came home from school and had wet your pants. Do you remember that? You told me you'd fallen into a puddle, but oh, the look on your face!"

"I *did* fall into a puddle," I told her, outraged.

Her smile wavered just slightly. "Oh, Naomi, honestly! Why did you look so ashamed, then? I'm your mother, for God's sake; you don't have to fib."

I shook my head, refusing to say another thing on the subject. Suddenly I was beginning to doubt my own version of events; it seemed possible that I had lied all those years ago and had fooled myself into believing otherwise. I guzzled my wine, furious.

"Ha!" said my mother. "You know I'm right."

Fortunately, she seemed to have forgotten what had started the quarrel in the first place, and sat smugly drinking her martini. We were quiet for several long minutes, looking out over the lake, where motorboats with their engines turned off drifted slowly by and fishermen cast lines across the calm water. It was a beautiful evening, but I felt irritable and uncomfortably cold. All around us, glasses clinked and people laughed and chattered. My mother sighed. "Oh, Naomi. I can't believe summer's over already. A whole winter without my radio show will be the death of me, it really will." She gave me a sorrowful look.

I was still angry, but reached out and patted her knee anyway. "Oh, Mama. You'll never die."

She gave my hand a squeeze. "Oh, well, I certainly hope that's not true," she said.

We walked down Line Drive in the darkening evening, my mother leaning into me. Her feet had never quite recovered from her bunion surgery; she walked with a rolling, precarious gait, like a child on new roller skates. It pleased me that she needed my help. The weight and heat of her body made me nostalgic; I thought of falling asleep on her lap when I was a child. Although that, to be honest, didn't happen very often.

"You're getting fat," she said, prodding my hip.

"I *am* fat."

We crossed into Train Line. Ahead of us, the queue of people waiting for Circles stretched right around the lecture hall and down toward the cafeteria. It was the time of day when light-colored clothes seem luminescent—shirts and skirts and socks glowed palely against the gray wood of Fox Hall. My mother had to stop and hitch up her panty hose. People turned and watched, then politely looked away.

Tony K., the hypnotist, was guarding the door. He was new to Train Line, but he had somehow insinuated himself into everything. He had a large belt buckle shaped like a sea turtle and a bad, overlong haircut. He'd already given the Sunday lecture twice, shown up at every picnic and barbecue and message service, and was angling to get himself a workshop next summer. It was galling, especially since he was such an unpleasant person. Every time he opened his mouth, all I could look at were his terrible, battered teeth.

"Miss Galina!" he yelped when he saw my mother. "Let me help you to your table. You're at number six tonight."

"That's all right, Tony. Naomi's got me. You man your post."

"Yes, ma'am." He gave me a wink. I didn't understand it at all. "Table two, Naomi." He gave us a bow and opened the door with a flourish.

"That man has no dignity," said my mother, when we were inside.

A dozen or so card tables were set up in the lecture hall, each with four or five chairs and a squat white candle in the center of it. The candles were the only lighting. In the interest of being aboveboard, none of the tables had tablecloths. Otherwise, it would have felt very much like entering an elegant, though barnlike, restaurant.

"Here I am, Naomi," said my mother, panting a little. "Get me a chair, would you?"

I pulled out an old wooden chair, the kind I liked.

"No! Not one of those. A *metal* chair. How many times have I told you?"

A few people turned and looked at us. I helped my mother into her chair, kissed her cheek, and quickly made my way to table two. It was farther over, near the back corner. Its candle was nearly done, the flame tall and smoking. I put my sweater on the back of the chair and went up front to get a fresh candle.

As I wove my way around the tables, I noticed Jenny, sitting in the dark. Her thin red hair was tied in a little knot at the back of her head, and her table had no candle. She looked pale and crabby.

"I'm getting candles," I told her as I passed. "Do you want one?"

"I prefer the dark," she said, with an unconvincing smile. Her hands were folded tightly in front of her. There was a rumor going around that she was sick, that she had a disease, but I didn't know what kind or even if it was true. Jenny did not confide in me.

Ancient Grace Batsummer had the candle boxes. She was trying to shove some leftover candles into a box that was clearly already full; the cardboard was tearing and she was muttering angrily to herself.

"I'll take one of those," I told her.

"One of what, dear?" she said, flustered. She was so tiny and shrunken her dress dragged on the floor.

"A candle. Please." Something about this evening was wearing on me, already. The flickering, pseudo-romantic light gave me a headache.

By the time I made it back to my table with the candle and a pack of matches, Tony K. had started letting people in. Two short, middle-aged women with matching perms were at my table, their purses on their laps.

"Hello," I said. "I'm Naomi Ash."

They nodded and looked at each other. One of them, the one with glasses, said, "Are we supposed to tell you our names? Or are you supposed to guess?"

"Well," I said. "I may never guess. But it's up to you."

They looked at each other again. "I'm Judy," said one with glasses. "And this is Ginny."

"Nice to meet you."

There were still three empty chairs. I didn't really like to do more than four, but so many of the mediums had already left town for the winter we had to double up. As it was, some people were probably going to have to be turned away.

A couple of teenagers came over. "Is this table two?" the boy asked. He had a long, rabbity face and a shock of blond hair. The girl was shorter, plump and nervous. She kept pulling her T-shirt away from her stomach.

I said it was and introduced myself again. Their names were Kevin and Elise.

I lit the candle and got ready. I let my hair down from its ponytail and shook it out, then took some deep breaths and closed my eyes.

"Fancy meeting you here," said a voice.

It was Dave the Alien, who worked in Train Line's cafeteria during the summers. He was a small young man with a surprisingly deep voice and no chin whatsoever. He did have very large, rather beautiful dark eyes, and I thought of him as Dave the Alien because an insane woman, a tourist, once insisted he must be an alien, because of those eyes. She had a complicated theory about aliens. Another Dave—Dave Wood—worked as Train Line's groundskeeper.

"Are you sitting at this table?" I asked, a little bothered but trying not to show it. Reading for people I knew could be tricky when they were mixed in with strangers, like this.

"You bet I am," he said. "I've been waiting for this. You promised all summer you'd give me a reading and you never did."

"Have a seat, then," I said, not too coldly, I hoped.

The hubbub died down. Tony K. shut the big wooden doors with a bang. Grace Batsummer tottered over to the podium at the front of the room. I could just see the top of her head behind it. "Welcome, all of you wonderful spirits," she said in her reedy old-lady voice.

"Microphone," yelled someone in the back.

Grace paid no attention. "Let's just skip the preliminaries, shall we," she went on. "Now. I'm going to say a little prayer. Bless us, spirits, and speak to us tonight. We're all ready and waiting. Amen."

Everyone at my table was looking at me. I hated this part, the beginning part. "All right," I said. "It would help if I could hear your voices first. If you could all just say a little something; I don't care what. Starting with Dave."

"Put the pressure on!" he said. "Okay. I work at the cafeteria. Or in the summers I do. Right now I'm unemployed and have too much time on my hands. Is that enough?"

"That's fine. Next?" Circle Nights tended to bring out a side of me I didn't like—the condescending, school-teachery side. It didn't seem to bother anyone else. I guessed they expected it out of a medium.

Kevin was in the chess club and Elise wanted to be a writer. Judy had four daughters and Ginny was planning a trip to Mexico at Christmas. I never told people to talk about themselves, but they always, *always* did.

"Thank you," I said. "Now, let's concentrate."

Judy looked panicky. "But—you're not going to let us ask our questions? I thought I was going to get to ask a question."

This always rubbed me the wrong way. I wanted to say, *I'm not a Magic 8-Ball.*

"I'm sorry," I told Judy. "I don't answer questions, at least at first. Please, let's focus ourselves." What I meant was, *Shut up.*

Before I closed my eyes I noticed my mother across the room. Her head was on the table, her hair perilously close to the candle flame, her shoulders heaving. The expressions on the faces of the people at the table were shocked and excited. I glanced over at Jenny. Her head was tilted back, and her sitters were holding their linked hands high above the table. I smelled nervousness and breath, and the wax of a dozen candles burning. Above us, the dark crowded down.

"All right," I said to my sitters. "Let's hold hands."

Elise was to my left, her hand plump and damp. With my fingertips I brushed her palm, using only the slightest pressure. I felt a shiver of something there, a heat and desperateness pushing back. Ginny's hand, on the other side, was cold and inert. I closed my eyes, and fell, right away, into a state of absolute concentration.

"Elise," I said. "Someone is here for you."

It was an old woman. She was dressed in a pale green wool suit and had white hair in a mannish cut. I could tell she hadn't been a spirit very long; there was an uncertainty about her, a waviness. Plus, once spirits get the hang of it they usually show up as younger versions of themselves. She was standing direct-ly behind Elise, her hands resting on the girl's shoulders, but I could see her clearly only with my eyes shut. I liked her. She was smiling. She said something, her voice fading in and out like a radio with bad reception. Spirit voices are always quiet, quieter even than my own thoughts, and sometimes it's hard to silence my head enough to hear them. The voice of Elise's spirit was on the very edge of my perception.

"I'm not getting a name, but she has short hair. She's telling you not to give up, I think. Does this mean anything to you?"

"My great-aunt," whispered Elise.

Yes, indeed. The woman nodded, her mouth opening and closing as if she was under water. *Stay a little longer*, I said to her, in my mind, but she faded.

"I'm sorry, Elise, but she's..." Then, in a sudden rush, I had what I can only describe as a vision. Sometimes, spirits will send me visions instead of speaking or appearing themselves. Elise's aunt was probably very shy. I saw Elise in her little bedroom, scribbling in a notebook, the walls pressing around her on all sides, the smell of the heavy fried dinner eaten hours ago, the hated buzz of the television in the next room, someone yelling very far away.

"Work hard at what's most important to you, though it seems impossible at times," I said. "You know what I'm talking about." Her grip on my hand tightened.

"Oh, *I will.*"

"Your aunt will always be with you."

Elise nodded. A tear slid down and hung at the end of her nose. The mistake many mediums make is to say too much. If you say the right thing, you do not need to ramble on.

Kevin was harder. I cleared a space for him, but no one turned up. I opened my eyes and took a quick peek. His face was a mask of contempt.

Well. No wonder.

I threw myself in harder. Finally, an old man, his back to us.

Kevin wants to talk to you, I said, as politely as I could.

Rotten kid. He was working on something, a radio or a clock or a toaster, maybe, and he wouldn't turn around. *Goddamn kid never so much as called...*

Spirits don't usually hang on to their earthly resentments for long. *He's sorry, now.*

No he's not! he shouted.

"Seems you had a rocky relationship with your grandfather, Kevin," I said, opening my eyes again.

The boy just looked at me, his face impassive. Two spots of color had risen in his cheeks, though, so I figured I'd hit home.

You're not just whistling Dixie. The old man had turned around now, and I could see what he held in his hands: a small china lamp with a pink shade. The man yanked a chain and it lit up. I had no idea what to make of that. When I looked back up at the man's face, it was much younger, almost handsome. He was smiling, and tears poured down his cheeks.

"I know you won't listen to me, Kevin, but it would do you good to try and set things right with him."

"He's dead," said Kevin snottily.

I sighed. "That doesn't matter." I was about to give up on these two. The man was beginning to fade out, and Kevin was just bristling with rancor. "Concentrate on the living, then. Your grandmother..."

That's it. His grandmother. The old man was back, brighter than before, holding his lamp out in front of him like a beacon.

My lady love, the old man whispered.

"None of us is here forever, Kevin. You don't want things to end bitterly with anyone. I want you to go home and call your grandmother, all right? Send her some flowers or something."

He blushed. I moved on.

The older women were easy, very similar. Crowds of spirit women bustled around, all overflowing with health advice. Don't overdo the medications, move your body once in a while, extra care with the teeth. I passed these on to Judy, who was shifting in her seat.

"You have a specific question, Judy?"

"Well, as a matter of fact I do. It has to do with my daughter. See, she's in with a bad crowd. I mean drugs, all of that! What I want to know is, will she be all right? And what am I supposed to do about it?"

Oh, Judy.

"Someone's watching over her," I said, and suddenly I knew this was true. Just above Judy's stiff hairdo, something radiated. "Someone loves her. Is it—it's not clear to me—is it your mother?"

"Oh!" Judy cried. "Oh, Momma just loved Roseanne!"

"Yes, well. Roseanne's going through some tough times, and there's more to come, but she'll get through them. You have to lay down the line, though, Judy. She needs to know how much she's loved."

That would be hard for Judy, I knew. The stricken, love-suffused look on her face told me I was right.

David I left for last. He waited, holding Keith's and Judy's hands gingerly, his eyebrows raised.

I couldn't find a way in. I knew a few things about him, about his crowd of older brothers and sisters, a bar in Wallamee he got beat up in once, his terrible wisdom teeth nightmare. But these didn't help; my mind suddenly felt restless and prickly, not receptive to anything.

Then, out of nowhere, I had another vision. It was an empty field in pouring rain. The rain came down so hard I could hardly see through it, but I could make out the vague shape of trees off in the distance. It was a cornfield, after the harvest. I saw myself running through the water-filled furrows, tripping and falling, then getting back up. It was strange; I was in my body and several yards away from it at the same time. The stubbled cornstalks raked at my ankles and made them bleed, and the watery field gave off a powerful smell of decay. Rain poured into my mouth and eyes, blinded me. Finally—though the whole thing couldn't have taken more than a few seconds to watch, it felt like forever—finally I fell and could not get up. I struggled for a short time, then the mud pulled me under.

Naomi.

It was Peter's voice. I jumped, and my eyes flew open.

All five of them were looking at me. "I'm a little tired," I said. "Give me a moment."

Peter had never come to me before. But the voice was his; I knew the way his mouth formed my name. I had feared it and I had longed for it, and I had never forgotten his voice. My heart surged in recognition.

I took a steadying breath and told David some hopeful things: chin up, you haven't found a job yet because the right one hasn't come around, etcetera, etcetera. I wondered if he could tell I was winging it. Usually they couldn't. But David looked disappointed.

Three syllables: *Naomi.* It was him. *It was him.*

Afterward, I shook everyone's hand. I gathered my purse and sweater and pushed in my chair. I was shaking a little. All around people were leaving—chatting and hugging and laughing.

"Naomi."

"Oh! Oh, Dave, I'm sorry…"

"No, no, it was me. My energy was all wrong. I'm sorry. My fault entirely." He hunched himself into his windbreaker.

"I was tired. I *am* tired. I'll make it up to you, any time you like."

He made a wry face, obviously pleased. "Well, all right. Hey, how about some time this week? I'll cook you dinner."

Oh, geez, I thought. "Maybe. You can call me."

"Of course. I will. Really, I really am sorry." He gave me a little wave, and I watched his narrow shoulders disappear into the crowd.

That night, after I walked my mother home, I thought I might watch the television news. Everyone else was in bed. From his room came the sound of Ron snoring, and occasionally I heard the squeak of Jenny's bedsprings as she rolled around, trying to make herself comfortable. I had never liked television. It embarrassed me to watch people mugging and singing on behalf of new cars and drain cleaner. I waited impatiently through the weather and a car accident or two and the endless shots of ponytailed girls running up and down basketball courts, but there was no mention of the body in the woods. I turned the TV off and sat there for a few minutes, listening to the sound of my breath in my nose, then got up and went outside.

I walked down Fox Street, toward the dock, until I could see the lake spread out in front of me, black as oil. Music floated across the water from somewhere. For a little while I argued with myself: *It's a woman, you heard what they said at the Safeway... they're most likely Indian bones, anyway, it's not Peter...Peter was not an Indian.* But as I stood at the edge of the lapping water, I gave it up. The bones were Peter's. Out there in the dark, on the other side of the lake somewhere, his grave was empty. I could feel it. Before, whenever I stood on the shore of the lake, I'd think I could sense him there, across the water. The presence of his bones had always been something I could take an obscure comfort in, a source of heat I could turn my cold face toward. But not tonight.

He came to me; he said my name. Why? Could the disturbance of his bones have shaken his soul loose, the way prodding a dead animal might release a cloud of flies? I didn't think so. He had come to me for a reason. To warn me? Maybe. Maybe he meant to taunt me.

I wanted to hear his voice again. I wanted to *see* him. If I tried hard I could see his face in the shadows of the hills beyond the lake, his features alive and shifting, and I could see him in the ripples on the water. The shape of his body was outlined in the trees above my head. He was everywhere, everywhere. Inside me, something trembled and broke free: love—love and horror.

4

invisible

During the night a storm passed through. Asleep, I interpreted the noise of rain to be a train I was riding, though in waking life I'd never been on one. I didn't know where I was going or where I had been, but the train rocked from side to side as if it was going very fast, and the landscape out the windows was blurred. An old man leaned close to me.

It's going to crash, he whispered. He nodded his head toward the window. *If I were you, I'd jump.*

Oh, I couldn't do that, I said.

He shrugged. *Well, I can.*

And, scampering like a leprechaun over the seats, he climbed up to the window and leapt out. His coat billowed out behind him. I gasped awake.

I was lying on the living room couch. It was still dark; I had no way of telling what time it was. When I'd come inside after my walk to the lake, I hadn't felt tired enough to go to bed, so I'd turned the television back on and watched some of a late-night talk show, though I must have fallen asleep in the middle of it. Someone, Ron no doubt, had turned the television off during the night. It seemed he also pulled an afghan over me. This touched me, though I was a little bothered to think he'd seen me sleeping. I hoped I'd kept my mouth closed. I fell quickly back to sleep, my jaw clenched tightly shut.

When I woke again, it was to a peculiar sound: a persistent scratching. I listened to it for a long time before opening my eyes, trying to figure out what it was. My mother, scraping the black from her toast? A dog, wanting in? But I no longer lived with my mother, and we didn't have a dog. Finally I opened my eyes, but saw nothing that solved the mystery. The room was filled with a dull gray light. The place was a mess; tools were scattered around from the latest renovation project—Ron was building a new bannister—and magazines about health and vegetarianism and the men's movement covered every surface. None of this stuff was mine; I kept my things upstairs, in my rooms.

With the afghan still pulled around my shoulders, I stumbled into the kitchen. Nothing there, either. But when I looked through the glass pane of the door to the back porch, I saw Ron. He was sitting cross-legged on the porch floor, scraping hard at a small animal hide that had been stretched and nailed to a board on his lap. His curly head was bent in concentration, and he didn't see me. I recoiled, backed quickly away, and sat down at the kitchen table.

It didn't take me long to figure it out. Jenny had remarked a few weeks before that Ron had run over a beaver in his truck—the jaunty brown truck that, as my mother once pointed out, looked just like Ron, with its rear end sticking up in the air—and, consumed with guilt, he decided that the best way to honor the animal was to cure its hide and make a ceremonial drum out of it. Jenny had mentioned this in way of warning: unless I wanted to know what a dead beaver smelled like, I should stay out of the back shed.

It wasn't until this point, actually, that I remembered myself, and remembered the day before. It came back to me in a rush—the body in the woods, the news article, Peter's voice. My heart skittered. For many months after Peter died, I felt the same way when I woke up each morning, remembering everything anew.

The train dream, the beaver hide, Peter's bones. Together, they seemed to possess a secret and complicated meaning, one just out of my reach. I stood up and began making my coffee and toast, trying to clear my head. And as I busied myself, the world did indeed seem to fall back into its customary patterns. The rain tapped lightly on the window, and the smell of coffee filled the kitchen. First I'd eat breakfast, then take a shower, then go to work.

But just as I was sitting down to eat, the phone rang. We had an old-fashioned rotary phone whose fierce jangle never failed to startle me. I swallowed a mouthful of toast, and it rang again.

It was my mother. I knew this even before I answered it, because she was the only person who ever telephoned our house this time of day—she had no qualms about calling whenever it occurred to her. Sometimes I wondered if she thought that I, like one of her spirits, sprung into life only in reference to her.

"Yes?"

"Naomi, have you read last night's paper?"

Uh-oh. "Not yet."

"Well, go read it. There's an article on some bones they found in the woods outside Wallamee. I want to talk to you about it. I think I know whose they are."

"Mama—I can't. I have to go to work."

"Not now!" she said impatiently. "Come over for supper tonight. Six o'clock. Bring Vivian. Honestly, I'm so excited I'm having palpitations."

She hung up.

Mechanically, I finished my breakfast. Ron was still out on the porch, scraping away. The sound of it had become somehow reassuring, and I sat there for a little while, listening and imagining the poor beaver's last minutes, the screeching of Ron's tires, the look on his face. Then I went upstairs and got ready for work.

Outside the rain had mostly stopped, and as I stepped out the door a sun-sized hole appeared in the clouds, allowing Train Line a brief but dazzling spell of illumination. Everything glittered. Perhaps, I thought, heaven had opened up a trapdoor for me. It seemed likely that at any moment someone would reach down and drag me up through it.

As I made my way uphill toward the library, however, it began to rain again.

ᏆᎧ

I worked all day. By three I had a tidy stack of newly cataloged books, including one called *Natural Philosophy*, which was a science text from the 1880s and not a philosophy book at all. Its deceptive title had apparently gotten it onto our shelves by mistake. Still, I found it absorbing and quite entertaining—it was illustrated with drawings of dour, bearded men conducting experiments in frock coats—and it kept me from thinking too much about the unburied bones across the lake. One chapter described the nature of light: a vibration of ether, it said. Some troubled reader had scrawled in a margin *Where is God in all this?*

I closed the book on my finger, uncertain where on the shelves it belonged, if anywhere. I was suddenly intensely aware of the physical world around me: the dust motes spiraling through the air, the relationship between the weight of each book and the force required to lift it. *There is something to be said for the concrete world*, I thought. Carefully, I erased the marginalia and gave the book a place in the philosophy section. The scientific method, I decided, was in fact a very serviceable philosophy.

Bolstered by this idea, I put on my sweater and locked up. Today was the first day of school, and I would be spending the rest of the afternoon with Vivian. Every day at three during the school year the bus dropped her off at the front gate, where I'd sit and wait for her on a squat concrete pillar, one of two put there to stop cars from smashing into the gatehouse as they rounded the curve. A gatekeeper worked here in the summer season, taking money from tourists and selling programs, but now the gatehouse was boarded up and the wooden drop-gates stored for winter. Years before, I'd spent a couple of summers as a gatekeeper, on the early morning shift. I remembered it would get so cold I'd have to turn the space heater on, and shed layers of sweaters as the day warmed. No one came through the gate until nine or so. Until then I'd read, or just stare at the trees and the empty road and the bit of lake I could see from the window. Mist hung over the water. We had a radio in there, but I didn't listen to it.

I walked down the hill and sat on my concrete pillar. Vivian had spent much of the summer with her grandparents; it had been a few weeks since I'd seen her. I was looking forward to having her again, but I felt too preoccupied to take much pleasure from the thought of it. From here, the approaching cars looked as if they were speeding toward me, then turning away just seconds before running me down. I felt as if I was narrowly escaping death over and over again, and I found this exhilarating.

When the bus pulled up, the roar of yelling children came with it. That sound—the pent-up, malevolent hilarity of school-children—still made me uneasy. Poor Vivian was the last child off, stumbling after a pack of Darva Lawrence's blond grandchil-dren, with her lunch box and tote bag and raincoat. It had rained all morning—for hours the rain trickled down the library win-dows—but now the sun was out and the air steamy and warm. Vivian was wearing a blue sweater with a steam engine on it, the sleeves pushed up past her elbows.

"Hey," I said, holding out my hands for her things.

"Why do you say 'hey'? You're supposed to say 'hi,' or 'hello.'"

"Well, all right. Hi!"

"Hello," said Vivian.

She wouldn't let me carry anything. We walked home across the grounds, Vivian making wide circles around the puddles.

Vivian had been an odd, funny-looking baby, and now she was an odd, funny-looking little girl. She had thick, small glasses and a peculiar way of laughing; she'd bare her teeth and roll her eyes and not make a sound. Her curly black hair was in two small pigtails, round as meatballs, over her ears. I was finding it dif-ficult to slip back into Vivian-mode; everything I said to her felt stiff and inappropriate.

She told me her new teacher was named Miss Strunk and that she had to sit next to a boy she didn't like.

"Why don't you like him?"

"He's mean. He shakes my chair."

"Shakes your chair?"

"Like this." She pantomimed a mean boy shaking a chair. "Then I almost fall out."

"Sounds to me like he likes you."

She grimaced, showing her small gapped teeth. "I don't think so," she said.

Back at the house I got her a snack, a plastic tumbler of grape juice and some squares of cheddar cheese. Ron was in the kitchen with nothing on but a pair of boxer shorts, grinding herbs with a mortar and pestle. "I don't know how you can drink that stuff," he said to Vivian.

"I like it," she said, gulping her juice.

He shook his head. "It tastes funky to me."

"Funky?" I said.

He picked up his mortar and poured the gray powder onto a sheet of paper. "You know what I mean. Just...funky. Rotten. Like someone made it in the dark." Ron was obsessed with food. He was like a person on a perpetual starvation diet, which I suppose he was. He was always drinking brothy things he called "infusions" and trying to get me to taste them. You could not eat a thing in our kitchen without fielding a comment from Ron. I wanted to ask him about his beaver pelt but could not come up with a good way to broach the subject.

"I like it," said Vivian again, kicking her heels against the table legs.

"That's good. I'm glad everyone's different," Ron said.

This was one of my favorite times of day: afternoon light filling the kitchen, and no one in a hurry to do anything. For several minutes the only sounds were Vivian's rhythmic kicking, the scrape of the pestle, and someone's distant wind chime. I wiped the toast crumbs off the counter and emptied the draining rack of dishes.

"I don't like the name *Strunk*," said Vivian after a while. "It makes me think of a skunk."

She told us how they were going to be studying Indians in the third grade, and that Miss Strunk told the class that she would try to see if they could go on a field trip to the excavation by the lake.

"But maybe not. She wants to make sure it's an Indian first."

Ron took an apple from the refrigerator and began chomping on it. "That doesn't sound very respectful to me," he said. "When I pass over, I won't want a busload of third-graders walking all over my bones."

"Would we walk on bones?"

"Of course not," I said.

"You *might*," said Ron. "But if I were your mom, I wouldn't sign the permission slip, I can tell you that."

This conversation was making me tense. Though I had my back to him, I could sense Ron looking at me. Lately, he'd been giving me long, appraising glances. It gave me the impression that since he was almost done renovating the house, he needed a new project, and would like very much to renovate me.

"You know," said Ron, "you two have a lot in common."

Vivian looked up at me, then back down at her plate of cheese cubes. "We both have brown hair."

"That's true. But I was thinking that you're both only children. You don't have brothers or sisters. That's unusual."

"It's not so unusual," I said.

"Actually, it is. I can't think of anyone else, off the top of my head. I have four sisters, Jenny has a sister and a brother…"

"My mother says one is more than enough," said Vivian, proudly.

"It must be lonely though. I'd be."

"I'm never lonely," I said. This was true, I believed, but it had come out more vehemently than I intended. I sounded defensive, as if he had hit a sore spot, which he had not.

"Never?" asked Ron.

"Not really." I turned to Vivian. "Homework time. Hop to it. I know you have some."

"I wish I had a sister," she sighed.

Her only homework, claimed Vivian, was handwriting. I cleared a place on the kitchen table for her, and Ron wandered off into the living room with his tall, murky beverage. While I drank my coffee and watched Vivian work, I felt myself sinking into something of a torpor. This state was caused not, I realized, by calmness or relaxation, but by panic: both my body and mind balked at the thought of discussing the skeleton with my mother over dinner. I wanted to close my eyes and slump to the floor. I found, however, that if I sipped my coffee at perfectly regular intervals I could keep panic from overtaking me, and thus remained upright.

When she was done with her cursive *A*'s—she had to start over twice, because her vigorous erasing tore holes in the cheap paper Elaine bought her—Vivian showed them to me. They were heavy and dark and misshapen: chains pulled from a sunken ship. But every single one was there.

"Good job," I told her, raising a leaden hand to pat her head.

"Thank you." Her bangs stood up from her forehead like a row of fuzzy trees.

Vivian sat in front of the television while I did a crossword puzzle and watched the clock hands creep inevitably toward six.

At a quarter to, I gathered Vivian's things and we walked to my mother's house. Dark clouds were beginning to pile up in the sky, but down below the air was still and clear as a block of glass. Most of the time I found it difficult to see Train Line objectively—the shabby houses and giant trees were more familiar to me than my own face, and I overlooked their flaws as I did my own—but with Vivian's hand in mine I saw the world frankly: the broken picket fences, the plastic sheeting tacked up in place of storm windows, the garish, brightly colored spheres that sat on pedestals in so many front yards. My mother had a red sphere in hers. It shone like a giant planet among the weeds and broken bird feeders. As we passed it, Vivian reached her hand out but stopped just short of touching it.

Sometimes, when I looked at Vivian, I would think it was a good thing I didn't have my own child, because my own child wouldn't be Vivian and would therefore disappoint me.

∽✢

We arrived at my mother's house to find her in an ebullient mood. She wore a tight, flamingo-colored dress and had piled her hair on top of her head. Sweat beaded her upper lip.

"Come, come," she said, ushering us into the kitchen. "Your timing is impeccable. I've just pulled the chicken from the oven. My, Naomi, you look nice this evening."

A slow blush moved up my neck and into my cheeks. I didn't, in fact, look nice. I hadn't washed my hair in several days, and I was wearing a sweatshirt with bleach stains on it. Was she trying to be sarcastic? I couldn't tell. My mother's good moods could be more bewildering than her bad ones.

But at dinner she was solicitous and polite, and she didn't mention the skeleton, so I began to relax. I asked her about her radio show.

"You mean," she said, "is it still canceled? Yes, it is, for now." She gave me an energetic smile.

"For now?"

"Mmm."

I didn't press it. Instead we chatted with Vivian about school, and then I found myself telling her about the strange dream I'd had the night before, with the train and the old man. She listened attentively, then said, "Well, that's about Jenny Butler, of course."

"What do you mean? How?"

"Haven't you heard? She's sick. Everyone knows that, but it's worse than we thought. She found out last week." My mother was far more plugged into Train Line gossip than I was, and she didn't always think to pass it on to me, which was slightly frustrating. Her best friend was a medium named Darva Lawrence, who had bleached-blond hair, a smoker's cough, and sometimes, fake eyelashes. She was always materializing at my mother's back door, loaded down with info.

"Found out what?"

My mother raised her eyebrows—which were plucked into thin, penciled fermatas—and gestured toward Vivian, who was distractedly prodding her potatoes with her finger, then mouthed a word at me. It looked like *dander*.

Dander? I mouthed back.

Can-cer, she repeated.

Oh.

"What kind?"

She shook her head; she either didn't know or didn't want to say. "The kind you don't want to get," she said.

It wasn't Darva who gave her the information, she said, it was Troy, who got it straight from Ron, who was the only person Jenny had told so far.

"So officially, I don't know," I said.

"Probably not."

"Still," I said, "I don't know how that connects to my dream."

My mother rolled her eyes. "The train is the train of life. You're afraid Jenny's going to jump off it. Jenny *Butler*—a butler's usually an old man, right? You must have known on some level how sick she is."

"Hmm," I said. I wasn't sure I bought it, but it wasn't worth arguing about.

When we were finished, my mother and Vivian went into the other room to watch television and I washed the dishes, thinking about Jenny. From the little window over my mother's sink I could see right into Tony K. the Hypnotist's house. He appeared to be having a get-together. Ron passed by the window carrying a glass of pink wine, and a little later I spotted Dave Wood eating something. A couple of people I didn't know were there, too, and so was a woman who went by the name "Beachsong." Her real name was Gina Saletta; I'd gone to school with her. She was one of a group of girls who came up to me one study hall during seventh grade and told me they liked my outfit. I was newly overweight at the time and none of my clothes fit at all. The outfit was a brick-red pantsuit with a butterfly print. In those days of polo shirts and crewneck sweaters, I had to admit I looked absurd. My mistake was in thinking no one would notice. When I got home that day I changed out of the awful things, balled them up, and stuffed them in a grocery bag with some rocks. When it got dark I ran out to the dock at the end of Fox Street and threw the bundle into the lake. I don't remember much else from seventh grade.

The dishwater was dirty and cold, but that was all right. I was done. I drained the sink and wiped it down, then cleaned off the counters and the table. *They didn't invite me,* I fumed. I should be used to it, I thought, but I was not. *It's not like I'm a newcomer or a beginner or old, or something…*

I squeezed out the sponge and leaned over the sink again, realizing, suddenly, that Jenny was most certainly there—everyone I'd spotted was a friend of hers—and that the meeting was probably about her. The top of someone's head—was it red hair?—was just barely visible over the windowsill. Then, as I was looking over at Tony K.'s, careful to look down if anyone happened to glance my way, the lights went out. They were having a home circle, I figured. It occurred to me that with the lights out they'd be able to see me but I wouldn't be able to see them. They were invisible—seeing but unseen. I went into the living room, picked up the newspaper, then quickly put it down again. I'd had just about enough of newspapers.

Against my better judgment, I told my mother what I'd seen. She and Vivian were flopped across each other, watching a quiz show. She looked up at me sharply.

"They didn't invite you," she said.

"Apparently not."

She turned back to the television, sighing. "I probably wouldn't have invited you, either. Why aren't you friendlier to people? I didn't teach you to be such an ice queen."

I pretended I hadn't heard her, and feigned great interest in the game show, my arms crossed tightly over my chest.

When it was time to go, my mother helped me bundle Vivian out to the Oldsmobile. I was holding the driver's side door open, waiting for Vivian to get her stuff together, when my mother said, "Let me drive."

"You're coming?"

"And I'm driving."

This was alarming. I drove Vivian home every Tuesday, when Elaine worked late, and my mother had never wanted to come before. I slid into the passenger seat and pulled the seat belt across me, grateful for the dark that hid my face.

We rumbled down Rochester Street and out of Train Line. I had to admit, my mother was a good, natural driver. She seemed to be paying more attention to her reflection in the rearview mirror than to what was going on around her—every time I borrowed her car, I had to readjust the mirror so that it reflected what it was supposed to—but she spotted a shadowy trio of deer alongside the road long before I did, and stopped to let them leap past us. Her earlier exuberance had flattened somewhat after dinner, and now she was thoughtful and preoccupied, tapping her fingers on the steering wheel.

We dropped Vivian off—she looked so small and hunched walking up the blacktopped driveway in the bright flood of motion-sensor lights—and then, instead of heading home, my mother turned down Vining Road. She wanted, she said, to take a look at the excavation by the lake.

"It's dark," I said, trying not to sound nervous.

"I don't see why that should stop us."

She slowed the car next to the unpaved driveway, which was now blocked with sawhorses. Yellow crime scene tape fluttered between them. My mother parked and turned off the lights.

"Police ribbon," I said, glancing at her.

"Ancient Indians, my eye," she said. "Let's get out."

"Mama! It's *dark*..." But she had her door open and was heaving herself through it.

I followed her through the dried-up milkweed and Queen Anne's lace to the edge of the woods. From here, we could look through the trees and down a steep embankment. The embankment smoothed out into a clearing, and there, at the very bottom, were lights. Also some machinery, the half-dug foundation, piles of dirt. It was hard to reconcile this vision with what I remembered about that day; nothing looked the same but the shallow slope of the ground as it dipped toward the lake. I'd expected to feel something, seeing this. I thought I'd feel like I was standing in a collapsing house; I thought the earth would give way beneath my feet. But oddly, I felt very little. Mostly I was cold. I rubbed my arms.

My mother was breathing heavily from the exertion. "Darva was telling me about it. Her husband knows one of the police. Apparently they got another forensics specialist to look at the bones this afternoon, and he said they couldn't be terribly old. I guess there's ways they can tell."

There was movement down in the clearing; perhaps they had a watchman. I stepped a little farther into the woods, trying to see, and walked right into a barbed wire fence. It gouged my shin. "Ouch. Watch out for the fence, Mama."

"He was *mummified*," she said. "Partly, anyway."

"He?"

"They can tell that, too. Don't ask me how."

My mother stood with her hands on the wire, peering through the dark. Then she closed her eyes, took a deep breath, and exhaled. It was less an exhalation, though, than a moan: long and low. It unnerved me.

"Mama," I said, taking her arm. "Let's go back to the car."

"Shhh." She batted me away.

So I waited, hugging myself to keep warm. I still didn't recognize the place at all. The barn would be somewhere off to the left, but it was hidden in the shadows, and all I could see of the lake was a string of lights on the opposite shore. It was possible to think that I had nothing to do with what was going on down the hill.

My mother swayed a little and her dress rustled in the weeds. Then she gave another moan, even longer and lower than the first, and then she sighed deeply.

"They're right," she whispered.

"What?"

"That he's a man. A white man..." She frowned.

"Not an Indian?"

"Definitely not," she said, shaking her head. Then she reached out and touched me on the arm. Involuntarily, I jumped. "Can you get through?"

"God, no. It's too cold to concentrate."

"Well. I can't seem to get much more, either. Let's go, then."

We turned and waded back through the weeds. I got into the driver's side of the car and my mother dropped heavily into the passenger side. "Don't take off just yet," she said.

I turned the engine on and switched the heat up to high.

"You're going to think I'm nuts," my mother said, adjusting her dress beneath her thighs. "But I think I know who it is. Whose the bones are. I think they're my brother's."

Again, I felt myself jerk, as if shot through with electricity. "Uncle Geoffrey's?" I asked, dumbfounded.

"Oh, for God's sake, Naomi! No, not Geoffrey's! Don't be stupid. He's still alive. I mean Wilson! I think they're Wilson's bones."

Wilson was her eldest brother, the one who left home and disappeared when she was a child; she hadn't seen him since the forties, in New Orleans. I'd only ever seen one picture of him—a skinny, smart-alecky boy sitting on the bumper of a very large car. My mother's glasses glinted in the light of the dashboard. She didn't speak for a few moments. Then she sighed.

"Well, all right, I know. It's pretty far-fetched. It's just an idea I have."

I'd never heard her sound so unsure of herself. "Well, it could be him," I said, dubiously.

"It doesn't matter. It's somebody." She sat up, turned in her seat, and looked at me. I could almost hear her confidence come roaring back. "And you know what? I'm going to save my career."

I revved the car. "I don't understand."

"Naomi! *Pay attention!* If I can figure out what happened here, just think what it will do for my career! They'd think twice before canceling my radio show, that's for certain. Someone was killed and buried and the spirit is *out there* looking for a medium, I can feel it. I'm sure of it."

I turned to look at her. My mouth fell open.

"Maybe I could even write a book," she mused.

After a long minute I nodded. "Maybe," I said, and put my foot on the gas.

As I drove, she told me what she planned to do: she would continue to visit the site two or three times a week, then go home and meditate for an hour. Surely, she said, now that the spirit's bones were disturbed, and people were curious about them, it would be receptive to contact. She would also do some traditional research, look up unsolved cases at the library, go to City Hall and look at old deeds to the land. The more information she could gather, the closer she'd get to the spirit's vibration…

No, I thought, reeling.

"Gosh, just look at that house," she said, interrupting herself and prodding the window with her thumb. I took a deep breath and looked. Every window of a big Greek-revival-style house was lit up, revealing glimpses of chandeliers and woodwork and different wallpaper in every room. There were some beautiful houses along Wallamee's Main Street, big immaculate Victorians with tower rooms and cupolas and porches as big as my mother's entire house. In the daylight you could see how intricately painted they were, with different colors for every part of the window frames. One was pale blue with indigo and gray and violet trim. That was my favorite. They all had big front windows with lots of panes and lace curtains. You couldn't see much of the insides, and I had never been in one. I imagined bright light and glass bowls full of flowers. When I was younger I had wanted to live in one of these houses more than anything. I'd forgotten that feeling until now. It seemed like you could live a certain kind of life in one of these lovely, solid houses—a respectable life. I used to wish my mother would marry a man who owned one. Or, if that didn't work, perhaps I would. I didn't expect that neither of us would marry and that I'd end up living a couple of blocks from where my mother did, in the very first house in Train Line we found.

"It's beautiful," I said. She nodded, staring out the window as we passed it. I used to wonder if she, too, wanted the kind of life that would allow her a Victorian house, a yard, beautiful curtains. Now I wondered again, missing those lost lives.

I stopped at a red light. A large crowd of well-dressed people crossed the street in front of us, having just left the restaurant on the corner. They were laughing, obviously having a barrel of fun. "You know what?" my mother asked me, watching the people going by. "I have this astonishing feeling. I don't know if it's Wilson or not, but there's something special about this spirit, Naomi. It's going to change our lives."

❧

My mother liked to say she'd been born a medium. That might be the only way to explain it. Certainly, there was nothing about her particular upbringing that encouraged spiritualism. Her name was Patsy then, and I can't help but think of her as a different person from Galina, Mother Galina, who came later. Her father owned an office supply shop and her mother, who was to die, lost and confused, so many years later, was always a school librarian. She had two older brothers, Geoffrey and Wilson, and a pet pack rat named Walt Junior, after her father. They weren't poor but nobody had much money then. In pictures, she is long-limbed and glowering, her wrists poking from sleeves, her socks down around her ankles. She looks a bit like I did, but more boyish, more fierce.

When she was twelve, Wilson ran away. This was, until the death of her mother, the big tragedy of her life. Wilson was her favorite brother, her favorite person in the world. He worked as a delivery boy around town and would sometimes bring my mother along with him, and they'd turn on the radio in his old Ford and they'd sing along with it. Wilson knew every word to every song. He taught my mother the most shocking dirty words he knew. He had a million girlfriends.

But one day after supper he announced that he was leaving. It was 1946 and Wilson was seventeen; he'd missed being in the war by just a few months, and it wrecked him. He'd decided to Go North and Experience Life. He was going to hop a freight, he said. Their father stood up to try and stop him, to grab and shake him or bar the door, but it was too late. Wilson vanished into the night. And that was the very last anyone had ever seen of him.

People vanish. My mother knew this; she knew that people died and moved away, but never really understood it before then. She'd never really thought of it as a permanent state, as something irreversible. She walked around thinking that any minute there'd be Wilson, grinning and singing and bearing presents. But it never was. For three years she walked around thinking he was there, just around the corner, or watching from a balcony, or trundling by on a streetcar. It made her feel better to imagine him that way, lurking just out of sight, seeing but un-seeable.

She was fifteen, in the middle of failing her first year of high school, when she found the peacock. She'd been sent home after lunch for hurling her sandwich at the lunch monitor and was

INVISIBLE

wandering through the neighborhoods near the river. She was
sitting in an alley on a broken wooden chair when she heard
what she thought was a baby crying, a peculiar, sorrowful kind of
cry. There, in a cardboard box behind a tobacco shop, she found
the peacock. Its tail was raggedy and sparse, as if someone had
plucked almost all the feathers out. It was dirty, too, but still
beautiful, its body gleaming like something made of a strange
blue metal. It didn't move when my mother picked up the box. It
didn't move or make another sound all the way home.

She snuck into her brother Geoffrey's bedroom and looked
up peacocks in his encyclopedia, and found out that it could eat
seeds and corn and bugs. It would have to look for bugs on its
own, but she found a bag of birdseed in the back shed, and she
sprinkled a handful around the peacock's box. It pecked at it. My
mother crouched down next to the box and watched it, close
enough to see the tiny seedlike nostrils in its beak and the ring of
bird skin around each of its small black eyes.

The peacock lived in their yard for nearly a year. They named
it Hector. Every morning it cried for its seeds and corn, and every
evening it cried from loneliness until my mother came out and
sat with it, under its perch in the cucumber tree. It wasn't satisfied with anyone else, and half the time it would chase Geoffrey
right back into the house. This was enough to make my mother
like the bird a great deal. But it also gave her dreams. From almost the first night the peacock lived with them, my mother began having wonderful, vivid, sometimes even prophetic, dreams.

Once she dreamed she got an A on a math test, for the first
time ever, and then she did. Another time she dreamed that a
boy named Ralph LaRoux would ask her to a dance—a miracle
if there ever was one—and that happened, too. Most of the time,
though, she dreamed about Wilson. There was Wilson riding the
rails, wearing a greasy wool hat and a moth-eaten beard; there
was Wilson working as a lumberjack in Canada, eating pancakes
outside a log cabin. She even dreamed of him sleeping with a
woman, once. Each of these visions—because she was sure they

– 73 –

were more than dreams, now—had a feeling in them, too. It was a feeling of *rightness*. She wasn't sure how else to describe it. It was a feeling that the visions were coming to her to reassure her, to announce to her that Wilson was fine and that life was moving forward as it should. My mother, who read obsessively, began to wonder if she was a witch. She'd read that witches sometimes had familiars in the shape of birds, usually crows or owls or something, but why not a peacock?

Eventually Hector's tail feathers grew back, and then one morning he was gone. My mother felt sure he had struck out on his own, maybe to search for a peahen, or perhaps just to Experience Life. It wasn't until she was grown up that it occurred to her he might have been stolen. At the time she just thought, *Ah, Hector's moved on,* and that was that. Because by then she'd saved up her allowance and bought a Ouija board, and though her visions became less frequent after Hector left, that sense of rightness never left her. She realized she could know some things.

My mother began in honesty, and ended in fraud; I began in fraud, and ended in something at least close to truthfulness.

❧

By the end of that week, the forensics specialists and archaeologists, working together, had discovered a few facts about the body at the construction site. I followed the story in the *Wallamee Evening Observer* and watched the evening news. So did my mother.

It was a male, they said, between twenty and twenty-eight years old, and most likely Caucasian. He had been buried for more than three years but less than fifteen, probably about seven years. The body was partly mummified. Fatty tissue had been preserved in the area of the skull, the spine, and the arms. There was not much to help identification—a little dental work, but no bones had ever been broken. There was no obvious sign of the cause of death.

The only reason murder was suspected, the news stories said, was because of the place the body was buried. How could a body show up there by accident? One theory entertained was that the man had drowned in a bog years before, and that the land had dried up since. That theory only lasted a day or so, until Mr. Hennessey, owner of the property, said that the clearing had been exactly the same since he bought it in 1954, and no one could have drowned in it then unless they'd gone and dug themselves in.

5

cryptesthesia

I was working in the library on Friday morning when a police officer came around to talk. It was only nine-thirty, so the library wasn't open yet, but from where I sat at my desk I could see him come up the stone walkway. He was a small young man with a pale stubble of hair. I unlocked the door and let him in.

"Miss Ash?" he said, holding out his hand. "Officer Peterson. I've been going around talking to folks this morning. We're doing a little investigation across the lake there." He gestured with his head. His hair was so short you could see right through to his skull, which was lumpy and coarse. "Would it be all right if I came in?"

"Sure," I said, shutting the door behind him. "We can sit in there." I showed him into the reading room and sat down in one of the big wicker chairs.

"This place is real old, isn't it?" said Officer Peterson. He held his hat behind his back and peered at the spirit photographs on the walls. He stared for a long time at one by a man named Mr. Skoog; it was of two normal men shaking hands, with the tiny face of Edgar Allan Poe looking over one man's shoulder. The floorboards squeaked under Officer Peterson's feet. The reading room was my favorite place in Train Line. It had tall windows and wicker chairs with feather cushions and two large oak tables with lamps on them.

"It was built in nineteen twenty-five."

"That's old." Officer Peterson looked about twenty-two. His face was still stuccoed with acne.

He asked me what my job entailed, exactly, and said that a couple of people had told him I might be a good person to talk to. Was it true that I saw a lot of the people who came through Train Line?

"Yes, I guess so. Though I don't necessarily look at them."

"What do you mean?"

"I mean I'm a librarian. I mostly only notice people who annoy me."

He laughed a little at this, unsure if he was supposed to. "But you worked at the gatehouse, too."

"That was a few years ago."

"We're talking about a few years ago."

"Yes, then."

"Does anyone stand out in your mind? Anything odd or peculiar about anyone?"

From one of the windows I could see the gatehouse, just down the hill from the library. The geraniums in its window boxes were dead. I tried to think.

"Well, you know, an awful lot of strange people come through here."

"For example?"

"There was man who had conspiracy theories. He'd hang around the gatehouse all day, telling me things. The government had a file on him, the army flew over his house every day in planes undetectable by radar."

"Describe him." Officer Peterson sat down and took a little notebook out of his pocket. He held a pencil in an odd way, between his thumb and pointer finger.

"Short, muscular. He had a tiny ponytail. Dark hair. Maybe thirty. He talked too fast. I think his name was Paul."

"And this was…?"

"Oh, I don't know. Eleven or twelve years ago."

"Do you know what happened to this guy?"

I shook my head. "People come and go all the time here. If I'd never seen him again I wouldn't think anything of it. I don't think anyone would." This was true. When Peter went missing, no one in Train Line seemed to notice. That hadn't surprised me, but I'd expected Peter's family would come looking. For years I waited for them, my gut lurching every time the phone rang, but I'd never heard from them. I rubbed my forehead, pretending to think about Paul. "I might have seen him two summers in a row."

"But only in the summers."

"Not many people are around in winter."

"Would you call this winter?"

Startled, I turned and looked out the window again. "I don't know. Yes, I guess I would. Everyone's left for the year. Or a lot of people have. More will leave before Christmas."

"But you don't leave."

"No."

"How about the rest of your…business? Any unusual customers?"

"That's private."

He nodded slowly, marking that down in his book. "Okay, then. Anything else you recall, unrelated to business?"

I racked my brains. I told him about the old Australian woman who claimed she was walking around the world, and how after she'd been lurking around for three days someone found her sleeping under a bush behind the lecture hall. I told him about the man who called up the main office and told them he was about to come down with a gun and shoot everyone, because we were all Satan worshippers. He said he'd heard about that one.

"How long have you lived here?"

"Twenty-one years."

"Since you were real little."

"Yes."

"And you've never left?"

"Not for any length of time. I went to Cape Cod with my mother once, and some other little trips like that."

"Do you like it here?"

"I'm not sure what that has to do with your investigation."

He shrugged. "It probably doesn't have anything to do with it. I'm just trying to get to know you. Is that all right?"

"That's fine," I said. Officer Peterson, I noticed, had wide, almost beautiful shoulders, and a narrow girlish waist. I came close to imagining putting my hands around it, then stopped myself.

"Good. So, *do* you like it here?"

"I do."

"What do you do for fun?"

"I have friends. I go for walks. I read books."

"No hobbies?"

I did not understand why he was asking me these questions. They made me irritated and hot. I told him about Vivian and my mother and the details of my job. While he walked around the reading room I explained the theories behind spirit photography. He seemed to get bored with me all at once.

"I guess I've taken up enough of your time." He tucked his pencil in his pocket but made no move to go. "So," he said. "So tell me something."

"Yes?"

"Is this all for real?"

"This?"

"This whole town. Is it real? Or is it all fakers?"

I looked at him right in the eyes. "It's real," I said. "It's as real as you are."

❧

After Officer Peterson left, I couldn't concentrate enough to read. I still had an hour before the library had to be open, so I locked up and went to the cafeteria for a cup of coffee.

CLOSED! said an index card taped to the screen door, BACK IN FIFTEEN MINS.

So I took a walk up the path that ran around the edge of Train Line, behind the last row of cottages and through the woods. The trees were tall there, huge spreading firs and maples.

It was, supposedly, one of the few stands of virgin woods in the county. It smelled delicious: damp, fresh, but decayed. This path connected up with the one that led to Illumination Stump, where message services were held in summer, but I took another branch, one that led to the pet cemetery.

It always struck me as strange that there was a pet cemetery in Train Line, but no cemetery for people. When people died in town, they were either sent back to where they came from— lots of people had houses somewhere else, many in Ohio, for some reason, and many in Canada—or were buried in Wallamee. Spiritualists were fond of cremation, too, and of scattering their ashes. But pets could stay.

The paths in the pet cemetery were arranged in a series of loops, with some loops the exclusive domain of one family. The Lawrences had numberless German shepherds, and they were all here, each under its own concrete tombstone. Their names had been scratched with a stick into the wet cement, CINDER, 1966– 1972; BARBARELLA, 1979–1982 (hit by a car; I remembered that); POOPER 1976–1988. I'd never had a pet, myself, so I hadn't buried anything here. One of the minor controversies at Train Line was whether there are animals on the spirit plane. Most of the mediums were—like my mother—softhearted where animals were concerned, and believed there are. I tended to believe that spirit is a human thing, exclusively, but opening my mouth on that subject would gain me no friends.

I walked around, checking to see if there were any new graves. There was one, a very small one marked with a tongue- depressor cross, under a spiraea bush off the main path. I knelt down to take a look at it. SNIPPY it said, in ballpoint-pen ink. 1996–1998. Oh, no.

Snippy was Jenny's bird, a fat green-and-yellow budgie. I didn't like birds, birds in cages especially, and Snippy in particu- lar. Jenny kept it in her room most of the time, but sometimes she'd bring it downstairs and let it fly around the living room, where it would smash into lamps and try to attack its reflection in the mirror, then leave white streaks across the glass. And it screamed. Jenny was devoted to it. She thought the bird was cute, the way it screeched when we turned the radio on ("Oh, listen! Snippy's singing!"). Most of the time I wanted to kill it. If it was absolutely still and quiet I could see how you might call it "cute," with its little tilted head and its pointy little beak, but it had no purpose other than to make noise. Once when it wouldn't shut up I put its cage in the closet, and then forgot about it and left for the day. Jenny never mentioned it, but I wondered what she did when she came home and found it gone.

But now Snippy was dead. I hadn't even known it was sick. I was up before Jenny so I hadn't seen her this morning—I was, in fact, avoiding her—but she must have buried the bird sometime since. The arm of the tongue-depressor cross was stapled on. It must have been my stapler, and the tongue depressors Ron's. What a tiny, careful grave. Of course, there was something absurd about it—tongue depressors!—but nevertheless it gave me a bad feeling. When I stood back up again I felt dizzy, and the trees spun. The pet cemetery, I decided, was not charming at all, but tragic. It made me think of something Peter used to ask me, something he brought up often. How come, he asked, spiritualists get so upset when someone dies? Why do they care at all? If it's just a "change of form," and all that? Usually I told him, we *don't* get that upset. But once in a while I said, well, we can't help it, we can't help but miss the body sometimes.

"So, there is no death, but death is sad," said Peter. "They call that a paradox in my neck of the woods."

"You and your pair o' ducks," I said.

I was walking back toward town when I spotted someone up the road ahead of me. I slowed down, trying to figure out who it was. It didn't take long—he was wearing a cop uniform. My friend Peterson.

He was reading his notes, his head bent over his notebook, walking distractedly along Seneca Street. He scratched his pim-

ply cheek, stopped, and looked around. I stepped behind a tree. I
didn't want him to think I was following him.

But I did follow him, all the way down Seneca and into
Ferd's Groc-n-Stop. When he'd been in there five minutes or so,
I went inside and bought a box of doughnuts, pretending not to
notice him. He was sitting at the back counter with a cup of coffee, laughing it up with the old guys.

From the benches outside the Forest Temple, which was next
door to the grocery store, I had a good view of the front entrance.
I sat there, eating a doughnut, until Officer Peterson came out.
An old guy came with him, and pointed him down Seneca Street
toward Fox. He shook the old guy's hand and walked off. At Erie
Street he turned right, then disappeared into the candle shop. It
would look funny if I hung around outside, so I took a slow walk
around the block, saying hello to Ron as he jogged by, his wire-
rimmed glasses bouncing on his nose.

"You have a message on the answering machine!" he called
back to me. "Don't forget to check it!"

"Thanks!"

I spotted Peterson walking resolutely down Fox Street. He
went right past my house, around the cafeteria, and up Rochester
Street. He stopped about halfway down, then checked his notes.
He walked a few more feet, slowed down, looked both ways,
then turned in at my mother's front gate.

My mother's!

෴

I went back home. Jenny was nowhere around. The message on
the answering machine, it turned out, was from Dave the Alien.

"Naomi! Sorry I missed you. Could you be at work already?"
His voice sounded artificially energetic. "I know it's, ah, short
notice, but how would you like to come over to my place for,
ah, dinner? You won't have to bring anything or even give me a

reading"—I cringed—"or, well, whatever. You have to eat, right? So you might as well. Give me a call or something."

Suddenly I noticed that I had a terrible headache. I washed my hands in cold water, which sometimes helped, and thought that maybe I would just lie on the sofa the rest of the day. I could put a sign on the door of the library: GONE HOME SICK. I never took sick days.

Then I thought of Officer Peterson, and how he could walk by and see the sign on the library door and think he rattled me so much I just fell to pieces and had to go home. So instead I took four aspirin and a glass of water, went back to the library, and slept at my desk until three-thirty. I only woke up once, when the mailman came with the gross of index cards I'd ordered.

"Thank God it's Friday, huh?" he said, dropping the box on my desk with a bang.

♋

When I was a child, I believed in everything, without even trying. But in the years after my grandmother died, I found faith to be a trickier thing, something that could wriggle away the minute I had my hands around it, like a wild animal. It wasn't a sudden transformation. I gradually grew embarrassed of my mother and her clothes and her exotic mediumship. When we first arrived in Train Line, she was exclusively a trance medium: no more trumpet, no more slate, no more gusts of perfume or ghostly voices. She'd fall down on the table with a thump, her mouth hanging open, groaning like a cow with a stomachache. In a minute or two she'd sit up, but it wouldn't be her—spirits would be controlling her, speaking through her. At first I thought it was scary but important; later I came to see it as gross, indiscreet, and my distaste evolved into skepticism. I sulked in my room when she held home circles and told her I was going to become a news anchor when I grew up. She laughed at me—literally laughed—and said I had to be a blonde. I threw my shoes at her.

At school in Wallamee I wanted clean-cut, wholesome-looking friends. I fell in love with fresh air and tennis shoes and Baptists. I had a friend named Becky Bell, who taught me Sunday school songs. But I was known as the spooky girl, the girl with the spooky mom who wore spooky clothes. In a small town a reputation like this will stay with you for the rest of your life, no matter what you do. They'd never, ever let me on the softball team, even if I could hit the ball, which I couldn't. By the time I was fourteen I realized I needed to try a new tack: capitalize on what I had. I told my friends—a handful of misfit girls—that I would hold a séance.

After school one afternoon, we met in the cemetery behind Wallamee Junior High. It was March and the grass was still patched with wet gray snow. The sky was clear blue and the wind was cold. Recently, a teacher in our school had died, a man named Mr. McGlynn who taught history and was famous for his meanness. He just didn't come to school one day, or the next, and when some other teachers went to his house to look for him— he was divorced and lived alone—they found him lying on the floor, dead, surrounded by gin bottles. None of us had had a class with Mr. McGlynn, but the drama of his life and death intrigued us. Other students told us about Mr. McGlynn's shaky hands, the alcohol on his breath; how the import of these details wasn't noticed until it was too late. The poor man was buried right out behind the school.

We sat in a circle, about twenty feet from the fresh mound of dirt over Mr. McGlynn. There was no stone there yet, just a small metal sign from the funeral home and piles of flowers from Wallamee Junior High. I realized that I didn't really think Mr. McGlynn would show up and that I had backed myself into a corner: my friends expected a show. All the tricks I knew—the spying confederates, the books of information on all the regular customers, the universal truths that sound like amazing insights—couldn't help me now. Still, there was no backing out of it. One of my friends, a chubby girl named Sharon who had a lazy eye, started to cry as soon as we sat down.

"It's all right, Shar," said my friends, patting her arm. They were nice girls, sensitive and awkward and benign. We waited until Sharon got herself together. I felt the damp ground soak through my skirt and my underpants. We held hands and closed our eyes.

I knew the lingo. If nothing else, that impressed my impressionable friends. I said my mother's prayer, And there is no Death, and there are no Dead, etcetera, and asked that we all keep ourselves hospitable to the spirits surrounding us. They liked that, I think—hospitable—as if we were part inn, part hospital, opening our doors to dead Mr. McGlynn. After a few minutes of silence, I threw my head back and started talking.

"He's with us," I said.

Sharon began to moan and shake.

I told them that he was glad he was through teaching, that he hated it, and he hated all the kids, too. Just the loud, popular kids, actually; he liked the quiet students. I told them that he said we should be nicer to Miss Ludlum, the frail, frightened young woman who taught us typing, because she'd had a tragic life. I hinted at miscarriages. I went on a long time. I said that Donna, my skinny, odd-looking friend, would find true love before any of us, and that Marie would have a difficult life but would be wildly successful one day. I told them that Mr. McGlynn wanted us to study more in history. They bought it all.

And later, when I went home feeling half-fraudulent, half-brilliant, I thought, *Well, why shouldn't they buy it?* Had I said anything patently false? Or harmful? And how was I to know whether the thoughts that came to me *weren't* Mr. McGlynn's?

For several months I gave readings and held séances at school, after school, at parties, in the pink-and-yellow bedrooms of popular girls, in the basement rec rooms of rich kids. I affected a mysterious look: loose hair, dark clothes, a slow smile. I quit forcing myself to talk to people when I didn't have to. I made sure, though, that I didn't go too far.

It wasn't long before my mother found out about what I was doing. She feigned nonchalance.

"Darva Lawrence told me that you gave Teeny an excellent reading," she said one day at the beginning of the summer. I'd been flopping around the house, bored out of my skull. "She wouldn't stop talking about it. Maybe you should try working a message service sometime."

Teeny was a tough girl, a year or two older than me, and though her mother was a medium, Teeny never took any flak for it. I'd given her a truly inspired reading the week before. We all crouched in an alley behind the Ha-Ha, and I said that a spirit who called herself Nana was telling me how misunderstood Teeny was. You can usually hit some kind of pay dirt by telling people they're misunderstood, or that they have an undeveloped talent—they're two of the universal truths of mediumship—but it must have struck a particularly resonant chord in Teeny. I saw in her big mean face how wholly misunderstood she felt, and when I told her about her sensitive side, how it needed to come out before she'd ever find true love, she started crying. So did a couple of her mean, leather-jacketed pals.

I knew, when I gave her the reading, that it would get back to my mother sooner or later, since Mrs. Lawrence was my mother's best friend. Besides lurking around each other's kitchens, they met once a week for the lunch special at the Italian Fisherman, on the wharf in Wallamee. When we were younger, Teeny and I went with them—Teeny always ordered french fries and applesauce and coleslaw, and she'd kick me hard under the table if I looked at her—and sometimes we'd be thrown together with the same babysitter if our mothers went out on the town. I hated her, really. And she'd never had a good word to say to me until the reading. Seeing that there was a sensitive side to Teeny Lawrence took more empathy than I'd known I had.

With my new hobby out in the open, and my mother giving no sign that she'd laugh at me, I talked to Troy Versted about working a message service. If he was surprised, he didn't say so. He just shook my hand, said Welcome, and put me on the schedule for a lunchtime Illumination Stump meeting later in the week.

∽◦∾

Summers, there were three message services a day in Train Line, the beginning of each signaled by the clanging of the lecture-hall bell. The first was at the Stump at noon, another at the Forest Temple at four, and the last one was at six-thirty, back at the Stump again.

Illumination Stump was in a clearing in the Violet Woods, accessible only by a short walk under towering maple trees and pines. The original stump had been sealed in concrete in order to preserve it, but it still looked like a stump. It was surrounded by a frilly border of petunias and, on holidays, miniature American flags. Facing it were rows of wooden benches painted gray. A sign nailed high on a tree said PLEASE OBSERVE SILENCE AS THIS IS A PLACE OF WORSHIP. During a message service, visitors sat on the benches and mediums gathered in back, behind them. In the old days, the rumor was, mediums stood right up on the stump, but now that was considered dangerous, as many of the mediums were elderly, so these days they stood next to it. They'd take turns going up front, where they pulled messages out of the air until Troy or whoever else was mediating gave them the time's-up signal: a finger across the eyes.

The morning before the first time I worked the Stump, I sweated and paced and changed my clothes three times. I settled on a black sundress with tiny buttons down the front and put my hair back in two silver clips. My mother had agreed to go after me, so that if I flopped she could flop too, and thereby lessen the effect. She encouraged me to come up with some interesting topics ahead of time ("How about sea travel? I haven't heard that one in a while. And jewelry! No one ever mentions jewelry, but you know, it's very important to people…") but I snootily told her I thought that was cheating.

"Oh, please!" said my mother, rolling her eyes.

We walked together through the dappled shade of the Violet Woods. Here and there alongside the path were marble benches, installed by the Victorians so the weak and consumptive could take a little rest on their way to the Stump. A spring of healing waters on the grounds drew crowds during the early part of the century. I imagined the pale young ladies making their way through the woods, skirts trailing, cheeks pinkening in the fresh air. I tried to feel them. I could not feel them. I was a fraud, a fraud, a fraud.

We got there early and gossiped about the new summer visitors, the regulars, the other mediums. My mother pointed out a woman—a wizened old lady with an orange dress and a matching hat—for whom she'd read the night before.

"She's gone through six husbands. *Six.* Some divorced but mostly widowed. She's like Henry the Eighth, or what's-her-name, that actress. All those men were just crowding around me last night, each trying to get his two cents in. She thought it was the funniest thing. Her name's—now what is it?—Ginger. That's why she wears that peculiar color."

A man lurched by, leaning heavily on his cane. "Darva told me about him. A former rocket scientist! Honestly. But he was in an accident and got a touch of brain damage. Anyway, if anyone says science, he's the one you want."

My mother's archenemy, Winnie Sandox, stood in front of us and looked around for someone to talk to. She was small and round and had a big puff of hair. Her blouse fluttered.

"Look what's deigning us with her presence," whispered my mother. "Ugh."

Troy said a prayer and Grace Batsummer started us off. She was old even then, as most mediums seemed to be when I was a teenager, before the New Agers began showing up. Grace was a very good, very clever medium, with a dry sense of humor and original things to say.

"Now, I sense a problem here in terms of—how shall I put it—productivity. It's coming to me in the form of a garden, you see. It's a garden with lovely flowers, vines and leaves and lush foliage, but—where's the fruit? This is for you, dear—yes, you with the darling hat. You know what this garden is, don't you? I know you do. It's you, dear."

The sun was right overhead, burning through my hair. Squirrels jumped from tree to tree above us, the thin branches bending under their weight.

After Grace there were two others, visiting mediums I didn't know, then Troy gave me the signal. I walked up front, my eyes straight ahead.

"This is young Naomi Ash, one of our newest mediums," said Troy. "We're so happy to have her. All right, then, Naomi."

I should have looked at my mother, or at Troy, or at the squirrels or even at Winnie Sandox, but instead I looked at the audience. The faces across the first row were bored, dubious, and self-absorbed. Someone looked at his watch.

"Thank you," I said.

For the first few minutes I repeated stuff I'd heard a million times—*someone named Mary...an illness...they're watching over you*—but after a while I found a groove. I picked a promising-looking person in the back, a plump thirtyish woman with a shiny black bob and white teeth. I told her about someone lost, someone she hadn't heard from in ages and ages, and she nodded right along. I gained confidence.

"You have to reestablish contact with this person. They're still on this plane, and they're thinking of you. It's a she, am I right?"

She nodded vigorously.

"And she needs you..." Suddenly, I could see this person: a laughing young woman with pretty clothes and long, sun-streaked hair. She appeared in front of me like a reflection in a pane of glass, transparent but real, and when I closed my eyes I could see her even more clearly. And she *wasn't* dead—I knew this with a certainty I would be hard-pressed to explain. I was so surprised: a real vision! I gasped a little. "You'll need her, too, later, but right now she's the one in need. You can help her. She'll never make the first move—it's all up to you." The woman turned a little pink, embarrassed, and looked down at her hands.

Then Troy drew his finger across his round blue eyes.

I stumbled to the back, my eyes on the ground. It was my mother's turn, then, and I didn't hear what she said but there was no doubt it had to do with sea voyages and jewelry. Every cell in my body was thrumming. I felt so *certain* about what I'd said to the woman in the back. She just *had* to find this person, whoever it was. She leaned toward a man next to her and whispered in his ear, and I thought, *I've done it.* I've connected with this woman. This wasn't true mediumship, yet, since no spirits were involved, but something else, something close—telepathy, maybe. Still. A weird little buzz of electricity hummed in my chest, and I imagined it was a kind of power line, linking me to the black-haired woman. I connected. Perhaps I wasn't such a big faker after all. It made me so happy I almost died.

◠◡◠

That evening, after Vivian went home, I poked through all my clothes and tried to find something to wear to dinner with Dave the Alien.

I'd spread everything I owned across the rumpled blankets of my bed, and the overhead light was on. Usually I just wore a dress of some kind and a sweater and forgot about my clothes entirely. But all my dresses, and skirts and blouses and stockings and sweaters, seemed to have fallen apart overnight. There were frayed bits of string where there used to be buttons, belts were missing, hems dragged, seams opened up. There were stains and pills and moth holes. Some didn't smell very good. It hadn't happened overnight, of course. But the thought that it had been

happening for a long time and I hadn't even noticed was worrying. That morning, during the interview with Officer Peterson,
I'd been wearing a green, supposedly pleated, skirt, but the pleats
had fallen out some time ago. The collar of my flowered blouse
was bunched because I hadn't bothered ironing it. Fur from my
mother's cats covered me from head to foot; I even found it in
my hair. The elastic was gone in my underclothes.

Dave the Alien doesn't care, I told myself. You don't even *like*
Dave the Alien.

That wasn't exactly true. I liked him fine. At first I'd thought
I would try to get out of dinner, but I'd promised him, because
I knew he wouldn't leave me alone until I did. It had been
a very long while since I'd been on a date, though. It didn't
come naturally.

I ended up choosing a skirt and a bulky blue sweater. They
weren't very snappy. But they looked clean, and they didn't have
much fur on them. So I put them on and walked to my mother's
house, borrowed her Oldsmobile, and drove to Wallamee.

Dave the Alien's place was the upstairs apartment of a mint-
green house in a run-down part of town. He'd told me to go
right in and walk up the stairs, so I did. It was so dark I had to
feel my way along the wall with my hand. The house smelled
old: bad pipes and rotting wallpaper and leaky gas furnaces. Also,
garbage. Light glowed around the door at the top of the stairs. It
flew open.

"I heard you!" he said. "What, can mediums see in the dark?"

"I couldn't find a switch."

"There isn't one. Sorry. Here." He reached over his head and
pulled a string. A dim bulb illuminated me. "Welcome. I hope
you like spaghetti."

Dave had dressed up. He was wearing a white shirt and
khaki pants. A gold chain glinted from his open collar and he
smelled like cologne. He poured a can of beer into a glass and
handed it to me. "Have a seat."

I sat.

While Dave cooked—I realized how often I seemed to be watching other people cook these days, and how rarely I seemed to do it myself—he asked me a series of questions. I answered them, and was beginning to feel as I had that morning, with Officer Peterson, when it occurred to me that I could just turn them back to Dave.

"What do *you* like to do in your spare time?"

This, possibly, was what Dave was after. He answered in great detail.

"Well," he said, "cars are my number-one pastime, but as you can guess, I also like history. My specialty is the Civil War through World War One. Which is what brought me to Train Line, incidentally."

He described his major at Bonaventura College in Wilson County, Pennsylvania. He somehow got back to cars, and had to turn off the gas under the spaghetti sauce so he could show me his collection of framed prints of antique automobiles, which covered the walls of his bedroom. Other than the prints and the unmade-up mattress on the floor, there was nothing else in the room. I was glad when he turned the light off and we went back to the kitchen.

"Would you like another beer?" he asked, holding open the fridge.

I would.

The food was fairly tasty—spaghetti, white bread with garlic butter, and an iceberg lettuce salad. I recognized this meal from an earlier, short-lived period in my life: a year or two when my mother was dating, and bringing the dates home to meet me. She always served this meal. It was the sure bet, the no-risk supper. I twirled the pasta around my fork, bit, sucked.

"Shit!" cried Dave. A tendril of saucy noodle clung to his white shirt. He peeled it off, threw it onto his plate in disgust, and jumped up to wash the sauce away. "Pardon my *français*," he said, dampening a rag and mournfully daubing at his chest.

"Let's go talk in the other room," he said when we were finished. "I'll get you another beer."

"Oh, I'd better…" I started to say, but took the fresh can.

In the living room there was a sofa and a matching easy chair. I sat in the easy chair, leaned back, and raised the built-in footrest. Dave sat on the sofa.

"Hey," he said after a minute or two. "You want to see my star machine?"

"Star machine?"

"Another one of my hobbies. Astronomy. I just bought this thing."

He went to a closet and pulled out a bulky black object. It looked like some kind of globe with a power cord.

"I'm going to turn the lights off. Don't be scared." Then he hit himself in the forehead with the palm of his hand. "'Don't be scared'? Look who I'm talking to!" He plugged the thing in and snapped off the lamp.

It certainly was dark. I felt better right away; my face relaxed out of the stiff half-smile I'd been maintaining. The star machine gave off tiny pinpricks of light. "Neat," I said.

"No no no. I have to focus." I saw, in the dim light of the star machine, that Dave was craning his neck and looking upward.

"Oh. I get it."

Constellations resolved themselves across the bumpy plaster of Dave's ceiling.

"It's like being outside, but with all the comforts of home. Here," he said, thumping the carpet with his hand. "Get down here so you can pretend you're lying back in a field."

"I'm pretty comfy."

"Come *on*."

I climbed, a little woozily, out of the easy chair. The floor was hard in comparison. It made me feel as if I was lying on a basketball court, not a field.

"See the Dipper?"

"The big one. Yes, sir."

All of a sudden I saw his plan. He was moving incrementally toward me. His hand, glowing palely in the starlight, was a mere four inches from mine.

"Ouch," I said, sitting up.

"What?"

"Nothing. A zipper." I rubbed the back of my skirt, vigorously. Discreetly, I shoved over a few inches. After a couple of minutes, Dave followed.

I began to feel very, very bleak.

We had inched ourselves almost halfway around the room when Dave, frustrated, got up and flicked on the lights. I climbed guiltily back into my easy chair and picked up my beer from the carpet.

"Well," said Dave.

"I like your machine," I said, blinking.

On the wall, I noticed, there was a photograph of a rock band, a few more car prints, and a poster from a Train Line workshop last summer: "The Power of Color."

I gestured at the poster with my drink. "Did you go to that?"

He blushed slightly. "Yeah, I did."

"How was it?"

"It was all right. You remember, I had to get someone to fill in for me at the cafeteria for a couple days."

"Oh, right."

"I mean," he said, "it was interesting, that's for sure. All that about what color you should paint your car and different colors for different days of the week and depending on your mood. I didn't totally buy it. I mean, some Fridays I just *want* to wear a red shirt."

"I hear you."

He was thoughtful a moment. "You remember that lime-green Datsun Peter Morton used to have?"

"Peter...Morton."

"That quiet guy with the glasses? Didn't you used to go out with him?"

"Oh, yeah. Uh-huh."

He gave me a long, steady look. "Yeah. I thought so. Well, did you know I bought that car from him?"

"*You?*" I remembered Peter telling me he sold it to a high school kid. It was the kid's first car—Peter liked that idea and gave him a discount.

Dave smiled. "I was sixteen. That car ran freaking *forever.* Lime green is supposed to be the worst color of all for cars."

"How did you know I...?"

"I went over to Train Line to pick up the papers from him. You were sitting on the steps of the house, reading a book. You looked exactly the same."

"Really? That was an awful long time ago."

"I know." Dave took a swig of his drink. "I liked the way you looked. I remembered you."

"That was an awful long time ago," I said again, feeling stunned.

"Yeah, well. It wasn't like I was sitting around waiting until I thought I was old enough. I was in the army, then college, etcetera. When I started working at Train Line and you were over in the library, I thought I'd sooner or later make a move. You don't exactly make a guy welcome, you know."

"Hmm."

"What is it, anyway?" he said, leaning toward me. "I don't mean this in an offensive way, but are you...you know, uninterested in men? I know a lot of the mediums over there swing that way, and that's cool."

"I don't think I'm a lesbian."

"I'm sorry, tell me to shut up if it's none of my business, but have you actually dated anyone since that Peter guy? I've asked a few people and no one seems to know."

"You've *asked* people about me?"

"Sorry!" He flushed, looked at his hands. "Just a few questions. I wanted to make sure you were available, that's all."

I sat there, chewing on my thumbnail.

"Oh, man," he said, getting up and crouching next to my chair. "I'm really sorry. I should never have said anything. If you need me to be patient, I can do that. Really." He smiled a rueful, understanding-man smile.

I thought to myself: *What was I thinking, coming to dinner?*

"I do need that," I said, trying out a sorrowful smile of my own.

"Hey!" he said. "I've got dessert! Do you like chocolate cake?"

"I love chocolate cake," I lied.

∽✦∽

When I got back to Train Line, I parked the car in my mother's driveway, stuck the keys in her mailbox, and walked home. I wasn't even the slightest bit drunk anymore. I wished I was. My shoes clattered loudly over the gravel streets, and a cold breeze tangled my hair. Train Line was pitch dark, and silent except for the wind blowing leaves.

I'd hoped Ron and Jenny would be in bed when I got to my house, because I wanted to drink some warm milk without being interrogated about my "date," but there were lights on downstairs. I sighed and peered in through the narrow window by the front door. Jenny was on the couch, reading, her small head bent in concentration. She looked like a child. I unlocked the door and went inside.

"Hello," I said, hanging my coat on the rack. Jenny didn't answer. She had her flannel pajamas on and was wrapped in an old brown afghan, and the cover of her book was hidden by her hand. I took my shoes off. Finally she looked up.

"Snippy died," she said. Her face was pale and her lips were alarmingly white.

"I know. I'm sorry."

She didn't ask me how I knew, but nodded, biting her lips. "I guess I should say *passed over*." She said this with startling bitterness, which made me uneasy.

"I'm sorry," I said again.

"*You* didn't kill him," said Jenny. Her face, which had always been thin and irritable, looked like it was about to crack in half. Her eyes were rimmed with pink and her white lips quivered. "*God* killed him. It makes no sense at all. Why would God want to kill my bird? Why would he even bother?"

I was just standing there by the coat rack, my arms dangling. Did she want an answer? I didn't have one.

"Sometimes this place makes me sick," she said, gulping suddenly and covering her face with her hands. The book fell into her lap, and I saw that it was the latest best seller: *Stories to Warm the Soul.*

Jenny sobbed. For a long moment I stood there, sweat sliding down my back, knowing that I should go to her. Finally I did. I sat next to her on the couch and put my hand on her shoulder. Then I leaned toward her, awkwardly, and put my arms around her body. She was too thin, and she had a hot, stale smell. *Oh, no,* I thought.

I had the terrible impression then that I was holding someone who had already died. And I knew that it was almost true, that she was going to die soon, and she knew it, too, and that's why she was crying. Spiritualists talk of this kind of knowledge, the kind that comes without voices or visions or manifestations or any glimpse into the spirit world, as "just knowing." There's another word for it, one you find in old books about parapsychology: *cryptesthesia.* Sometimes just knowing is the truest kind of mediumship. Perhaps it's a spirit whispering in your ear, so gently you mistake its words for thoughts, and standing too closely for you to see it. Once I read about a little Italian girl going to bed a few hours before she would die in an earthquake. Her mother was helping her put on the socks she wore to bed, and the little girl asked, "Why are you putting on these death-socks? My death-socks."

Jenny cried for several minutes, not leaning into me but not pushing me away, either. I could feel her tense muscles loosen and grow tired under my hands.

For some reason I found myself thinking about Peter's lime-green Datsun, and how we drove that car fast down back roads on dark nights, and how sometimes we turned the headlights off. Dark shapes loomed out at us, and the road, still soft from the hot sun, was like velvet under the wheels. We didn't care what could happen to us, and nothing ever did. I ached for them, those nights, Peter whisking me safely through the blackness.

Eventually Jenny stopped and I leaned back. She wiped her face with her pajama sleeve and stood up, unsteadily, and walked into the kitchen. I couldn't help but glance down at her feet. They were blue-white and bare.

6

reconstructed head

A week went by, then another. The story of the bones fell out of the paper right away, and almost as quickly town gossip found new subjects: the wife of the manager of Train Line's single hotel, the Silverwood, left him for another woman; a famous psychic was said to be trying to get church membership so she could buy a house on the grounds; and so on. I felt less relieved than perplexed by the story's swift vanishing. Was all news so temporary? It gave me the sense of plots unfolding behind my back, of armies assembling just over the next hill. My mother, even, had little to say about it, though I had not seen much of her in the past weeks. She seemed to be lying low.

And I hadn't heard from Peter, either. Sometimes I thought I was about to. Walking across the grass to the library, or half-dozing on the sofa, I'd get an impression of him: the smell of his hair, or the feel of his waist under my hands. These would vanish almost before I was aware of them, and left me feeling haunted and bereft. *What do you want from me?* I'd ask, desperate to know, to oblige him, but terrified, too, that he'd answer.

Then, one afternoon two weeks after they'd found the bones, there was a photograph of the skull in the *Observer.* Next to this picture was one of the skull covered with a clay skin. It had fake eyes and hair and was sculpted to look real. It wore a peculiar expression: its mouth was smiling but its eyes were blank and wide open, like a store window mannequin's. They had it set up on someone's lab table, no body, just the ragged edge of a neck. A FAMILIAR FACE? asked the headline.

But it was Peter. There were his small, sharp cheekbones, his long chin, his high, narrow forehead. I had never noticed those things about him before. If someone had asked me to describe Peter, I'd never have thought to say *small cheekbones, narrow forehead,* but when I saw them I knew them intimately. The hairline was wrong—Peter had a widow's peak, which I used to envy— and of course, the hair itself wasn't even close, either. Peter's was wavy and black and lifted straight up from his forehead, as springy as the outside of a coconut; it didn't flop over to one side like the hair in the picture. The nose wasn't small enough. Peter's nose was pointed and delicate.

I covered the picture of the clay head with my hand and looked for a long time at the bare skull instead. I was in the kitchen, the only one home, my toast getting cold in the toaster. Outside, the sky was full of forbidding purple clouds. I remembered sitting at this same table years before, in the same house, watching Peter eat. He was so skinny, you could see all the different pieces of his jaw move when he chewed. He had pale skin that the veins showed through, and a face that came to a point, as if his head had been pushed into the corner of a room, and sleepy, snobby eyes. Somehow, there was more of Peter in the skull picture. Maybe it was the teeth: a tad too long, overlapping a bit in front.

But would anyone recognize him? I couldn't tell. The clay head clearly belonged to someone very different from Peter: a chunky, slow, poorly groomed person. He looked like a hick from around here, which Peter definitely was not. You'd have to be intimate with Peter's bones, I decided, to make the connection. You'd have to have felt his face in your hands. You'd have to have rubbed headaches from that forehead and slid your tongue along those teeth. As far as I knew, no one else around here had done those things, least of all my mother.

I found a pair of scissors in the kitchen drawer and snipped the pictures out. I didn't know what I wanted to do with them, but I wanted them. Unfortunately, the newspaper now had a hole in it, and I wasn't sure if Jenny and Ron had read it yet. Too bad, I thought, and slid the paper to the bottom of the recycling box. The pictures I took upstairs and put in my underwear drawer.

But then I pulled the drawer open again, took the news clipping out, and stared hard at the clay face. Here he was, back once more, in this strange new physical form. What would this head say to me, if it could talk? Maybe, *You loved me once.* Maybe, *Don't forget.* Or maybe something else entirely.

∽✴∽

The reconstructed head was big news in Train Line. Suddenly, the bones were a hot topic again. Ferd at the Groc-n-Stop cut out the picture and taped it to the cash register. Everyone had a theory.

"Power vacuum salesman," said one of the old men who hung around there. I listened to them while I shopped for food. "He came right into my house and threw dirt on the wall-to-wall carpeting. This was I don't know how long ago. Fella wouldn't leave! I wouldn't be surprised if he threw dirt on the wrong rug, and it was all over."

"Nah, nah," said his friend, the postmaster. "I knew the guy, but fat. Used to drive all over the place on a tractor. He was too fat for a car—remember him? Police pulled him over for drinking and driving, and he hid the beer can down between his big old thighs."

A teenager named Desmond Wallace was hauled in for questioning. Desmond was a thin, dirty kid whose family lived in a house a little way down Line Drive. Once, he killed someone's cat and nailed the body to a tree along the path to Illumination Stump. No one saw him do it, but everyone knew it was him. He had dropped out of school and now ran around with a little band of junior-high-school Satanists, who apparently looked up to him. The police caught him snooping around the excavation site, and his friends told the officers that Desmond was obsessed with the bones, talked about them all the time and even hinted that he was responsible. They let him go, though, since it was clear that, at seventeen, he couldn't have been older than twelve when the body was buried. Some people thought that twelve was plenty old enough, knowing Desmond.

But there was no way it was him, according to my mother. She, too, had cut out the pictures of the skull and the reconstructed head, and pressed them between the pages of her address book. She came by the library the morning after the paper came out and showed me.

"Now, doesn't he look familiar?" she asked, putting her glasses on and squinting at the piece of newspaper.

"Hmm. As a matter of fact he does. He looks like the mannequins in the Sidey's window."

"Come now, use your imagination. Picture him with different hair, or with a beard maybe."

I thought for a moment. "Well, with a beard, he's the spitting image of Mr. Shaw, the high school shop teacher."

"Isn't he still teaching?"

"I believe so."

"Then you're no help at all, are you?" she said, slipping the pictures back into her address book.

"Sorry."

She took her glasses off and folded her arms, frowning at the stack of uncataloged books on my desk. *Tiny Spirits: Stillborn Children in the Afterlife* was on top. "I don't know why you've been so negative lately. You're just radiating negativity."

"I'm sorry," I said again.

"Oh, it's probably my fault. I've been distracted. I can't tell you how this thing has taken over my mind!" She rubbed her temples. "It's all I think about. I dream about it. Do you remember Watergate, how every time we'd turn on the television, there it was? You couldn't escape it. Well it's the same thing here. Worse even. I don't recall that I dreamed about Richard Nixon."

"You're obsessed."

"Or possessed," she sighed. "It's good though; I need a project. Next week is my last radio show. They're throwing me a 'retirement' party down at the station. We're all pretending I'm just retiring. It helps us remain polite."

"Are you still hoping they'll have a change of heart?"

"Actually," she said, perking up, "I have a better idea. What do you think of this: a *television* show?"

I raised my eyebrows, waiting for her to explain.

"I know the people at WRUK from the times I was interviewed on the *Morning Show*. They'd be receptive, I think, especially if this investigation works out. I was thinking of a program with more or less the same format, except with a studio audience instead of call-ins."

"Well, that would be great," I said, careful not to radiate any more negativity.

"It certainly would," said my mother.

I rolled an index card into my typewriter to show her that I had things to do. While I clacked away she walked around the reading room, looking at the photographs on the wall. She stopped at one and rapped it with a knuckle. "Those were the days, weren't they? Look at how many people are listening to that lecture!" She put her glasses on and peered at it more closely. "It could happen again, you know. It's almost the end of the century, people are searching…"

"Mama."

"Yes?"

"A police officer came around a couple of weeks ago. He was asking about the bones. You didn't happen to talk to him, did you?"

"A police officer? Oh, I heard about that. No, I didn't talk to him. Why do you ask?" She looked at me right in the eye.

Suddenly, and for no reason that I could tell, I found myself suspicious of her. *She's lying,* I thought. *She's keeping things from me.*

"Why?" she said again.

I turned from her, shrugging. "He said he was going to talk to you, that's all. I wondered what he said." This was difficult to say, because my mouth had gone dry. I felt myself beginning to panic. I fought it down. If my mother noticed, she made no indication.

"Hmm. I wish he had talked to me. I'd like to find out what they know. It would be nice to get it from the horse's mouth for once, instead of from that wretched *Evening Disturber*..."

She chatted on for a few minutes, then picked up her purse and left.

When she was gone, I turned off the typewriter. I couldn't type; my fingers were sweating and slipped off the keys. I'd *seen* Officer Peterson walking up to her house. I'd seen him go through the gate. Was it possible she wasn't home? That was a Friday; her radio show was a repeat on Fridays, a day off for her, so she wasn't at the station. She could have been grocery shopping, or at Darva Lawrence's, though it would be awfully early for her to go out. Maybe she was only pretending not to have recognized Peter in the skull...maybe she knew.

I pulled myself together. I wiped my hands on my thighs and turned the typewriter back on and typed several cards, and then I felt somewhat better. Of course my mother didn't know! And she would never know. She was probably still convinced the bones were her brother's. She was a terrible medium, anyway—a fake.

If she only knew what *I* knew.

༄

Everyone was obsessed with the reconstructed skull, even Vivian. One afternoon we were going for a walk, kicking the first fall leaves, when I noticed she was touching her face with her fingers, prodding her eye sockets and feeling her chin.

"What are you doing?" I asked.

"What?"

"With your face." I mimicked her, and she frowned.

"I'm trying to feel my skull," she said.

I couldn't help but picture that: the big, childish dome of her forehead, the delicate jaw and tiny teeth. "That's gruesome."

"What does 'gruesome' mean?"

"Gross," I said, though that didn't seem quite right.

She was silent a moment. "Andy Paulson is gruesome."

"I'll bet."

We were heading for the lake, and Vivian had a plastic bread bag full of crumbs for the swans. She swung it around. "What would people look like if they didn't have any bones?"

"Like sacks of jelly, I guess."

"Could they walk?"

"I doubt it. Maybe they could slither a little bit."

"Do ghosts need bones?"

"Ghosts?"

"How can ghosts walk if they don't have bones?"

I shrugged. "It's a mystery."

She didn't seem satisfied with this answer. She peered out over the lake, looking for the big dirty swans that usually hung around the dock. The lake was choppy and gray, and the wind blew right through my sweater. Across the lake in Wallamee, they were harvesting grapes. I could smell them. The grape harvesters were big bizarre machines; tall enough to arch right over a row of grapes, shake the daylights out of it, and fling the traumatized fruit into a hopper. You didn't need to harvest these grapes by hand—they were dark, leather-skinned Concords, the kind Peter and I used to steal from the field behind Train Line. We'd pinch them until their insides burst out and suck the flavor from the skins.

Vivian turned the bread sack upside down, dumping the crumbs into the water. "Stupid swans," she said.

This was something new in Vivian: a grim impatience, an angry willingness to be defeated. She used to be so *dogged*.

"Well, geez, Viv," I said. "Give them half a chance. Maybe they're out visiting their friends or something."

"I don't care."

How I hated that. "Don't say you don't care."

"Why not?"

"It sounds ugly."

She just shrugged, not caring or talking now.

We were heading for home, trudging gloomily up Fox Street, when it started to rain. It came down suddenly, as if someone had just thrown a sprinkler switch. Vivian lagged behind me. "Hurry up, Viv!" I called to her, and stood waiting.

When she caught up she came to me and looked me in the face. "Hurry up, Viv!" she said in a nasty, sarcastic voice.

For several seconds I just stared at her, unable to believe what I'd heard. She glared right back. Without even thinking about what I was doing, I slapped her, hard, across the cheek.

"Do *not* speak to me that way," I said.

She barely flinched, but continued to glare at me, her left cheek growing red and hot. I turned and walked quickly back to the house. Vivian followed several minutes later, quietly hanging up her jacket and lying down in front of the television, cradling her injured cheek in her hand.

Horrified at what I had done, and panicky to think of what would happen if Vivian told her mother, I drank cup after cup of coffee at the kitchen table and finished the crossword puzzle in record time.

If Vivian did tell her mother, it didn't get back to me. But I couldn't stop thinking about it. In my head I slapped her over and over. I slapped her until she fell down. My hand felt huge and fiery. For several nights, I slept with it clamped between my knees, hating it and what it could do.

⚘

It was the middle of the night, long after we'd all gone to bed. I was dreaming my drowning dream—in the high school pool, crowds of boys swimming above me and blocking my way to the surface—when the phone rang. I sat straight up. The glow-in-the-dark dots on my clock were no longer glowing so I couldn't be sure of the time, but judging from how deeply asleep I was it must have been three or four. I had an extension in my room, and I reached over and picked it up just after Jenny did. I heard her soft voice say Hello.

"Is this Naomi? I'm looking for Naomi," said the other voice. It was my mother.

"I've got it," I said.

"All right," said Jenny, and she hung up.

There was a click, a pause, and another click, which must have been Ron seeing if it was for him. Then quiet.

"Mama, what's wrong?"

She was crying. She made little choking sounds into the phone.

"Mama! What is it?"

"I had a dream. You were lost. You were with your father, and I couldn't find you..." She cried, snuffling and blowing her nose.

"Mama, I'm right here. Do you want me to come over?"

She gasped out a laugh. "Oh, God, no. It's all right. I've just never been so...discombobulated by a dream. Oh, Naomi, it was horrible. I was so lonely. It was...like you never existed. Like I'd made you up."

There was a pause while she blew her nose again and got herself together. "All right. All right."

I picked up my clock and tried to read the hands. "Did you say my father was in it?"

"I think. I'm sorry. It's boring to hear about other people's dreams."

"No, no, it's fine."

"When I woke up, I didn't know what was real. It was the same feeling as when my mother passed over, and I'd wake up and remember all over again that she was gone."

"Why don't you drink some milk or something? I can come over."

"No," she said firmly. "I'm fine. I'm sorry I woke you up."

"It's all right."

She hung up without saying good-bye.

I got down under my blankets and tried to sleep. Usually, if I woke in the night I could go back to sleep immediately, but after my mother's phone call I had the creepy sensation that there was something fluttering in the corner of my room, something like a bat, and it kept me awake. Every time I opened my eyes and checked, nothing was there, but the feeling didn't go away. Maybe, I thought, it's a spirit. I cleared my mind and tried to contact it.

What do you want? Leave me alone, I want to sleep.

It didn't answer. But after a minute or two it began to moan. The sound it made was like my mother weeping: dry, hacking sobs. I pulled my pillow over my ears, but the thing wouldn't stop. It didn't make any sense to me; I had no idea what it was. Maybe it was a demon, but I didn't believe in demons. It seemed neither spirit nor animal, but like a thing in between, a thing incomplete, like the ragged neck of the reconstructed head.

Eventually I must have fallen asleep, because I woke up when it got light. Ron was stomping around downstairs, and the newspaper hit our front door with a bang. Morning. Whatever the creature was, it was gone. But the feeling it left me with was a sick and horrible one: like guilt, or regret. It was as if what I had done all those years ago had come back to life, and was trying hard to fly, howling, into the world.

∽✌∾

In order to be a practicing medium on the grounds of Train Line—that is, to be able to hang out a sign and charge money for individual readings in your own house—you had to be approved and registered by the Train Line board of directors. You'd have to present yourself to the board, state your beliefs and philosophy of mediumship, and then hold a circle. It was a rigorous process. Every year, more mediums failed than passed. I failed two years in a row and was nineteen when I finally got my registration.

I spent those years living with my mother, finishing high school and practicing my mediumship on friends. In the summers I took jobs. It was because of these jobs that I never gave up on being a medium; I knew I'd never make it in the world if I had to have a job. The summer after I graduated from high school I worked at a tomato-packing plant outside Wallamee. I was a sorter. The other sorters and I had to climb up to a huge conveyor belt contraption—we had to duck under steel girders and go up ladders—and sort the tomatoes as they tumbled past us. They were all hard as baseballs, and green. Our job was to pick out the defective ones and the ones with any trace of red at all. Red tomatoes went on another conveyor belt, eventually to be made into ketchup, and the defective ones were tossed down a chute. These were smashed or gouged or had weird prongs, like green fingers, or else had "cats' faces." The woman who trained me had an accent of some kind, and was hard to understand.

"See," she said, pointing to a cleft in the bottom of a bad tomato, "this is a cat's face." It looked like a navel, intimate and odd. "If the cat's face is bigger than a nickel, throw them out."

Fow dem out, she said.

Somewhere at the head of the conveyor belt there was a sprayer that coated all the tomatoes with a slippery wax. It made the tomatoes hard to grab and puckered my fingertips. For what seemed like hours the tomatoes rolled by, and I'd frantically snatch at the rejects, grabbing and tossing them into the chute, becoming so hypnotized that when the conveyor belt was shut off for some reason—usually because a supervisor had noticed too many bad tomatoes getting by, or too many good ones in the chute, and needed to yell at us—I'd have to catch myself to keep from falling over. Once I cut my finger on a piece of metal. Something about the wax spray kept the wound from healing, so blood trickled from my finger for a long time, smearing the tomatoes. No one had told me what to do if I was bleeding, so I did nothing, pleased to imagine piles of bloody produce in the supermarket.

If it rained hard, as it did often that summer, the pickers wouldn't be sent out into the fields and there'd be no tomatoes for us to sort. Those days we'd climb a ladder up to the loft, just under the warehouse roof, and fold sheets of cardboard into boxes. With the machines shut off, it was quiet enough to hear the rain on the metal roof and to talk. Some of the women—all the sorters were women—had worked in the packing plant for thirty years. *Thirty years.* They had strange, awful lives.

"So I says to him, if you're gonna live like a raccoon, you can just go live in the goddamn woods! So he did! He took his shit out to the woods and built himself a hut. I ain't seen him since." The woman who said this was tall and thin and had the look of someone who smoked instead of ate. Her skin was leathery and her eyes colorless.

I could see my life going that way. No one would ever hire me to work in an office; I was not cheery or outgoing, and I couldn't type. My fingernails stayed dirty no matter how often I washed my hands. There was no point in living, I knew, if I was going to continue being a tomato sorter. I'd one hundred times rather be dead. Every day, as I got on my bike to go to work, I'd cry so hard I couldn't see.

But I kept going, that whole summer, until the very last day when there were only a few mostly bad tomatoes, and they sent us home early. I thought I'd feel good, getting through the whole summer, but I didn't. I felt like I'd just gotten out of prison, having paid for a crime I didn't commit. I couldn't tell anyone about this feeling. I knew what they'd say.

What, you think you're too good to work?

Well, yes. I did.

But I couldn't live with my mother forever. At night I'd lie in bed, thinking, *Something has to change, something has* got *to change,* but I couldn't think what it was. My mind chased itself in circles. I could leave Train Line, but then what? Work as what, do what? It was when I realized that nothing seemed worth doing, that I couldn't even imagine a worthwhile life, that I got scared.

Once I spent an entire day lying on top of my bed, staring out the window at the sky. I knew that pretty soon I'd have to get up and go downstairs and eat the dinner my mother was cooking—chicken patties, I could smell them—and I couldn't stand the idea. There'd be a glass of water by my plate and the salt and pepper shakers shaped like corncobs, and she'd tell me all about her day and what everyone said and then we'd watch the television news. The thought of it made my head roar.

It was in the middle of this roaring that I heard my first voice. It wasn't a spooky voice, or even an ethereal one, but a practical, somewhat bored one. It sounded exactly as if someone put her mouth right up close to my ear and said, in a slightly hushed tone, *"Wake up, Naomi Ash."* The voice was so real I thought I could feel the heat of breath on the side of my face.

Until that moment, I had never really believed in spiritualism. I sort of believed. I pretended to. I enjoyed the attention I got when I worked message services and sat for séances, and sometimes I felt the thrill of connection, but part of me held back. I didn't want to be like my mother, with her eager, delighted face and pushy advice. I dallied in spiritualism. And that was the problem. My life was a dalliance.

But when I heard the voice in my ear—it said nothing earth-shaking, and it wasn't a voice I recognized—I knew that all I lacked was conviction. The people sitting on the Train Line board of directors saw that; they saw that I didn't take myself quite seriously, that I was hanging back. And it occurred to me, too, that if I wanted to I could dismiss the voice as a daydream, or, if I chose to, I could believe in it. Belief was a decision I could make.

That evening I ate my mother's chicken patties and listened to her gossip and sat on the sofa with her, watching television, but I was different. I had become a medium. All it took was that small shift.

For the next few months I threw myself into my mediumship. At home circles and message services, I worked so hard I sweated and trembled and gave myself migraine headaches, the worst pain I'd ever known. Sometimes I'd go home afterward and lie on the floor of the bathroom with the light off, the headache beating at the back of my eyes, until I threw up in the toilet and began to feel a little better. I heard voices all the time, those months. Sometimes I recognized the voice—my grandmother, occasionally—but usually it was a strange voice saying things I didn't understand. *Try again, Lily, when the table's bigger!* I heard once. Another time it was, *History is blasphemy, darling.*

Because I accepted everything I heard, I heard more. The connection was clear to me. For a while things came in such a rush I had trouble sorting them out. It was like sitting in a room surrounded by people having conversations: sometimes a certain word would catch my attention, and the voice would, for a minute or two, carry above the others, until another voice drowned it out. This would go on for as long as I let it, as long as I concentrated. It was the most exciting thing that had ever happened to me.

I never doubted the validity of what I heard. Whether it was strictly *true* or not didn't matter, because truth, I knew, could be interpreted a thousand ways.

❧

I passed my board exam the spring I turned nineteen. It was a cold, drizzly afternoon, and I met the board of directors in the paneled exam room behind the main office. All the Train Line old folks sat in folding chairs around a long, flimsy table—a heavier table might never levitate—and they greeted me when I came in. Grace Batsummer gave me some coffee in a paper cup.

"Good to see you again, Naomi."

"Think the sun's gone in for good?"

"Hello, my dear."

"Hello, Naomi, dear."

As Troy read out the rules and procedures for the exam—they were long and detailed and I'd heard them twice before—I looked at the photographs on the walls. There was a picture of Train Line when it was just a big white tent in the woods: TRAIN LINE CAMP MEETING proclaimed a banner draped between two trees. Young ladies sat in the grass, their white summer dresses billowing around them. All the men wore top hats. There was a picture of a horse covered with paper flowers, a little girl on its back. I knew I was going to pass my exam.

"So, Naomi," said Troy. "Tell us the forms your mediumship takes."

"Clairaudience, mostly. Some clairvoyance and clairsentience."

"Clairaudience!" said Robin Blackthorn. "That's new for you, isn't it?"

"Yes."

"Could you describe for us how you intend to use your talents?"

I told them I believed that the fear of death distracted people and prevented them from living their lives in the ways they were meant to. I hoped, I said, to ease that fear.

They nodded. They'd certainly heard that before.

Grace Batsummer asked the next question. "Why, in your opinion, do spirits bother with the so-called Living? Why linger around this plane at all?"

"Well, first of all, I believe that the two planes are not all that separate. I believe that the spirit plane and the material plane are intertwined. Spirits bother with us because they can't help it; we're all around them. Just as some of us can't help bothering with spirits."

There were some low chuckles. "Very original," said Troy.

Grace folded her knobby old hands on the table. "So you're saying that spirits just…*show up*? That they have no real intentions toward communicating with us, that we bump into them like strangers at the supermarket?"

"No," I said, trying to smile. "Not exactly. I meant that we are as important to spirits as they are to us. Some people have the idea that the spirit plane is *higher*, somehow, and that spirits condescend to us. I don't think that's the case. They want to speak to us to comfort us, and we speak to them to comfort them."

"I can see that," said Robin, nodding.

"Do you *really* think those on the spirit plane need comforting, Naomi?" asked Grace.

"Um, yes," I said. "If—if my mother passed over, I know she'd take comfort in me, in my life…she'd want to see me, to know I was okay." As I was saying this, I realized I had no idea if it was true or not. It had to be; it had to be. "I guess I'm trying to say that spirits all have unfinished business here on this plane," I added a little dubiously. "It is a comfort for them to see us carry it out. And—and we need each other, the dead and the living. Our lives are meaningless without the afterlife, and well, their lives are meaningless without the…antedeath."

"The antedeath!" yelped Grace.

"Remember, Grace," said Troy. "There are no right answers or wrong answers here."

"I know," she said, leaning back, only slightly disgruntled.

There were some more questions. These I answered quickly and confidently, occasionally glancing out the window to make sure I was really here, that it was really happening. It was.

"Okay, then, let's get started," said Troy.

Grace lit three white candles and spaced them evenly down the table. We held hands—the old men on each side of me both had dry, papery, ice-cold fingers—and I led a short prayer.

"Blessed spirits," I began.

After the prayer we let go of each other, and the room was silent for several minutes. A car crunched by on the gravel outside, and water dripped from the roof, splashed on the windowsill. I thought I could hear the hum of a television in the house across the street; I thought I could hear radio waves. I felt as if I could hear anything, if I listened.

The voices started.

"Um," I said. "There's a Lowell here. I don't know if that's a first or last name."

"First," grunted old Edgar Phinney, on my left. "My brother."

"Right." I listened for a minute or two. "A dog's here with him."

"Barnabas."

"Yes."

I listened harder. Voices poured down on me.

I told Edgar Phinney that Lowell was building a house with his own hands, out of sticks and mud and grass and rocks, and that the house would have five windows, and through one of them I saw a little girl with gray eyes. The dog had his own house, across the street. As soon as he was finished, Lowell would burn love letters in the fireplace.

Then I said I had someone named White. No one claimed him, at first. White wanted to tell us all about a woman he called Twilight, how she was dying of neglect. I cried in the middle of this one. Robin said, quietly, that she thought she knew who I meant.

There was more. A girl with no arms, a baseball player. It was possibly the strangest circle I'd ever led.

But it was the truest one, too. I felt shaken at the end of it, much more than usual, and when they sent me outside to discuss the exam, I had to sit down on one of the wet stone benches under the cedar tree and put my head on my knees.

Troy came out looking for me. His face was long and pale and his hair seemed to float over his scalp. "There you are, dear. Congratulations. You passed."

I signed some papers in the office, shook everyone's hand, and put on my coat. Grace pulled me aside as I was heading out the door.

"Listen," she said, whispering. "Don't take this the wrong way. But get a haircut and buy some new clothes before you hang out your sign. You don't want your customers thinking you're hard up. Do you?"

I shook my head, wrenched myself from her grasp, and fled.

❧

My mother lent me her wood-burning kit, and I found a small pine board behind the garage. I traced my name in pencil several times before I got it right, then carefully burned it in. NAOMI ASH, MEDIUM, it said, in block letters.

❧

For the first season I was registered, I lived with my mother and shared her séance room. She only gave a few readings on her busiest days, and my business was slow at first, so it wasn't difficult to schedule around each other. I made sure I signed up for every message service and every Circle Night I could, and slowly got more customers. When I wasn't busy, I hung around on the porch of the Silverwood Hotel. It was the social center of Train Line, late summer evenings, and we'd play cards and listen to the band play by the lake and watch bats swoop down. That was where I first met Ron, although at the time he lived in Cleveland and was only visiting for the summer. I met an aura reader there, too, and we became good friends, despite my mother's disapproval. His name was Nelson Karp and he was not very handsome. His eyes bugged out. But we soon became allies, making fun of the obnoxious tourists behind their backs and taking picnic lunches out on the lake. Nelson had invented his own language, and he taught me some of the words.

"Wribble kloffer," he said to me one day, as I was rowing the boat.

Wribble, he said, meant "beautiful." *Kloffer* meant "woman."

"Oh," I said.

But he was shy, or else very perceptive, because he didn't push it any further. On the last day before he left to go back to college, he gave me a yellow rose and said, "I tried to be a gentleman, but it wasn't easy."

I kissed his thin cheek. "Thank you," I said.

He blushed a little and stared intently at something in the distance behind me. "I know you're not into this, but you really do have the most amazing aura I've ever seen. It's pink with violet and yellow flecks. You should wear pink."

"Thank you," I said again.

When Nelson came back the next summer, he brought a friend.

"Naomi," said Nelson, blinking his large blue eyes and wiping his skinny palms on his shirt. "Meet my friend Peter Morton."

❧

Though they don't often admit it, let alone advertise it, it's fairly common for state police and sheriff's departments to hire "psychics" to help out with difficult investigations. Usually these are missing-persons cases rather than regular criminal ones, since psychic evidence doesn't fly well in court. But Winnie Sandox—my mother's nemesis—often bragged that she worked with the FBI on a famous child-kidnapping case, and once Robin Blackthorn helped to track down members of a local drug ring. Mediums could make a lot of money this way, or at least get publicity. Or so I'd heard. Still, I was surprised when Officer Peterson called me up, saying he was looking for a medium to help with the investigation.

"I don't really have much experience with that kind of thing," I said, startled. I'd been watching television, a nature show. Lately,

I'd seen quite a bit of television. For the last day or two, ever since my mother had called in the middle of the night, I'd felt nervous and restless, and the dull noise and flicker of it soothed me. On the screen, a herd of gazelles stampeded by.

"Well, actually, your mother's the one we were looking for. Madame Gail—Galina Ash, right? The one on the radio."

"Um, yes."

"Is she out of town or something? We've been trying to get a hold of her for a couple of days, and there's no answer. There's no answering machine, either."

"She takes the phone off the hook a lot."

"Uh-huh. Well, do you think you could get her a message? Tell her we'd like her help, and that she should call Officer Peterson or Officer Ten Brink at the state police department. ASAP."

"ASAP," I repeated.

"That's right," he said. "So how's it going at the library?"

"Pretty uneventful."

"You must like it that way."

"I do."

"Good. Good. You pass that message on to your mother. I can trust you, can't I?"

"Of course." On the television, a leopard came out of nowhere and pulled down one of the gazelles. They showed it again, in slow motion. "Officer Peterson?"

"Yes, Naomi?"

"Can I ask *you* a question?"

"That depends. What is it?"

I took a deep breath. The leopard was eating the gazelle now, his muzzle-fur spiky with blood. "Didn't you already talk to my mother? I—I thought I saw you at her house."

Peterson's voice dropped an octave. "Were you following me, Naomi?"

"No. I just—"

"You were following me. I saw you." He paused, and I could hear his beard stubble scrape across the receiver. "But to answer your question: that's none of your business, Miss Ash."

"All right. Good-bye."

"As it happens," said Peterson, "your mother wasn't available, but I had a nice chat with the man who answered the door. His name, if I remember correctly, was Trevor, or Troy or something."

"Thank you."

"Curiosity satisfied, Miss Ash?"

I hung up. God, I thought. What an awful person.

I put on my windbreaker and walked over to my mother's. It was drizzling a fine, sleety rain. Talking to Officer Peterson had made me warm, as if I'd had something hot to drink. The back of my neck itched with sweat. He had taken a dislike to me, for some reason. This shouldn't have bothered me, but it did, because his hostility had come out of nowhere. It was unfair, I thought. It was unprofessional. He reminded me of those leering boys from high school, boys who didn't even know me, who catcalled and made ironic kissy lips when I walked past them. And I felt as I did then: befuddled and humiliated. Rain soaked through my stupid cloth shoes.

A limousine was parked out in front of my mother's house, taking up most of the width of Rochester Street. Its driver snoozed in the front seat. I walked around it and went in the front door, making enough noise to let her know I was there, then sat down to wait for her in the kitchen.

She came in about twenty minutes later, dressed in a blue satin gown and matching nail polish. "Newlyweds!" she said. "Did they expect me to doom and gloom them? Lucky thing they're a good match, or I'd have had to lie. So what are you do-ing here?"

I told her about Officer Peterson's message. She stared at the refrigerator a moment, then opened it and took out a bottle of wine. It was actually less a bottle than a jug, a squat green one with a small round handle at its neck, and it was two-thirds empty.

"My goodness," she said. "Have some? We ought to celebrate."

"Sure."

She poured wine into two plastic tumblers. I sipped at mine; it was cold and dank. I remembered the tumblers from when I was a child. We'd brought them from New Orleans, God knows why. Maybe my mother thought we might have needed them on the bus. They made me sad whenever I saw them.

"Well," I said. "Are you going to do it?"

"I am, I guess. It's what I wanted." She gave me a weak smile. "But suddenly, I'm nervous. Do you think I should?"

"Why not?"

She shrugged her big satin shoulder. "I don't know. It seems like a very large undertaking, all of a sudden."

I drank more wine, ransacking my mind for ways to talk her out of it. Appallingly, I had finished the glass almost before I realized what I was doing. I glanced at my mother to see if she'd noticed. She hadn't. She was drinking her own wine with careful determination, frowning, as if it were a potent medicine.

"Devil and the deep blue sea," she mused. "If I don't do it, my career could well be over. But if I do it, and fail miserably..."

She peeled back some foil from a pan of cake on the table and stabbed at a piece with a fork. *If only Peterson had called* me *instead,* I thought, a little jealously, *my problems would be solved....*

"Well," I said. A plan was forming in my head, almost as I was speaking. "I have an idea. If you're interested."

She looked at me expectantly, her broad cheeks already pink with wine.

"I'd like to help you. I know they didn't ask me, they asked *you,* and I wouldn't take any credit. But if we put our heads together...I'm sure we'd come up with something. Anyway, it wouldn't hurt."

She drank the rest of her wine. *Say yes,* I begged silently.

"I didn't think you cared about any of this," she said.

"I want to help you."

"Hmm," she said. "You're jealous, aren't you? It's all right. I'd be too." She paused a long moment, and then went on. "Well, see, I *have* made contact with the spirit."

My stomach leapt. "You have?"

She nodded.

"Then who…?"

"That's the thing. I don't know. He doesn't even know. Have you ever heard of such a thing? The spirit seems to have forgotten who he is."

She told me how it happened: That morning, she was coming home from shopping in Wallamee when she had the urge to drive past the excavation site again. She was just going to park and meditate a little, but instead she found herself getting out of the car and walking down the rutted path toward the lake. She'd only gone about thirty feet when she tripped and fell. She hit her knee on a rock, and she must have whacked a nerve because a sudden, excruciating pain exploded in her, and she saw stars and thought she was going to faint. Almost as suddenly the pain ebbed, and as she sat there gripping her knee and wondering if she'd ever get up again, she heard a voice.

Use the Ouija, it said.

Hitting her knee like that must have done something to her mind, made it more receptive, she said, because she'd visited the site several times and hadn't heard peep one, but this voice was loud as anything. Still, she couldn't believe the spirit would say *that*.

What? she asked it.

Use the Ouija.

After that, nothing. My mother sat there for a while and tried to gather her bearings. The fall had taken so much out of her that she had to crawl back to the car on her hands and knees, and pull herself up by the door handle.

"Oh, my," I said.

"Thank goodness no one drove past."

Back home, she dug a Ouija board and a planchette out of my old bedroom closet and took it down to the kitchen. She taped the pictures of the reconstructed head onto the planchette, drank a few glasses of wine, then got down to business. At first she got a lot of garbage: random letters and a few three-letter words: *DIP, BRA.* Then she asked the spirit straight out, *What's your name?* And the planchette sprung into action.

DON'T KNOW, it said.

Are you a man or a woman?

NO ONE NO ONE NO ONE.

"And then," said my mother, "when I asked what happened to him—I'm presuming it's a he, since that's what the police say, and he certainly seems masculine—the planchette flew off the table and smashed against the wall. The legs broke off. I had to tape them up. See?" She reached behind the row of coffee and flour tins on her counter and showed me the planchette. Each of its three legs wore a bandage of masking tape. She put it back.

"More wine?" she asked. "I'm feeling decadent."

"No thanks."

She filled her tumbler to the top and stood there to drink it, holding on to the edge of the sink. "What I've come up with so far won't be enough for the police, that's for sure. Now that I have a sense for it, I'm sure I'll contact the spirit again. But I need a name."

"You need a name," I agreed.

She closed her eyes and drank.

Was this all a lie? It was so hard to tell with my mother; her lies and truths were constantly masquerading as each other. You could lift up one of her lies and find a truth beneath it, then find beneath that truth another lie, and spend your whole life pulling away layers and never get to the bottom of it. How easy, I realized, it is to become paranoid, to see every story as a trap for you to fall into, every person as a leering high school boy.

"I love you, Mama," I said.

She opened her eyes and gave me a puzzled smile. "I love you, too," she said.

Was I drunk? I didn't know. The room was hot and shimmered. My mother, with her glowing face and bright-blue dress, seemed huge, monumental: big enough, even, to hide in.

"I want to help you," I told her again. My eyes were springing small invisible tears.

She nodded. "Well, then, I suppose we can work together. It can't hurt, can it?"

I could only say no.

7

there'd always been deer heads in the ha-ha

This is what I couldn't help but wonder: how many people remembered Peter Morton?

I did, and my mother probably did, too. She never forgot anyone, and usually remembered their birthdays, the names of their children and pets, and could do a good imitation of them, too, with accents and gestures and favorite sayings. Dave the Alien didn't know Peter well, but well enough to remember that I was his girlfriend, so that counted. Who else?

His family, of course. They were from Oregon: Portland and Eugene. His father died when Peter was in high school; his mother remarried a few years later. There was an older sister. I'd never met them, but from Peter's descriptions I imagined them as a brilliant, good-looking, somewhat cold family. Their houses were full of pianos and typewriters and Oriental rugs, and small white-paned windows without screens. I imagined coffee mugs left on bookshelves and desks that folded down out of the wall. It rained a lot in Oregon, the fine kind of rain, after which the sun came out but didn't burn. His mother was the pianist. Both the children took lessons, and they both turned out to be accomplished, though lazy, musicians. The dead father had been a doctor, an anesthesiologist, who left them lots of money, though the family had plenty already. Peter was angry with his mother for remarrying, and his sister was angry at him for being angry. His mother called once or twice during the time I knew Peter, but his sister didn't. They had stopped speaking years before.

Some months after Peter died, his mother sent him a birthday card. In it was a photograph of her with her new husband, a ruddy, fat man, and a collection of blond stepchildren. The card itself had a picture of a South American blanket on the front, and nothing printed on the inside, but his mother had written *Happy Birthday, Petie,* in a precise, excruciating backhand. I resealed the envelope and sent it back to her, with a note telling her the same story I'd told everyone else: that he'd dumped me and left Train Line with no forwarding address. The following summer, when I went to Cape Cod with my mother, I sent her a typed postcard with Peter's faked signature, telling her he was working as a waiter and had met this cool Mexican girl, and they were going to the Yucatán together. He'd had a fantasy about doing this, I knew. I remembered standing in front of a mailbox with my shoes full of sand, holding the postcard over the slot before finally dropping it in. Seagulls cried above me. It was probably the stupidest thing I'd ever done. To my surprise and immense relief, I hadn't heard from her since.

Peter lived in Train Line for a year and a half. Probably half the people who were here then were still around, at least now and then; some, like Edgar Phinney, had died, others, like Nelson Karp, had moved on. Troy would remember Peter; he never forgot anything. Teeny Lawrence, too. She'd wanted to date Peter at one time, though she wasn't his type at all. Her mother, Darva, might also remember him. How about the others, Robin and Winnie Sandox and Grace? Or Ferd at the grocery store, or the women who worked in the cafeteria? Could ten years erase a not-very-significant someone from your mind?

The answer, I suspected, was maybe.

❧

My mother called Officer Peterson the next morning. He seemed pleased that she'd agreed to work with him, less pleased that I was going to be involved.

"I didn't plan on hiring the entire Ziegfeld Follies," he told her. "This is a low-key thing, all right? Just a little consulting."

"Don't worry," my mother said. "My daughter's very low-key."

They discussed particulars. My mother wouldn't be paid, but if her help proved useful she'd receive 50 percent of any reward money. There was often reward money involved in missing persons cases, sometimes a great deal. My mother hadn't thought of this before. "You, of course, would get half of my share," she said generously. She'd called me at the library right after she talked to the police. I could hear her breathing heavily into the receiver. She always breathed heavily when she talked about money.

"Oh, Mama, please."

"I'm just being practical," she said. She told me we had an appointment to meet with Officer Peterson at the state forensics lab in Hollington at the end of the week. "We'll be able to see the actual bones! And touch them, too, I hope. I told Peterson it would be helpful if he lent me a bone or two to meditate on, but he said that was out of his jurisdiction. Maybe there'll be a little one I can slip into my pocketbook."

We'd try the Ouija again right after our trip to the lab, when the "vibrations" were still fresh.

"That sounds good," I said. I couldn't remember the last time I'd used the Ouija. High school? Junior high?

"I'm glad you'll be there," said my mother. "I'm too old for this."

❧

Later that afternoon I took Vivian to Maxwell's for french fries and Coke, to reward her for getting a hundred on her spelling test. We were speaking again, but not much. As we walked, it occurred to me that one day Vivian would be too old for a babysitter, and there would be no reason for us to see each other. Maybe we could be friends, I thought, consoling myself. I pictured a teenaged Vivian telling me about her latest boyfriend, us giggling over sundaes at her favorite hangout—but the girl

I imagined was not Vivian, and the laughing confidante was nothing like me.

Vivian got to Maxwell's before me and stood waiting at the door. She wouldn't go in alone. She had once, and the bartender made her cry by demanding to see her ID. She had trouble recognizing when she was being teased. She didn't look at me when I reached past her to push open the door. It was a quiet afternoon, and the only other person in the bar was Troy Versted, the Australian medium, who was puffing on a small cigar. Smoke hung in the air like ectoplasm. He waved at us from his barstool as we sat down.

Vivian ordered her french fries—I made her do it herself, and told her to look the waitress in the eye—and then I gave her some quarters for shuffleboard. She trotted off, and after a few minutes Troy slid into her seat, across from me.

"I came here to meet your mother, but look who I found," he said, gently tamping his cigar in the ashtray. "We have a martini date."

We were sitting by the big front window, looking out over the lake. Large drops of rain slid down the glass. The bar smelled of stale smoke and beer and fried appetizers and rain. I couldn't think of anything to say to Troy. I smiled at him instead.

"You look pretty," he said.

"I do?"

"Rain in your hair. Did your mother look like you when she was young?"

"She was skinnier. I could show you pictures."

Troy nodded. "That's right. I remember. I suppose she wasn't much older than you are when she first came here." Troy was wearing a pale-blue-and-white golf shirt with matching pants. Another little cigar stuck out of his shirt pocket. "Funny, mediumship does that to women sometimes. They get bigger and bigger. Men get bony." He patted his own gaunt chest.

"I hate it," I said.

"Oh, you shouldn't. Many men like a woman with a rump."
Mini min, he said, with his accent.

"Well, I've never met one." Peter certainly didn't like it.

"What about me?" said Troy.

"Okay, one."

Across the room, Vivian's shuffleboard puck went flying off the table. It hit the floor with a bang. She chased after it and caught it just before it rolled into the men's room. Troy chuckled. He lit up his cigar again, sucked on it, and blew the smoke out behind him.

"So, I hear your mother's working with the coppers."

"Mmm-hmm."

"Traitor!" He waggled his eyebrows. "The coppers are a medium's worst enemy. Whatever is she thinking? Has she forgotten what her brothers and sisters have gone through? Has she forgotten the years of oppressive fortune-telling laws? Back when I lived in the city, cops once confiscated my Ouija board, told me I was a charlatan. I'd have gone to jail if they'd found any money on me. Good thing I'd spent it on booze."

I couldn't tell how serious he was. Troy with a Ouija board? "You're not really mad?"

"Ah, no," he sighed. "Jealous, I suppose. My career is going to hell in a handcart, too, but I'm too old to care, really." He coughed a rattling, old-man's cough and squinted at me through watery eyes. "So. Have you heard the latest?"

"About the skeleton? No. I don't think I have."

"They think they know how the poor bloke died."

"Really." Our french fries arrived then, so I leaned back, blinking and bracing myself for this new information. The waitress clunked down a crusty bottle of ketchup.

Troy reached over and took several of my fries. "Apparently, it was a brain injury," he said, chewing.

I drank some Coke, trying to keep the shock from registering on my face. "Hmm. I wonder how they can tell something like that from a skeleton."

He shrugged. "Oh, they have their ways! A little crack, I think it was, a hairline crack in the skull. Wasn't obvious at first." He touched his own temple with his long, bony fingers. "Blunt instrument. According to my sources, anyway."

I called for Vivian then, and it seemed my voice echoed in my head, as if I were shouting in an empty theater. I put my napkin on my lap, fussed with my knife and fork, straightened the arrangement of condiments on the table. When I looked back up, Troy was staring at me, examining my face with his medium's frank gaze.

"Am I making you nervous?" he asked, grinning.

"Of course not."

"It's a scary thought, though, isn't it? A murderer in our midst."

"Hush," I said, indicating Vivian, who came wandering over. But it was too late.

"Who's a murderer?" she asked.

"I am!" growled Troy. He picked up a spoon and brandished it.

Vivian smiled, delighted. "Who did you kill?"

"Time. I killed Time!"

I ate my french fries quickly. Troy, I decided, was the real thing. He could see right through me. "Eat up," I told Vivian, who was still fooling around.

"French fries are fattening," she said, making a face.

Troy guffawed. "The truth comes out!"

I felt myself blush. "Fine," I said. "Let's go."

Troy was still chuckling, lighting another of his awful cigars, as I paid the bill and steered Vivian out the door. Let him get drunk alone, I thought, the miserable old alcoholic. Then I remembered that Troy had said he was waiting for my mother. My mother hadn't said anything about it. Were they...*dating*? A headache crawled into my skull and lay down.

The ditch along Line Drive was deep and full of leaves. Vivian climbed down in and waded through them. They reached her thighs.

"I can't wait until Halloween," she said. She took a big handful of leaves and threw them into the street. "I wish it was tomorrow."

"What are you going to be?"

"A witch!"

"That'll be fun," I said. It was still cold and drizzling. My headache was waking up, stretching its arms and kicking the backs of my eyes. I couldn't stop thinking of my mother going to bed with Troy. "Are you going to be a good witch or a bad witch?"

She thought for a minute. "Just a regular one."

"You have to be one or the other."

"Which kind gets to have a broom and a big hat?"

"I think those are the bad witches."

"I guess I'll be bad, then."

We walked through the gates, circled the park, and stopped to look at the fountain, with its naked gold baby holding the showerhead aloft in the rain. The water was turned off for the winter and leaves floated in the pool beneath. Through the trees, I noticed someone with a big umbrella come around the corner of Rochester Street. It was my mother, heading for Maxwell's. At this distance she looked old and awkward and slow, though it was obvious she was hurrying. She was paying attention to the ground, careful not to step in any puddles. She didn't see us.

Not long ago, I thought, I'd have been so happy to see her, I'd have run to her, helped her over the puddles. But I did not feel that way anymore. Now she seemed sneaky and secretive and out for herself. It enraged me. My whole body throbbed with emotion. Was I jealous? How could I be? I certainly didn't want to date Troy.

"You know why I want to be a witch?" Vivian asked. She poked at the water with a stick.

"Because they can do magic?" I guessed.

"Nope. Because they can live forever," she said. "I read that in a book."

That evening I had a private client scheduled, and I thought about canceling. My head still ached. After Elaine picked up Vivian, I lay on my bed for a long time, trying to figure out how I could possibly derail my mother and Officer Peterson. I was just sitting here waiting to be caught, for Peter's name to surface, for someone to say *I know what happened.* I could force the Ouija, tap the planchette toward other letters, but I'd have to have another story and another name, and they'd have to be convincing. If I just created a lot of dead ends, I'd do nothing but draw attention to myself. But any other name would lead, eventually, to a dead end…. What I'd have to do, I thought, is build a parallel universe. A universe in which there is a me, and there is a Peter, but one in which we part amicably, and the skeleton belongs to an anonymous no one….

I fell asleep for a little while. Then it was too late to cancel my appointment, so I washed my face in the deep-blue bathroom sink, changed into some clean clothes, and went downstairs to wait.

Odette was right on time, and she brought someone with her: a tall young woman with pale brown hair and a plain, pinched face. Odette herself was middle-aged, chunky, and French. She'd come to the United States when she was nineteen, freshly married to an American serviceman from Wallamee. She couldn't have imagined Wallamee from France. She must have pictured white frame houses and friendly shopkeepers and a village green. Instead she found streets and streets of poorly weatherized houses, their cheap siding peeling off, their yards full of old toys. She stayed married to the serviceman until he died, but she never shook the feeling that her life had taken a wrong turn the moment she first saw him. Her spirits were all French, and they reminded her of the farm she grew up on: the stone floors, the parrot, the bowls of sweet coffee.

"This is Wendy, my niece," said Odette, removing her coat. I helped her and hung it on the coat tree. Wendy made no move to take hers off. "Thank you, Naomi. Wendy lost her baby. It was not right when it came out and did not last the month. I told her you will make her feel better." Wendy looked down at the floor.

"Well, I can't promise that," I said carefully. "It is very difficult when a baby passes over. But come upstairs."

I led them to my séance room at the end of the hall. I loved this room. I loved the small beveled glass doorknob, the old-fashioned brass key that rattled in its lock, and the heavy way the door swung when I pushed it. I loved the way it smelled: sweet, like the old fabric of the curtains, and slightly dusty. It was the room I did my best work in, and so I felt a small flood of happiness whenever I entered it. Odette made herself comfortable in one of the blue wingback chairs and gestured for Wendy to sit in the other one. I entered them in my logbook, sat down on the low wooden stool I used for readings, and we got started.

At first everything was fine. I found Wendy's baby right away, and told Wendy that the child was in its great-grandmother's arms, and that it was happy and was with her all the time. I talked about the stuffed bears everyone had brought the baby in the hospital, and a particular undershirt the child had, one with tiny sheep on it. Wendy did not break down and cry as I'd expected, but that was all right. The first sign I had that something was off-kilter was the expression on Odette's face: she was nervously glancing back and forth between Wendy and me. Odette was never nervous.

"Is something…?" I began, but stopped when Wendy's fists slammed down on the table.

Slowly and emphatically, her face wrinkled in anger, she said, "You stinking fraud."

I did not respond. Once every few years I had a customer get angry, and it had been a long time since the last one. Sad people are like soufflés: they might look perfectly solid, but if you're clumsy you'll flatten them. Keeping my mouth shut and letting her speak would be the best tack. I looked at my folded hands while she berated me.

"I'll bet you read the obituary page every single day, don't you? You just rub your hands when there's a big car wreck or a house fire full of dead children. More business!" She let off a little shriek.

Odette tried taking her hand, murmuring, "Wendy, love…" but Wendy shook her off.

"They're all just better off dead, aren't they? The afterlife is so fucking happy! Why don't we all kill ourselves? Why don't you?"

I stood up, walked to the door, and held it open without saying a word. Odette scrambled out of her chair. "I'm so sorry, Naomi," she said.

"Shh," I answered.

"I have no idea why I came. My child is dead. It's all right to be depressed; I'd be *nuts* if I wasn't depressed…" She trailed off. Odette took her upper arm. "Let's go, dear." This time Wendy acquiesced. She stood up and stumbled to the doorway.

"We can show ourselves out," said Odette, pink-faced. It was clear she was mortified. But as they passed by, Wendy lunged at me. She sprung up like a jack-in-the-box, and I didn't have time to raise my arms to protect myself. One of her hands hit me under the eye and a fingernail raked my nose. I fell against one of the blue chairs. Wendy ran down the hall, Odette hurrying after her.

"Forgive her!" Odette cried from the stairs, but I wasn't sure who she was talking to.

When they were gone, I washed my face in the bathroom and examined my small wound in the mirror. It was a gouge about three-quarters of an inch long. Not small at all, actually; it was big enough that I would have to explain it. I dabbed at it with a wad of pale-green Kleenex. It took several minutes to stop bleeding.

I felt terrible. I felt many things—physically sick, humiliated, furious, and depleted—but they all added up to terrible. Back in my bedroom, across the hall from the séance room, I buried my face in my stale bed sheets. I was too tired to cry. Nothing Wendy had said was true, except that I did read the obituary page. And I'd heard about her baby. But so had everyone. What was wrong with that? I kicked off my shoes, and they banged against the wall.

But I hadn't connected to Wendy, not at all. Perhaps it was the baby business—I'd never lost one, never had one, never even gotten pregnant. It was hard for me to feel much on the subject. The reading had been *real*, I was sure of it—I'd seen the child, the great-grandmother, the little shirt—but something was missing. What was it? Empathy? Had I ever had it? Maybe not since before Peter. For so long, all I'd felt for people was, well, *envy*. Envy for their lives and their loves and the spirits that gathered around them....

What was it my mother called me? *Ice queen.*

God. I was so tired. It suddenly seemed impossible to carry my secret any further. I couldn't do it. I couldn't! I sat up, breathing hard. I would call my mother—that's what I would do!—call my mother and say, *I'm sorry, Mama. Mama, I did something.*

God! The telephone ached to be picked up.

I didn't do it. Not telling was such a powerful habit that it froze my tongue and kept my phone-dialing fingers curled into fists at my side. It would take a force more powerful than I to confess. It would take Peter himself showing up, huge and glowing and righteous in the middle of Train Line, pointing his finger at me and shouting my name.

◦✕◦

The first time I saw Peter, standing in my mother's yard next to poor Nelson Karp, I didn't think much of him. He was almost as thin as Nelson, and paler. He had thick, round glasses and black hair that stood up from his forehead. But his hands, when

I shook them, were warm, square, and strong. Nelson's were skinny, his fingers like spiders' legs.

"Nice to meet you," I said. "Do you want some iced tea?"

Nelson did. I showed them into the kitchen and poured us three big glasses full. I cut up a lemon and found the sugar bowl and even ran out to the yard for some sprigs of mint. I'd spent the morning being bored out of my mind—it was still too early in the season for there to be many tourists, and I didn't have any readings scheduled that day—so I was glad for the company. Also, I was wearing my favorite sundress and was happy to have someone see me in it.

Both boys were shy and as polite as Mormon missionaries. Nelson did most of the talking. Apparently he'd found a girlfriend.

"Diane's spending the summer in the city," he said. "She might come visit in a few months," and, "She's not the New Agey type, but she's quite interested in the work I've been doing with Kirlian photography."

Peter, who'd been sitting quietly with a half-smile on his face, caught my eyes with his. One eyebrow twitched. I narrowed my eyes, just slightly. He slowly moved his head back and forth. I'd never seen such an expressive set of eyebrows in all my life. Nelson kept talking, unaware we were laughing at him.

I stretched my arms over my head and put my bare feet on the table edge. My sundress shifted across my thighs.

"So, Peter," I said, when Nelson ran out of things to say. "Where are you staying?"

"He's got a room on the third floor of the Silverwood," said Nelson.

"Communal toilets, huh?" I said.

"Just the way I like it," said Peter.

Nelson blushed. "The rooms are pretty cheap, but not bad. I stayed there my first summer. Tell Naomi about your night, Peter."

Peter shifted his chair up and put his elbows on the table. "Well," he said. "This may not sound like much of a story to *you,* if what I hear about you is true."

"Nothing you've heard is true," I said.

"Good. Because I want you to be as surprised as I was. So. Last night I went to bed around ten o'clock, early for me, but I'd gotten up at four to drive from New Jersey."

"You went to Princeton, with Nelson, then?"

He nodded. "I had a book to read, a very very boring one, but I have to read in order to fall asleep, no matter how tired I am. So I was reading, reading, reading, listening to all the bumps and creaks in the hotel, and the wind blowing branches against the window, and I got just a tiny bit spooked."

"As well you should."

"Well, yes. But I have this compulsion I'm embarrassed about, and I have to tell you for the sake of the story. I have trouble sleeping unless my bed is against the wall. I mean *right* up against the wall. Especially if I'm in an unfamiliar place. So I got out of bed, shoved the bed tight against the wall, and got back under the covers, feeling much much better. In about ten minutes I was out cold. I hadn't even shut the light off.

"But then, I don't know how much later, I was awakened by a loud bang. My eyes flew open. There was no one in my room, no apparitions whatsoever, so I sort of staggered out of bed, shut off the overhead light, and staggered into bed again. I fell asleep right away.

"When I woke up the next morning, though, I couldn't find my book! I looked under the covers, on the floor, everywhere. You know where I found it?"

I shook my head.

"It was on the floor *underneath the bed.* And the bed was at least three inches from the wall."

"So..."

"So what must have happened was this: I fell asleep reading, the book still in the bed, and then sometime during the night someone—or something—shook my bed so hard that the book slid *off* the bed and fell down between the mattress and the wall! The sound of it hitting the floor woke me up."

I smiled. "It must have been a pretty heavy book."

"It was. *The History of Greece.*"

I didn't say anything for a while. The day was so quiet I could hear the sound of boat motors out on the lake. There was something about Peter's story that rubbed me the wrong way, though I couldn't put my finger on it.

"It was his first paranormal experience," said Nelson. He took his glasses off and polished them with a small cloth he got from his shirt pocket. Sweet, serious Nelson.

"Well, Peter Morton," I said, leaning onto the table and looking him straight in the eyes. "I'm going to tell you something, and I want you to promise me you won't forget it the entire time you're here. Do you promise?"

He flickered his eyelashes, looked down at his hands, then back up at me. The skin beneath his eyebrows grew pink. This, I realized, was how he blushed. "Sure. Yes. I promise."

"Spiritualism," I said, holding the edge of the table, "is our answer to death. It's not a joke. It's not even close to a joke."

He glanced at Nelson. Nelson's mouth was shut tight.

"Okay," said Peter, nodding slowly. "Okay, Miss Naomi Ash. I'll remember that."

⁓✦⁓

That summer, I was a big, suntanned, lazy girl, with a lot of black hair I pinned to the back of my head. I'd mostly gotten over the incessant clairaudience and headaches of the year before, though I still sometimes spent whole days with the shades pulled down, wet towels over my face. I scheduled readings for the afternoon and evening, so I could spend the mornings at the beach in Wallamee. At first I went with Teeny Lawrence. She wore bikini bathing suits in blinding colors and ate potato chips from a can.

Children galloped past us, spraying our towels with sand, and
Teeny screamed blue murder after them. It wasn't long before I
was going to the beach with Peter Morton. Nelson knew enough
to leave us alone.

Peter didn't seem to like the beach, though. He didn't have
any shorts, so he rolled his pants up around his knees, and refused to take his T-shirt off. The brightness of the sun on the
lake made his eyes water. But he wouldn't admit that he'd rather
be somewhere else, so we kept going; he spent the time lying on
his side on the beach blanket, reading. Sometimes he'd sit up, his
elbows on his knees, and watch me sunbathe. I pretended not to
notice, but I could feel his eyes move over me.

One day we dumped the sand out of our shoes, rolled up our
towels, and walked to the Ha-Ha for sandwiches. We'd known
each other for almost two weeks by this time, and we saw each
other every day, but he still hadn't made any moves. He walked
several feet away from me, his hands in his pockets. Once in a
while he would stop, pick up a pebble, and wing it at a tree.

We were crossing the bridge at Wallamee Creek when he
asked me a question. "Naomi. Why didn't you go to college?"

I shrugged. "I didn't want to. I never felt the urge. Why?"

"No particular reason. It's just that everyone I know goes to
college, or will go, or has gone. Everyone does, that's all."

"Not everyone."

"I guess not.

We leaned over the railing and watched water tumble over
rocks.

"I mean," he said after a minute or two, "it's not like you're
dumb."

"No," I said. "It's not."

The deli section of the Ha-Ha was in the back, past the racks
of candy and fishing supplies. We got in line. Peter looked
uncomfortable.

"Have you noticed," he said under his breath, "that there are
deer heads on the walls in here?"

"Yes," I said. Of course there were; there'd always been deer heads in the Ha-Ha. I told him how once, a few years ago, my mother ran into a deer with her car out on Vining Road. Instead of leaving the carcass there to rot, she brought it to the Ha-Ha and had it cut up. We ate venison burger and venison stew and venison everything for months. We had no idea what they did with the head. It might well have been the one hanging above the cashier stand.

This stunned Peter into silence.

For the first time, I found myself looking around at the Ha-Ha and actually seeing it. Flies buzzed and died against the windows, and their tiny corpses littered the sills. Whole squares of linoleum were missing from the floor, revealing the patchy concrete beneath. Some of the cans and boxes on the shelves, with their crushed corners and faded labels, could have been twenty years old. This was the gift Peter gave me: the ability to escape myself. Though it might not have been a gift at all, but a curse.

We got our egg salad sandwiches. They were wrapped in white paper and accompanied by a little sack of chips. From the glum look on Peter's face I knew what he was thinking: *hepatitis B.*

"I've eaten sandwiches here a thousand times," I told him. "I promise it won't kill you."

He looked at me dubiously. "If I die, you can have my books."

"Thank you," I said.

We ate on the tiny square of lawn that passed for Wallamee's War Memorial Park. Peter leaned up against a skinny maple tree, relieved to be out of the sun. I asked him what, exactly, he was doing in Train Line.

"Nothing," he said. "I'm here to do as close to nothing as possible."

He'd finished his history degree at Princeton in the spring, he said, and was going to graduate school in Boston in the fall. He had a scholarship and a teaching assistantship waiting for him. "But I almost can't stand the idea, I'm so burned out. I don't want to work, I don't want to travel. I want to do nothing. Nelson told me Train Line was a good place for that."

"I guess that depends." I talked about my own last year, getting my registration and doing endless message services and being laid up with headaches half the time. I'd never spoken to him about my mediumship before, and after a few minutes I began to feel self-conscious. I stopped and prodded my sandwich.

"Go on," he said. "Please." And he took my hand.

It was hard to speak with my hand clamped between his, so I just shook my head.

"Please?" he said again.

"No. That's all." I waited a moment, struggling to get a hold of myself. "You think we're wackos, don't you?"

He looked at me for a long time, then frowned and looked away. "No. I have to admit I thought that before I got here. And for a little while afterward. But I don't now."

"Hmm," I said.

"I mean it." He gave my hand a squeeze and rolled away across the grass, staring up at the tree branches.

❧

Soon we were kissing in the woods, holding hands under tables, lying for hours on the narrow, lumpy bed in Peter's hotel room. The room was tiny, with a sink and a chair but no desk or table. Books and clothes covered the floor. Through the window floated the voices of the people on the porch below, chatting and complaining and cracking themselves up.

"This place disturbs me," Peter said one afternoon. We were lying half-dressed in front of an oscillating fan, trying and failing to get cool. The temperature was in the nineties outside, even hotter in here, and stuffy.

"The point is to disturb you, I suspect."

"Not how you think," he said. He pulled a T-shirt on and crouched next to the window, looking out. "I haven't seen anything I couldn't explain. The messages at services are pretty general, you know. And there've been no materializations, nothing like that."

"What's so disturbing, then?"

"The people here. Some are a bit odd, but no one's downright crazy. And, for the most part, no one's stupid."

"*For the most part,*" I said. "I like that."

"You know what I mean. These people are smart and nice, and about the most earnest people I've ever met. They're not trying to trick anyone or make a lot of money. Which means—"

Below us, the gang on the porch erupted in laughter. Someone had a deep, honking laugh, like a foghorn.

"Which means what?" I asked, when the noise died down again.

"They really believe in it."

"Duh."

"You're not listening to me," he said grumpily.

"Sorry."

I stood up and buttoned my skirt. I didn't have much patience for this sort of thing. Believe it or don't believe it, I wanted to tell him, but don't make me listen to you muddle through it.

"Naomi!" He turned to me, desperate. "I'm sorry. It's just that there's something here I'm not getting." His hair was flattened on one side of his head and stuck out on the other.

I wasn't very nice. I put my sandals on and tied my hair up. "Give me a call when you figure it out," I told him, and walked right out the door.

⚭

He didn't call for almost a week, but I thought about him the entire time.

Though I would never have admitted it to Peter, there was a part of me that was falling in love with the idea of going to college. I had no idea what Princeton looked like, but I imagined buildings with Gothic windows and towers and an observatory, one that would open up on clear nights and poke its telescopes at the moon. The library would have green reading lights and the kind of book stacks that reached so high you had to climb ladders to get to the top. I would write with fountain pens if I went to college, I thought, and I'd study my textbooks for hours and hours, until I was kicked out of the library or my eyes went bad, whichever came first.

Naomi Ash, College Student, was a very different person from me. I knew that, dropped suddenly from an airplane into a college campus, I would not be able to do it. I'd go to my room and want to sleep the whole time. At parties I'd spill drinks on my dress and have to flee, stained and mortified. In classes I'd be so afraid of not understanding what the professor was saying that I'd spend the whole time staring out the window at the beautiful campus or else drawing tiny pictures in my notebook. But I wanted to be someone else. I'd never felt this way before, but something about Peter brought it out in me. I wanted to be like him: quiet, studious, and full of information. I wanted to know things.

Actually, Peter never did call. I'd turned off my bedside lamp one night, and had just pulled the sheet over my shoulder, when something hit my window screen and bounced away into the night. It happened again, then again, so I stood up and squinted out into the dark.

"But soft, what light through yonder window breaks?"

I knew that from high school.

Peter was wearing a white shirt and his pale-blue pants. Standing there out in the street, he practically glowed. *"It is the east,"* he said, and went on to recite the whole damn soliloquy.

I pushed the screen up and leaned out on my elbows to watch him. He was making a fool of himself. Anyone watching from a porch or window or yard all up and down Seneca Street could hear him. Even I knew it was a cheesy thing to do: clichéd, sentimental, silly. It seemed out of character for Peter, who was such an intellectual, and so serious. But it knocked me for a loop.

"Naomi?" he called when he was through. I didn't answer. "Naomi? Am I going to have to repeat it?"

I fell in love that fast.

❧

And as the summer wore on, Peter changed. He shoved his history books underneath his bed and began hanging around the library, reading up on spiritualism. A lot of what he read annoyed him.

"Did you know, Naomi, that after the Fox sisters admitted, *admitted*, they were dropping apples and cracking their toes to make the rappings, people refused to believe they were fakes?"

"Well," I said. "They were only fakes in one sense of the word."

"What is that supposed to mean?"

I explained. It is possible, I told him, to begin with what may seem to you like fraud, but have it acquire truth. As an example, I asked him if he'd ever been in a horrible mood and then gotten out of it by smiling.

"Maybe, I don't know. But I see what you mean. Go on."

At first, I said, that smile is a fraud. You're not in a good mood at all. But then, because you're smiling, you are. Is that smile still a fraud?

"Hmm," he said, dubious.

"Plus, most mediums end up fudging a bit, now and then. People pressure you to come up with something, no matter how crummy your day's been or how rude they are or anything." I told him about the intercom in our house in New Orleans, and about poor Miss Beryl. A lot of times, I said, what seems most faked to you can turn out to be the most true, and the most helpful. That, anyway, was how I saw it.

But what changed his mind, in the end, I think, was me. He came to message services and Circle Nights and watched me. Once I even had a message for him. It was during the four o'clock meeting at the Forest Temple.

I liked the Forest Temple—it was made of white painted wood, just an archway with a back on it, rather like an over-sized shrine, with the words FOREST TEMPLE in old-fashioned green lettering—but it was right off Seneca Street. From the platform I could see tourists walking by with their dogs, and the old men coming in and out of Ferd's grocery. It made it hard to concentrate. Peter sat in the back, the shadows of leaves moving over him.

"Peter. I have your father."

Did I? I had a presence. I wanted it to be Peter's father, and it might have been. Sometimes a presence was all I had to work with.

I told him something fairly general: how much he loved Peter, how Peter should study hard but remember there are things more important than school, and that he had to be careful not to become too self-absorbed.

"You know what I mean," I added.

Afterward, Peter came up to me, furious. "My father would *never* say anything like that," he said, eyes narrowed. "Fucking *never*." There was a bright-red splotch on each of his sharp cheekbones.

"How do you know?" I said, just as angry. "Just because he never *did* doesn't mean he didn't want to. And what he said was true, wasn't it?"

He didn't say anything. "Peter," I went on. "I don't have a father, either. I know it's hard…"

He turned and kicked one of the benches, emptied now of old ladies and impressionable teens. "You never had a father," he said bitterly. "I had one and lost him. It's not the same at all." He took a breath. "Look," he said, calmer now. "I want to believe this. You don't know how badly I want to believe this stuff. But I can't."

"If you want to, you can."

He looked at me, anguished. His eyes filled with tears. And then, while I watched, Peter's face fell apart. It was almost as if the structures that held it together, the jawbones and snooty brow and arching nose bone, had been taken away and replaced with a meltable substance—wax, maybe, or ice. Something was happening to Peter; something in him was breaking down. It didn't last long. After a few moments he pulled himself together. But that face was never quite the same.

"Fuck," he said. "I'm in love with you."

After that, Peter relaxed a little. He took the Kirlian photography workshop that Nelson was teaching and told me he wasn't even going to bother thinking up a scientific explanation for the strange, bright auras on the film. He met me for lunch after message services, and we discussed the good parts and bad parts, sharing pie and coffee. He even seemed to gain some weight. Everything about him softened; his hair even lay flatter against his head.

The first time we had sex, I didn't like it much. Peter was thorough and clinical and removed. "It's like you're hammering nails into the wall," I complained. He was good-natured enough to laugh. But the sex changed, too, and before long we were having it up against trees in the woods, and in my rowboat, and in the bathtub on the third floor of the Silverwood. Our times together became charged. I'd slept with boys in high school—a long-haired soccer player named Ryan Forbes, and a boy named Preston Venn, who was obsessed with computers—but it never interested me. Having sex, I thought, was not much different from playing volleyball or swimming laps in the pool: a lot of effort for nothing. I had trouble concentrating on it. But sex with Peter was its own form of concentration, like concentrating with your body and mind and eyes and mouth all at once. I'd never felt so absorbed.

We noticed that the places we'd had sex seemed, every time we came back to them, weirdly haunted. If we passed a spot in the woods where we'd done it, something hummed in our ears, and the air felt thicker. This erotic fog began filling Train Line, rolling off the lake and out of the woods and filling up places we'd never been, let alone had sex in. It rolled out of the Silverwood bathroom and down the stairs and into the lobby, where old women sat crocheting with their purses on their laps and old men read back issues of *Spirit Light Monthly*. Soon we'd barely have time to walk up the wooden porch steps, set foot on the lobby carpet, before we nearly suffocated with the thought of making love. Anything could set us off; the swirly pink-and-yellow spirit art in the cafeteria, the sound of wind blowing through pine branches. Poor Nelson Karp left for Princeton early, as soon as his workshop was over. His missed Diane, he said—she never did come and visit.

As fall loomed, we became more and more preoccupied with each other. My readings and messages were all for Peter, though I had to pretend, most of the time, that they were for someone else. It was only Peter's mind I was in, and only Peter's spirits that held any interest for me. And, for Peter, I was the only thing he wanted to look at, see, or touch. His history books were lost somewhere beneath the bed.

It was the end of August when he had to leave. His teaching assistantship at the university was about to start, and he'd been getting letters about his scholarship that he opened, read, and dropped on the floor of his room. We both felt it coming but didn't say anything, until one afternoon Peter asked me if I'd drive him to the train station the next morning.

"There's no *train station* around here," I said. We were in the grocery store, looking for ballpoint pens. Peter hadn't written a thing all summer, he said, and all of his pens had dried up. He figured he ought to have some when he got to Boston. "They tore up the rails years ago, when I was a little kid. And no trains had run on them, anyway, since I don't know when."

He looked at me sadly. "Port Gilbert. I called."

I spent the night with him. We had mournful, self-conscious sex, then lay awake the rest of the night without talking. At four we staggered up, deeply cold in the dank morning air, and carried his lumpy duffel bags down to my mother's car. For a spooky town, a town obsessed with death and spirits and trances and clairvoyance, it seemed awfully conventional that morning: all the lights were off, everyone was in bed under blankets, waiting for the sun to come up so they could cook their breakfasts. In the car I turned the heat up to high, and we rumbled down the gravel and potholes of Seneca Street, past the glimmering lake, and out onto the road.

"Good-bye," whispered Peter. "Good-bye, good-bye." His thin face was green in the light from the dashboard.

I'd never driven to Port Gilbert before. It was only an hour and a half away but I had no reason to go there, ever. Peter had asked directions from the person at the station, and they were easy to follow, at first. I zipped down the highway. No other cars were out, only semitrucks. They roared past us in the dark.

"Oh, my God," said Peter. "Did you see that?"

"See what?"

"That semi driver had a clown mask on."

"Are you kidding?"

He insisted he wasn't. It was, he said, the creepiest thing he'd ever seen. "A malevolent clown mask, too. It had a huge smile but devilish eyes."

"Maybe it's a sign."

"I hate to think of what."

We got to the Port Gilbert exit of the interstate with plenty of time to spare. "How about a doughnut?" said Peter. A brightly lit cube of glass and plastic beckoned near the off-ramp. DAY-LIGHT DONUTS said the sign. Beyond it, the sun edged up over the horizon. "Perfect," I said.

We had two glazed doughnuts and two cups of coffee. Flies landed on the orange countertop, and around us, everyone was weird. The counter boy was so fat you could hardly see his eyes. An old man grumbled incoherently into his mug of tea. And an overdressed woman lounged across the seat of her booth, kicking her high-heeled foot in the air, saying nothing but giving us smoldering looks.

We were glad to leave.

But somehow we'd gotten ourselves turned around. Instead of the main strip, we were on a residential one-way street, rattling over the brick paving. Then we were speeding down a hill, Lake Ontario in the distance ahead of us, spread out like a flag.

"I'll ask for directions," said Peter, hopping out and running into a Ha-Ha store. He was back in half a minute. "Follow that bread truck," he told me, pointing at a big white van. "He told me he was going right past it."

The bread truck went down alleys filled with pallets and Dumpsters, it cut through parking lots, it made sudden turns without signaling. I had the feeling we were getting farther and farther away from the train station all the time. We passed a house that was on fire; the bread truck drove onto the sidewalk to get around the fire engines. We did the same.

All of a sudden the bread truck stopped, tooted its horn, and a white-clad arm waved at us from the side window.

"This is it, I guess," said Peter.

We'd stopped at a big square building that had rows of greenish windows and a giant, round, handless clock over the double doors. It looked like a cross between a warehouse and a cathedral.

"Uh-oh," I said. "The train's already here."

I turned off the car and helped him pull the duffel bags out of the back. We had time for a hurried, nervous kiss before he went galloping into the station, laden with luggage. But he'd only just disappeared behind the doors when the whistle blew, and the train slowly began pulling out of the station. I got back out of the car and leaned against the hood.

Three minutes later, Peter came out again. He dropped his bags on the dirty sidewalk. Then he didn't walk toward me, he ran.

"You missed it," I told him.

"I don't know what I was thinking," he said, over and over again. His arms were tight around my shoulders. "I can't leave. I don't think I can ever leave."

"Never?"

"Never," he said. "Never ever ever."

We drove home. Peter left his hand in my lap the whole way. Other cars were out now, families and commuters and school buses, and we listened to the local radio station as we got back onto the interstate. "Good morning, early risers!" said the deejay. "It's a beautiful day!"

It was. The sky was clear and cloudless, and the sun was up, so bright and glaring we felt like we were driving straight into it.

8

witch

I took the boat out on the lake again. I hadn't done that much in the last few years—my boat was rusty and had some leaks in the bottom I didn't know how to fix—but the morning before my mother and I were to go to the forensics lab, I thought it would feel good to be alone for a little while, away from every living soul. In summer the lake was always choked with thick green algae, impossible to row through, but the colder fall weather had brought clear water. I rowed hard for a bit, then stopped and drifted. Now and then I'd have to bail out the water with a yogurt container of Ron's I'd brought along.

From the lake, Train Line looked like an island. I hunkered down in my boat, windbreaker zipped to my chin, and looked out at it: the pointed rooftops poking out from the trees, empty flagpoles, shuttered windows. There was Winnie Sandox raking leaves; there was old Francis Liggett smoking his pipe in the middle of his lawn. Other times I'd gone out on the lake, I'd seen people taking walks, and going out to their cars, and having cocktail parties on their patios, but they never noticed me. It was as if the lake was a wall to them. I could have waved or even shouted, but they'd look around, look up at the trees, and still never see me. There I was, completely out in the open, but invisible. Spirits must feel like this, I thought.

After a while I stopped rowing and ate some chicken-flavored crackers from a box. My fingers were wet and numb from bailing, and my hair was whipping around. It was too cold to be out, but I liked it there and thought maybe it would be better if I were to lie down in the bottom of the boat, since I'd be out of the wind. I spread the tarp on the bottom and gently lowered myself down, holding on to the oars.

It *was* warmer there, and quiet. The only sound was the clunk of water lapping the metal hull. Without a horizon the sky looked strangely depthless, like a lid. I ate some more crackers, imagining how odd the boat would look from shore, if anyone bothered to notice.

When I stood up again, fifteen or twenty minutes later, I lost my balance. That had never happened before. I must have stepped too close to the left side of the boat, because it tipped sharply, and when I flung myself to the right side I overcorrected. The boat flipped over, and I splashed like a big sack of junk into the water.

It seemed like a long time before I came back up again. Under my windbreaker I was wearing a heavy cotton sweater, my pants were wool, and my shoes were clunky leather loafers. I kicked and struggled against my suddenly weighty clothes for what must have been a whole minute before my face broke the surface. I spat and gasped and pushed my hair out of my eyes. My cracker box bobbed in the waves three feet ahead of me, but the boat was gone. I couldn't believe it. It took so little to sink the boat; it took nothing, a tiny miscalculation. I swiveled around in the water. There were the oars, but the boat had vanished. And the shore, I realized, was awfully far away.

I nudged my shoes off with my toes and floated, trying not to panic. Though I'd never been much of a swimmer, I could do the back float all day, I thought. But the water was choppier than I'd expected, and waves kept washing over my face, and the current—what there was of one on Wallamee Lake, anyway— seemed to be pushing me in the wrong direction. I had to roll over and dog paddle until I got tired, then rest and float, then dog paddle again. Swimming in a full set of winter clothes was harder than I could have imagined. I got myself out of my jacket and sweater, but left my pants and undershirt on. Ten, fifteen minutes went by, and the shore didn't seem any closer. I kicked and flailed, fluttered my feet as fast as I could.

While I was swimming, I calmed myself down by trying to imagine the bottom of the lake. Was it smooth and sandy, or rocky and muddy and littered with rowboat hulls? I knew of a few boats that had gone down in Wallamee Lake. Eighty or ninety years before, a boat full of teenaged girls from Train Line sank, and in their long dresses and lace-up boots they didn't have a chance of swimming to shore. There were seven of them, and every one drowned. I didn't know if they found any of the bodies or not, or if they all sank. When I was a little girl, a retarded boy from Wallamee stole his father's rubber raft, took it out on the lake, and was never seen again. Was the bottom of the lake covered with bodies? I wondered how far down the bottom was. I imagined a cross-section, me dog-paddling on top, yards and yards of cold brown water beneath me, then the lake floor, with its mud and sunken boats and dead things.

Fish bumped me with their cold snouts. Bits of algae clung to my hair.

I wasn't going to make it. The cold became a suffocating blanket that wrapped my head and face until I could hardly see and could hear nothing but the sound of my own breathing. Let go, I thought. Just sink.

I couldn't.

If your faith is so strong, I told myself, why not let go?

There would be a funeral, closed casket, whether they found my body or not. Lots of people would come, many of my customers, unless the weather was bad and then they wouldn't bother coming out; they were mostly old, after all. My mother would be devastated, Troy and Dave the Alien and Ron and Jenny stoic. Elaine wouldn't allow Vivian to come, and would tell her some lie about how I'd moved out of town, or something. After a little while someone new would rent my rooms. Well, that might take some time, months even, since it was winter. But next summer I'd be a distant sad memory, my rooms cleaned out and my furniture given to the Ladies' Rummage Shed, and a cheerful new person would be living there, someone who'd get along wonderfully with Ron and Jenny, and they'd stay up late drinking herb elixirs and laughing. My mother would get over it. I'd come to her séances. Or would I? Maybe I'd go to hell. Or maybe I'd just be gone, utterly and completely vanished, even more gone than Peter, whose mystery, at least, was keeping him vital.

Then my feet touched bottom, and, somehow, my head was still above water.

Washing ashore I felt as huge and slow as a sea monster, my hair and clothes dragging like plates of armor. Miraculously, I was only a few yards from where I'd put out. I lay on the bank with my face in the soggy grass, so cold I could hardly feel it. But then I could feel it, so I sat up and wrapped my arms around my knees, teeth chattering.

Across the lawn of the Silverwood, Jenny walked by, wrapped up in a heavy wool coat and with a scarf around her head. Her hands were deep in her pockets. I thought about yelling for her, but suddenly felt embarrassed at my state: my undershirt clung like plastic wrap to my breasts, and you could see right through it to my safety-pinned bra. Anyway, she was on her way back from her reincarnation group, and I didn't want to hear about it. I'd heard enough already. Tony K. and Winnie Sandox were in it and had recently revealed that they had been, respectively, T. S. Eliot and Ptolemy Epiphanes, ancient king of Egypt. Reincarnation was a touchy subject in Train Line, and had been for a long time; officially, it is not a part of spiritualism, but few spiritualists are particularly doctrinaire. Many of the newer, and New Agey, mediums are all for it, but I'd always felt reincarnation raises a few more questions than it answers. Once, when I was just starting out, I told a woman at a message service that I had her father's father here, but she just shook her head emphatically. "Impossible!" she declared. "He reincarnated twenty years ago!" What can you say to that? Not much.

But Jenny liked the group and claimed that she'd been animals for most of her former lives, which caused a heated debate. There'd been some discussion, too, of where Jenny was headed next. Would she be rewarded for living a good life this time around with a better one? How soon would she reincarnate, and if she did, how would they be able to contact her? Would she have any say in the matter?

"I want to live this same life over," she'd told me that morning. "But more happily."

Something about that depressed me. I wondered, would I be in that life, too? I hoped not. Imagine living your life over and over again, making new mistakes each time and fixing them, your soul like a page of homework rubbed thin with your eraser. It was exhausting to think about. But perhaps less exhausting than the idea of spending an infinity in the spirit world, at the beck and call of the living.

Jenny turned up Fox Street, her head scarf fluttering in the breeze. The wind had picked up and changed direction, and now it came off the lake, turning the water coarse. I lumbered to my feet. When I slapped myself my cold flesh rang like a copper bowl, and I smelled like the lake. How odd to be alive! It felt like a mistake.

❧

My mother picked me up at one o'clock. I'd taken a very long bath and washed my hair twice, but I couldn't get rid of the lake smell, so I'd tried to disguise it with Jenny's lemon-scented bath powder. The combination was unfortunate: sweet and fetid. My mother didn't mention it, but as she drove down the interstate toward Hollington her nose twitched, and she gave me some curious glances.

"Are you taking care of yourself, Naomi?"

I told her I was.

The forensics lab was hidden behind a hill just off the highway. Like everything else in Wallamee County built since the fifties, it was low and uninspired. We parked near some police cars and hobbled across the gravel parking lot in our high heels. I had dressed up and my mother had dressed down, and consequently we met somewhere in the middle, both in sober navy blue. Still, as we stood in the cramped lobby waiting for Officer Peterson, surrounded by slim, uniformed people, I felt huge and overblown. I felt like my mother. She was examining her makeup in a little, tiny mirror, oblivious to the fact that no matter where in the lobby we stood, people had to go around us. I kept blushing, apologizing, shuffling out of the way.

Officer Peterson appeared from behind a cubicle wall, his hand extended toward us. His hair was freshly cut, as upright and stiff-looking as the bristles of a toothbrush, and his eyes gave nothing away. "Glad you could make it," he said. He seemed more polite than he had on the phone; perhaps my mother reminded him of his own.

He led us back through the catacomb of cubicles, past file cabinets and computer screens and people working at jobs I would never in a million years be hired to do, through a swinging door that opened to a wide, hospital-like hallway. Our shoes clicked and echoed, and the air smelled like the high school biology lab, like the preserved crayfish I dissected sophomore year. Formaldehyde. I remembered how hard it was to get that smell off your hands. It would get in your hair, taint your sandwich at lunch.

Peterson stopped outside a door with a glass mesh window and pushed it open for us. We entered a bright room full of sinks and drawers and metal tables, and a short man in a white coat eating from a small bag of chips. Peterson introduced him as Dr. Freeze.

"That's F-R-I-E-S," said the man, crumpling his empty chip bag.

"Oh," I said.

"They're the ladies I told you about," said Peterson. "Here to see John Doe."

"Right, right." He stuffed the bag into one of his pockets and rubbed his hands together, then pulled what looked like a handful of white balloons from another pocket. "You'll want gloves," he said, handing us each a pair.

We snapped them on. It was at this point that I began to feel a little dizzy, as if the hard tile floor had suddenly acquired some give. I reached for one of the metal tables.

"Don't!" cried Dr. Fries. "Don't touch anything yet. We don't want any cross-contamination."

I took some deep breaths.

We followed Dr. Fries to the back of the room, where there was a whole wall of wooden drawers. He pulled one out and extracted a plastic bag full of small brownish things. "Now, does it matter what bones you look at? This is a hand. Skull's down the hall." He reached in again and pulled out another bag. "This is, um, looks like another hand. Let's see…foot…" He put the bags on a table and opened a new drawer. "Here are the big bones… ribs, legs…" He looked up at us inquiringly.

My mother cleared her throat. "I was hoping to see the back bones. There's a lot of power in the spine."

Dr. Fries shook his head. "Sorry, no can do on that. There was some flesh preserved there, and we've got it refrigerated across the hall."

"All right then. These will do." She indicated the bags on the table. "Let's try a hand."

He nodded, put the other bags away, and brought the hand bones to a glass tray on the counter. He carefully shook the bones from the bag and pulled a gooseneck lamp over the tray, then flicked it on. The bones looked like nothing so much as a few pieces of dog kibble.

"No squeezing or scratching, please," said Dr. Fries. Then he gave Officer Peterson an ironic salute and wandered back across the lab.

My mother picked up one of the small brownish lumps and cupped it in her hand, then closed her eyes. She stood there, swaying, for a minute or so. While Peterson and I watched, she made a fist of the hand with the bone in it, and brought the fist to her forehead. She exhaled deeply.

"Hunhhhhhh," she said, opening her eyes. "Well. Aren't you going to try, Naomi?"

I reached for a bone. Close up, it actually did look like a bone, a tiny one. I wasn't sure what I was supposed to do, so I held it in my gloved fist and gazed out into space, frowning. Peter's hand! I'd loved his hands. Square, broad, fine black hairs, scraggly cuticles. It seemed impossible that this was all that was left of them; in fact, it seemed impossible that they could be Peter's, and that he was dead. Obviously I'd been fooled, somehow. The lab slipped out of focus.

"...left-handed, they think," Peterson was saying, and my mother said, "How on earth can they tell that?" and Peterson said, "Dominant hand's usually bigger," and I was on my knees on the hard floor.

"Whoop," said Peterson. He slid his hand under my arm and steadied me.

"Sorry...I...um."

"What's wrong? What's wrong?" cried my mother. She knelt down and looked me in the face.

"Lost my balance," I said. "Here." I handed her the bone, hauled myself up—with Peterson's fingers digging into the soft flesh under my arm—and made a controlled lunge toward the nearest sink. I vomited hugely into it.

"Did you see something? She saw something," my mother said.

Would an innocent person have vomited in this situation? I wasn't sure. I hung over the sink, coughing and running water, in order to give myself some time to think. Had I reacted too strongly? Maybe. Maybe I had. The bones weren't disgusting, weren't scary at all.

"Naomi...?" My mother put her hand on my back.

"He was buried facedown," I said.

Though at the time I could not have said why I revealed this, why I chose a detail so telling and possibly dangerous, it was clear to me later. A good medium will always tell you something true before telling you something less than true—it only takes one true sail to float your ship of lies around the world. If you tell someone his grandmother's maiden name, he will listen to the rest of your message with an open heart, even if it's unmitigated nonsense. A medium ought to be a mistress of timing, a duchess of pill-sugaring, a queen of liars.

"I had a vision," I said. "He was face down."

My mother handed me some Kleenex from her purse, then turned to Officer Peterson. "Is this true?"

"Well, I'm not sure I can disclose that information." He scratched his bristly head. My vomiting seemed to have impressed him. "I mean, I don't know offhand. That might be privileged information."

"Write it down, then," said my mother. "We might be getting somewhere."

Peterson dutifully scribbled something on his pad, then asked, "All right. Anything else?"

"Well..." said my mother. "I had a vague impression of—I know this sounds strange—a sort of feeling of *money*. Perhaps a lot of money passed through this man's hands? Or maybe he was killed for money. He might have been a rich man, or a bookie. Or deep in debt."

"That wouldn't surprise me," said Peterson.

I washed my face with cold water. What had I done? Perhaps nothing. Perhaps those earthmovers tumbled the bones over and over before dragging them out of the soil. Perhaps no one knew whether he was face down or up or sideways or anything. I dried my face on my sleeve and smiled at Officer Peterson. It was all I could do to wrench the muscles of my mouth into position. I did not feel well at all.

"You might want to get some air," he said, sticking his pencil behind his ear.

Back outside again, I leaned against a bright orange Dumpster and threw up once more. The air smelled like formaldehyde.

"That was a real vision, wasn't it?" asked my mother, crunching toward me across the gravel. She had a can of cola from the machine in the lobby, and she handed it to me.

"I guess so."

"You guess so!" She stood there with her hands on her wide hips. "You know, it's so rare for me. I hardly ever have visions. I have to try and try and I'm lucky if I get a fleeting *impression* or an *image*. You don't know how frustrating it is." She looked so sad in her sensible pumps, her hair askew. She never made confessions like this, and I didn't know whether to believe her.

"Oh, Mama…"

"I had such hopes."

"It's not over yet."

"I know."

We got in the car. My mother drove and I sipped the warm and bilious cola. We took hilly back roads, which was a mistake; I made my mother stop after a while so I wouldn't be sick in the car. She pulled off the road next to an old cemetery. It was about the size of someone's kitchen, full of white limestone markers too weathered to read. I got out and sat on the grass.

My mother called to me from the car. "All this upchucking reminds me of when you were a little girl."

I nodded.

"If you're still sick later, you should come stay with me tonight."

"I won't be. I feel better already."

"But if you are."

"All right. Maybe."

It was cold, there on the grass. I wondered who cut it. The stones must have been a hundred and fifty years old; who could care enough about them to cut the grass? I reached out and ran my hand over one of the markers. It was rough, rougher than it looked. Poor Peter, I thought. Not even a headstone.

The trunk of my mother's car popped open then, and she climbed out of her seat and got something out of it. It was a Ouija board. She waved at me with it.

"No time like the present!"

"Oh, not now, Mama."

"Look." She lumbered over with some difficulty. "You're vulnerable now, the vision's fresh. Let's try it."

I was too tired and queasy to argue. When I shut my eyes, I could feel the rocking of the waves on Wallamee Lake. My mother leaned against a headstone to help herself down.

She arranged the board between us and said a short prayer. The graveyard was on top of a hill, and Wallamee County was spread around us on all sides: the lake a silver finger, trees turning color, ribbons of highway winding in and out of sight. There was a steady wind. With our fingers resting on it, the planchette was a little wobbly.

"Okay," said my mother. "First think of the bones. Think of the vision you had, the way the body looked. I'll try to get in touch with the spirit from the other day…"

Before, I thought I'd take control of the board. I even had a name: *Andrew,* because it could be a first or a last and it was common but not too common. I thought I'd very gently pull and tug the planchette, spelling out A-N-D-R-E-W and vague answers to the questions my mother asked. But I was crumbling. The hill, the graveyard, the lake so small and far away, the worn-away names, all filled me with incoherent emotion. My fingers shook.

"You, the one buried by the lake many years ago. Are you ready to talk to us?" My mother's voice, loud and out of place here, was immediately caught by the wind and tossed away.

The planchette jerked slightly, then slid to YES.

What made it move?

This question, this ridiculously obvious question, had never occurred to me before. I wasn't moving the planchette, not consciously, anyway. And if my mother wasn't, either, then that meant a spirit had entered us, *both of us,* and that we were no longer in control of our own hands. It was normal, it happened all the time, but now it struck me as awful and strange that we would allow this to happen, that we'd give up our bodies this way.

"What's your name?"

The planchette moved with surprising speed. *N-O-T N-O-W.*

"How did you die?"

W-R-O-N-G-F-U-L-L-Y.

Tears slid down my face and dripped off my chin.

"All right, I've been patient!" yelled my mother. "Tell me your name or we're through!"

The planchette slid to *P.*

Oh, God. What was happening? I felt, with sudden conviction, that I *was* moving the planchette around, that it had been me all along; that my mediumship had never been anything but me turning my face away from my own fraudulence.

E-T-E

But if it was me, why couldn't I stop?

R

The planchette paused, then went on. It meandered for a few seconds, then stopped at *S.*

"Oh, very funny!" shouted my mother, and she picked up the planchette and flung it into the hayfield behind us.

"What?" I cried. "What happened?"

"Didn't you see?" she said crossly, picking up the Ouija board and looking like she was going to Frisbee it into the hayfield, too. "It was spelling out *Peterson!* All this work and we're the butt of some stupid joke!" She looked at me. "What's wrong? Why are you crying?"

"I don't know. I feel weird." Peter's middle name, of course, was Samuel.

"It's too much, isn't it?" she said, sighing. "I feel like I've been fooled with ever since this started. Maybe I'll take a break and try something new for a while. Help me up, would you?"

I held my mother's hands and pulled her to her feet. What I was feeling could not properly be called relief; it was too tenuous and unreliable for that, like a paper boat on rough seas. I'd been convinced that once Peter's name was out, everything would be over; and that the cataclysm that was sure to erupt from this disclosure would annihilate me, and my mother, too. But here I was helping my mother into her car, buckling my seat belt, making plans for dinner. It was the end of the world; it was an ordinary day. This was a lesson I should have learned ten years ago, when Peter died. The worst thing in the world can happen, but the next day the sun will come up. And you will eat your toast. And you will drink your tea.

∽

And then, for two weeks, nothing.

Day after day, the weather was warm and the sky empty of clouds. The trees around the library turned a deep blood red, so when the sun shone through them, the light that filtered into the reading room was pink. It was quite beautiful. If no one was in the library or downstairs, in the museum, I'd sit outside on the stone bench beneath the trees and read.

But there was, often, someone in the library. A young man doing research on the history of Train Line came in every couple of days, and, three or four afternoons in a row, an overdressed woman with dark, ponytailed hair spent an hour or so in the reading room. I thought she must be on vacation, because she seemed bored, and always asked me to recommend a book for her. I gave her *Series of Letters from a Medium, "J"* and *Spirit Art: Prehistory to Today*. She said she found them incomprehensible.

"Well," I said. "Try this one." I handed her a book on spiritual healing.

"I'm tired of reading," she said, drumming her fingers on my desk.

So I unlocked the basement door and let her wander around the museum by herself. She was down there until it was nearly time for me to go home. She was dusty and delighted when she came back up.

"Those slates are amazing!" she said. "And all that equipment! What was that machine, a dynamistograph? Bizarre!"

I explained to her how it worked: the machine would be shut in a windowed room, so that observers could watch from the outside without disturbing it, and the spirit would enter the cylinder in the center of the machine. A lettered dial on top could spell out long communications with the spirit. The woman nodded, her attention already somewhere else. With her chewed fingernails and wide hazel eyes, she reminded me of Peter. People didn't often remind me of him, because he was so different from everyone else I knew. She had Peter's thin mouth, too, and lips the color of her skin.

It didn't frighten me. Instead, it made me miss Peter.

"Are you here on vacation?" I asked. Suddenly, I didn't want her to leave.

She rolled her eyes. "I wish! It's awfully quiet around here, isn't it?"

"In the fall it is. It's worse in winter. But in summer the place is a madhouse."

"I like madhouses," she said.

She wasn't looking at me. Her nervous eyes scanned the shelves behind my head, looked down at my desk calendar, peered out the window. Peter was never that nervous. He exuded an extreme calm. But sometimes he ignored me in the same way, caught up in his own thoughts, running ahead of our conversation with his new ideas.

Before the woman left, she turned to me and asked, "Are you Naomi?"

"Yes. Why?"

She shrugged. "No reason. I've heard about you, is all."

There wasn't much I could say to this, so I said nothing.

I watched through the glass door as she walked down the steps. She stopped at the end of the walk and looked both ways, wrapping her arms around her. A falling leaf caught in her hair. She didn't seem to notice, but turned and walked smartly up the gravel road, moving on to the next thing on her agenda.

When she was gone, I sat at my desk and wished I'd asked her to have coffee or something. She didn't really seem like someone I could talk to, but still. I thought, *I really need some friends.*

Outside, leaves fell.

∽◦∾

The week before Halloween, I drove Vivian to the Murphy's Five and Dime in Wallamee to buy her a witch costume. Elaine had asked me to.

"There's going to be a party at her school," she'd said, "and a parade, you remember all that. They sent home a flyer, which I lost, of course. Go ahead and get her one of those plastic ones in a box, if you want. I'd really appreciate it. And of course I'll reimburse you."

When I was a little girl, all my costumes were from the Woolworth's and came with those cheap plastic masks that smelled good inside. I loved the thin elastic string over my ears, the way my breath condensed inside them, the way every expression on my face was hidden by that frozen plastic sneer. We didn't have parties in school, but I went trick-or-treating with a big gang of neighborhood children, and we came home with popcorn balls and apples and peculiar candy bars you never saw the rest of the year: Full Dinner Bars and Honey Chews.

But I had bigger plans for Vivian. This, I thought, could be my opportunity to make it up to her. I made her lie down on a piece of newspaper so I could trace her body, and then we designed a witch dress. It would be long and black and would have draping sleeves and a bright green lining. Vivian insisted on the green, though I told her orange was the more traditional Halloween color.

"So?" she'd said, belligerent. The tone in her voice made me want to spank her. I didn't.

But we'd made up by the time we got to Murphy's. Big rubber gorilla faces and cardboard tombstones filled the windows, and inside it smelled like wax lips. I liked Murphy's. The floors were made of wood and creaked, and you could buy anything there: a Naugahyde wallet, a wig, rat traps, a Chinese checkers set, sympathy cards, walkie-talkies, old lamps, tiny spiral notebooks, a paint-by-numbers kit. Old white-haired ladies, twins, worked there, and if you were under twenty-five or so they'd follow you around the entire time you were in the store. Their white bangs were curled up with rollers. They wore pale-green smocks.

Vivian found a wig with long blond hair and put it on her head. She looked like a miniature nearsighted country singer.

We gathered our supplies. We got yards and yards of black and green fabric, a thick black cord for a belt, and some green face paint. Vivian insisted on the blond wig and wouldn't believe her own hair was much more suited to witchcraft. We also bought a bag of candy pumpkins. "I can throw them at people!" said Vivian.

As we were leaving the store, hauling our giant puffy plastic bags, a nun was coming in. I held the door for her.

"Why, thank you, dear!" she said, her round, velvety face creased from years of smiling. It was a rare thing to spot a nun in Wallamee. She was followed by an old man who looked very much like her; her brother, maybe. "You have a good afternoon," she added.

I couldn't help but wonder what a nun would think of all this, the whole black-cat, grinning-pumpkin, floating-skeleton spectacle. I watched her as she waddled down the aisles. She pointed, chuckling, at a stuffed Frankenstein. Her brother leaned over and patted its head. I wondered, then, what she would think of *me*.

Vivian and I spent the next few days putting the costume together. It was harder to line a dress than I'd expected, but I managed to do it after a lot of ripping and pinning, and then we spent an entire afternoon searching Train Line for the perfect stick to make into a broom.

The days were getting shorter. It was dark during the long hours I lay awake in the morning, unable to sleep and unwilling to get up. I thought if I lay perfectly still, my body would become so numb and bored it would fall asleep, but instead I just stopped being able to feel it. I felt like a pair of disembodied eyes propped up on my pillow, staring up into the dark. Sometimes, fixing my eyes on the light fixture, I imagined the ceiling was sinking—slowly, slowly—down toward me, and, being a mere set of eyes, I couldn't do a thing to stop it.

Peter? Peter! I called to him.

No answer.

A few days before Halloween, Dave the Alien showed up at the library. I was Windexing: the glass-topped end tables, the telephone, the locked bookcases, the windows. This was one of my favorite library duties, along with putting acrylic covers on books.

"If you're too busy, I can leave," said Dave, plopping himself down in an upholstered chair. He didn't look very good; his hair was dirty and he hadn't shaved.

"I can talk and Windex."

"You must be a genius!" said Dave, grinning. He lowered his voice slightly. "I hope you don't have any bad feelings about our dinner a few weeks ago. Because, you know, I don't."

"None at all," I said, spritzing a tabletop and wiping it with a paper towel.

"Good." He ran his fingers through his hair. "Umm…"

"Yes?"

"What are your plans for Halloween?"

"Sleep."

He laughed: too hard and too long. Dave was a lonely man. It gusted out from him like a smell. "Because, see, there's a costume party I was thinking of going to. If you'd like to be my 'date.'" He made quotation marks in the air with his fingers.

"'Costume party,'" I repeated, noncommittally.

"I think I want to go as a televangelist." He described his costume: he'd find a bad powder-blue suit, a Bible, and shaded glasses, then grease his hair back and wear a cardboard television over his head.

"Wow," I said. "That's creative."

"I thought so," he said. He stroked his hairy chin and looked me over. "You'd make an awesome prostitute."

"What?"

"I mean that in a good way. See, if you dressed as a call girl, we'd be a perfect pair."

"I'll think about it," I told him, spraying the cabinets.

He tapped his shoes on the wooden floor: *tappada tappada! tappada tappada!* "Oh, by the way!" he said. "Did you hear I finally found a job?"

"Great!"

"I took your advice. I didn't settle for anything that wasn't right."

"My advice?"

"You remember. At Monday night Circles?"

"Oh."

"*Oh.* I'm working at Big Ed's Video, over on Marquis Street." I looked at him. "Well, great."

"I get three free video rentals a week, and a thirty percent discount on every one more than that. Plus a raise after four months."

I nodded.

"So…maybe you'd like to come over for videos sometime?"

"Maybe," I agreed.

He sighed deeply. I stopped working for a minute and leaned against the windowsill to stare out the window. The sky was bright, bright, bright.

"Do you have secrets, Naomi?"

I didn't turn to look at him. "Everyone has secrets."

"Maybe so. I don't know as I do."

"Why do you ask?"

"Because," he said, "either you're a really dull person, or you have huge secrets. And I'd bet money on the latter."

"Well. Don't bet too much."

"I wish," said Dave, more forcefully, now, "I *wish* you'd be straight with me. If you don't like me, tell me to get lost. If you do like me, just show it or something. All right?"

I felt myself blush. I'd thought I didn't care whether he liked me or not. But I did, very much. Suddenly I felt frightened and unmoored. "I'm sorry," I said quickly. "I do like you."

"All right," he said. "All right."

⌒⌒

The night before her big party and parade, I got Vivian's costume ready. I folded the dress and the wig and put it in a plastic bag, and reinforced the pointy hat with black electrical tape. I gave her detailed directions on applying the face paint.

"And make sure everybody gets *one* of these candy pumpkins before anyone gets seconds. Got it?"

"Okay, okay!" crowed Vivian, nearly hopping with excitement.

In the car on the way to her house, she held the witch hat on her lap and told me all the things she'd do if she really *was* a witch.

"I'd turn invisible and go inside people's houses," she said. "I'd watch them eat their food."

"That's a strange thing to do."

"Then I'd turn my mom into a chicken!" She kicked her feet out and threw her head back against the seat, laughing as if this was the funniest thing she'd ever thought of. She bared her teeth like a rabid cat. "Then I'd turn my dad into an egg!"

"Now you're getting silly."

"I'd turn you into a ball of mush!"

I pretended to cry. "That's not—boo-hoo—very nice."

"I'm sorry," she said. She looked thoughtfully out the window. "Actually I'd turn you into a queen."

"Much better," I said.

I thought about her the next day, as I worked through the stack of books I was cataloging. I remembered wearing my costume to school in first grade—I was a clown—and how we each had to step in front of the class and make the class try to guess who we were. I loved my teacher, but I remember standing in front of the class, my curly black hair showing behind my mask— I was the only one in the class with curly hair—and feeling angry that the poor woman felt obliged to pretend she didn't know it was me. Everyone knew who I was. And *I* knew *they* knew. The charade humiliated me.

Around ten o'clock the phone rang, a startling racket. The library phone didn't ring more than once a month this time of year. It was the principal of Vivian's school.

"You're the babysitter, right?" she asked. "The parents left this number for emergencies."

"That's right. There hasn't been an accident…?"

"Oh, no—ha ha—nothing like that. A little misunderstanding. I'm afraid Vivian's costume is—um—inappropriate." The woman said they'd sent home strict instructions that scary costumes were forbidden in school. It had been the policy for two years now. Instead, the children were encouraged to dress up as characters from children's literature. "We have the cutest Rats from NIMH this year," she said. "And an absolutely darling Moby Dick."

I didn't know what to say. "Well, nobody told me."

"I suppose not. We *did* send home flyers."

She suggested I bring Vivian a new costume as quickly as possible, so she didn't have to miss any of the fun. Meanwhile, she'd be catching up on homework in the principal's office.

"I'll see what I can do," I said.

I closed the library and ran to my mother's house, certain that Elaine had planned it all, undermining me for her own mysterious reasons. My mother wasn't home, and neither was her car. *Crap*, I thought. I wondered if she'd started working with Officer Peterson again and pictured her touching bones at the forensics lab, or wandering the excavation site with her fingers at her temples.

From her house I called Dave the Alien. I got him out of bed.

"Sorry," I said, and described the emergency.

"So you want me to give you a ride to Murphy's, then to the elementary school?"

"Then back home again. If you have the time. I guess I could ride my bike."

He yawned noisily into the phone. "Oh, no," he said. "I can do it. For a price." The price, he said, was going to the costume party with him. "And dressing up as my Lady of the Evening."

"Oh, come on!" I said. I hemmed and hawed for a while. Dave was silent.

After a minute or two I relented.

"Great!" said Dave, fully awake now.

He was at my house in minutes. His hair stuck up and he smelled like bedclothes. "Hop in," he said, holding open the car door for me.

David seemed excited to have a project and flattered that I'd called him in my hour of need. He drove quickly and a little recklessly around the lake, chatting about the dream he'd had that night. "And you were in it! You were eating macadamia nuts from a jar. I didn't remember the dream until I saw you. Weird, huh?"

"Too weird," I said.

Murphy's had just opened when we got there. An old woman was in the costume aisle ahead of us, poking through the masks with her black-gloved fingers.

"You go ahead and find a costume," said Dave. "I have a rendezvous with destiny." He headed off toward the bathrooms.

Pickings were slim. There were skeletons and wolf-girls and Brides of Frankenstein, and a few oversized clowns, but not much acceptable in Vivian's size. I asked one of the green-smocked women behind the counter if there were any others. She shook her head. "Had a run on Dorothy of Ozzes last night. Cinderellas went like that, too. All we got's what you see. Most people buy their costumes ahead of time, you know."

I looked some more. On the very bottom, underneath a pile of Grim Reapers, I found a Wonder Woman costume in a faded box. I took it out to look at it: what looked like a set of red and yellow pajamas with a plastic face mask. But it was Vivian's size. *Excellent,* I thought, and tucked it under my arm.

"Hey," said Dave. "Look what I found." He held out a pair of spike heels, fishnet stockings, a blond beehive wig, and a spangly red dress. "Ooh-la-la."

"Oh, no."

"Please let me buy them for you. Please? You owe me."

"Okay, okay. But those shoes are about four sizes too small."

We bought the costumes and headed over to the elementary school. Vivian was in the principal's office, but she wasn't doing any homework. She was crying, her green face pressed into her spelling workbook. "Viv, Viv," I said, patting her head.

"We got you a Wonder Woman costume!" said Dave. He pulled it out of the sack with a flourish.

"NO!" yelled Vivian.

Behind her desk, the principal shrugged. She was a mannish woman with a square head. "She's been like that since this morning. Maybe you'd better just take her home."

"Mmm," said Dave. "I smell a cafeteria lunch."

"Ravioli with peach slices and pumpkin bread."

"Mmm," he said again.

We ended up taking Vivian back to my house. I had to carry her out past children lining up for lunch: a crowd of Davy Crocketts and Little Bo Peeps. Vivian hid her face in my hair. She'd mostly stopped crying. Now she was just moaning, as if she'd broken her leg and pain was shooting through her with every step I took.

❧

Elaine called and apologized the next day, a Saturday, Halloween. "Sorry to put you through all that trouble. I honestly didn't know about that silly policy. It seems pretty crazy, don't you think?"

I was getting dressed for the costume party. The dress barely covered anything. I'd never worn heels that high before, and they made me feel like a great big tottering bird. "I'm just worried about Vivian," I said, grabbing the door frame for balance.

"Oh, she'll be fine. Her dad's going to take her trick-or-treating. I just hope I can get her back into that witch costume. It's darling, by the way."

Dave was going to be by any minute, so I got Elaine off the phone and slapped some makeup on. My mother'd lent it to me. I put on lipstick and glittery eye shadow and fake lashes, then decided to forgo the perfume. It was something called "Celestial," and about half the mediums in Train Line wore it: a sort of mediumistic signature scent. When I'd gone over to her house to get the makeup, she seemed a little depressed. Her radio show was finished, now, and the people at WRUK weren't excited about the television show idea. She was still working on them, but she didn't hold out a lot of hope. I hadn't seen Troy around much lately, either. She didn't get up from the sofa the whole time I was there.

When Dave arrived at my door, he had his cardboard television over his head, "*Bay*-buh!" he said in a thick, fakey Southern accent.

"I forgot to ask where we're going."

"Elk's Club Trophy Room!"

The Trophy Room, it turned out, was over the fried chicken place on Railroad Avenue. We had to go inside the restaurant, past the counters and tables full of chicken eaters and the vats of bubbling grease, through a big double doorway, and up a narrow staircase. When I smelled the chicken I wanted to stay there.

The room did not look like it was over a chicken restaurant: there were chandeliers and velvet curtains and a multicolored sphere of lights. The dance floor was parquet. There were lots of vampires and vampiresses and devils and she-devils; also a gorilla or two, a Queen of Hearts, some zombies, an Abe Lincoln and a Winston Churchill.

"I'd never think to dress up as Winston Churchill," I told Dave.

"I think that's supposed to be W. C. Fields. See the nose?"

"Ah."

We danced. Neither of us could actually dance—we didn't know any steps and had no rhythm at all—but we moved around. I found I couldn't move too much, or else I'd lose my balance. Dave managed to dance much as you'd think a televangelist would: a lot of shaking arms. People looked at us and point-ed. I felt horribly self-conscious at first, but then it faded. My clothes helped, I think. It became easy to pretend I was someone else entirely.

"Do you know anyone here?" I asked Dave, panting.

"Hmm." He looked around, then pointed at a woman dressed as a potato. "She works at the desk in my dentist's office. I think I've seen that man she's with come into Big Ed's." The man was wearing a tuxedo and had huge, lovely wings on his back. There was a witch there, too, a sexy witch dancing with her broomstick. She made me think of Vivian. I hadn't really stopped thinking of Vivian, but now I was reminded of her with such force it made me queasy. I thought of her sad green face, her moaning.

After half an hour, the music stopped. I staggered toward a row of theater seats along the edge of the room.

"I'll get you a drink," said Dave.

Sweat dribbled beneath my wig. One of the zombies took the seat next to mine, and his dirty bandages touched my arm. I recoiled.

"I'm not a real zombie," he said.

"Oh, I know."

"This first break is for Funniest Costume, I believe," he told me, and pointed at a small stage on the other side of the room. An emcee-looking person was trying to fix his microphone into a mike stand. When he got it to stay he tapped on it several times with his ring. "Okay! Prize for funniest costume goes to the Car Wreck! Congratulations, Car Wreck! Let's give her a hand."

The Car Wreck, a young woman covered with sheets of shattered safety glass, a smashed bumper, a broken headlight, and dollar bills, received her trophy and took a bow. Her bumper hit the floor with a thud.

"I don't think that's funny at all," said the zombie.

Dave came back with the drinks. "What a coincidence! I brought you a zombie, and here you are sitting with one!"

The music started up again and the zombie lumbered off. I sipped my drink. It was sweet and strange, and hit me between the eyes.

"Well," I said, dizzy already. "Well."

We danced some more. We switched partners with the angel and the potato for a slow dance, and I got to run my hands over the soft, feathered wings that rose from the angel's shoulders. He rested his hands on my hips and stared right into my eyes. "Did you know that angels have the sexual characteristics of both genders?" he whispered. I had never expected to find myself in the arms of a man so handsome, and could only smile and smile, embarrassed.

Things were beginning to run together. Sometime during the evening I lost track of my shoes, so when we won the trophy for Best-Matched Couple, I had to go on stage in my stocking feet. A Book and Bookmarker threw us threatening looks. As the evening wore on I grew to like Dave quite a bit. He felt good to lean against.

I don't remember much about the rest of the night. I remember going back to Dave's apartment and lying with him on the sofa. We kissed and hugged and Dave said, over and over, "Please don't change your mind tomorrow, *please* don't change your mind." I remember throwing up in the toilet. Then I was waking up on the sofa and it was morning and Dave the Alien was cooking eggs in the kitchenette. It was the smell that woke me.

"Oh my God."

"Think of it as a slumber party," said Dave.

Actually, I didn't feel sick. I ate some of Dave's eggs and drank some juice and cringed at the thought of his lips on mine. He gave me a few searching looks that I managed to evade. He was nice, though, and didn't bring it up. He displayed our trophy—a small plastic urn—on the shelf over the stove, and then he drove me home. The streets of Wallamee were empty and strewn with toilet paper and candy wrappers. "Aftermath," said Dave quietly.

He dropped me off at the gate, not even trying a good-bye kiss. The air felt cold and vigorous, and I was glad the whole stupid, excessive holiday was over. Dave had lent me a pair of basketball sneakers, but I was still wearing my hooker dress and carrying my wig under my arm. No one was out. I kicked leaves and took in big lungfuls of air. I am a cruel, cruel person, I said to myself.

When I rounded the corner of Fox and Chadakoin Streets, I saw a police car parked in front of my house. My first instinct was to run. I could hide in the woods, I thought. I could make my way to the highway, hitchhike, jump into the back of a truck...

But running away would mean admitting everything, and I knew then that I could do anything but that. So instead I gripped my wig with both hands and forced myself through the door of my house.

My mother was there, with Officer Peterson and a petite, severely coifed policewoman. They looked startled to see me come in.

"Naomi," said my mother. Her voice had a slight shake. "This is Officer Ten Brink, and Officer Peterson, of course."

"Hello," I said, shaking their hands.

"I let them in," said my mother. "When you weren't home, they came to my house…" She looked around, uncertain whether to stay or leave. "I'll go make coffee," she said, and hurried off into the kitchen.

"Sit down," said Officer Peterson, which was odd, since it was my house.

I sat. Officer Ten Brink thumbed through an accordion file on her lap and handed something to Officer Peterson, who handed it to me. It was a photograph of Peter.

"Can you identify this person?" asked Officer Peterson.

It must have been Peter's high school graduation picture: his face was fuller than when I knew him, and he had thicker, perhaps even blow-dried, hair. He wore the kind of sport jacket he would not be caught dead in later: it had gold buttons and terrible wide lapels. He was smiling.

"It's Peter Morton," I said.

I repeated my story again. I knew Peter for a year and a half or so, then he left, and I hadn't heard from him since. We'd broken up. We'd had a fight; that's when he left.

"A violent fight?" asked Officer Ten Brink.

"Oh, no," I said. "Just arguing. I don't even remember what about."

"And when was this?"

I pretended to think. "Summer, maybe late summer, 1988."

"Ten years ago, then. Did he give you the slightest indication of where he might have gone?"

I shook my head. "No. Well, I got a postcard from him. From Mexico, I think. That was about a year later."

He nodded. "That fits, more or less." He explained: Peter's mother had died a few years before, and his sister had been trying to find him ever since. She'd contacted the police departments in the places she knew he'd been, and after the discovery of the bones by the lake, they'd notified her.

"But she says the mother was in touch with him for at least a year after he left here. There were postcards, and apparently some phone calls."

I'd sent the postcard, of course, but the phone calls were impossible. I nodded, though, fixing the look of concern on my face. They said they came up with my name through a friend, a Nelson Karp.

"So, anyway," said Peterson. "We don't have any real good reason to think Mr. Morton's our John Doe, but we're checking it out. The sister isn't *real* eager to dig him up, so to speak. They didn't get along too well."

"Right," I said.

My mother brought in the coffee. Her face was gray.

The police took just a few sips of their coffee, then shook our hands again and thanked us. They'd be in touch.

"And Mrs. Ash, you let us know if you have any of your 'hunches,' right?"

My mother nodded mutely.

They left, and I was alone in the living room with my mother. I drank my coffee very quickly, letting it burn my mouth.

"Peter," said my mother.

I was shaking, so I set the mug on the floor.

"Naomi," she said. "What was his middle name?"

"I don't…"

"*What was his middle name?*"

"Samuel," I whispered.

She nodded. She knew this. "Peter S. Morton," she said, folding her hands and looking past me, out the window.

The room seemed cold. I pulled the hem of my dress down as far as I could, tried shifting it around to cover more of my body, but I still felt naked. My stockings were torn. The wig slid onto the floor.

9

she was more than a glimmer

I kept some of Peter's things. There was his wallet, which I took from the back pocket of his khaki pants before I buried him. In it was five hundred eleven dollars—five hundreds, a ten, and a one—and fifty-three cents in change. I never spent any of it. There were several cards: his Princeton student ID card (he was growing a mustache when it was taken, an awful, smudgy-looking thing); his New Jersey driver's license (grimacing at the camera, his hair tall and bushy); a Visa card that had expired in 1989; a business card for a used-book store in Hollington. My business card was in there, too, for some reason, perhaps because of the phone number he'd scrawled on the back. It wasn't my phone number. A few months after he died, I called it. It was a pet shop in Wallamee. Was he thinking of buying a pet? Or did he meet someone who worked there? I had no way of knowing. The wallet was well organized, no receipts or paper clips or handfuls of pennies. There were no photographs of anyone, either.

I had his wristwatch, too, which he wasn't wearing before he died. He might have been getting ready for bed before I came over to my mother's house, where he was staying. I found it in the bathroom, on top of the toilet tank. It was an expensive watch, I could tell; I vaguely remembered Peter telling me it had belonged to his grandfather. It was gold, with fine hands and Roman numbers and a dark leather band. It stopped running after a day and a half, because no one wound it. I also kept his glasses, the lenses so thick they made me dizzy to look through, and a pair of his wool socks, a pencil, a third of a pack of chewing gum, his comb, his razor, a tube of athlete's foot cream, his nail clippers, some keys to I didn't know what, a few books, and a pair of binoculars.

All this, except for the binoculars and the books, I kept in a box under my bed. It was one of those Christmas gift boxes, covered with teddy bears in Santa hats, about a foot square. I tied a red ribbon around it and hid it behind some shoe boxes and rolled-up blankets. The door of my bedroom was always locked, but the box never stopped making me anxious. The rest of his stuff—clothes, mostly, and some of the books—I put in taped-up paper bags with some rocks, then I rowed out to the middle of the lake and dumped them. I'd have preferred to burn them with some leaves and yard waste I'd collected from my mother's yard, but leaf fires had been prohibited here since the thirties, when one set a whole neighborhood of Train Line on fire. For months afterward I worried about the bundles, and found myself scanning the shore for signs of rotting clothes and swollen books every time I went out. But I never found anything.

I used the binoculars. When I was a little girl I had a pair of plastic binoculars I got in a box of cereal, and though things appeared rough and blurry through them, they did work: they brought the distant close. For two or three years before she died, my grandmother played double bass in an orchestra. I used to bring the binoculars to the theater when she played, and by squinting a little I could even make out her expressions. It was, in general, a stiff and gloomy orchestra. The violinists sawed away liked carpenters, the horns squealed, the triangle had bad timing. My grandmother, heaving over her double bass, was the only musician who ever moved or swayed. I don't know if she was any good or not, but to me she *looked* good. I imagined the others were angry at her, resented the way she emoted, thought her a big phony. I worried a bit that she *was* a phony. Still, hearing the music and watching the way it translated across my grandmother's face was one of the first things that actually moved me as a child. It was almost too difficult to watch, but fascinating, too. At home, my grandmother was as stiff and gloomy as anyone. It was as if my cheap plastic binoculars let me see inside her, and what I found there betrayed her.

Peter's binoculars were, of course, top of the line. They were sleek and black and oiled, and had a delicious, pharmaceutical odor. They came in a case with a little maintenance kit: a set of fine cloths and a small spray bottle full of glass cleaner. The smooth leather strap felt good around my neck, and I liked the way they bumped heavily against my chest when I wore them. No one asked where I got them, but if they had, I'd have said that Peter left them for me. That was, essentially, true.

If I sat on the dock at the end of Fox Street and looked out over the lake with my bare eyes, I could see the shapes of houses and buildings in Wallamee. The downtown was a few blocks inland, but I could make out the long blue roof of the Italian Fisherman, where my mother and Darva Lawrence used to go for lunch, and the broad orange back of the Catholic church, and some boathouses and cottages. There was often a bluish haze obscuring the far shore. If the weather was clear I might just be able to see the shapes of people or cars. I had good vision.

But with Peter's binoculars, I could see everything. Birds, flying across the water, looked like cutouts from a field guide: one-dimensional and detailed and precise. I could see the way every leaf on a tree on the other side of Train Line moved independently of the others, and even had its own shadow. Grass and weeds and peeling paint looked beautiful and delicate through the binoculars. The lake, I realized, never stopped moving.

I could even see in windows. Usually it was hard to distinguish much: maybe a vase full of flowers on a sill, books propping open a casement, an arm or face moving past. There was a row of apartments in a converted warehouse near the restaurant in Wallamee, and they fascinated me. I often thought that if I'd had a different life I might live in an apartment like one of these. Some had window boxes, and all had unusual seven-paned windows. Inside they had white walls and dark wood molding and, from what I could tell, Murphy beds. The idea of hiding my bed during the day delighted me. I didn't like the look or smell of beds, and I thought I'd like to live the kind of life in which they were invisible. In the very end apartment there was a woman who looked a little like me. She had similar long dark hair, and was stocky, too, though her hair was curlier than mine and she was shorter. Sometimes I saw her sitting by the window, reading or eating. She had a white cat who spent a lot of time sleeping on the windowsill, and a strange piece of art on the wall: a black-and-white mermaid holding a big red heart. A man was in the apartment sometimes. He was better looking than Peter and appeared to talk a lot—his hands were always moving and gesturing. I was deeply jealous of the woman and watched her often. But one day in the spring I spotted her and her boyfriend looking out at the lake with a pair of binoculars, too. By the way they moved them I could tell they were bird-watching: some geese were on the lake that day. They passed the binoculars back and forth, pointing and exclaiming at the dull brown birds. They didn't see me, but they could have. Soon after that I stopped watching her. It wasn't that I was afraid of getting caught spying, but knowing the woman had the power to watch me, and didn't, made me feel as if what I was doing was boring and sad.

I continued to watch other things, clouds and leaves and water and birds, but I was tired of people.

෮෴ඁ

The summer I met Peter it thundered every afternoon. It reminded me of New Orleans, it was that hot. All day long the clouds above us would gather and threaten, and by three or four it might break into storm. There might be lightning and ripping thunder and tremendous, sudden winds. But more often the clouds would just continue rumbling on into evening, and by the time the sun went down the sky would have broken up enough to let the last of the sunlight stream through. It was portentous weather.

By the time he missed the train and decided to stay in Train Line, it had cooled off, and hurricanes wandering away from the southern coast swept the tips of their long arms over the county. It rained and rained. I moved out of my mother's house and rented two rooms from Welchie Pratt, and Peter got his room at the Silverwood back. During the fall he worked off part of his rent doing painting and repair work around the hotel, and when it closed up for the winter in late October, he moved in with me.

We were happy for a while. At least, I was. Welchie Pratt went to stay with her invalid sister for several months, so we had the house to ourselves, and I spent a lot of time painting and fixing up my séance room. I never had more than three or four readings a week in the fall and winter, though, and I didn't work at the library yet, so Peter and I could sleep late and make each other elaborate breakfasts. He had been a vegetarian before, but now he ate bacon and pork chops and steaks. "This," Peter said often, "is real life." He liked going for long walks along the lake, breathing in wood smoke, watching wild turkeys and grouse through his binoculars. He sometimes brought books with him, and more often than not ended up in Maxwell's, reading and drinking Irish whiskey. He'd come home with cold cheeks and hot, sweet breath, and we'd have sex against the living room wall. This ended when we ran out of money.

I hadn't realized how much I had depended on my mother to support me. In the summers my mediumship brought in scads of money, and so did hers, and we were not excessive people so money was not much of a problem—ever. Of course, she owned her house, and that made a big difference. Our rent wasn't much, but my earnings barely covered it. I told Peter he needed to find a job.

"Of course," he said. "I've been planning on it."

But he couldn't find one. He wouldn't mind doing something with his hands, he said, but since he had no experience, the few construction jobs left by that time of year went to other people. He said he couldn't work in a store; it would depress him too much, and I had to admit it was hard to picture him selling things, ringing up change, smiling when people were rude to him.

He decided to start a tutoring business. He drove to the Super Copy in Wallamee with a five-dollar bill I gave him and made posters, hung them around town, and waited for the phone to ring. It did, eventually, but only three times. He saw each of these students once a week in our kitchen. Two were high-schoolers needing help with calculus, so Peter read a *Calculus Is a Snap!* textbook from front to back one weekend. The other was a woman going back to college after fifteen years who needed help with her papers. This project energized him for a while. It didn't bring much money in, however. One evening we were sitting in the living room with the heat off, trying to eat spaghetti sauce on bread, when Peter broke down crying.

"Hey," I said. "It's all right."

"It's not, it's not, it's not," he moaned, putting the food on the floor and covering his face with his mittened hands. We were bundled up, blankets to our chins. I didn't mind so much. My mother and I lived this way, on and off, during our first few years in Train Line. It appalled Peter, though. He couldn't believe it when the telephone was disconnected. "How can they do that?" he kept asking me. "What if there's an emergency?"

He cried for several minutes, and though I thought I should comfort him, something held me back. His sobs were broken and cracked; they staggered, faltered, collapsed.

I listened to him awhile, and when he quieted down I asked him something I'd been meaning to ask for some time: didn't his family have money? And if that was the case, shouldn't he have a little, too?

They did, he said, catching his breath, hiccuping, but his share wasn't coming to him until he was twenty-five, almost three years off. And there was no way he'd actually ask any of them for money, he added roughly.

We ended up borrowing money from my mother to get through that crisis. Over Christmas I made a bundle at a psychic fair and got a store in town to sell gift certificates for readings, and that helped, too. But it was an endless winter. It was cold for long periods, so cold that the snow squeaked underfoot, and if Peter cried outside, his lashes froze together. The sun might come out just long enough to start the snow on the roofs melting. The icicles were the biggest I'd seen: some like stalactites reaching all the way to the ground, some like frozen waterfalls. Icicles built up so thickly along our porch roof they became a wall of ice. "Like living in an ice castle," I told Peter, whereupon he took the crowbar lying by the door and smashed the ice to pieces.

☙

In different ways, and for different reasons, Peter and I both became obsessed with death that winter. It started with a riddle he told me. We were standing on the heater, a two-foot-by-three-foot grate that got hot enough to melt the rubber bottoms of my slippers, but not Peter's, which were leather. Outside, a blizzard raged.

"So," he said, wrapping his arms around himself. "A man is found dead in a locked room. Windows *and* doors have been locked from the inside—the cops had to break the door down. There are stab wounds in his chest but no sign of a weapon anywhere. The only other thing about the room that's slightly out of the ordinary is a glass on the bedside table filled with pinkish water. How did he die?"

"I give up."

"Come on!" he said. "Try!" Peter had acquired a somewhat manic look in the last couple of months: his hair was out of control, and his eyes darted. Sometimes he forgot to shower.

I thought for a while. The heat billowed up my nightgown. "Really, I have no idea. I'm going to go make some corn bread, if you don't mind."

"Suicide, there's a clue."

"I still have no idea."

"He committed suicide by stabbing himself with an icicle. Before he died he put the icicle in the empty water glass, where it melted."

"I should have got that. It's horrible."

"It's my favorite riddle," said Peter. He skipped supper that night and spent the evening in bed, where I found him several hours later, asleep with his face in a book.

Then, maybe two weeks later, a child died in Train Line. I didn't know him well. He was a six-year-old named Brian Robinson and was related in some way to Winnie Sandox. He'd spent Christmas here, and on the day the accident happened—it was a few days after New Year's—he was playing in Winnie's yard, building a snow fort. It was one of those cold but sunny days we'd had on and off all winter. The sun warmed the roofs of Train Line just enough to allow a giant pillar of ice to loosen itself from the upper story of Winnie's house. The ice slid down the porch roof and landed where the child was playing. He didn't die right away. He lay unconscious in the snow for perhaps half an hour, his skull fractured, and when they brought him to the hospital and warmed him up, his brain swelled. He was in a coma for a week before he died.

It was an awful thing. There was a memorial service in the lecture hall, attended by the eight or ten households who were there that winter—more than usual had left town, it seemed. I went with my mother. Ice covered the small high windows, and even with the huge oil furnace roaring away while we prayed, we could see the breath gusting from our open mouths. Peter stayed home.

When I got back to the house he was drinking whiskey. He never got violent when he drank, but he would, occasionally, become argumentative. I was angry that he'd spent our money on whiskey but decided not to bring it up.

"Why is it," he asked, while I hung up my coat and hat and mittens, "that, if mediums really believe what they preach, they still freak out when someone dies?"

"They don't 'freak out.'"

"You'd think, if death were so great, that mediums would go around offing themselves whenever they got in trouble, or in debt, even. I mean, if the only difference between this plane and the other is that you can't bring your *stuff* with you, it's kind of like declaring bankruptcy. See what I'm saying?"

"No, I don't."

"No one has a memorial service for you if you declare Chapter Eleven."

"Blah, blah, blah," I said.

It did upset me, though. It was clear that spiritualism had lost whatever temporary charm it had held for Peter. He'd begun hiking across the frozen lake to go to Wallamee's miserable public library every couple of days or so; it took him an hour and a half each way. He said he was reading magazines. "My mind's gone to hell," he said. "I can't concentrate. I can't even handle the freaking *New York Times*."

But that winter, my faith in mediumship was stronger than ever. Every morning I woke up, usually cold, usually hungry, but terribly excited about the work waiting for me that day. The more I thought about death—death in the concrete, I mean, death as in being crushed by ice, as in being stabbed by an icicle—the more important spiritualism seemed to me. It was so important! Believing, as I was sure I did, in the spirit world, I was kept from thinking that life and death were without meaning. Peter didn't have that. Living in the half of the house we rented was like living in a cave, or a coffin, to him.

He didn't leave me, though. He could have gone back to Oregon, or hung around with old friends in Princeton. But he still loved me. At least, that's what I told myself. Why else would he stay? And we had sex quite often. It was a fierce business, with lots of pinching and scratching and slamming around. I always kept my eyes open, watching him, which is how I knew that he kept his shut, and that his mouth moved silently the whole time, as if he were praying for something.

∽✕∾

Spring came. It came in a sudden rush of water: rain poured down, snowbanks shrank, and puddles and rivulets flooded the roads of Train Line. Every day the ground breathed out the smell of relief. It was strange to see the battered grass again and strange to pry open the windows and let air flow through the house. We all shook ourselves and woke up a little. Peter and I started taking walks together again. The hard ground felt unbelievably good beneath my feet after walking on snow all those months. Peter got a haircut and his cheeks regained their color, at least for a while.

Peter kept a journal. He'd kept one since he was fourteen, several volumes of those hardcovered blue laboratory notebooks. I'd never felt much urge to read it. He wrote in it when he was alone; at the library, I suspected, or when I was busy. I figured they were "deep thoughts": observations on the beauty of nature and the stupidity of people, etcetera. There was a good chance, I thought, that I'd be embarrassed by what he wrote. Perhaps it was over my head, or perhaps it wasn't very intelligent at all.

So I don't know why I picked it up off his desk the first time and opened it. It was a mild, indeterminate spring day: warm but cloudy, no leaves on the trees but no snow, either. I was cleaning the house, happy that I'd survived the winter, and feeling that my life was changing. Whenever the seasons changed I felt that way. Life was opening up. I thought about growing a garden that summer. We had a small square of lawn behind the house, and I wanted to grow potatoes and carrots and maybe something like strawberries. Seed catalogs had arrived in the mail. I pored over them constantly, loving the way the pages smelled, drawing diagrams of my plot. The Silverwood had hired Peter to do some preseason painting and repair work, so he seemed slightly more cheery, too. That's where he was that morning. I expected him back in an hour or so, for lunch.

The first thing I noticed about Peter's journal was how regular and controlled the handwriting was. He wrote with a blue ballpoint pen, and every letter slanted the same way, and every page was filled: no margins. He'd pressed down hard, too, so that the pages were stiff and crinkly. I spotted my name.

...unlike Naomi, who hasn't washed her hair in a month...

What? I washed my hair far more often than that. Was he serious? I pulled my hair over my nose and smelled it. It smelled fine, like hair. I flipped through the pages.

As I read over the journal, I found references to my "large legs," "hairy legs," "man hands," and "vast behind." The nicest thing I found was from October; it referred to my "comfortably weighty presence" and "calm, simple soul." The entries became worse and more insulting as the journal wore on. The most recent was from the day before. In it he described a fantasy about having sex with someone else.

...she had a waist that fit in my hands as she rode above me, and we moved together, like waves peaking and crashing. Her slender, boyish hips held an ocean of pleasure, and I kept diving in, losing my breath...

This went on for several paragraphs. Then:

...when I awoke N. was snoring. When I nudged her to roll over, her big old arm flopped across my chest, nearly driving the life out of me.

I had to sit down, my finger holding my place in the notebook. Sweat broke out on my forehead and under my arms. It seemed impossible that he could write this and still live with me. True, he was grim and unpleasant much of the time. I had chalked that up to the weather and having no money. What had I done to make him feel that way? Anything?

At lunch I was subdued, but Peter didn't seem to notice. He complained about the idiocy of the people he worked with— "You'd think they'd know enough to keep all the tools in *one place,* so we could find them again. I spend half my time looking for the godawful tools…"—and expressed, again, his wish that people with low IQs would be banished to an island somewhere.

"What do you think my IQ is?" I asked him, suddenly wanting to know what he'd say.

"Considerably higher than the sum total of those fools at the Silverwood."

"No, seriously. What do you think it is?"

He gave me an impatient look. "How am I supposed to know?"

"I'm just curious."

He chewed on his sandwich. "I was tested when I was a child, and my score was off the charts. Of course," he added modestly, "I'm sure IQ testing for children isn't all that accurate."

Peter talked like this a lot. It had never bothered me before; it wasn't as if he did it in public or around people other than me. I thought he was just being honest. But he wasn't honest, really. Not after what I'd seen in his journal. It hit me with a peculiar force. Why was he so critical? Incessantly, smugly, neurotically critical?

After a few days I more or less forgot about the journal entries—that is, I never actually forgot about them, but I hid them away in the back of my mind—and threw myself into my work, my garden plans, the coming spring. I treated Peter with the utmost politeness—he didn't seem to notice anything amiss—until finally I felt normal around him. Now and then I'd recall one of the insults—*vast behind!*—and be shocked all over again, but this happened less and less as spring rolled into summer.

Part of me had stopped loving him. But another part of me desired him more than ever; I wanted to prove him wrong, somehow. I wanted to force him to love me, to want me, to fall under my spell. I wanted him to wake up one day, look at me, and think, *I was wrong.*

❧

In the late spring, and on into summer, something happened to Peter. At first it was just allergies. His eyes ran, his nose ran, he sneezed and coughed and stumbled bleary-eyed around the house. It was grass pollen, he said. At one point he got an infection in his throat from all the dripping and swelling, and lay around the house, shivering under quilts. Outside the air was lovely, the sun was warm, but Peter just stayed inside, sniffing. It disgusted me. I was surprised at the strength of my reaction.

"It would do you good to get some fresh air," I told him.

"That air is *not fresh.*"

"You're going to look like a cave worm if you mope around all summer in the dark."

"Why are you telling me this? Can't you tell I'm sick?"

I told him I couldn't sleep with him clearing his throat every twelve seconds—I timed it—and began sleeping on the sofa downstairs. I imagined him dying during the night. I'd be shocked, but I'd handle it. Trapped on the other side, Peter would be frightened and lost and utterly dependent on me. Imagining it was quite satisfying.

But even when the allergies lifted, Peter didn't believe he was better. There was something caught in his lungs, he said. He sat up at night probing his ribs. A doctor in Wallamee gave him a chest X-ray—which we couldn't really afford—and a clean bill of health, but by then the problem had migrated to his neck. "What are these bumpy things?" he asked me, running his fingers along his jawline.

"Glands."

"No, not there," he said impatiently. "Over *here.*"

I couldn't talk him out of his hypochondria, so I decided to change my tack. I began to humor him, even encourage him. "Have you always had that freckle?" I'd ask, poking the back of his hand. Or I'd tell him, "The whites of your eyes look awfully yellow today." I took a perverse pleasure in his reactions. He'd pretend to ignore me, but later I'd catch him staring at himself in the mirror, or looking up symptoms in a secondhand medical guide he bought at the Rummage Room. He called in sick at the Silverwood until they fired him. Every time he opened a door he had to cover his hand with his shirt before he touched the knob, in order to avoid germs.

I still took a peek at his journal now and then. Mentions of me were scarcer, but other interesting things replaced them.

> *I know it's ridiculous, but sometimes I'd swear there's poison in my food.*

And,

> *All day I've had an odd buzzing in my head. Possible stroke? Oh, God. I think I'm going to die.*

Some days he was better, others he was worse. I couldn't predict it. We went to the beach in Wallamee one Saturday, and he took off his shirt, jumped in, and swam for a long time. When he came out, he was happy and chatty and had a sunburn on his nose. The next day he sat in the kitchen in his long johns, reading the *Journal of the American Medical Association*—I had no idea where he found of copy of *that*—with all the stove burners turned up. For heat, he said. It was seventy-five degrees outside.

❧

My garden didn't grow. I watered it enough, I thought, and gave it some fertilizer, but the tomato plants withered, the carrots stayed tiny, and the lettuce bolted the instant it came out of the ground. The strawberries never showed up. I was horribly disappointed. I had failed at this one simple project, and now I had nothing to do all summer but work and hang around melancholy Peter.

It might have been the failure of the garden that caused my mediumship to take the new turn it did. It happened during a normal home circle, one I held every Wednesday night that summer: the lights low, the occasional noise of cars rumbling by outside, the sound of breathing and shifting in chairs. I was glum; I wanted to make something happen. So, after ten minutes or so I said I was in touch with a spirit named Martha, who was full of rage. This was a bit of an exaggeration. There *was* a spirit of some kind, I thought, but the rage came from me. I felt it, leaping up like a sudden fire.

"She might not be one of ours. She seems particularly hostile—a restless spirit. Can anyone claim her?"

No one could.

But before long, someone—a woman from Arizona who was visiting that summer—said she could *see* the spirit. It was there, she said, in the middle of the room, glowing faintly.

I stared. People claimed to see things all the time, but rarely did more than one person see the same thing—no one liked to admit that someone else saw it first, I think—and as it happened, I never saw the phosphorescent shapes that people said showed up at circles. But this time, after staring for a few minutes, hard, I did. Just barely. It was as if light had gathered from the shadows around the room and collected in that one spot. It was the kind of thing you might dismiss if you were in a mind to. I wasn't.

"Yes," I said. "I see her, too."

Other people chimed in. Oh, yes, they said. She's wearing a long dress. Her hair's up. She's carrying something—a basket? Yes, a wicker basket.

Did I actually see these things? I wanted to—we all wanted to. That was enough.

She stayed for perhaps ten minutes, then faded. When the home circle met again the next week, though, Martha was back.

This time, she was more than a glimmer. Someone said she could actually make out the hat pins in her hair, and someone smelled the perfume she wore. She stayed nearly half an hour, and—through me—told us about her life. She had been beaten by her husband, she said, and in the basket was a stillborn baby. Martha herself had died in childbirth. This electrified the circle.

It didn't take long before the rest of Train Line heard about Martha. People wanted to join our circle, but we wouldn't let them. It was a subject of immense speculation. Why me? I was hardly a physical medium. Some people thought it was a bunch of baloney, of course, but I didn't care. Our weekly circle meetings stretched to an hour and a half, then two hours, and we were all obsessed with Martha.

I liked the attention. But before long it got back to Peter, who, when I explained it, choked on his milk.

"*You're* doing that? Didn't that manifestation stuff go out with the nineteenth century?"

"Obviously not." And if he was going to be like that, I told him, I was simply not going to talk about it.

"Like what? Skeptical? Reasonable?"

And Martha wasn't the only one. Soon, there were others: a little boy who didn't talk, an old woman, a very old man. There was even one of the girls who drowned in the lake. She cried, cried, cried. To be perfectly honest, I wasn't sure if I ever saw much myself. Some glowing, some movement, perhaps. But my circle did, and for the first time I was extremely popular around Train Line. That summer I got invitations to every party, every development circle, every meeting of every kind, New Age or not. The board asked me to teach a workshop the following summer. There was talk of starting a public-access television program, which I would host.

This, I suppose, was the last straw for Peter. We began arguing about it, loudly, at night. It was fine, he said, to operate on faith, intuition, psychology, all that, but when we started dealing with the *physical,* then we were going over the line.

"Who is going over the line?"

"Spiritualists and all of you freaking New Agers!"

There was nothing I hated more than being called that, and he knew it, but I kept my cool. "Going over *what* line?" I demanded.

The problem, he said, was in trying to co-opt science. Why weren't religious people ever satisfied with their own spiritual niche? Why did they always feel like science had to be proved *wrong* in order for them to be proved right? That's when religion becomes garbage, he said. Materialization is garbage.

I gave him a big shove and he sloshed his milk on his pants. He looked stunned for a second, then his normal cynical look came back. "Real mature."

"Asshole."

It was odd how quickly our arguments reduced to name calling. We used to be able to discuss things, but not anymore. I had an idea. If Peter would only believe me, I thought, everything would be better. Not only would we get along, but his hypochondria, his morbid fear of death, would go away. He wouldn't come to any of my circles, of course, but maybe I could bring a circle to him.

That is how I began haunting Peter. My intentions, I swear, were good.

❧

There were tricks I remembered from my childhood: a bladder hidden beneath a piece of furniture that, when squeezed, would blow cool air across a person's ankles; perfume daubed on a lightbulb so that, when the light is switched on, a scent would fill the air apparently apropos of nothing; tiny bells installed in different parts of a room, so that the sound might seem to come from all directions. Those were the subtle things. Sometimes Peter didn't notice my tricks at all; sometimes he'd look around, confused. Only rarely would he say anything. We were sitting in the living room one evening in July, watching the television news, when he asked, "What's that smell?"

"Smell?"

He sniffed. "Are you wearing perfume?"

"You know I don't wear perfume."

"Hmm."

The next day, when he was out, I washed and dried the lightbulb, rubbed it with a little vanilla extract, and replaced it in the lamp. If he noticed, he said nothing. It didn't matter. My point was to undermine the world he was so damned sure he understood.

After a few weeks of this, I got bolder. I cooked up a complicated ruse: I whispered his name over and over into a small tape recorder and brought it to bed with us. While we read I kept it hidden in my nightgown. Twenty minutes or so after we turned the light off, I rolled over, stretched, and slipped my hand with the tape recorder under a corner of Peter's pillow. I could tell by the way he was breathing that he was dropping off, so I gently pressed Play.

It only took a few minutes before he began to rouse. I quickly switched the machine off and rolled over, sliding it under my own pillow. Peter sat up, looked around, then lay back down again.

I did this every night for more than a week. Some nights Peter slept through the whole performance, but once, he even yanked his pillow away while my hand was still under it. I'd been expecting that, though, so I'd hidden the tape recorder in my sleeve.

"What?" I said. "Did you have a bad dream?"

"No! It's nothing." But he sat up in the dark for a long time, breathing hard.

Most of what I did was simpler: I moved his things around, stole things and replaced them, left strange or disturbing objects in unlikely places. I put a crow's feather on our front steps, where he'd find it when he went out for his daily walk, and I balanced a penny on the toe of one of his shoes while they sat in the hall. I made sure I did nothing so obvious he'd ask me about it. Once, I left a mouse skull in his sock drawer, but removed it when I realized I'd gone just a hair too far.

∽⌒

It worked. Peter's hypochondria, which had never really gone away, came back in full force. He spent nights wracked with a nausea that neither culminated in vomiting nor abated. He complained of itchiness and sweats, and the frantic look he'd had all winter returned. Finally, over a lunch of peanut butter on bread, I told him I had something to tell him and that he should promise not to get angry.

"What is it?" he said, angry already.

"You're not going to like this, but I think you should know." And I told him that a spirit had been hanging around the house a lot lately and that I had a feeling it was his.

"You know I don't believe in that garbage."

"I know," I said calmly. "But I do. And I just thought you might be interested. Sorry I opened my big mouth."

He stared at me, his eyes red-rimmed. "What do you mean, it's *mine*?"

"Well, just that I think it knows you. *He* knows you. A relative or a friend, maybe."

"I don't believe in that garbage," he said again.

We ate our bread. Peter got peanut butter all over his hands but didn't seem to notice.

"One other thing. Can I tell you?"

"No!" he almost shouted.

"All right." I waited a few minutes. Then, picking up crumbs with the end of my finger, I said, "The spirit keeps saying the name 'Billy Friday.' Do you know anyone with that name?"

Peter turned his head and looked out the kitchen window. His eyes, I could tell, were filling with tears. He covered his face with his hands, then slowly got up, went into the bathroom, and shut the door.

Billy Friday was the name of one of his cats when he was a child. It was killed by a dog who left it under a blackberry bush in the backyard, where six-year-old Peter found it days later. He'd never told me the story. I read it in his journal.

꙼

But in the end, I did go too far.

By August, the attention I'd been getting in Train Line for the Martha circles had faded. I should have known; people are faddy, and once the novelty wears off they're onto something new. A woman who went by the name Sheree began "channeling" a spirit called Ta-Ne, who, because he was from Atlantis, had lots of enlightenment to impart. Suddenly, my Wednesday night circle was buying Sheree's tapes and telling me all about them.

"You know, Naomi, you're really limiting yourself. You should try contacting larger, more universal spirits. They have important stuff to say, you know."

Of course, I had to be polite.

"Atlantis?" I said. "*Atlantis?*"

A television talk show flew Sheree to New York City to appear on a whole special program about channelers. I watched it one morning in my pajamas, aghast.

"Peter!" I cried. "Look!"

He was dozing at the table. He picked his head up and gazed blearily at the television. Sheree was sitting in an armchair, her platinum-blond hair hanging over her face, and she was speaking in a goofy, low voice. "...because we're all brothers and sisters..." she said, and, "...a golden staircase awaits us..."

"Oh, come on," I moaned.

"That's what your mother does, isn't it? That trance stuff," said Peter.

I yelped. "As if! Peter, that guy's supposed to be from an *imaginary place*. It makes no sense at all."

"I don't see the difference." He shrugged and shuffled off to the kitchen.

I could have argued with him, but I didn't. Instead I decided it was time to make my next move. That night, I told Peter I had a message for him.

"Who called?"

That afternoon he'd gotten a haircut. His hair lay smooth over the back of his head, and his sideburns flew high over his ears. He looked good, neat and together, for the first time in a while.

"No one called," I said. "I don't mean that kind of message."

"Then you must know I don't want anything to do with it."

"It's from your father."

Peter gave me a wild-eyed look, then covered his ears and ran out the door.

⤬

He came back just before dawn. I'd been sitting up for a long time, but I'd finally given up and gone to bed. I woke to the sound of him throwing things into his duffel bag.

"What are you doing?"

"I'm going to go stay at your mother's."

"You can't do that!" We'd been house-sitting for her while she was at a retreat in Ohio somewhere, watering her plants and slowly eating all the food in her cupboards.

"Of course I can," said Peter angrily. "In fact, she's *glad* to have someone staying there. I called and asked. Where I can't stay is here, with you."

"What do you mean? Why?"

He threw one of his shoes at me. I caught it and threw it back. "I've figured you out," he said. His face was contorted. "I know what you've been doing."

There were many things I could have done at that point. Screamed and argued, cried, fallen at his feet. Instead I kept my pride, got back into bed, and let him go.

✑

But every morning and every evening I went over to talk to him. He wouldn't listen to me. I tried calmly explaining to him the difference between what I'd done and fraud. He would have none of it.

"But, Peter, your father *does* want to contact you. It's true. I'm sorry if you felt tricked…"

"I never felt tricked."

I had lost him, I had lost him. He decided to move to Cambridge, where he'd work as a research assistant, or something, until the spring, when he'd start graduate school. He took all the money out of his bank account in order to buy a truck to move with. "I'm getting myself together," he told me. "I suggest you do the same."

At home I cried long and hard and hated myself and spiritualism and Train Line. I spent whole days digging in my dead little garden, trying to coax the plants back to life, chopping away at the lawn that kept trying to reclaim it. The sun burned down on my head. When I went back inside the house, my light-adjusted eyes would be nearly blind, and I'd lie down on the sofa and stare at the dull white August sky.

The full significance of what I had done gradually dawned on me. The tricks I'd played on Peter had not undermined him at all. They had undermined me. It was as if I had carefully dismantled my own faith and built a tacky outhouse with the bricks.

✑

It was an accident.

It was an accident, because when it happened it came out of nowhere. It was an ordinary day. The sky ached to rain, and the wind off the lake smelled like fall, like the ketchup factory in Wallamee. I wore the black-and-white sundress I'd worn almost every day that summer and picked the only two tomatoes from my garden. I sliced them and ate them for lunch, sitting on the back steps with the plate on my knees. They were the best things I'd ever eaten. I wished Peter was eating them with me. He'd agree, tell me how amazing they were. That morning, when I saw him at Ferd's grocery buying salami, he'd ignored me.

The day was hot, so when I lay down on the sofa that afternoon I trained the box fan on me and fell asleep. When I woke up it was dark, and I was cold and disoriented and my ears roared from the fan's artificial wind. Welchie Pratt was due back in a week or two, but for now she was still at her sister's, who'd finally died. The house was quiet and dark and empty.

I sat in the kitchen, feeling groggy and achy. I wanted to enjoy this solitude but I couldn't. There was no ice cream in the freezer, and flies tapped against the window glass, and the refrigerator hummed on and off. I had a headache. I knew I was going to go over to my mother's house and cry in front of Peter, and I hated myself for it. I found a sweater, put my sandals on, brushed my hair, all the time cursing my stupidity and weakness.

The walk over there was like any other: bits of gravel got caught between my foot and sandal, and I had to stop and shake my leg until I dislodged it. The sound of televisions floated from open windows. A dog barked at me. I was still grumpy from my long, windblown nap, but the walk made me feel a little better, and by the time I got to my mother's house I was sure I'd be able to control myself. I wouldn't beg or plead this time. I would just talk to him, because I was lonely, and surely he was lonely, too.

He let me in without looking at me, just opening the door and walking away. The house was stuffy and smelled like something burnt—dinner gone bad. All the overhead lights were on. I asked him how he could stand that.

No answer.

He went into the kitchen and began washing dishes. I sat on the tall stool and asked him when he was planning on leaving.

Still no answer.

I could feel it coming on, that terrible desperateness I'd wanted so badly to avoid that night. I looked around the kitchen for something to occupy myself, something to fix or clean and distract me. The room was spotless. Peter dried his last plate in silence and put it in the cupboard.

"I have a secret to tell you," I said.

He walked out of the kitchen, headed up the stairs. I followed, three steps behind. My face was level with his rear end. In the old days, I'd have tried grabbing it, and he'd have run up ahead of me.

In my childhood room, Peter sat down on the bed and took off his shoes. One of the laces had broken, and he took a new package of laces off the beside table and opened it up. I leaned against the doorjamb.

"You don't think you owe me anything, do you? Not even an answer to a simple question."

Finally he answered. His face was a mask of revulsion. "You don't think a year of my life is enough? I gave you that. That's a year I fucking crumpled up like trash, and fucking threw out the window."

I slapped him across the face. He grabbed my wrist and pushed me away.

We stared at each other from across the room. "Peter," I said—I couldn't help it, I knew it was wrong, it was pathetic—"I want to tell you…"

"Don't you ever give up?" He shook his head slowly, amazed.

"I've read your journal," I said.

Peter put his shoes back on. They were good, expensive shoes, the kind you can order from a catalog for a hundred dollars, but they hadn't been polished in a year. They looked like they'd been carved from wood. I hated them. Peter turned his back to me, and his shoulders began to shake.

I could do something about this, I thought. I could make it up to him. I knew how it would feel, too; falling into each other's arms like we did that first summer, kissing at first, making love.

I imagined it so sharply it hurt. I stepped toward him, put my arms around his waist, lay my head against his damp back.

He spun around suddenly and shoved me hard toward the wall. What I'd thought was sobbing was anger. My head hit the edge of the door molding hard enough to disorient me for a moment, but if it hurt I didn't notice.

"You are such a fraud," said Peter in a choked voice. "You're a fraud and you know it, too."

God, I hated him. I picked up a book from the dresser and threw it; it hit him on the shoulder. "You don't know anything!" I screamed at him.

The room was small, with a ceiling that sloped at one end. The air was always close in here, and it smelled like old paperbacks, and the single window cranked open only with difficulty. It was the room of my childhood, and I knew everything about it. The window screen had a certain bitter taste if you pressed your mouth to it; a trickle of dark water slipped down the wall and across the dresser when it rained. It was my room, but Peter's stuff was scattered across every surface now. Stupid, heartless stuff—packages of Kleenex, allergy medicine, socks—next to my china dogs and the candles I made in a craft class when I was twelve. He fouled everything. He made everything of mine look poor and tacky.

"I hate you!" I shouted. "You think…!" I threw at him whatever I could grab, all the ephemera of my childhood. A pocket dictionary, a handful of pens, the stuffed dog I'd brought from New Orleans and never named, a coffee mug. It rained around him. He put his hands out to stop it. I threw harder: my tape player, which struck him across the chest so hard the door popped open and a tape fell out, and the glass jar of pennies I'd collected as a child and brought to Train Line with the stuffed dog. Peter and I had taken and spent the silver coins, many of which were minted the year I was born, because my grandfather used to save them for me. It was a heavy jar, the size of a pineapple and with a similar shape, and when I hefted it at Peter it did not seem like a dangerous object. It was just my penny jar. He saw it coming and turned from it. It caught him on the temple and he fell.

I screamed. The way he dropped seemed permanent, his spirit yanked from his body like a magician's handkerchief from a sleeve. How could it be? I covered my mouth with both my hands to stop the screaming. Forces pulled at me; one toward Peter and one away from him, and so I was stuck where I was, staring at the small amount of blood collecting by his face. It came from his ear, I think, or perhaps his nose. There was only a little, on the blue linoleum.

How could it be?

My hands moved over my body. I was still here, hot and panting.

I went into the bathroom and found a washcloth, dampened it, and cleaned the blood from the floor and from Peter's face. Then I returned to the bathroom and rinsed the cloth, hung it from its nail over the tub, and went back to Peter. He was lying on the bed.

What happened? Had I imagined him on the floor? Had he gotten up? His head was near the center of the bed, far from the place I thought I'd wiped clean. I knelt on the floor and felt for dampness. There was none. Could it have dried?

I put my fingers, slick with sweat and humming electrically, on his throat to feel a pulse. I didn't feel one. I couldn't even find a vein.

❧

Memory is unreliable. I would like to say with certainty that I called an ambulance then and sat waiting for it half the night, but it is equally possible that my wishing it were so is what put the memory in my head. No ambulance came, of course. I have tried so hard to remember that phone call, to recall whether I dialed the wrong number, or whether I gave the wrong address, or whether I was perfectly clear and the confusion was on the other end, or if in my distraction I never called at all. But I sat at the table waiting, and I'm sure of this, because I made a cup of tea and spilled some boiling water on my hand, and as I sat at the table, waiting, I watched the burned place blister and turn white. The pain was a point of clarity. I slept with my face on the enamel tabletop and in the morning I went outside.

Train Line. All around, the same things. The houses looked sleepy and surprised. Ragged blue chicory flowers grew around the telephone poles and in weedy places, and some kind of small, hairy, orange flower poked out of lawns. I took a walk and soon found myself in the Violet Woods. The air was heady, the woods tangled with jewelweed. The clearing around Illumination Stump was deserted. I sat on a bench. Crows hopped along the ground. Leaning forward, my head resting on the bench in front of me, I prayed very long and very hard for an explanation for what was happening.

I sat until evening, when fireflies flashed their cold lights in the trees around us. *There is no Death, and there are no Dead.* I told it to myself over and over until it felt true. Faith could be the rope that pulled me out of this chasm. *There is no Death, and there are no Dead.* And Peter was still Peter, my mother would still love me, and I could go on.

Back at my mother's house, I cleared up Peter's things, turned off the lights, locked the door. I went back to my apartment and took a warm shower, then lay in bed, thinking how I would get Peter down the stairs, into the boat, and across the lake. My mother, far away at her retreat in Ohio, was asleep in a rented bed. She would be home soon, and I couldn't wait. I missed her terribly.

10

sisters

Every religion has at its source a person confronted with the inexplicable. Spiritualism has Kate and Maggie Fox, two stern-faced young women who lived in the small town of Hydesville, New York, in the 1840s. Their portraits hung in Train Line's main office, and in the library, and in the lobby of the Silverwood Hotel. I remember seeing their stubborn, unbeautiful faces when I was a child, with their thin lips and heavy hair, and asking my mother who they were. She didn't want to say. "They were the first mediums," she said, pulling me along, "but not really. Jesus Christ was the first medium." But they were everywhere, so I knew they were important, and bit by bit I pieced together their story.

In the spring of 1848, the Fox family—Mr. and Mrs. Fox and their daughters, who were twelve and fifteen at the time—began to be disturbed by weird noises echoing through their tiny rented house: knocks and crashes and bangs that were sometimes so loud it seemed as if someone must be throwing objects against the walls, or pounding the floors with his fists. It was terrifying, at least at first. But after a couple of weeks of this, of sleepless nights and restless haunted days, one of the girls had had enough. Snapping her fingers, the twelve-year-old, Katie, cried out, "Mr. Splitfoot! Do as I do!" *And he did.*

Maggie tried it, too, clapping three times. Three raps echoed hers. When the girls' mother asked the spirit to tell the ages of her children, he did it, including those of the four grown ones and a baby who died. Suddenly they were bubbling with questions: Are you alive? No answer. Are you dead? Two affirmative raps. Did someone hurt you? Yes. Did someone kill you? Is the killer living? Are you buried beneath this house? Yes, yes, and yes.

Neighbors were summoned. They heard the raps and were thunderstruck. One of them came up with the idea of reciting the alphabet and asking the spirit to rap when the correct letter was reached—a kind of oral Ouija. The spirit then told them more: his name, Charles B. Rosma—or was it Ross? Or something else? No one was sure—and that he had been a traveling peddler, killed and robbed by a previous occupant of the Fox house named John Bell. Mrs. Fox and her daughters went to stay with a relative, and the next day, investigative committees were formed among townspeople, and the Foxes' cellar floor was dug up, but the hole kept filling with water and nothing was found. Much later, someone claimed to find some bits of teeth and bone, but this was never proved.

Then, a former servant of the Bells came forward. She told a story of a peddler who showed up one day and vanished suddenly, leaving behind some new thimbles and an old coat that Mrs. Bell took to wearing. The servant remembered stumbling over freshly mounded soil in the cellar not long afterward. She, too, had heard ghostly raps. Someone else said that the summer the peddler went missing, the Bells had bad, evil-smelling water for months.

Mr. John Bell, the accused, was outraged. He denied everything—there was no peddler, he said, and no murder and no secret burial. And no evidence, either, at least nothing from this world, the only world that counted in a court of law.

At any rate, the Fox sisters were caught in the uproar. After a few months, they moved to Rochester, but the knocks followed them, and they discovered they could communicate with spirits other than the murdered Mr. Rosma. They began to tour the country, charging lots of money and drawing enormous crowds, and so Spiritualism was born.

But that, unfortunately, is not the end of the story.

People began accusing them of fraud. The girls were examined by a group of professors of medicine, who discovered that Maggie could not produce any raps when her legs were being held. Many years later, she confessed: it *was* all a fraud, they'd made the raps by cracking their toe and knee joints. Her sister confirmed it. But by that time it was too late. Spiritualism had spread across the world, there were thousands of mediums, hundreds of spiritualist churches. Train Line was a bustling town with dozens of buildings and a two-hundred-year charter. There was nothing to be done with the Fox sisters' bit of information. When they recanted their confession a few years later, they found that few people paid attention to that, either.

Old Charles B. Rosma was forgotten; he disappeared into the slippery space between the knowable and the unknowable. Everything we forget goes there, eventually; the dreams we don't bother to recall, the people we meet once but whose names escape us. I thought Peter would stay there, too.

⚬⚬⚬

When the police had gone, that morning after the Halloween party, I sat for a while on the sofa in my living room. The sofa was the only piece of furniture from the days of Welchie Pratt that Ron hadn't yet replaced. It was a musty orange thing, sunk in the middle, springs poking through. I wanted to take my hooker dress off, but I could not make myself get up and do it. Behind me a window was open, and a cold draft blew against the back of my head.

My mother sat down three feet away from me, staring raptly at a poster Jenny had hung above the television. It was of a polar bear moving across some tundra, white on white, only its black nose marring the landscape. Jenny told me once that polar bears cover their noses with their paws when they sneak up on seals, in order to make themselves more completely invisible.

"It's not him," I said at last. My voice was steady and did not shake. "Peterson said it couldn't be him."

"It fits, though," said my mother. She swept her hand across her face, as if brushing away spiderwebs.

"No, it doesn't fit at all." I said this firmly, then got up and walked around the room, touching things. Almost nothing in this room was mine. There were Jenny's little figurines, Ron's candlesticks and magazines and cassette tapes: *Frog Talk* said one, and *Rain Dances* another. I was always uncomfortable leaving my things where other people would have to look at them, possibly disliking them and wondering why I had to fill rooms with evidence of myself. Dust clung to everything. The road out front was unpaved; dust got everywhere if you didn't stay on top of it.

"I'm sorry," she said.

"There's nothing to be sorry for," I said. "It's not Peter."

"Oh," said my mother. She looked sick and confused.

"Anyway, even if it is, what's that got to do with us?" Somehow, my face relaxed, and I managed a small smile. "He left here. I even got a postcard from him."

"You did?" she asked, hopefully.

"Yes. From Cape Cod. It had a clam kind of thing on it. A cartoon. He said he was going to Mexico."

"You never told me that." She searched my face. "Do you still have it? That would be evidence."

"Of course I don't have it! That was years ago. I threw it away."

She sighed and picked at some threads poking out of the sofa. She was wearing a loose cotton housedress covered with pink flowers, and I pictured her cleaning her house, dusting and obliviously singing to herself, when the police came to the door.

"Mama," I said. "What is it?"

"Oh," she said. Her face was strained, like the face of someone carrying a load almost too heavy to bear. "I found things."

"You found things?"

She nodded slowly. "In the house, when I got back from Ohio. Things he left."

"What things?"

"Underwear!" she said, as if the thought of it was surprising to her still. "Three pairs of boxer shorts. And some maps and some keys in a drawer. I thought it was strange, but you know, the things you forget when you move in a hurry."

"Well, then, so what?"

"He also left his diaries."

The word *diaries* made me think of the one I kept for a sporadic year when I was nine, the five-and-dime diary with the shiny orange cover and the cheap lock, which I had to open with the tip of a ballpoint pen because I lost the key. Girls kept diaries, hid them under their pillows, tied them with ribbons, and at first I did not connect them with the blue-bound lab notebooks Peter kept his journals in. I stared blankly at my mother, unable to believe that Peter had a *diary,* and then, when the memory of those journals washed over me, unable to believe I had forgotten about them.

"They were under the sink, wrapped in a paper bag. It just never made sense to me that he would leave them here, even by accident. It was so odd..." She rubbed her face hard with both hands.

"Did you read them?"

"No. Not really. Enough to know what they were. I sent him a note through his mother asking where I should send them, but I never got an answer. So I hung on to them."

"You never said anything to me about it."

"Well," said my mother. "You made it pretty clear you didn't want to talk about him, if I remember."

I left the room, went into the kitchen. I began to clean up frantically, piling dishes into the sink, throwing the scattered sections of newspaper into the recycling box. What I had to do, I decided, was get the journals away from my mother. I had to get them out of my mother's house and burn them, or pour acid over them, or destroy them in some other way. How much had she read? Who had she told? That they existed was intolerable.

She came up behind me, wrapped her arms tight around my chest. "It's all right, it's all right if it's him," she whispered. "Anything could have happened when he left here. It's all right…"

I got out of her arms and pushed her away. "I want you to give me those diaries," I told her.

She backed away from me, shutting her eyes and putting her hands over her ears.

"Please, Mama!"

But it was clear she did not want to hear me doing this; I was implicating myself, and though a tiny part of me knew it, I couldn't stop. I turned and ran out the back door. Halfway across the lawn I slipped and fell—the stupid hooker dress was as tight as a sausage casing, nearly impossible to run in—but I got up and kept running, down Fox Street, over to Rochester Street, up to my mother's house. I pounded across the porch and tried to open the door. Locked! She never locked the door, never since I could remember, I didn't even have a key. I ran around the house to the back door—locked, too. The windows were shut tight. I tore at a screen with my fingernails, tried to pry it up so I could get at the real window and break it maybe.

"Naomi! Stop it!"

It was my mother, gasping and red in the face, leaning against the porch railing.

"Please, stop it! People are watching!"

I wheeled around. Rochester Street was empty, all the houses up and down were Sunday-morning quiet, shades down, curtains drawn. The sky was a blank gray void.

"Who?" I cried. "Who?"

She didn't answer.

I understood, then, the true horror of the world: it is that once a thing is done, it can never be undone. A universe of wishing can't uncrush a bug, or unspeak a word, or erase even the tiniest action from the past's ledger. The past is fixed and unalterable, a tyrant, and none of us has any power against it. How can we do anything, how can we live, knowing this? My mother came to where I stood among the trampled ivy that grew around her house. This time, when she pulled me into her arms, I did not resist. Her heart thudded hard through her pink-flowered dress.

"Please don't read them," I said into her hair.

"I won't," she said.

∽

When I got home again, I slept. It was a strange half-sleep; I heard Ron in the hallway telling Jenny that he needed to go to Wallamee to buy some caulk to fix the kitchen sink, and I dreamed she answered by saying that he shouldn't bother, because a tornado was coming and it was heading right for our house. I woke up confused and with a headache. The clock said it was almost one in the afternoon.

I took a shower. Usually I wouldn't touch anyone else's bath products. I was sure they kept track, and would notice the scent of it on me. Today that did not seem to matter. I used Jenny's thick mud-colored shampoo and her translucent soap, which looked like a piece of foamy green glass. The smell of tree bark and pinesap, Jenny's scent, rose in the steam around me. While I ran the soap over my body, I thought about Officer Peterson and Officer Ten Brink. Officer Peterson, I suspected, kind of liked me; Officer Ten Brink did not. But women like her—those spunky, scratchy-voiced, energetic types—never did. She reminded me of the gym teacher I'd had in high school, the one who gave up on trying to make me play volleyball and let me hang around in the weight room alone, where I'd occasionally drop a dumbbell on the floor to let her think I was doing something. Officer Peterson was different, more like the tall, popular vice-principal. He might overlook things, if he liked you.

Peter Morton had been all wrong for me. I should have known that the minute I met him. He was too sulky, too brooding, too self-absorbed. Someone like Officer Peterson would have been better. A calm-eyed country boy. A practical person—head full of nothing but ordinary facts and simple opinions. Or even better, no opinions at all. A mind as plain as a field of wheat. That's what I wanted.

I'd been standing in the shower for so long, soaping myself and fantasizing about Officer Peterson, that the water had gone cold. I put the soap down and got out, dried myself roughly with a towel, and yanked a brush through my hair. In the mirror my face was round and ruddy, my hair dark and stringy, my eyes...strange. For a long, disturbing moment I didn't recognize them. Once, in a magazine, I'd seen paintings in which the artist had given his human subjects the eyes of animals—there was a woman with the round, baleful eyes of a cow; a little boy with bird eyes; someone else with the peculiar square pupils of a goat. That's how I looked to myself. I squinted. Who was that?

You're a murderer, came the voice of Officer Peterson in my head.

Yes, I thought to myself. The thought was a terrible relief. *Yes, yes, yes.*

ॐ

After I was dressed, I went for a walk around Train Line and found myself standing in front of Troy's house, looking up at his kitchen window. Behind it, the old man appeared to be cooking. He moved back and forth, concentrating on something presumably on the stove, his white hair fallen across his forehead. I had put on a dress and a sweater after my shower, which wasn't enough. I was cold. I rubbed my arms, watching Troy.

After several minutes he turned and peered out at me, then signaled me to come inside. I unlatched the front gate and walked up the steps.

"Hoping for an invitation?" he asked, holding the door open for me.

"I didn't think of it, but maybe I was."

The house was warm and steamy and clocks ticked from every wall. He had cuckoo clocks and school clocks and wristwatches hanging from their cracked leather bands, and grandfather and grandmother clocks and, in the parlor, an hourglass on a huge oak frame. Once when I was a child Troy turned it over for me and I timed it with my new digital watch. The last grain of sand fell through the aperture an hour and one second later.

"It's off by a second," I told Troy.

"It's your watch that's off, dear," he replied.

The clocks had all come from his father, an undertaker and medium in Australia. "It's not me who's obsessed with mortality," he liked to remind visitors. People liked to make assumptions about Troy's psyche based on the presence of the clocks. "It's not the time aspect that's significant, Troy," I'd heard Tony K. the Hypnotist tell him once. "It's that *you* control every single timepiece. None are electric, are they? They depend on you for life. It's that you're a control freak, Versted." Or, "They symbolize your father to you, that much is clear." It was my mother who said this. Troy just smiled and shrugged, conceding that he did keep them around for sentimental reasons, but mostly just because he was used to the sound they made. The whirring and clattering and chiming would have driven anyone else insane, and it would be a shame to break up the collection. Only a few were set to the right time. Others, I suspected, were set to some Australian time zone, but most seemed randomly set. It occurred to me, as I was taking my shoes off in the entryway, that every clock was accurate for some place on the globe—or would be, if time wasn't standardized.

"Do you like mulligatawny?" Troy asked, hurrying back to the kitchen. "It's just about finished. I can take some Snickers bars out of the freezer for dessert, too."

"I've never had mulligatawny. It smells interesting, though." It did.

"Straight from the Colonies," he said in his Britishest voice.

The smell, I realized, was curry: something I'd had once or twice at a potluck and liked well enough, but not the kind of thing I normally ate. I felt suddenly and deeply relieved to be here, with Troy, who knew nothing of Officer Peterson or the investigation. Or did he? I might never discover how much he, or anyone, knew. He stirred the soup with a wooden spoon and put slices of white bread into the toaster, then stood and peered into the bright orange slots as they toasted.

"Hurry, hurry!" he whispered at them.

"You must be hungry," I said.

Troy glanced at me. "I certainly am. I have an atrocious metabolism. If I don't eat all the time I turn mean."

I smiled. "I wouldn't want to be around for that."

"You certainly would not."

When the toast popped up he scraped a little margarine over each piece and cut them into triangles, then set the table. I sat down, suddenly dizzy with hunger.

"Sorry if I'm not much of a conversationalist at the moment," said Troy, pouring soup into my bowl. "No talk when hungry. Eat! Then Troy talk."

We sipped from our spoons. After a few mouthfuls, Troy's face visibly relaxed. His forehead smoothed out and his jaw loosened.

"So," he said, wiping his lips with a paper napkin. "What brings you here this fine fall afternoon?"

"Actually, I was just going for a walk. I didn't mean to invite myself over. Though I appreciate it. Thank you."

"Mysterious forces at work, I suppose," he said. "Because, as a matter of fact, I wanted to talk to you."

"Really? What about?"

"Oh, um." He looked down and quickly scooped several spoonfuls of soup into his mouth. "It's a coffee-and-dessert subject, I think. We can wait until then."

With his lowered head and tidy, nervous motions, Troy suddenly reminded me of someone. I couldn't put my finger on who. Of course, he could have just reminded me of Troy; I'd known him for years, eaten dozens of meals with him, here or at my mother's house or at Maxwell's. Other places, too. Troy was a fixture. But no; it wasn't him I was thinking of. This shy, embarrassed version of Troy reminded me of someone else—I'd never seen Troy shy before—but who?

My grandfather, of course. With his face hidden in his soup bowl, all I could see of Troy was his white hair and narrow shoulders: my grandfather's exactly. My grandfather! Somehow, over the last twenty years, Troy had grown as old as my grandfather was when we left New Orleans. By now, my grandfather would be nearly a hundred, but he'd died a year or so after we left. He had a live-in companion for the last several months, a young man from Spain, to whom he left everything: the house, the furniture, the meager bank accounts. The young man, whose name was Carlos but who preferred to be called Charles, was deeply embarrassed by this, and offered to split everything with my mother. He called several times, apologizing.

"Please, we share?" he asked. "We share, please?"

Nothing doing, said my mother. "It belongs to you, Charles. It's all yours. You deserve it."

"You take some furniture."

"Absolutely not," said my mother.

How angry my grandfather must have been. It had never really occurred to me before. He died angry.

"Are you all right, Naomi?" asked Troy, touching my hand.

"Oh, yes, I'm fine." I smiled at him. "I was just thinking of my grandfather. You remind me of him."

His face took on an exaggerated unhappy expression. "Am I that old? Oh, dear. How old are you, anyway, Naomi?"

"Thirty-one."

"Really!" He seemed truly surprised. "You don't look more than twenty-five. But it's been that long, hasn't it?"

"I guess it has."

"You're lucky. You have that round face. You won't wrinkle for a while."

I shrugged. "I don't really care about that."

He chewed his toast and gazed at me. "But you should. In a way. I don't mean you should be vain. It's just that you're in the bloom of life. You won't be this young forever. You should get married. You should leave here, Naomi."

Leave here! What a thought. I used to want to leave Train Line so badly; all through my teens I read travel books and road-trip novels. I'd fantasize about getting in a car and driving some-where, just anywhere. Peter did that once, he and Nelson Karp, one summer vacation from Princeton. They had a guidebook of roadside attractions, and they drove from one attraction to the next for weeks, eating at truck stops and sleeping in the back of Nelson's van at state parks and rest areas. Their favorite place wasn't a roadside attraction at all, but a town called Ozona, in Texas. The whole state, Peter told me, was desert and grasslands, flat and dry and uninspiring. But when they got off the interstate at Ozona, it was suddenly lush and full of trees, huge oaks and Norway maples. He and Nelson ate at a restaurant that looked like a converted legion hall—they sat at card tables in folding chairs, and the walls were covered with calendars from local busi-nesses—and the food they ate was surprisingly delicious. They had pancakes as huge and pillowy as mattresses, and huevos ran-cheros, and tortillas that came in a sombrero-shaped basket.

We would do that, Peter used to tell me. He and I would travel together. We'd go west and swim in the Pacific Ocean, he'd show me the Grand Canyon and the rain forests of Oregon, and in California we'd pick warm lemons from trees along the side of the road.

We didn't, of course. But Peter would talk me to sleep some nights with these stories, at least when we first fell in love, and sometimes later, too, when we got depressed about the cold and being poor. I remember wanting to travel so badly it made me cry; I imagined my hands so full of lemons I'd have to fill my shirt with them, the load of them as heavy as a sleeping child against me.

I looked back up at Troy, smiling, my eyes filling with tears. "Maybe I should travel."

"Oh, you should!" He slapped his hands on the table and leaned toward me, his face bright. "Europe! You'd love it. I can see you bicycling through Provence. You'd eat bread and cheese under poplar trees. Or trekking in Nepal! That seems to be what all the young people are doing, these days. You could bring me a yak-fur hat."

"I would. I definitely would."

He nodded. "I'm in my settling stage, myself. I had a fairly itinerant youth. Even the thought of packing a suitcase tires me out. I want my things, my people, around me."

"Spirits, you mean?"

"No. *They're* everywhere, of course—one can't exactly escape them. I meant the solid folk. You know."

I nodded, though I did wonder who he meant. My mother? He didn't have any family, as far as I could tell. We ate quietly for a while, and when we were finished I stacked the plates and bowls and carried them back to the sink.

"Don't you dare wash them!" cried Troy. "If I don't do the washing up I won't have any thinking time. I love my thinking time."

"All right. Let me do something, though."

"Go ahead and slice up the Snickers bars. They're in the freezer behind the juice."

While I hacked away at the rock-solid candy bars, Troy made coffee. "I meant what I said, you know. You shouldn't be hanging around here with all of us golden-agers. You need to meet people."

"I do meet people."

"There's that David character from the cafeteria. I've seen him looking at you. But I think you know what I mean. How do you know what's out there unless you look? How do you even know if you like someone like Mr. David Cafeteria if you don't have a nice array of men friends to compare him to? I'm sorry if I sound like your father. Or your grandfather, I suppose."

"That's all right. I'm sure you have a point."

"You just gave me a shock, telling me you're over thirty." We carried the coffee and candy bars into the parlor, where the sound of cuckoo clocks was exploding from the walls. "Lately I've been setting all the cuckoo clocks to the same time. The racket is stimulating."

I chewed on a piece of candy. "Thirty-one's not that old, you know."

"Of course not. Heaven forbid. It's just another reminder that time is whistling by."

"As if you need one!" I said, gesturing to the giant hourglass.

"Yes, indeed. The good thing about clocks is that they're not linear. They go around and around and start fresh every day. It's quite reassuring." He put his coffee on the end table and clasped his hands on his knees. "I'm going to tell you something you might find shocking. Promise me you won't run screaming from the house."

I set my own coffee down. "Of course I won't. What is it?" I braced myself.

"I'm in love with your mother. I might ask her to marry me. Umm, no. I *will* ask her. But I suppose I'm asking your permission."

"Troy! But…you've known each other forever!"

Inside me, something was breaking into a thousand pieces. *He wants to marry my mother.* It was preposterous. *He's in love with her.*

"Well, it hasn't been *quite* forever. Anyway, things change, people change. I don't know how to explain it."

"Troy, it's…it's….I don't know. It's wonderful. You don't need my permission, though. I *am* surprised."

"I thought you would be." He smiled: a relieved, bashful grin. "Galina's been a little busy and preoccupied lately. I haven't seen as much of her as I'm used to. And I miss her. I guess I only just realized how used to her I've become." Embarrassed, he threw several chunks of candy bar into his mouth and chewed noisily.

"So…when?" I asked.

"When?" He looked startled.

"When are you going to ask her?"

"Oh. I'm not sure. We have a date on Friday—Pizza Village. Do you think that'll be romantic enough? I'm afraid if we go to a white-linen-tablecloth sort of place I'll be too nervous to say anything."

"She loves pizza."

"*That* I am well aware of."

I drank the coffee and rocked in my chair, gripping the mug tightly so that my hands wouldn't shake. The last time my mother had gone on a date with a man, years ago, she came over to my house afterward to tell me about him—his thin mustache, his shiny narrow tie, how he wouldn't shut up about his son's new sports car—and we'd had a good long laugh about him. I felt a stirring nostalgia for that evening, a nostalgia so powerful my ears rang.

Now that he'd got his secret off his chest, Troy seemed more at peace. He fingered the doily on the end table and stared into space, saying nothing for a long while.

"I suppose I should be going," I said. "Thank you for the mulligatawny. I'm warm all through, now."

"Good, good!" He stood up quickly to walk me to the hallway, where I slid my shoes back on. "There's one other thing I need to ask you, though."

"Yes?"

"What do you think she'll say? Do you think she'll say yes?"

"Oh, Troy." I took his hand—a thin and veiny old thing, the fingers yellowed from years and years of cigars. "Of course she'll say yes."

He gave my hand a squeeze. "Good," he said again, nodding. "I've always wanted to be someone's father."

And with that, he shut the door behind me.

❧

Already it was getting dark. I walked from Troy's house to the lake, where bugs hovered and pricked the water's skin. The air was clammy and smelled like mushrooms.

This is good, I told myself. Troy loves her, and now you are free of her.

But I did not want to be free of her. I wanted her to love me and no one else.

Out on the water, a small brown duck floated in circles. I picked up a pebble and threw it at the duck. It missed and dropped into the water with a tiny plop, and the duck didn't seem to notice. It paddled around and around and around, and now and then I glimpsed the bright orange flash of its feet beneath the water. I wanted to affect it in some way, I wanted it to fly off or quack or dive under. It wouldn't. I thought I might find a bigger rock, really pelt the thing, but I realized that was not what I wanted at all.

My empty heart was collapsing in on itself. A lonely life is a crime without witnesses, it is a movie playing in a locked theater; can you ever really be sure what happens in it? Can you be sure that it happens at all?

I am here! I am here! I wanted to yell at the duck. But there was no point in that. The duck was smart; it knew I did not matter, in the scheme of things.

11

premature burial

When I woke up the next morning, I felt inexplicably full of hope. There was no good reason for this, but the sunlight that came through my windows looked cheerful and kind, and my heart was light. As I washed and dressed and made up my bed, I planned my day with something close to relish—a morning of work, a good lunch at the cafeteria, more work, then Vivian. The previous morning's scene with Officers Peterson and Ten Brink seemed distant and small, unworthy of the agony it had caused, like a childhood illness. I had survived it, and as far as I knew so had my mother. It was survivable.

And I did have a good day, though I was distracted while working by the sound of branches tapping insistently against the library windows, and by a restlessness I could not quite contain. I kept getting up, looking out at the lake, sitting down again, getting up. I left early for lunch. I bought a hot sandwich at the cafeteria, brought it down to the lake, and ate it on the dock. The wind had picked up and the waves were tipped white.

Though it had begun to rain by the time I left to meet Vivian's bus, I had enough of a good mood left not to mind that I was dressed poorly for the weather. Rain plastered my hair to my head and cascaded off the gatehouse roof. I stood a few yards away, under a large pine tree, and I began planning what Vivian and I would do that afternoon. We'd make popcorn, I thought, and work on the Vivian and Naomi paper dolls we'd cut out of tag board: our project before the witch costume debacle. I was designing a whole nineteenth-century wardrobe for mine, using the photographs in the library for inspiration, and Vivian was making a cheerleader's outfit for hers. We spent hours decorating the clothes with crayons and colored pencils.

After ten minutes or so I heard the rattle and groan of the bus as it downshifted around the bend, but it didn't stop. It slowed down, paused briefly, and then picked up speed and roared off over the bridge. I noticed, as it sped past, that someone had written FUK YEW in the steamed-over back window.

I waited for a while, imagining that Vivian had missed her stop and was perhaps kneeling on the floor of the bus right now, gathering her dropped homework and lunch box and umbrella and booksack, and would stagger up to the front in a minute or two and have the bus driver drop her off down the road. But this did not transpire. I watched as the bus turned at Dean Road on the other side of the bridge, and then it disappeared over the hill.

This had happened before. Once, on the first day of second grade, Vivian had gotten onto the wrong bus, and it was only after a series of frantic phone calls to the school that she finally showed up on my doorstep, tearstained and exhausted. Another time, Vivian was home with hives, and Elaine had forgotten to call me. I decided that this had happened again, so I trudged back home and called Elaine's real estate office. Water dripped off me and pooled on the linoleum as I waited for someone to answer.

"Thank you for calling Downtown Realty. None of our service representatives is available to come to the phone right now, but if you leave your name, number, and a brief message, we'll call ya right back! Your call is so important to us!"

Hmm.

I called the school next. The school secretary couldn't help and told me the teachers were in a staff meeting. But if I left my name and number, she said, Miss Strunk would call me as soon as she could. I said that would be fine.

So I made the popcorn and melted some butter and sat at the kitchen table eating it by myself, waiting for the phone to ring. Ron came in and joined me. He took a large handful of popcorn and chomped it down.

"Greazy," he said, showing his shiny palm.

"I like it that way."

"I do too, as a matter of fact. But, oh, Naomi, your poor heart!"

"I don't care about my heart."

He took another handful. "That's not a very good attitude. Where, by the way, is Vivian?"

"I don't know. She didn't get off the bus. I'm waiting for someone to call and tell me why."

"I always used to hate the school bus," said Ron, shaking his head. "It was worse than the boys' restroom. Did I ever tell you about the hell I went through in school?"

"I don't think so."

"I had thick glasses and an overbite and I was so skinny my pants hung off my hipbones—you wouldn't believe the pictures of me then. They used to take me by the arm and the leg and throw me down the stairs."

"Oh, Ron!"

"*Ronald,* then. I couldn't walk down the aisle of the school bus without getting tripped. Most weeks something of mine would get tossed out the window. I'd have to get off at the next stop and search through the weeds for my hat or book or whatever it was, then walk the three, four, five miles home. I can't tell you how happy I am to be an adult."

"I'll bet."

"Do you think Vivian has that kind of trouble in school? Because she's an odd one, you know. Those creeps can spot an odd one a mile off."

I shrugged. "I don't know. I really can't tell. She doesn't tell me much. I don't think she's very happy in general."

He shook his head sadly. "The terrible part is, we can't do a thing about it. Adults, I mean. We have no effect at all. My parents would sometimes call the school—if I came home so bloody and battered I couldn't hide it from them—or, worse, they'd call someone else's parents." He rolled his eyes. "It just made it worse. Incalculably worse."

I stood up and got some water from the faucet. "I don't know. I like to think I make a difference to Vivian."

"I'm sure you do," he said, kindly. "It's just that you won't be able to take away her misery. No one can do that but Vivian."

Ron had wandered out to the yard to work on his compost—he turned and watered it once a week, adding whatever substances he thought would hurry its decay—and I'd finished all the popcorn and washed the dishes before Miss Strunk called. She had a breathless, high-pitched voice.

"Miss Ash? I'm sorry to take so long to get back to you. Actually, I'm calling from my car. What a day!"

The line was dense with technological fuzz. "Sorry to bother you. I was just wondering if Vivian got on the bus this afternoon. She never showed up at this end."

"She didn't?" The signal vanished for a moment, and when it returned Miss Strunk sounded very far away. "...another bus, not her regular one. I think, anyway."

"She got on a different bus? On purpose?"

"As far as I could tell. The bus drivers take care of all that, you know, the permission slips and all that. You should really call her parents. Sorry if I'm not much help."

"You've been plenty of help," I said.

Strunk, Strunk, Strunk, I thought when I hung up. It really was a terrible name.

～∞～

I did, finally, manage to reach Elaine, after spending ten minutes on hold listening to the local talk radio station. A rerun of my mother's show was on: *The Mother Galina Psychic Hour, Encore Edition.*

"Stop crying, dear. He's with you all the time, he's watching over you!"

"But I miss him!"

"No, you don't, dear, you can't, because he's not gone. Now listen…"

"Oh, Mother Galina, I'm so lonely!"

This continued for some time. I was quite relieved when Elaine's loud and chirpy voice came on.

"Hi, this is Elaine. How can I help you today?"

"Hi, Elaine, it's Naomi. I'm calling because Vivian…"

"Oh, my goodness! I can't believe I forgot to tell you! Oh, shame on me!"

"But what—"

"Oh, Naomi, I can't believe it. We found another babysitter for Vivian. Much closer to home, on my way from work—it's just so much more convenient! And there'll be other kids there, and a snack…"

"Another babysitter?"

"Well, really, it's a daycare center, but a small one. You know, intimate. And so close to work and home…"

"But Elaine…"

"And I figured, you know, with this investigation and all, you must have a lot on your mind…"

The investigation. Elaine chattered on, but I didn't hear her. Instead I stared out the window, watching Ron dig at the compost with his yellow rubber gloves. He squatted on his heels, his frizzy head bent, picking through the rot to find what had refused to decay. He pulled out a root, a handful of pebbles.

Very gently, I hung up the phone.

◦❦◦

I did not know what to do with myself. My first instinct was to call around, find out which daycare center Vivian was at, and then go get her. Of course, they wouldn't let me do that, and besides, there probably was no such place. They couldn't accept children on such short notice, could they? More likely Elaine had persuaded her husband to watch her for a few days while she looked for a new babysitter.

I walked around the house, pulling at my hair and imagining poor Vivian plunked down in front of some Disney video, homework forgotten in her booksack.

When this all blows over, I thought, *Elaine will come to her senses and give Vivian back, and everything will be back to normal.*

But maybe it wouldn't blow over. That was beginning to seem like a very real possibility. I needed to pull myself together and think.

∞

My mother didn't want to lend me the car, but I convinced her that I needed to get some things for the library from the office-supply store. She handed over the keys with a worried look.

"You're not coming to Circles, then?"

"No," I said.

The rain had mostly stopped, but the wind had picked up, hurling wet leaves into the windshield as I made my way around the lake. I set the wipers to intermittent. Along the shore, willow branches waved in the wind like skinny arms. The water itself was dark gray and cruel-looking, and sent waves over the bank and into the road.

I had mostly just wanted to drive around and think, but the closer I got to Wallamee the clearer it became to me that my real plan was to go see Vivian. I was pretty sure she'd be at home, and if not, perhaps her father would tell me where she was. I wanted to tell her not to worry; anything they'd said about me was wrong, that I still loved her and would be her babysitter again soon. It was not fair to uproot a child like this. And if I knew Elaine, she'd lied to Vivian, told her terrible things to make her comply.

But first I stopped at the office-supply store and bought enough sticky notes and labels and typewriter ribbon to last me out the decade.

Then I headed up the wide, bland avenues that made up the development where Elaine and her husband lived. There were no sidewalks, because there was no place to walk to from here, and the trees were no more than saplings clutching desperately to their green fertilized lawns. People here did unnatural things to shrubbery. Every house was flanked by an army of green bowling balls or cones or cylinders that looked like nothing else alive. It was Train Line's opposite, the anti–Train Line. Elaine's house, a low brick-and-stucco "home," as she and her real estate cronies would call it, was nearly invisible behind its wall of evergreen. The driveway was black and smooth and freshly tarred, the lawn plush. From the outside, you'd never guess at the place's dank, ill-furnished, cigarettey interior.

I thumbed the doorbell and waited. From somewhere deep within, chimes played a familiar tune. There was a large picture window some ten feet from the door, and although I stepped back and craned my neck, I couldn't see in. Elaine's husband was home, though; his car, a humpbacked sporty thing, was parked in the driveway next to my mother's. I rang the bell again.

It was a few more minutes before the husband answered. He needed a shave and a hairbrush and didn't look happy to see me.

"What do you want, Miss Ash?" A beery odor wafted from him.

"Hi." I smiled. "I just thought I'd stop by and say hello to Vivian. She, umm, left some things at my house and I—I thought I'd let her know she should stop by and pick them up sometime."

He frowned. "What kind of things? Why didn't you just bring them with you?"

"I should have, I know!" My grin hurt my face. "Actually, I didn't plan on coming here, I was just in the neighborhood and…well, you know, there's some, umm, schoolwork, a sweater I think. A few things like that."

"I'll let her mother know. Good-bye, Miss Ash."

He tried to shut the door but I grabbed the knob and pushed. "Please, can I talk to Vivian? I just want to let her know she shouldn't worry about—her things."

"She's not here. Take your hand off the door or I'll call 911." And he gave the door such a sharp shove I nearly fell backward off the concrete stoop.

"Then where is she?" I cried out, but the door slammed and I heard the lock click in place.

I doubted he would really call 911. What would he tell them? A woman knocked on his door and talked to him? I stepped off the stoop and made my way around the enormous shrubbery to the picture window. Standing on the tips of my toes, I could only barely see in. The room was dark but there appeared to be a television glowing just out of my line of sight. The opposite wall was covered with mirrors, and I saw the top of my head and my eyes reflected in them. I looked silly and a not a little desperate.

Then suddenly Elaine's husband was there, rapping on the glass with his hairy knuckles and mouthing something at me. I stepped back into the bushes and he gave me the "take a hike" sign with his thumb, and so that's what I did.

∽✵∾

Back in the car, I shook the rain from my hair and tried to pull myself together. My thoughts were piling on top of each other and I was sweating. "How can people *live* here?" I said out loud, to no one.

I drove the car around the neighborhood, lost myself temporarily in the maze of loops and cul-de-sacs, then drove out again onto Vining Road, which curved around the north side of the lake. I felt a little bit better right away. Weeds and bushes pressed close on either side, and here and there through a gap in the trees I could see the lake, gray and reassuring, and, from this distance, calm and flat as the sky. I cracked the window open a bit so I could smell the air. It was rank with the odor of wet earth.

The place I buried Peter was not far from here. I wondered if the police were still guarding it, or if they were satisfied they'd found all the pieces of the skeleton and had decided to let the construction resume. I hadn't even driven by since the night my mother dragged me out here.

I parked next to the dirt driveway that led down to the clearing. A couple of pieces of yellow crime scene tape still fluttered from the trees, but the sawhorses that had blocked the way before were now pushed aside. I slid the car keys into my pocket and hiked down.

If there had been anyone there, I'd have turned back. But the site was silent and looked abandoned. I climbed down the steep dirt path, sliding on rocks with my inappropriate, slick-bottomed shoes, but managed to make it to the bottom without killing myself and followed the path toward the lake. Several yards from shore, a yellow backhoe crouched like a reptile next to a pit—the foundation, I assumed, and where they'd found the skeleton. A stiff breeze blew. I rubbed my hands up and down my arms. I'd forgotten to put a coat on and was chilled. Nonetheless, I waded through the tall dead weeds to get a closer look at the hole.

It didn't look like much. The construction men were part way through the foundation when they'd had to stop: two of the walls were straight and smooth, and most of the floor as well, but the two other walls were crumbled piles of earth and rock. Four stakes painted bright orange stuck out of the dirt, connected by string to form a crooked rectangle. That's all there was to show where Peter had lain for the last ten years.

It would be easier to get over there, I realized, without my stupid slippery shoes. I took them off. Then I squinted up toward the embankment to make sure no one was coming. But it had begun to rain hard again, and I could make out nothing through the thick line of trees.

Stepping down, I sank to my ankles in the muck, then climbed over the piles of dirt to Peter's grave. I touched the orange sticks, plucked the dirty string. It looked less like a place where someone had been exhumed than someone's vegetable garden, before any of the seeds had sprouted or plants been put in. The dirt itself was darker and richer than most soil. I didn't know why I'd come here, except just to see the place again. The rain came down harder, flattening my hair and soaking my dress. It was a funny thing, but I remembered something I hadn't thought of in a long time, since I dug the hole ten years before: an airplane had flown over my head that afternoon. It was a jet, just a tiny shape in the blue sky, with a vapor trail that streamed and fattened behind it. What had the passengers seen? The flat mirror of Wallamee Lake, surrounded by green and brown squares, maybe thready black highways in between. Me? Not likely. As I went about my task I'd have been as small and insignificant as the eye of a germ, as the toe of an ant. Teeny, tiny. Practically nothing. Thinking of this helped me get through that day. I'd put myself on that airplane. I couldn't even see what I was doing. It hardly mattered at all.

I turned to go. But as I did, the earth beneath my feet gave way. The whole unfinished side of the foundation, saturated with water and disturbed by my stomping, slid into the bottom of the pit, bringing me and the stakes and the string with it. I fell to my knees and tried to grab at something, but there was nothing to grab. It was like dreams I'd had of falling—tumbling out of windows, over waterfalls, down elevator shafts—the same few panicked moments that seem long enough to live your whole life in. By the time I stopped I was half sunk in mud. There was mud in my eyes and hair and mouth, where it had the rotten, gritty taste of bad fish. I struggled up and climbed to firmer ground, and spat and shook myself and cried.

At first I thought if I stood out in the rain long enough, it would wash me clean. It did no such thing. I wandered around the clearing, crying, feeling like I had spent my life working up to this day, the day I would lose everything and end up covered with mud and falling to pieces at a construction site. The rain began to let up a bit. Beyond the trees, cars on Vining Road flicked on their high beams. Soon, it would be dark.

◈

When I got to my mother's house, she wasn't home. Was this the night Troy was going to propose to her at Pizza Village? I couldn't remember. I'd managed not to get much mud on the car seats by digging a blanket out of the trunk of the Oldsmobile and sitting on that, but it wasn't until I was home that I realized I'd left all the sticky notes and labels and typewriter ribbons in the car.

◈

The next morning, as I was dressing for work, I told myself firmly that I would not do anything else rash. I would continue my life exactly as I had until Labor Day—working, going to circle meetings on Mondays and lectures on Sundays, eating slices of pie in the cafeteria, reading the newspaper, and chatting with people. Occasionally I would watch television and occasionally I would go over to my mother's house. I could make a life out of that.

I brushed my hair furiously, trying to get rid of the grit that seemed embedded in my scalp.

But as I stood on the steps of the library, fumbling in my coat pocket for the keys, I knew I didn't have the heart to catalog today. I didn't really want to go home, either. I dropped my things inside the door, locked it from the inside, and went into the reading room, snapping a couple of shades up to let in the weak November light. Then I pulled one of the overstuffed chairs close to a window and sat in it, missing Vivian.

After a while I fell asleep, my legs hanging over the armrest and my face pressed into the dusty upholstery. I'd been thinking about Vivian's house when I dropped off, trying to imagine what her life there was like, and when I began to dream it was of that house. In my dream, I owned it. It was filthy—sticky black dirt everywhere, overflowing ashtrays teetering on every end table and piles of junk mail sliding to the floor whenever I turned around. The whole place smelled like garbage. So I cleaned it. I was extremely thorough, squeaking Windex everywhere, kneeling down to scrub baseboards. And the more I cleaned, the more light poured into the house. The bad smells vanished. Something was baking in the kitchen, and somebody, my husband, presumably, was taking a shower in the bathroom. Though I didn't see him, or anyone else for that matter, I heard the pounding water, him singing over it. At one point I stretched, raised my hands over my head to get the kinks out of my back, and realized I was pregnant. My stomach bowed out in front of me like the sail of a ship. Of course I was pregnant. I'd known it all along. I walked, swaybacked, to the front door and threw it open. It was spring. I loved it. I loved my unborn baby, I loved my house, I loved everything.

A terrible banging sound woke me up. It took a few minutes before I was awake enough to figure out what it was—someone knocking on the front door of the library, shaking it and rattling the knob. I was frightened at first. Who could so desperately want to read dusty old spiritualist books?

It was my mother. She was cupping her hand over her eyes and peering in through the window in the door. I unlocked it and let her in.

"Oh, Naomi! You're all right." She had that wild-eyed look she sometimes got when I was a child and came home bleeding or with torn clothes.

"Of course I am. Why wouldn't I be?"

She shook her head, then put her arms around me and gave me a quick hug. It felt strange, for a moment, to realize that my belly was flat and I wasn't pregnant after all. Grief rocked through me.

"Will you come to the cafeteria with me? I need to talk to you."

So I put my coat on and followed her down the hill. To my shock, it was snowing. I had forgotten about snow. Since the morning it had gotten much colder, though it was still warm enough that the flakes melted when they hit the ground. They grazed my face and hands like flying insects.

My mother seemed energized, though with panic or something else I couldn't tell. At the cafeteria, she picked up an orange plastic tray and bought us two slices of pie and two cups of coffee while I sat at a corner table, waiting. Part of me was still caught up in my odd dream.

When she sat down in her rickety chair, the coffee sloshed onto the tray. My mother seemed hardly to notice. She leaned in toward me.

"People are saying terrible things, Naomi."

I gazed at her steadily to show I didn't care about what people were saying, then looked down at my coffee. It was old, burnt, and when I poured milk into it, it turned the color of ashes.

"You don't believe them, do you?"

"Of course not!"

"Then you should ignore them."

My calm unnerved her, I could tell. I ate a little pie.

She turned and looked out the window, where giant flakes were whirling down. "I believe in you, Naomi."

"That's fine."

"You are my daughter. I have made the decision to believe in you."

"All right," I said.

She picked up her fork, put it down, picked it up again. "Officer Peterson called this morning and told me that my help on the investigation is no longer welcome. He said that if any of the information I have already given them proves useful, I will of course be compensated, but since the investigation has come so close to home it would not look good if our partnership continued. So he said." She gave me a wry smile.

"Close to home," I repeated.

"That's what he said. I asked him what had changed since Sunday, but he wouldn't tell me."

She bent her head over her pie, and when she did I noticed that her hair was coming in gray at the roots. Though I sometimes teased her about dyeing her hair, I didn't like to see it turning gray, because it looked like forgetfulness, or neglect, or illness.

"I am a suspect," I said.

My mother looked up at me, alarm in her eyes. "No, Naomi. No, you aren't."

"Yes, I am. I am a suspect."

I sat back, seeing how this felt. It did not feel bad; it felt right, it felt like things were falling into place at last. I took a deep breath, and my lungs expanded more fully than they had in a long time.

"Don't say that. Don't say that." My mother made two fists and placed them on the table. "Look," she said. "I have a plan. We need to leave here for a little while. We can go home again."

"Home is here."

"No, it's not," she said, bitter. "We should never have left New Orleans. This is a hateful place. We have no one here."

"What about Troy?"

"What about him?"

"Did he ask you to marry him?"

Startled, she said, "He did, as a matter of fact."

"And what did you say?"

"I told him I couldn't possibly. Not now. I told him you and I were going on a trip together. He wanted to come, but I..." She put her face in her hands.

For a strange and fleeting moment I wished she were dead. What a terrible thought. But I did—I wanted her dead, I wanted her gone, because I could not stand her suffering; it filled me with loathing. *There's no suffering on the spirit plane,* I thought. But what did I really know? And almost immediately I recognized that it wasn't her I loathed, but myself.

"We're not going anywhere," I said. "I'm sorry, Mama." Then I stood up, kissed the top of her head, and left her there.

∽✕∾

She was right, though; people were saying terrible things.

When I took the library's mail to the tiny Train Line post office—it was like a paneled tool shed, with room for two medium-sized people to line up at the counter; everyone else would have to stand outside—the postmistress, a Miss Rita Raymond, would not even glance at me as she weighed and stacked and affixed postage. Once she had been a kind of friend, with kindly words for me on even my dourest days. Within a few days, I noticed that no one would make eye contact with me, not even Ron. People coming toward me in the street swerved, or turned around, or suddenly realized they were late and passed me at a rapid, distracted clip. The effect was odd. I found myself touching my face, my neck, making sure I was still there.

In the Groc-n-Stop I heard someone say, "... surely can't allow a murderer to live here. I mean, talk about PR problems..." I was kneeling on the floor, going through the boxes of macaroni and cheese to find one with a price tag, and I was hidden from the speaker, but I recognized the voice: Tony K. the Hypnotist. Pain shot up through my knees, but I stayed there until I was sure he'd gone. Later the same day, someone I didn't know was talking about me in the cafeteria—"She was a babysitter, imagine that!"—until someone else I didn't know spotted me and gave her friend a nudge.

Still, I walked carefully and slowly and with my head up. I took my arrows as if I deserved them.

∽✕∾

When it happened, I read about it in the paper, like an ordinary person:

MYSTERY MAN IDENTIFIED

(Wallamee, NY) Thanks to careful police work and a sheaf of dental records, a positive identification has been made in the Lake Side Grave Mystery. The bones are those of Peter S. Morton, of Portland, Oregon, purportedly a summer visitor to the area, who was last seen approximately ten years ago....

It wasn't even a headline story, just a sidebar, and I imagined that people reading it felt a vague sense of disappointment that the skeleton was not from a local person after all. Certainly, if he had been local, it would have made the headlines. There was no mention of me. If this was a good sign or a bad sign, I didn't know.

I was sitting on the porch in the wan November sun. A week had gone by since I'd seen Vivian, though I'd driven slowly past her school during recess and tried to catch a glimpse of her in the mass of running, screaming children in their identical pink and green and blue winter coats. Without her, I felt like I was going through life with one eye shut, or with huge mittens on; I felt clumsy and not quite there. I had hours to sit on the porch, or read the newspaper, or refill my coffee mug over and over. It occurred to me that I should get another job. It seemed like a daydream, though, something that would happen in another life, not mine. Me, Naomi Ash, filling paper bags with hot greasy food, or me in a turquoise smock, turning old people in a nursing home, seemed about as real as my paper doll trying on different crayoned outfits.

The bones were Peter's, definitely Peter's. Why did this shock me? At first I didn't recognize the sensation moving through me, slowly as Novocain. But I was truly shocked. I must have harbored some hope that it was all a paranoid fantasy of mine, that the discovery of the bones was a terrible coincidence, that everything I'd told the police was true. Oh, God, I'd wanted it to be true.

A cloud moved over the sun. A dying bee crept across the porch floor, heading for the steps, though it couldn't have known they were there.

~✿~

One morning that week I cataloged a book called *The Human Vivisection of Sir Washington Irving Bishop, the First and World-Eminent Mind-Reader.* It was a thin, pamphlet-sized monograph bound in faded blue paper with gold lettering, dated 1889. It was written by Bishop's mother, Eleanor Fletcher Bishop, and told the story of her son's bizarre death. Washington Bishop was a mind reader, one who performed stunts like this one: someone—preferably a prominent, well-known, and liked person of the city he was performing in, the mayor, perhaps—would hide a brooch or a hair pin or some other small object within a mile radius of an agreed-upon starting point. Bishop, with his hand tied to that of the person who'd hidden the item, would then rush about the city, invariably finding it within half an hour. Sometimes, he'd head straight for it, veering from the most direct route only when a building or river or some other immovable structure required it. However, these acts of clairvoyance took a lot out him, and often after such a performance, Bishop fell into a kind of cataleptic fit. He'd barely make it back to his room before succumbing to a deathlike state: his breathing would nearly stop, his heartbeat slowed to just detectable levels, his skin turned gray and cool. Anyone who knew Bishop would never mistake this state for death, however; he—like many Victorians—had a morbid fear of premature burial and spoke of it often. In the latter years of the century, all kinds of devices were patented to prevent such an occurrence or to catch it before it was too late. I'd seen them in other books. One, I remember, involved a sensitive air bladder placed on the chest of the deceased; any movement, even the slightest breath, would cause a bright red flag to pop up and signal to passersby that an exhumation was in order, *tout de suite.* Other devices involved megaphones and air tubes and lightbulbs—the only thing worse than waking up in a coffin underground being, presumably, waking up in a coffin *in the dark.*

Washington Bishop's big fear, worse even than being buried alive, was that of premature autopsy. He carried a note with him stating that under no circumstances should his "corpse" be subjected to autopsy, or packing in ice, or prodding with electrodes. However, stated Mrs. Bishop in her monograph, an autopsy is exactly what happened, not eight hours after his final mind-reading performance. It was carried out in secret—I couldn't tell by whom, but it appeared to be initiated by a cadre of jealous, less-successful mind readers—and it wasn't discovered until shortly before the funeral. A friend was helping the distraught Mrs. Bishop prepare her son for the service, combing his hair, when he dropped the comb. It disappeared. A little probing revealed that Bishop's head had been sliced open and his brain removed; the comb had fallen into the empty cavity. Well.

The brain was eventually retrieved and buried along with the rest of Bishop, but his mother wasn't satisfied. There was supposed to be *no* autopsy, yet one had occurred. Mrs. Bishop was convinced by this time that her son hadn't died at all, but been murdered by the crazed "vivisectionists." This turned out to be a tricky thing to prove in court. If he seemed dead, tested dead in every way, how could someone say he simply wasn't? How could Mrs. Bishop be so sure?

A mother simply knows, said Mrs. Bishop, claiming for herself the psychic powers that killed her son.

☙❧

On Saturday morning I got a phone call from Peter's sister. I was in my pajamas, fixing an English muffin that I planned to eat upstairs in my room, when Ron handed me the phone.

"Moira Morton," he said.

I set my muffin down and took the phone cautiously. It was several seconds before I could say Hello.

"Hi, I doubt you remember me. We met at the library last month. I hope you're not busy today, because I'd really like to meet you for lunch. Moira Morton, Peter's sister?"

"Right," I said. I recognized her voice: the woman at the library. "Of course. Today's actually kind of busy."

A long silence. Then: "All right, I understand that, but can you meet me for lunch? I can be there at noon."

"I don't know." *

She sighed impatiently. "I'm coming at noon, then. Meet me outside the library."

I hung up the phone and stood there for a moment, wondering what I had gotten myself into, and then the phone rang again. Again it was Moira.

"If you have anything of Peter's, books or anything, I'd like you to give them to me," she said.

"All right. I'll look around."

"Good," she said.

She showed up at exactly noon, in a black minivan that looked like a government vehicle. It rolled down the narrow leafy road toward the museum. I was watching for her out a side window. I'd put my hair up in the closest thing to a French twist I could manage, and I was wearing a pink cotton sweater and a pink-and-blue plaid skirt. I hadn't taken a shower, which I regretted now; my fingernails could have been cleaner and I suspected I smelled odd. Sometimes when I got very nervous I'd sweat, and I was nervous now. I sniffed myself and thought I could detect a faint oniony odor. I'd just have to keep my arms clamped to my sides all day. In my purse were two books of Peter's: a biography of Tycho Brahe and the plays of Aristophanes. I hadn't wanted to give them up, but I did want to make Moira happy.

I was already outside, locking the front door of the library, by the time the minivan had come to a complete stop. Moira got out and slammed the door. She was wearing a suit made out of a nubbly, woolly material, and her black hair was swept off her forehead and tied in a loose ponytail. She walked up to me with her arms folded, her eyes not quite meeting mine. They were hazel, darker than Peter's, and sat above Peter's small sharp cheekbones. The expression on her face was neither hostile nor friendly; she looked, as she had in the library, rather bored. I wondered what she did for a living. Something in an office, I'd have bet; something with numbers instead of people, a job that let you be as rude as you liked, as long as you dressed well.

"I suppose I should ask what this is all about," I said. I tried to say it lightly, with some irony, but it came out stiff and frightened.

"Lunch, as I believe I told you," said Moira. "Did you bring those things I asked for?"

I opened my purse and took out the books. "I brought these…some Greek plays, and a biography of Tycho—"

"Is that it? Two books? He didn't leave anything else?"

"No. Why…?"

She sighed impatiently. "Well, let me put them in the car."

I handed them over. As Moira tossed them into the back seat of the minivan, I wished I'd lied, said he'd left nothing. I wanted the books back. I had been planning to read them someday; I wanted to learn from them.

Moira returned, wiping the book dust from her hands onto her skirt. "So, where do people eat lunch in this place?"

"There's the cafeteria."

"Oh. I've been there. Well, all right."

We walked down the hill, Moira a step or two in front of me. The ground was frozen hard and tricky to navigate. I slipped and stumbled a little and broke out in a fresh sweat. The cafeteria, as it turned out, was closed.

"Shoot," I said. "This time of year you just can't predict."

"Where else, then?" Moira's nostrils had turned pink in the cold, just like Peter's used to.

"There's Ferd's. The, umm, Groc-n-Stop."

We tramped up the road. Ferd's was, as usual, cramped and steamy. There was no place to sit and not much to eat as takeout, but Moira seemed very interested in the freezer full of ice-cream novelties. She reached in and pulled out a shape unidentifiable beneath its thick coating of frost.

"I'll have one of these," she said.

"I guess I will, too."

We paid for our novelties and went outside, where I managed to scrape away enough frost to see that I had a Fudgie Cone. Moira had a raspberry Ripple Cup. I peeled the paper off and at tempted to take a bite, but it was rock-hard, and my teeth could find no purchase.

"Why don't you show me around," said Moira.

"All right. Sure."

We walked, gnawing at our ice cream, and I began to relax somewhat. I pointed out the sights: the Memory Garden, the trail to the Stump, the Silverwood Hotel, the Lecture Hall. For weeks now I'd felt as if Train Line were my enemy, as if the town itself—the trees and gravelly roads and houses—were pitted against me, but for now they seemed returned to their old selves: dull and benevolent.

"That's the Crystal Cave," I said, pointing to a large half-renovated house sided with plywood.

"Let's go in."

The bell tinkled as we entered, and I gave a little wave to Francesca, the large, very butch woman who owned the place. She nodded to me, somewhat coolly. The shop was filled with rocks—crystals and geodes, and jewelry made from them—and things like tiny bubbling electric fountains and wind chimes made of copper pipe. I remembered when the store opened: the summer Peter died. No one thought it would last, but it had expanded several times. There was room after room after room of glittering junk.

In the warm air my ice cream was acquiring some give, and I ate it quickly. I wadded up the wrapper and put it in my pocket.

Now that I had nothing to occupy my hands, I began to feel my creeping nervousness return. Moira was poring over a display of turquoise jewelry, huge gaudy pieces that reminded me of wads of chewing gum. Her Ripple Cup had disappeared, and her fingers were laced behind her back so tightly, I noticed, that her knuckles were white. This frightened me.

"Naomi," she said, not turning to look at me. "Tell me. How's Peter?"

I was not sure I heard her correctly. "Pardon?"

"I said I want you to tell me how Peter's doing. In the afterlife. That's your business, right? So. How is he?"

We were in the next room over from the cashier's desk, where Francesca was sitting and sipping from a mug. She could see us, and certainly hear us, too. I blushed.

"I'm sorry—I don't know. I can't—he hasn't contacted me. Not really."

"Hmm. I wonder why."

She still hadn't turned to look at me, and without seeing her face it was impossible for me to tell how sarcastically she meant this. I began edging away, looking intently at some tiny chunks of amethyst. A hand gripped my upper arm, hard. I jumped.

When I turned to her, Moira's face was not filled with rage, as I'd expected, but with sorrow. This was so shocking I couldn't breathe for a moment. Tears welled in her eyes, and her mouth twisted. Francesca was watching us with great interest.

"My mother killed herself," whispered Moira. "She was diabetic and stopped taking her insulin. My father died years ago. And now Peter's dead. Naomi…" The tears dripped down her face and her fingers were beginning to hurt my arm. "Naomi, I don't understand how this happened. Can't you tell me how this happened?"

A voice came booming over from the cashier's desk. "How can I help you girls?" it said.

"We're just leaving," I answered.

I managed to pull Moira, who was now crying hard and without restraint, through the door and into the street. After a couple of minutes I pulled a Kleenex from my pocket and offered it to her. She didn't take it, but instead wiped her eyes and nose with her fingers. "I was so mad at Peter," she said, sniffing and pulling herself together a little bit. "I was mad that he ignored my mother all those years. He was always like that. He never bought anyone presents, he didn't remember anyone's birthday. I never liked him. But I didn't think he was *dead*."

She broke down in tears again. I was shivering; my teeth chattered. The wind was cold and I hadn't dressed warmly enough. In fact, I'd dressed for an Easter brunch, right down to my white strappy shoes.

"Naomi," cried Moira, "what's going to happen to me?"

"I—I don't know."

"No! No, Naomi. I mean, I want to know what's going to happen to me. I want you to give me a reading."

"A reading?"

"Please. I want you to tell my fortune. Please."

Normally, the word *fortune* would have made me wince, but I did not correct her. "All right," I said.

I led her to the Violet Woods and down the path to Illumination Stump. Though regular message services hadn't been held here since September, the benches weren't yet packed away for winter. I gestured for Moira to sit down. Without the leaves and the flower boxes full of petunias, the clearing seemed empty and desolate, like a bombed-out church. I stood next to the stump and rubbed my forehead.

"All right, Moira, just—center yourself. Try to concentrate." She squeezed her eyes shut and folded her hands. "Okay," I said. "Okay."

I tried hard. I focused on everything I knew about her: her mother, her father, Peter. I thought of her face and how her mouth looked when she was crying. But for the longest time, I heard no voices, and no one came to me. I was about to give up and just say something, say anything, when I saw it: Moira dancing. It was summer, she was wearing a flowered dress, her hair was long and loose. It looked fake and unreal, at first, like a detergent commercial, but soon more details came clear. A picnic table; a band with fiddles and banjos; friends all around her.

Then another one. This time a group of children, staring up at the sky in wonderment as a flock of geese honked overhead.

Then Moira, older, on a Ferris wheel, gasping with pleasure, someone's arm around her.

There were a few others—a dog running through a hayfield, a baby swaddled in blankets, a table with pizza boxes on it—and by the time I finished, Moira was crying again, silently.

And she would have all these things. Perhaps not exactly as I saw them, but similar things, good, happy things that I would never have. She was beautiful, after all, and her life was not yet ruined. My heart ached with envy.

"You will be successful," I told her. She glanced up at me, her eyes teary. I wanted to make it up to her, to give her everything I had. "You'll—you'll never want for money or friends. You will live a long and comfortable life. You will be happy."

12

hands that melt like snow

I walked Moira back to her car. It had begun to snow as we emerged from the woods; by the time we got to the library it was coming down in giant wet flakes. It was like walking through curtains, long sheer curtains that parted in front of us and closed behind us, layers and layers of them. I could barely make out the shapes of the trees that lined the road or the houses behind them. Moira said nothing to me on the walk, and I couldn't even guess what she was thinking. I waited on the library steps as she got into her car, started it up, and drove slowly down the road and out of Train Line.

After that, it was quiet.

❧

Things stayed quiet for a couple of days. The police didn't show up again and Moira didn't call. One afternoon I sat on my bed and slid the ribbon off the Christmas box that held Peter's things. Outside, an inch or two of new snow was melting already, dripping off the eaves, though the sky was heavy as a wool blanket. I left my window open a crack so I could hear the outdoors: the dripping, the squirrels chattering in the trees, the rare car that crunched by.

The box was covered with dust and fuzz, so I wiped it clean with the corner of my bedspread before I opened it. I took the lid off and set it beside me. Each object was as familiar to me as if I'd looked at it every day; I'd inventoried these things in my mind so many times since the day he died. The gray wool socks smelled of the inside of the box—cardboard and dust. His glasses rested high on my nose, the earpiece digging into my ears. I took them off. The tube of foot cream was still soft and smelled medicinal. I rubbed a little into my hands. I touched the cards in his wallet and counted the money. The wristwatch fit my wrist, so I guessed at the time, set the hands, and wound it.

What I was doing, I realized, was trying to decide what to bring with me when I left.

I didn't really know I was thinking of leaving, until then. But after that I could think of nothing else. Of course I was leaving. What else? My bedroom suddenly looked different. It was no longer *my* bedroom; it was just a place I rented, and when I was gone someone else would live in it. I imagined that—my clothes gone from the closet, the pictures off the walls, no more books on the floor. I imagined days and nights when the room would stand empty, no one turning on a lamp or even opening the door. Until one day when someone would move in, and obliterate me.

The money, of course, and the watch. I wouldn't need to pack the watch because I could wear it. I could wear the socks, too, but I wasn't sure yet where I was going, and it might not be the kind of place I'd want to wear wool. And of all the objects, the watch had the most of Peter in it, except, perhaps, for the glasses. I remembered how it looked on Peter's wrist. He had lightly hairy arms and hair on the back of his hands, black silky stuff I liked to smooth with my fingers. His skin was a shade or two darker than mine, his hands were beautiful: long and square and delicate and strong.

I took the watch off and examined the back of it. Someone's initials were etched there—*JCM*—and a date, *12-25-35*. Peter's grandfather, I supposed. In the fine crevices made by the etching was a tiny amount of dark dirt. I scraped a bit out with my fingernail and put it on my tongue. It had no taste at all.

In the end I brought everything: the watch, the money, the foot cream, even the terrible jar of pennies, which had rolled under the bed that day but somehow didn't break. I couldn't bear to part with any of it.

⚮

My mother invited me to dinner. She left a message on the machine; I played it in the empty living room. Ron was out, Jenny upstairs. My mother's voice sounded unusually formal, as if she and I were only acquaintances, but friendly ones. On the way over I stopped at the Groc-n-Stop and bought a jelly roll for dessert. Ferd did not look me in the eye when he handed me my change, and I thought, *This is the last time in my entire life that I will shop here.*

She had set the table with candles and a vase of dried flowers. I was struck with the sudden conviction that she had meant to call someone else, Troy probably, and had called my number by mistake. "Why...candles?" I asked her, standing in the kitchen with my jelly roll. She wore a loose green dress made out of something like furniture upholstery, and her face was unhappy.

"Oh," she said, looking at the table. "I wanted it to be nice for you."

She'd made fried chicken, my favorite thing, and there were the peas in cream sauce you can get frozen, another of my favorites, and red wine in tall tumblers. I put my jelly roll on the counter and hung my coat in the closet. When I put my hands to my head to feel my hair, I found it was hanging in thick tangles that I could not rectify with my fingers. I patted it down as well as I could.

"One light, one dark?" she asked as I sat down, with her tongs in the colander of chicken parts.

I nodded. We ate.

I'd never eaten fried chicken by candlelight before, nor washed it down with so much wine, and I was amazed that the food found its way down my throat, past the constriction that had formed there. The meal was so beautiful and good that I kept eating long after my mother had stopped. She watched me. When I finally looked up at her, she covered her mouth with her hands.

"What's wrong?" I asked.

"Nothing," she said, but put her hands down, and then went on. "I was just thinking about when you were a baby. It was so hard, you know. I used to wake up in the night with horrible thoughts. There was one—it obsessed me for months—I thought, what if someone broke in and murdered all of us except you? We'd be lying there dead and you'd be alone in your crib for God knows how long, because no one would bother to come check on us…for a week or two, possibly."

"It never happened, Mama."

"Yes. But what if it *had*? I remember hoping that if a murderer did come in, he'd kill you, too, so you wouldn't be alone all that time, waiting for us to come and get you. I'd picture you holding on to the crib bars and crying, then giving up on crying and just lying there, and how quiet the house would be. I couldn't get it out of my head. I couldn't stand it." Her face had collapsed, as if what had held it together had at long last given way. "Love like that is horrifying."

I put my fork down. "Mama…"

"I still love you that way. That's what I'm saying. I—I never minded the thought of dying until I had you. Now I'm terrified…"

Why does anyone have children? Mothers and daughters are put on Earth to tear each other's hearts out.

"Mama. Why are you telling me this?"

Her poor exhausted face. "I wanted to tell you that I read those journals."

I knocked my plate to the floor. It bounced on the linoleum and chicken bones scattered in all directions. The cats came running.

"Don't," said my mother. "Don't. Please. It's all right."

"I asked you not to read them."

"I know. I'm sorry—I know. I shouldn't have. But I couldn't stand not knowing, Naomi. And I still don't. But—"

"But what, Mama?"

"But I heard—someone told me the police are getting a search warrant. Your house or mine, both. I don't know."

"Mama, what did you do with them? Where are they?"

"Don't worry about them. I got rid of them. I—I burned them."

"I don't believe you," I said.

"Naomi, I just want this to be *over*..."

"You gave them to Officer Peterson, didn't you?"

"They said they'd get a search warrant—that if I had anything, I should just give it to them up front. Naomi—I want them to think we're cooperating with them—"

"You just want everyone to like you! You don't care about anything else. You just want your stupid radio show back."

"That's not what I want! That's not—I just can't stand it. I want it to stop."

"You think I did it," I said. I picked up my knife and jabbed it hard into the table.

"Did what?" she cried. "What did you do, Naomi?"

I couldn't answer her. I wanted to come up with a lie, a perfect lie, but she would know.

She put her hands on her head, weaving her fingers into her hair, as if she was keeping her skull from flying apart. She groaned.

"Mama," I said, unable to look her in the eye. Instead I looked at my hands, my fat, chapped, nail-bitten hands. "Would you hate me if you knew I did it?"

"Tell me how it happened," she said.

So I told her, truthfully. Before I was finished she was sobbing.

"Thank you for telling me," she said, but then she began to shriek.

I led her upstairs. I put my arm around her and led her to her bedroom, to her bed, and helped her down and took off her shoes. She lay there, crying brokenly, and I lay down beside her. I took her fingers and kissed them. "Shh," I said. "Shh, shh." She put her arm around me and pulled me close. "Oh, Naomi," she whispered. "Oh, my love. Please, let's go back home." I kissed her wet face. She put my fingers in her mouth.

Eventually she fell asleep, and after a longer time I did, too. I had strange, brief dreams of large things bearing down on me. When I woke up I didn't know what time it was and I was freezing cold. I got up in the dark and found a blanket in the closet, then lay down again, wrapping it around us.

"Mmm, Franklin," murmured my mother, snuggling close. Franklin was my father's name.

⌘

It was barely light when I got up. My mother was asleep, snoring lightly, her hairdo crushed into her pillow. I pulled the blanket up over her shoulder and went downstairs. The kitchen table, I noticed, was still covered with our dinner dishes, the candles had burned themselves down to nothing, and my jelly roll waited, uncut, on the counter. Maybe she'd eat some for breakfast, I thought. I hoped she would.

Train Line was cold and silent, like an abandoned space station. I'd been here twenty years and hadn't made a mark—hadn't planted a tree, painted a house, built a gazebo. Train Line would not miss me. Hundreds, thousands of people had come through Train Line and gone again, some had even lived out their entire lives here, and Train Line mourned none of them. Any affection I'd felt for this town was misplaced. A town is a heartless thing, unfaithful and forgetful. It will never love you back.

⌘

I spent the day getting ready. First I called information and got the number for my uncle Geoffrey, in New Orleans. There were two Geoffrey Ashes and I called both. The first number was out of order. The second was my uncle. I knew it before he finished saying, "Hello?"

"Hello!" I said, working hard to keep the tension out of my voice. "Bet you don't remember me!" And I told him who I was.

His voice warmed up instantly. "Why, hello there! What a... what a treat to hear from you! How are you? How's Sissy?"

I told him how wonderful we were, how wonderful everything was. And I told him how I was thinking of relocating to the New Orleans area, how I wanted to continue my job search on site, and did he have any recommendations for places to stay?

"Oh, my goodness, you'll stay here, of course! My daughters have moved out, I'm rattling around in all this empty space... what field did you say you were in?"

"Um, communications," I said. "But I'm thinking of a change, so I'm flexible."

"Why, this is just marvelous!" He sounded genuinely thrilled. "I haven't heard from your mother in, gosh, ten years, probably. Is she still in the spiritual business?"

We chatted for a little while, and when I hung up I felt as if I'd set something large and unstoppable in motion. It occurred to me that Uncle Geoffrey, excited by my phone call, might call my mother. I would have to leave soon, before she knew what I was doing.

Ron had a road atlas. I slid it out of the bookshelf, took it to my room, and spent a couple of hours devising a route south and copying it onto several sheets of paper, which I stapled together. I packed Peter's things, and some clothes and a few books and some food I could eat on the road: apples and salami and cheese and cookies. I spent the rest of the day fooling around. I read magazines and made popcorn and tried to nap. Ron asked me if I was sick.

"Maybe I am," I said, rubbing my forehead. "There's not much to do at the library, actually."

"Ah," he said, nodding, but the look on his face was unconvinced.

Night fell. I thought obsessively of travel: speeding down dark highways, sleeping in locked motel rooms. It seemed ridiculous that I hadn't gone months ago. I was meant to travel, I knew it. Finally, at nine o'clock, I gathered my things.

I was standing in the living room with the lights off, my duffel bag over my shoulder, when Jenny appeared on the stairway. She hadn't been feeling very well lately and had spent much of the last few days in bed. I'd almost forgotten she lived here.

"Are you going somewhere?" she asked, her voice wavering. There was just enough light coming from the streetlight outside to make her visible. She was wearing a long white nightgown and no robe. Her reddish hair fell across her face.

"Oh," I said. "I guess I am."

"Where're you going?" She sat down on the step, pulling her nightgown over her feet.

"On a trip. I'll be gone a while, I think."

She nodded. "Is it because of the investigation?"

"I don't really want to talk about that."

She nodded again, sighing. "I hope everything works out for you."

"Thanks. And for you, too."

I knew I should leave soon, but it was suddenly very hard. Jenny leaned her head against a banister pole. She'd lost weight. She'd never replaced Snippy. I'd meant to spend more time with her, get to know her better. Suddenly I wished I could go back and do it again.

"Good-bye Naomi. I'm sorry we didn't become better friends."

"I am too. Good night, Jenny."

"Good night, good night, good night," she said, turning and going back to her room.

⚬⚬⚬

I crept out the back door and around the house behind ours, then found myself on Davis Street. I took the long way to my mother's house, avoiding the bright lights. It was drizzling unpleasantly. Invisible puddles covered the road, and by the time I got there my feet were soaked. I hid my bag behind her car, then knocked on the back door. After several minutes, she answered it.

"Naomi!" She seemed shocked. Uncle Geoffrey probably hadn't called her, then. She was dressed up. I wondered if she had guests.

"Can I borrow your car, Mama? I'm sorry to bother you so late. I need to run to Wallamee for some things…"

"Things?" She looked confused and frightened. "What do you need? Naomi, what is this all about?"

"Nothing, Mama!" I forced a smile. "I need some…female things. The Groc-n-Stop is closed."

"Oh." Her face softened. "All right. Hold on. I have company…" She didn't ask me in, so I stayed on the steps, drizzle filling my hair. She returned with the key.

"Here you are. Drive carefully, it's slick out there." I took the key from her warm hand.

"Thank you. Mama, I…"

"Go on. I have company."

I wanted to cry.

"Naomi? Are you sure you want to…?"

I shook my head. "Bye, Mama," I whispered.

She stood back and let me go.

I got into the Oldsmobile and put my seat belt on. Then I remembered my duffel bag, so I got back out, hefted the bag onto the passenger seat, and tried again. My mother, I noticed, was watching from her window. I didn't wave. I took Peter's money out of the bag, put half of it in my pocket and the rest in the glove compartment, then started the car. Like a pirate ship with its sails down I slipped through Train Line, navigating rocky shoals and inlets until I was on the open road, free.

Wallamee was nearly empty, and the traffic lights through the middle of town had switched to blinking yellow caution lights. I didn't need to stop or even slow down as I headed for the interstate. But as I neared the street that Dave the Alien lived on I felt a powerful urge to visit him and say good-bye. He was probably at work, I thought. A video store would be open late. But I wanted to see him. It would be a pity to leave him without a word or an apology.

Both floors of the house were dark. I went inside and up the unlit stairway, anyway, and knocked on his door. There was no answer so I knocked again, hard.

"Minute," came a muffled voice, far away.

The door opened. Dave had pale-blue striped pajamas on and his face was sleepy. Still, he looked very surprised to see me.

"Are you all right, Naomi?"

I noticed that I'd been crying. I wiped my eyes with my hands. "Yes, I'm fine. I'm sorry to show up like this. It's just that I'm leaving on a trip and I wanted to say good-bye first."

"Come in. Can I get you something?"

I shook my head.

He turned on the overhead kitchen light and we both blinked in the glare. "Have a seat," said Dave. "Where are you going?"

"I can't say. But I wanted to talk to you."

"All right." He pulled his chair close to the table and looked at me, expectant. His long face was pale, his freckles dark, his upper lip in need of a shave. Dave was a good person. He was the kind of man who'd get married young, have children, and stay married until the very end; a man with reasonable expectations and a kind heart.

"I'm sorry about Halloween," I said miserably.

He laughed. "Oh, no. Don't be. I had a good time."

"You did?"

"A very good time."

"Well, I'm glad." I blew my nose. He patted my hand.

"I guess you didn't, though, huh?" he asked.

"I did. If it didn't look that way it's because I've been preoccupied lately."

"I know."

I looked at him. Of course he knew. Dave was as plugged into the Train Line gossip as anyone. "Is that why you haven't called?" I asked quietly.

"No. That's not why. You didn't want me to call again, Naomi."

He was right. Poor Dave. "You're an excellent reader, Dave. You should be a medium."

"You think?" He smiled. "But I'm not mysterious enough. Every thought I have might as well be written in lights across my forehead. I'm Mr. Transparent."

"Mr. Transparent. Like a sideshow act."

"Mr. Transparent and his lovely wife, Mother Ash! This is your last chance, ladies and germs, to see the world-famous couple before they leave on their tour of Europe, China, and the Sandwich Islands! Step right up and take a gander!"

I laughed. But in saying it he'd made it true for a moment, and I imagined the dinky little trailer we'd live in, and the smell of the sideshow tent, and our friends the Rubber Man and the Nail-Eating Woman. We'd have a child with its own remarkable talent, utterly unlike ours: it would be a snake charmer, maybe, or a strong man.

"I'd enjoy that," I said, and meant it.

"Me, too."

I put my hands on the Formica tabletop. "I can't really stay. I just wanted to say good-bye." I hoped he'd try to talk me out of going for a little while, but he didn't.

"Okay," he said, standing up. "Do you need anything? Are you going a long way?"

"Pretty long. But I don't need anything, I don't think."

He looked around his kitchen, then opened a cupboard and took out a box of Fig Newtons. It was the only thing on the shelf. "Here. A meager offering. But it's all I can do with the short notice."

I accepted them. "Thanks. You're very generous."

"Ha. Well, good-bye, Mother Ash." He walked me to the door.

"Good-bye, David." I stepped out into the hallway and turned to look at him one more time. He wasn't very handsome, but suddenly I wished we'd had that child together, that snake-charmer child.

"Godspeed," said Dave.

I went halfway down the stairs and waved. He watched until I was gone.

∾×∾

I drove all night. I had highlighted my makeshift map in yellow marker and circled exits and rest stops in red. I kept it folded open on the seat next to me and referred to it now and then with the flashlight my mother always kept in her car. Though it was a pitch-black and moonless night, and the only lights shone from other cars and farms far from the highway, I had a sense of the landscape changing around me. Wallamee County was a series of flat valleys and low hills, but as I descended toward Pennsylvania, the valleys became narrower and the hills higher. They rose up invisibly around me. The air that came through the vent smelled different, too. More like cows and more wet.

Time went faster than I thought it would. I'd imagined that minutes would creep by while I drove and that the miles would slip beneath my tires as slowly as clock hands. But that didn't happen. When I first thought to look at Peter's watch—holding it by the window and waiting to pass under a light—three hours had gone by and I was well into Pennsylvania. I wasn't tired at all, which surprised me. I never stayed up this late.

The sky lightened. This was another surprising thing; how early I could tell the sun was rising. By three o'clock in the morning, the sky to the east had begun to look paler. It was as if a huge city squatted behind the hills, lighting up the night sky with its spotlights and billboards and marquees. But according to my map there was nothing back there except for some tiny towns and vast areas of emptiness.

By morning I was in West Virginia, and the highway began twisting and curling and heaving up and down over hills. All night I'd been thinking, half-subconsciously, about astral bodies. There is a theory among spiritualists—not a well-favored theory, anymore—that there was an "etheric counterpart" to the physical human body. This astral body could leave the physical one and travel around; it could visit dying relatives and come back with news of their demise, it could sit in on meetings when the physical person was sick in bed. Spiritualist scientists had done experiments on it. One I read about, back in the twenties, claimed that the astral body weighed something like two and a half ounces and that it was terribly, terribly thin: almost as thin as a shadow. Ordinarily the astral body never completely separated itself from the physical one. It was attached by a kind of cord, the astral or silver cord, which, like a piece of chewing gum, got thinner and thinner the farther the astral body traveled. And if the astral body made its escape through a window, and someone subsequently slammed that window, there'd be trouble. At best the astral cord would be damaged; at worst, severed. Without its astral body, a human would eventually wither and die.

All night I pictured myself at home, in bed, while my astral self drove the Oldsmobile down toward Louisiana. My silver cord must have been as fine as spider thread by this time; subatomically thin, perhaps. I imagined it fluttering through the gap between the car window and the frame, battered by semis and pickup trucks, and now, as the road curved and turned back on itself, winding around the body of the car like cobwebs. Sooner or later it would break. Back in bed, I'd feel a sharp but tiny tug, like someone plucking a hair from the middle of my chest, and then an emptiness. Maybe the colors of my room would seem to fade. Then I'd get colder and colder and weaker and weaker until I couldn't move at all. But the car would keep driving.

At noon I stopped somewhere in West Virginia, my whole body humming with exhaustion and the vibration of the car engine. It was a beautiful day. The sunlight shone cleanly through bare trees. I bought gas and a bottle of pop at a Stop-n-Save, then drove across the highway to a small motel.

There were motels like this one in Wallamee—pretty yellow clapboard, green trim, window boxes and brightly painted porch chairs—but most of them had been converted to retirement homes or Christian schools when the interstate bypassed the town. This one looked as if it had drawn a small but steady stream of customers every night for thirty years. There was a fenced pool in front. Though it was too late in the year to swim, no one had bothered to cover or drain it. Its blue water winked and trembled.

The girl behind the front desk told me that check-in time was two o'clock. The maids needed time to clean the rooms, she said, keeping an eye on the television set in the corner of the lobby. The girl was young enough to be in school, I was sure. I tried to remember what day of the week it was but couldn't.

"Well, I'm here now," I said. "What do you think I should do?"

"You could keep going, though there's not much down that way for a while. Or you could go to an early matinee."

So I left the car at the motel and walked toward town. The movie theater was a hexaplex, a large flat brown building in the middle of a parking lot, with a light-up sign of abbreviated movie titles, THE CLM was one, BLE LSITN another. I imagined years of windy nights in this West Virginia town, entire alphabets set to flight.

The movie I chose turned out to be an urban-office thriller. I ate some of my smuggled-in Fig Newtons and watched a copy machine plunge from the top of a high-rise building before I fell asleep, my head tilted over the back of my seat. I dreamed about Vivian. Vivian in an Easter dress, Vivian winning a trophy for something, Vivian running across a wide lawn toward me and throwing her arms around my neck. When I woke up the lights had come back on, and someone was shaking my shoulder.

"Ma'am?" said a girl's voice. "Ma'am?" I jumped and turned to her. She looked just like the motel clerk girl, only with a white shirt and a black bow tie and her hair up in a top knot. She was as startled as I was, her blue eyes wide and rimmed with mascara. "Ma'am," she said again. "The movie's over."

༄

In my motel room I slept deeply and dreamlessly, sprawled across the bedspread in my clothes and shoes. I woke up briefly at sunset and drank a glass of tap water. Outside, a family with arms loaded down with fast-food bags passed my window, and the sky beyond the hills was dark orange. I thought about getting something hot to eat: a box of chicken, maybe, or a fat hamburger and onion rings. I was dizzy with hunger, but even more tired, so I lay down on the bed again and pulled the bedspread over my shoulder and watched orange shadows move across the bumpy plaster ceiling until I fell asleep.

It was one in the morning when I got up, suddenly jittery with the idea that I had to get driving again. I took a shower and changed my clothes and ate a piece of cheese from a plastic Baggie I'd brought. The motel office was closed, so I slid the key through the mail slot in the door. I heard it clatter onto the rug.

Night took me across Kentucky and part of Tennessee. I went through a city by accident, but missed the name of it, since I was paying attention only to the highway number signs. I saw a giant spinning cow on a pole, billboards for suicide hotlines, a double semi painted with the name of someone who must have been a famous country musician: the letters were spelled out in airbrushed stars and lassoes. Bank signs blinked the time and temperature: 50°, 2:15.

I slept through another day in a motel room somewhere in Tennessee, waking up to eat an egg salad sandwich I'd bought at a gas station. It tasted like a mouthful of vinegar.

⌒⌒

It was night again, my third night of driving, when I came to a roadblock. I was in the middle of Mississippi, though I'd noticed nothing about the state except for a bad smell—like backed-up sewers. Now and then, far from the highway, there'd be a huge complex of brightly lit smokestacks. This is where the smell came from—sugar factories, maybe. I had driven myself numb and could think of nothing but staying in my lane, a safe distance from the car ahead of me, but now all the other cars had disappeared, and I was alone on the highway.

A cop with a glowing orange stick was standing in the middle of the road, waving his arms. Behind him the road curved, and I couldn't see what was back there, just some flashing lights—more cop cars, it looked like. I remembered, horrified: *I don't have a driver's license.* Perhaps it wasn't too late to turn around. Perhaps I could just run him over. Before I had a chance to do either of these things, I was putting on the brakes and the cop was walking toward me. I took a breath and opened the window.

"Howdy, ma'am. How are you this evening?" He was black and seemed very tall.

"I'm fine, thanks. How are you?"

"Not bad, considering. We got a real mess up there. Nasty accident. They got to clean up the road before I can let you through."

"I see."

The cop looked over at the passenger seat, at the map and the bags of food.

"Traveling, huh?"

"Mmm-hmm."

"All the way from New York."

"Yep."

"Well, well. You sure you're all right, ma'am?"

"I'm tired," I said, and it was true.

"Well, I won't keep you much longer. There's a coffee and doughnuts place not too far up the road. You might want to take a break."

"Thank you. Maybe I will."

The cop stood up and his walkie-talkie crackled on.

"All right," he said to me after a minute or two. "You can proceed."

I drove on, relieved. Just around the bend in the road there was a semi parked crookedly on the shoulder, its back doors flung wide open. People were milling around, not terribly urgently, and more police were arriving as I neared the scene. Something had spilled all over the road. It was dark and wet and had an odd but familiar smell, which I couldn't place. I drove through it cautiously, trying to keep from spraying whatever it was over the people along the road. Besides the semi, there were two other cars involved. One was upside down, sitting on its flattened roof, and the other was smashed from the front. This car was piled high with the dark wet stuff. A person was lying on the shoulder of the highway, blue jeans bloodied, his arms reaching up his head.

And then I was past it. Police lights flashed in my rearview mirror, but soon they were gone too. A few miles later an ambulance screamed by.

Dog food, I thought. The semi had been full of wet dog food. Though I had never owned a dog myself, I recognized the smell—like a dog's mouth.

Death is a horror.

❦

I drove for an hour or two more. It was becoming clear that though I'd slept all day, it wasn't enough. I daydreamed about my bedroom in Train Line on summer nights: the cool and shady quiet, the sound of neighbors' wind chimes, the smell of the lake. My longing for it felt like starvation. I would go back, wouldn't I? Any life besides the one inside this big black car was impossible to imagine.

Signs for an exit loomed up ahead. Nothing would be open, I thought; there were no big towns around here. The landscape was barren and unlit, with no hills. But I pulled off, anyway, thinking I could find a parking lot to sleep in.

But there was something open: a twenty-four-hour gas station and a doughnut shop. They were lit up like a UFO landing pad. Nothing on my trip had looked so welcoming. I pulled the Oldsmobile down the exit ramp and across the parking lot, then stopped under the wide green awning to fill my tank. There was no one else around, except for the shape of the person behind the cash register inside. It reminded me of my time at the Ha-Ha, and of being held up, and I wondered if the cashier wondered, even briefly, if I might be the one who'd do it.

I didn't. I wiped my hands on a stiff blue paper towel and went inside to pay. It was cool in there and smelled of fried things, chicken and corn dogs and doughnuts from the adjoining shop, and quiet music came from over the speakers. The cashier was a young boy with a pink face. He might have been sleeping, head on the checkout counter, until I showed up.

"Is the doughnut shop open?" I asked, handing over the money.

"Yup," he said. "Don't never close. Can't even lock the door— don't need to, you know, if you don't never close."

So I took my change and went outside to move the car, then came back to the doughnut shop.

The same bland music played in here, but even more quietly, and the smell of doughnuts was overwhelming: sweet and greasy and warm. The woman behind the counter asked if she could help me.

I looked over the racks and told her I'd like a custard-filled one with chocolate on it and a cup of coffee.

She put my doughnut on a small china plate, filled a cup with coffee, and handed them to me. I carried them carefully to a small table next to the windows, where I could watch people fill up their tanks while I ate. The table was shiny yellow Formica, and the chairs were hard orange plastic with metal legs. Outside, on the highway, headlights came and went.

I had taken a bite of my doughnut and was staring out the window when I saw, out of the corner of my eye, the shape of someone coming toward me. I turned to look. It was a man in a blue shirt and khaki pants, carrying his own doughnut and coffee and smiling widely.

"May I sit with you?" he asked.

I nodded.

It was Peter.

He didn't look any different. His hair was shiny and black, his sleeves were rolled up, his lashes were long behind his glasses. But at the same time he did not look twenty-two. He looked older, he looked my age, but he looked the same. This is the only thing that was odd.

He bit into his doughnut and continued smiling while he chewed. It was filled with lemon creme. Yellow stuff oozed onto the plate and powdered sugar clung to his lips.

I didn't know what to say. I sipped my coffee and took quick glances at him.

"I missed you, Naomi," said Peter.

My heart crumpled. I did not know what to think: whether I'd lost my mind, whether I was dreaming, or whether this was as real as anything could be. I wanted it to be real. I longed for it.

"Peter..."

He put his finger over his mouth. "Shh. You don't have to say anything."

So I watched him eat. He seemed to enjoy his doughnut a great deal. He chewed it slowly, licked his lips, and put it down between bites to drink his coffee. Peter would sometimes look like this, I remembered, when things had worked out better than we had planned, when circumstances had come together in a certain, perfect way. One Sunday morning the summer we met, we went on a picnic and found the perfect spot for it under a tree, and the weather was just warm enough, and he had the Sunday paper to read. I remembered there was a breeze and the ripples in the lake flashed silver. That time he'd smiled just like this: half to himself, half to let me know how happy he was.

But when he finished his doughnut, his smile faded. In the fluorescent light his skin was sallow and pale.

"Why did you do it, Naomi?"

I couldn't answer at first. When I tried to speak, my voice felt choked.

"I didn't..."

"I know," he said bitterly. "You didn't mean it. Why should I care about that?"

He wasn't wearing his watch. I was. I noticed the pale ring of flesh around his wrist and tried to push my sleeve down to cover the watch, but he saw it anyway and shrugged. Then he rubbed his hands down over his ribs, his stomach. His eyes filled with tears.

"I wanted to grow old," he said. "I wanted to grow old and fat!"

I cried out and reached for him. I grabbed his wrist and shoulder and pulled myself over the table toward him. He was as solid as anything, his skin was warm, and when I pushed my face into the place between his throat and his shirt collar I could feel the rough, shaved skin of his neck and I smelled him. He smelled like he always did, but I had forgotten that smell. It was sweet and peppery and like ironed clothes. With my fingers I felt the buttons on his shirt, opened one and slipped my hand inside. There was hair on his chest. It was his chest. I remembered the pattern of hair and how silky it was around his nipples. My hand came to life, feeling it. I wanted him, I wanted his body.

Abruptly he pushed me back into my seat. Tears pooled behind his glasses and ran down his face. "I *can't*," he said. He stood up and carried his empty doughnut plate and coffee cup to the front counter.

"Thank you," he told the woman, who nodded.

He headed for the men's room, wiping his face with the back of his hand. I got up and followed. When the door swung shut behind him I tried to open it and go in, but it only moved a few inches. Peter was standing on the other side, holding it shut. I tried throwing myself against the door, shoulder first, and I tried bracing my feet on the hard tile floor and pushing steadily. Nothing worked.

"Peter!" I whispered through the door. "Please, what's it like? Are you lonely? Is your family there? Please—tell me—"

I shoved and struggled with the door for what seemed like forever, but Peter was stronger.

Finally I gave up. I went back to my seat and finished my doughnut. Crumbs were scattered across Peter's side of the table. My coffee was cool. I drank it anyway.

When I went back to check the men's room, it was empty. There was a dirty urinal with a pink cake of something like soap in the bowl and one stall. Peter wasn't in it.

Back out in the parking lot, a wind had picked up. It was the kind of wind that blows just before dawn, a warm wind that smelled of car exhaust and fields and water. I took deep breaths of it and shook my hair out, walking back to my car.

If he had lived, I would have stopped loving him. I was so sorry.

13

after life

In the Train Line Spiritualist Museum there was a collection of
photographs that each showed a medium materializing a spirit.
I spent part of one summer cataloging them and filing the ones
not chosen for display. They were some of the strangest and most
grotesque pictures I'd ever seen. In one, a woman in a Victorian
dress lay back in her chair, arms slack at her sides, while a lumpy
white substance poured from the side of her mouth. Another
showed a woman with something stringy and gray spouting
from her ear. Sometimes the ectoplasm took the shape of wads
of fabric that draped itself around the medium's body. This substance—which was usually wet or sticky or gelatinous, but sometimes hard and dry—was gradually supposed to resolve itself
into a more human shape, and the result would be a perfectly
formed spirit, solid enough to slap your face. In a few of the photographs, you could even see the beginnings of a foot or face or
hand floating in midair. The theory was that a spirit merely borrowed some living material from the medium for a short time;
mediums claimed that the process of materialization was much
like that of giving birth. In fact, the semiconscious medium
would sometimes shout and groan, as if experiencing labor pains.
Materializing séances were a big fad for a while, though modern mediums consider them a bit over the top. Still, as I hurtled
down the highway that night, I couldn't help but wonder if I had
materialized Peter.

I didn't know how I could have. According to everything I'd
read, ectoplasm is incompatible with light, and the kind of fluorescent glare that illuminated the doughnut shop would surely

have caused the stuff to snap like a rubber band back into my body. But who knew anymore? The world was inexplicable, full of strange machinery. Perhaps I had done it! And perhaps I could do it again. Hope clutched at me with her wet and desperate hands.

⚬⚬⚬

Before I got to New Orleans, I passed through miles of Mississippi and Louisiana pine woods. The interstate was bounded on either side by trees as thick and even as hedges, and the land rolled gently up and down. Above, in the lightening sky, the stars winked out.

Then trees gave way to swamp, and the highway, supported high above the water by concrete pillars, smoothed out. From the car I could see the tops of dead trees, large birds flying, and once in a while, someone's house. A cold, skunky swamp smell blew in the car window when I opened it. The air was heavier here, and wetter. By the time I reached the city it was morning for real—rush hour—but it looked like dusk. Taillights glowed in the murky light that hung over the river. Now that I was here, I didn't know what to do. It was too early to show up at Uncle Geoffrey's, and anyway, once I got *there* what would I do?

So I drove around. Cars honked at me for going too slowly, and I found myself getting shunted into the same one-way streets over and over. It wasn't the city I remembered, but then, I didn't expect that city. My memories were made of sidewalks and backyards and trips to the grocery store. Certain vistas were as familiar to me as if I'd seen them every day of my life—looking up Saint Charles toward the middle of town, or down Canal Street toward the river—but there were big glassy buildings where I didn't think they belonged at all, and T-shirt shops on every corner. Some of them were already opened for the day. Maybe, I thought, they never closed. The air had a smoky, garlicky odor, like restaurants. It made me think of falling asleep in the backseat of the car when I was a little girl, coming home from somewhere, and waking up in the dark when the car stopped.

Eventually, unnerved by traffic, I made my way toward the Garden District, where Uncle Geoffrey and his family lived. I found the house without much trouble—three stories, surrounded by trees and banana plants—but I didn't stop. Instead I went to a park a few blocks away, got out of my car, and sat on a bench, eating the last of the food I'd packed myself so long ago. The sun came out and burned off the mist.

I was sitting there, squinting in the light and chewing the stale end of a peanut butter sandwich, when a person dressed all in green shambled up to me. I thought at first he was going to ask me for directions—that was the only reason a stranger would ever approach you at home. He had a big stick in his hand and a wadded-up bunch of tarpaulin on his back. His face was dark with dirt.

"Pardon me, ma'am," he said, giving me a crooked bow. He didn't sound like he was from New Orleans. He didn't sound Southern at all—then again, neither did my mother. "But I was wondering if by chance you had some change you could spare for a hot meal."

"Actually, I don't," I said. That was true; I'd left my money in the car, which suddenly seemed like a bad place for it. "Sorry."

"Not even just a *little* handful of change for a hungry man, a lovely young lady such as yourself?"

"I'm sorry," I said again. I took the last sandwich out of its plastic sack. "But you can have this, if you want."

He snatched it out of my hand and stormed off. I watched as, several yards away, he opened the sandwich up, sniffed at the contents, and then tossed the pieces of bread into a bush, grumbling.

When he was out of sight I went over to the bush and rescued my sandwich. I pressed it back together again and stuffed it into the sack. I wasn't going to eat it, after that. But I couldn't stand to leave it there.

Before I went to Uncle Geoffrey's, I walked around the neighborhood. *I'm home,* I whispered to myself. I wanted to believe it. And certain things swelled my heart: passing a small house shaped like the First Bank of Wallamee but painted pink and yellow, I smelled a sweet olive tree. The scent was like peaches, but better; it was a golden color exploding in my head. My knees wobbled and I thought I'd cry. What did it remind me of? I didn't know. Something. I put my hand on a wooden fence post to steady myself.

But so much else was strange. The cars parked along the curb were small and expensive and clean; none were coated with the sticky dirt that covered cars in Train Line from October to May. The people I passed were tanned and dressed lightly. There was no one as pale as I must have been. I turned my face to the hazy sun, feeling my skin drink it in. No one said hello, either, or made eye contact. A woman in heels clicked by, walking a cat on a leash.

By the time I got to my uncle's house, dragging my duffel bag, I was ready to go home. Probably I was just tired. Everything I'd seen in the last few days weighed on me. I thought of my mother, carless and lonely in her little cottage, and ached to see her. The front door of my uncle's house loomed like a wall. On the other side would be more unfamiliarity: people I didn't know wanting things from me, odd food.

Uncle Geoffrey opened the door before I'd gotten up the nerve to ring the bell. He must have seen me coming up the front walk. He was short, with very little hair and my mother's beak-like nose. He wore corduroy pants and a pair of furry slippers.

"Naomi!" he said, taking me into his arms.

I stiffened automatically, then put my free arm around him. He was fat and soft, like a little man made of bread dough, and slightly sweaty.

"So good to see you again, Naomi," he said over my shoulder. He sounded like he meant it. Then he pulled away, smiled, and took my duffel bag. "What a drive! Let me show you your room. Maybe you'll want to take a shower? Then I'll make you breakfast." He trotted on ahead, turning and grinning at me.

I followed him.

The house was beautiful. The rooms were sparsely furnished, big and plain and full of light. What furniture there was looked ancient and dark, like monuments. My room had violet walls and a bare wood floor. There was jar of fresh hyacinths on the windowsill.

"This was Imogen's room, until she got married. That was a while ago. She lives in Denver now. You remember her, don't you?"

I did but only vaguely. She was a tall girl with straight black hair, a few years older than me. My one memory involved a family picnic, in honor of my grandfather's birthday, I think. Imogen sat by a fence, tugging moodily at weeds, and she wouldn't give me the time of day. But I nodded for Uncle Geoffrey and managed a small smile.

"It's a nice room," I said.

"That girl loved purple. Her mother and I made her settle for lavender, but she'd have had it the most gaudy Mardi Gras shade of purple you'd ever seen." He took my hand in his and patted it. "Now, look. I'm semiretired now, and only go into my office a couple days a week. You'll see me at home a lot. But you think of this as your house as much as mine, all right?" He looked me in the eyes intently.

"What about Aunt...?" For the life of me I couldn't remember her name.

"Francie. Oh. Well. We've been divorced since Isabel was out of high school."

"I'm sorry."

"Oh," he said again, shrugging, and then he smiled. "Bathroom's across the hall there. You'll have it to yourself. Men's room's over yonder." He let go of my hand and gave me a quick salute. "Find me when you're hungry."

"Thank you," I said, somewhat stunned. I'd expected to have to answer all kinds of polite questions. But Uncle Geoffrey just trotted back downstairs, whistling.

I went into the room and shut the door. My grubby Adidas bag, sitting on Imogen's violet bedspread, looked like someone had drowned a litter of puppies in it. I picked it up and slid it under the bed. Cars rumbled by outside, but up here it was quiet. I moved the hyacinths to the bedside table, pushed up the screen, and leaned out the window.

Down below, people walked by. It was hard to imagine where they were all going. To restaurants, to work? Around the block and home again? A couple passed by, hand in hand, then a young man with a stroller. I was higher than most of the surrounding houses and could see the tops of the trees in the park I'd sat in that morning, and a distant glimmer of water. Was that the lake? The river? The ocean? I had no idea. I pulled myself back inside and sat on the bed. I felt too dirty to lie down, so for several minutes I just sat there with my hands in my lap. Exhaustion roared in my ears.

There was a tentative knock on the door, almost too quiet to notice.

"Come in," I said, standing up.

"I'm sorry," said Uncle Geoffrey. He poked his head in, but kept most of him in the hall. "I forgot to ask if you want anything."

"Oh, I don't think…"

"But if there's anything you need. There's clean linen in the bathroom, aspirin in the medicine cabinet…" He raised his eyebrows expectantly. His face was red and flustered but pleased. Clearly he wasn't used to guests.

"No," I said, shaking my head. "But thank you. I don't need a thing."

"Then I'll leave you alone." He waved again and was gone.

❧

I spent two weeks with Uncle Geoffrey. Every day passed in almost exactly the same way, from breakfast at the kitchen table each morning to coffee in the front room every night. In between the days stretched twice as long as they did at home. Breakfast itself seemed to last all morning; we ate courses and courses of toast and jam and tea and orange juice, trading sections of the *Picayune*. Uncle Geoffrey and I, it turned out, had a lot in common. We both hated small talk and could go hours without speaking and not even notice. We hated seeing the television on when it was light out. We loved pastries. We quickly became as comfortable with each other as an old married couple, but endlessly polite, and careful to stay out of each other's way.

My habit, after reading the classified section of the paper and circling a few ads, was to wash the breakfast dishes and walk into town. Though it was practically winter at home, the air here was still gentle and predictable; the mornings were cool, the afternoons warm enough to take my jacket off. It didn't rain much, and the sun was out for several hours every day. The walk from Uncle Geoffrey's house to downtown took nearly an hour, but there was no reason to hurry, and there was a lot to see on the way. I stopped in flower shops just to look and at newsstands to read the headlines. There was a neighborhood I especially liked to walk through, where café tables crowded the sidewalks and young men sat in sunglasses, their feet stuck out far enough to trip me.

In town, I was supposed to be filling out job applications and stopping by temp agencies. The second day I was there I applied for a job as a copy shop clerk and for another one in a film store. I told the truth on the applications, which was that I'd spent the last ten years as a babysitter and librarian in a spiritualist colony, because I was sick to death of lying. I couldn't stand the thought of making up a single other thing. Though I had given up my old life, I couldn't yet face making up a new one.

Mostly I walked around and looked. I bought myself little things with Peter's money. There was a shopping center near the river I spent whole days in, buying pretty candles and scarves, notebooks, things to eat. I sat on benches on the pier and watched huge freighters slide by. Sometimes I kept the gifts I bought myself, sometimes I threw them in the garbage, or dropped them in the gutter, disgusted.

One afternoon, drinking strong coffee from a tiny cup at a tiny coffee shop table, I saw someone who looked like Peter. My heart leaped up. He was passing outside, walking with another boy. In the sun his black hair was nearly blue, and he wore heavy, horn-rimmed sunglasses. I got up and leaned against the window, pressing my face to the glass to watch him go. There was something odd about his behind, and his walk seemed a little bouncy for Peter. Still. Was it him? I couldn't tell. My breath steamed the glass, and by the time I'd wiped it away he was gone.

I finished my coffee with shaking fingers. This is how it would always be, I knew. He would never be completely gone, but he would never, ever be with me.

∽⁓

Uncle Geoffrey was getting nervous. Every morning at breakfast, he watched uneasily as I pushed away the classified section of the newspaper and read the funnies instead. He noticed that some days I didn't go into town at all, but stayed in my room, or, sometimes, sat out behind the house in an iron garden chair, reading. "I know you don't have much computer experience," he said to me one morning, trying for nonchalance. "But if you wanted a job in my office I could get you some training. It's not all that hard, and I know you'd just pick it up."

"You don't have to do that." I smiled, partly to let him know I appreciated the gesture and partly because the image of me as a clerk in a law office was a funny one. "I'll find something sooner or later."

"Oh, I know you will."

"If you'd like me to pay for my room and board…"

"Wouldn't hear of it!" he said, throwing up his hands.

But that night I bought groceries and baked a quiche, which Uncle Geoffrey ate with cautious enthusiasm. For dessert we walked to the Donut King. He held the door open for me and insisted on paying, and we sat by the window, watching the sun go down over the city.

My uncle ate his doughnut and wiped his mouth carefully with a paper napkin. "I'm sorry I was never really in touch with you all, over the years," he said.

"Oh, it's okay."

"Your mother never got over our brother leaving, you know. She really worshipped him. I guess I was a little bit jealous." He paused a moment, uneasy, then went on. "He wasn't a very nice person. I know Patsy doesn't remember him that well, but he was awful to our parents. To everyone. He used to ask homely girls out on dates just for kicks, and then not show up. He'd make prank phone calls, tell people they won prizes. He was always happy, happy and cruel. What makes someone be like that? I just have no idea."

He fiddled with his napkin. "He was nice to Patsy, though. I should just keep my mouth shut. Don't tell her I said any of this, will you? I used to wonder if the whole medium business was just her way of trying to get him back, though God knows, Wilson's probably still alive."

"It's all right," I said.

He smiled and shrugged. "Here, I'll get you another doughnut."

He went up to the counter and came back with a coconut one. I could hardly swallow it: my uncle's kindness seemed so unreasonable, it made my throat tighten up. The setting sun glowed in his thin, curly hair, and he looked out at the street, shaking his head at it, like someone who'd never seen a street before.

∾⚬∾

The next afternoon, I came into the house to find my uncle hanging up the phone. I'd been outside most of the day, reading a book on botany, but now the sun was going down and it was getting cold, and my behind hurt from the hard iron chair. I kept my finger in the book to mark my page.

Geoffrey was standing by the telephone table. He hadn't turned the lights on yet, so the hallway was dark and I couldn't make out the expression on his face.

"I just called your mother's house," he said.

For a long moment, I felt that everything must be over. She told him, I thought.

"She wasn't there. I left a message on the machine."

I breathed a secret, relieved sigh and leaned against the paneling. My uncle rubbed his finger along his lips.

"I'm sorry," he said. "I don't mean to tell tales on you or anything. I'm just a little worried—I want things to go well for you. I hoped Patsy—Galina, I mean—could give me some advice."

"I'm fine. Really."

"All right," he said. But he did not look convinced.

❧

We watched television all evening, letting the malicious noise of it fill the room. It depressed me to see the shenanigans of the sitcom characters reflected in Uncle Geoffrey's glasses. His face was worried and sad; his lower lip pooched out and his cheeks were pale. After a while his eyes fluttered shut and his head began to nod. I couldn't bear to sit there any longer while he snored, so I got up and decided to take a walk.

I had my shoes and jacket on and was about to head out the door when the phone rang. It was my mother, I was certain; she would be returning Geoffrey's phone call. I stood there frozen in the hallway, not two feet from the telephone table. I wanted, suddenly and acutely, to hear her voice. I let it ring once more, and then I answered it.

"Hello?"

But it was not my mother. "Naomi," said a man's voice. "This is Officer Peterson."

Horrified, I hung up. Geoffrey came up behind me, shuffling in his slippers. "Who was that?"

I could only shake my head. As I stood there, mute, the phone rang again. I turned and ran out the door.

෨෪ඁ

It was a cool night, breezy, with a moon that reeled in and out of the clouds. I kept running for a few blocks, but soon lost my breath and had to walk. Beneath my feet the sidewalk was broken and bumpy, and it rose and fell sickeningly, like the ocean. *They know, they know, everyone knows what I did.* Officer Peterson must have searched my house, or my mother's house, and found something, perhaps tapping my mother's phone to find out where I was, or maybe my mother herself had told him everything. Anything seemed possible—it seemed possible, even, that the moon could roll out of the sky and crush me. I wanted it to. I wanted everyone who'd ever died to come walking out of the houses I passed and to take me into their arms.

The city at night was not the same as the city in daytime. Seeing it this way, lit from the inside instead of from without, confused and disoriented me, and it wasn't long before I found myself on streets I didn't recognize. Here was a shadowy park with blue streetlights, and there was a house guarded by statues of dogs. It made me think of my grandmother in the last few hours before she died, wandering lost through the city she'd been born in and had once known intimately. Had she felt this way? I ran my hand along an iron fence and imagined it was her hand, her long arm with its loose skin and the veins that wrapped it like ivy. I passed an open window, and the smell of cooking gusted out of it. People crowded by me, overflowing into the street, smelling of alcohol and perfume, laughing. Young men in baseball caps sloshed drinks onto the pavement. Cars roared by. The city spun around me, and inexplicably, my heart began to open.

This, I knew, was how my grandmother felt. Stripped of memory, of her past and her future, she had only what was around her: the weeds growing from cracks in the plaster walls, the litter caught in doorways, the trees reaching over traffic to clutch at each other, her cotton dress, her body. The unburdened heart sees everything. I saw the shapes of leaves and the shapes of shadows of leaves; I saw every doorframe and window ledge. My grandmother was happy the day she died. Stumbling across hot and busy streets, past shops and bars and offices all humming with mysterious activity, my grandmother must have felt real ecstasy—the ecstasy of saints, of ascetics and flagellants when they finally give up their attachments to life. We were wrong to think she suffered.

I'd never in my life felt so happy. I hadn't known my soul was capable of such a feeling! I ran and walked and ran. It was all strange, all new and perfect. And how beautiful it was—neon signs and architecture and things in shop windows, and people with their clothes and hairdos. I wanted it all. All over town, half-memories flew out at me. I thought of dresses I'd owned but couldn't remember how I looked in them, if they itched, or what happened to them. I passed a bar I thought I recognized—had my father taken me here once? I stopped at the door and peered in. It was smoky and at the back was a row of washing machines. The same old familiar bar smell rolled out at me, but I couldn't tell if it was familiar because I remembered it or because all bars have the same smell. He had carried me on his hip and bought me root beer.

And this house—tall and narrow and sad, with shuttered windows and a tiny front lawn of dirt. Or the one next door, with the porch slanting down so sharply that once all my marbles rolled off it and disappeared into the weeds. Hadn't I lived here?

I gripped my elbows and tried to see something I was certain I knew. That banana tree? It would have grown since then.

A car pulled up behind me and a voice called out. "Naomi!"

I turned. It was my uncle Geoffrey, leaning out from the backseat of a police car. His face was stricken and wet.

"Don't run, please!"

I didn't run. I stood, exhausted, as the two officers got out of the car and approached me. One was white and one was black, and they looked like nice men. I put my hands over my face and staggered into them. "I'm sorry," I said over and over. They led me back to the car, and my uncle pulled me into his arms.

"Hush," he said. He took my hands from my face and brushed away my hair. "Hush. It's not your fault. It was her heart. It could have happened at any time. Shh."

I sat up, pushed him away from me. What was he saying? What did he mean?

My mother, he said. My mother was dead. She'd had a heart attack in her kitchen, apparently making breakfast. Hadn't Peterson told me? Isn't that why I'd run off? Nobody had found her for several days, and then no one could find me, until Uncle Geoffrey left a message on her machine.

"It's not possible," I said. "If she was dead, I would know."

My uncle wept and blew his nose. "I'm sorry I called the police. I thought you were going to do something to yourself."

"If she was dead I would know."

But even as I said this, I was beginning to believe that what my uncle was telling me was true. We were in the back of a police car, and my mother was dead. I had stopped being a medium. I would never again be one.

"Is this where I lived?" I asked my uncle. The two officers were standing on the sidewalk, smoking. A mist was gathering over the grass. "Isn't that our old house?"

My uncle shook his head. "No, no. I'm sorry—your family didn't live anywhere near here."

Outside, the police were finishing their cigarettes, dropping them to the ground and stamping on them. In a few minutes the white one came back to the car and poked his head in. "Are y'all ready for a ride home, or what are we going to do here?"

"Home," said Uncle Geoffrey.

They got in and slammed the doors. The one in the driver's seat mumbled something into a radio, started the car, and pulled into the street.

We drove for a while. The city, from the backseat of the police car, looked rather ordinary: block after block of convenience stores and stoplights. I was surprised at how far I'd come. The two police officers were separated from us by a steel mesh that was bolted to the ceiling and sides of the car. I gripped this mesh with my fingers and leaned in close.

"Officers," I said. "I have something to tell you."

epilogue

Eve tempted Adam, and Adam was tempted, and because of this humans have lived ever since in a state of sorry exile from the Garden they believe is home. But some early spiritualists figured out how to get back in. After death, they said, the soul goes to the Summer Land, a place of flowery meadows and soft breezes and magnificent scenery, all created out of the deepest wishes of the dead. Nothing is denied them. If the dead want art, art galleries spring up, and if the dead want fresh, ripe fruit, orchards grow from the mountainsides. There are schools in the Summer Land, but no one has to go. At night, the dead can visit the living, who are free to join their dead loved ones while they sleep. After a lifetime of thwarted desire, the dead can at last indulge it, and thus the very thing that caused our expulsion from the Garden in the first place will lead us back into it.

I think about this sometimes and wonder what my mother's version of the Summer Land might be like. I picture a sumptuous restaurant, linen tablecloths and golden silverware, endless lines of waiters bringing her desserts, bowls of flowers on the table, a new dress for every course. She might never get tired of it. But if she did, there'd be a huge front porch with a wicker chaise longue, and some tall drinks, and books with pretty pictures for her to look through. She could never get enough of prettiness when she was alive.

It's hard to believe in such a place, though. Wouldn't there be conflicts? What if what you wanted didn't want you? What if your greatest desire was to be alive again?

Sometimes I imagine my mother coming back down here, and I wonder what she'd think. I've moved back into her house and have begun to fix it up a little. When I came back after my eighteen months in the Women's Correctional Facility, in Delphi, the place was in terrible shape: the weeds were shoulder high and the paint was entirely gone from the siding. Inside, the linoleum floors were peeling up, spiders had built nests in the curtains, and all the taps leaked, so there was the constant sound of rain. Kids had pelted the house with eggs and broken some windows, and rain and snow came in, and the furniture sagged and wept. I wasn't even sure if the house ought to be lived in anymore, but I had nowhere else to go, and to be perfectly honest, it looked no different from most of the others in Train Line. Things seemed to go from bad to worse while I was gone, but this observation might have been the result of my fresh perspective. The cats ran away when my mother died—Troy says he looked for months and never found them—but they returned a few days after I moved in. I find this miraculous, and a blessing.

For a long time I found it painful to think about my mother, and instead I thought obsessively of Peter, hoping, I think, that I was making it up to him by confessing and by going to jail. Perhaps I did make it up to him, in a way. His bones are now in Oregon, buried alongside his mother's and his father's.

I cannot forget him, but he no longer haunts me.

෴

It was a relief, actually, to be in jail at last. I wore a denim dress with a number on it. It was like being dead, a kind of afterlife in which my only desire was to be left alone—a desire that was granted to me. I worked occasionally, in the cafeteria or as a groundskeeper, but usually I had whole days to do nothing but read. The prison library was a disaster—nothing but self-help books as far as the eye could see—but Troy sometimes sent me books, and so did Dave the Alien, though this stopped suddenly when he met a girl at the video store, had a whirlwind romance, and got married. Ron sent me newsy updates about Train Line, and in particular about Jenny. Her health rallied for a while, then turned suddenly bad again, and she died a few months before I was released. Train Line renamed their children's beach after her.

I got mail from other people, too. People who'd read about the case in the paper wrote to me, some telling me I would burn in hell, others saying that if I repented all would be forgiven. Prisoners at other jails wrote with legal advice. Once I even got a Christmas card from Moira Morton. Enclosed was a holiday letter describing her year: she'd married in the summer, was pregnant already, and she and her new husband were relocating to Arizona, where he would work in aerospace. They were in the process of buying "a beautiful new home at the edge of the desert, where sometimes on nights with a full moon, the mournful howl of coyotes can be heard."

At the bottom she'd scrawled, "Your visions were true." I kept the letter.

❧

Of my two jobs—one at night, cleaning a medical complex, and the other during the day, as a gardener at a nursing home—I prefer my nursing home one. I like being outside and taking breaks on the patio with the old people, and I have discovered I have a knack for pruning and digging and trimming. I like it in the winter, too, when I drive the tiny snowplow up and down the walkways and water the houseplants inside. The cleaning job is also satisfying in its way—I polish chrome and empty trash cans, and I do it efficiently and well. I vacuum, too. I have a way of backing out a door, sweeping over my footsteps as I leave, so it looks like I have never been there.

One morning, I came home from work to find someone sitting on my doorstep. I was quite tired, ready for a bath and a long nap, and did not recognize her for several minutes. She was much taller, for one thing, and for another she was dressed in a bizarre outfit—a cape that dragged on the ground, and a long black dress—but it was Vivian. Her glasses were gone, contacts no doubt, but her curly black hair was the same, as was her skinny, hunched shape.

"Hi," she said, as if she'd just gone round the corner for a carton of milk.

Stunned beyond words, I unlocked the door and pushed it open for her. She went inside, holding up her cape so as not to trip, and I followed.

"Goodness," I said at last. "You've grown up."

"I'll be thirteen in two and a half months."

"Dear God."

Instinctively, I began rummaging around my kitchen, looking for something for Vivian to eat. "Would you like some cheese? I have some crackers, too…"

"Just crackers. I'm vegan now."

I fixed a plate of crackers, put some tea on to boil, and finally sat down to look at her. Though it's nearly impossible to see the future adult in a baby's face, the baby never leaves the adult, and I thought of the first time I saw her, in her high chair, with her rounded forehead and pot-handle eyebrows. These were exactly the same. She hadn't really changed much, though she looked prouder, more angry, and less lost. She also appeared to be wearing eyeliner.

"So," I said. "What are you doing here?"

"I'll leave if you want."

"No, I don't want."

She turned her head and looked around at the kitchen, and the living room beyond. "This house looks different from how I remember."

"I threw a lot of stuff out. And Ron helped me with the walls and floors."

"It looks better."

"Thank you." I got up and poured the tea. "So…"

"I want to be a medium," she blurted suddenly. Her face turned pink.

Oh, my. I stared down at my tea. "Does your mother know you're here, Vivian?"

"Yes. No. She doesn't care. She and my dad got divorced. I mostly live with him. My mother and I fight all the time. I mean, like cats and dogs."

"So, then, does your father know?"

"He lets me have my independence."

"I see."

She was breaking a cracker into little pieces and eating the fragments one at a time, picking them up with the tip of a licked finger. "I've been a Wiccan for two years," she said, "but what I really want is to be a medium. I have to be one. Can't you teach me?"

"You know, Vivian, I haven't been a medium in a long time."

Her mouth twitched. "Is that because you killed that guy?"

"Umm," I said, startled. "Sort of. Not really. It was when my mother died. It was—I don't know—complicated. I shouldn't be telling you this."

"Why not?"

"Oh, Vivian." I sighed painfully. I had a memory of her as a little girl, a toddler, half-asleep on my lap, bumping her head beneath my chin. "I'm glad you came to visit. But I don't know if I can help you."

"You have to help me!" she cried.

"I'm sorry," I said. "I'm tired right now. Can you let me think about it, and come back in a few days?"

"Can I come back tomorrow?"

"No," I said. Then, "Come Friday."

୦ତ

In the days after Vivian's visit, I felt restless, maybe a little dissatisfied. I found myself experimenting with the vacuum cleaner one night in the medical complex: was it quicker to vacuum in crisscrossing diagonals or overlapping stripes? Or perhaps taking sweeping strokes was more efficient, since a certain amount of time was wasted in getting the vacuum cleaner into position… and then I thought, looking out the tinted window at the lights along Lake Wallamee, *Oh, who cares.*

I hadn't missed mediumship before. And I still didn't, really, but there was something about it I *did* miss. I began to think that I probably won't be doing these jobs forever. I hadn't thought I would. I just hadn't thought about it at all.

After work on Friday she was waiting for me, dressed in more or less the same getup, only this time her dress was red. I noticed a three-speed bike leaning up against the fence.

"Did you bicycle all the way from Wallamee?" I couldn't help but picture it—her cape flying out behind her.

"Yes," she said.

"Well, come inside, then."

I made Vivian wait while I changed out of my work clothes and brushed my hair, nervously tugging out the tangles, then I went downstairs and led her to my mother's séance room. This was one room I hadn't changed much; like her room in New Orleans, its walls were velvet, the curtains satin. There was a tiny table and two chairs. The air smelled like dust. Sometimes I just sat in here, thinking about my mother. But lately there was less to think about; I went over and over the same memories, and each time they became less immediate and real, and finally neither particularly pleasurable nor sad.

"Cool room," said Vivian.

I handed her a grocery bag. In it were some of my mother's things: her trumpet, her Ouija, a set of slates for spirit writing, some books. As she took it, I had sudden misgivings. Being a medium would not make her happy. Perhaps it would, in the end, make her unhappier than ever. But I had no way of knowing, I couldn't see the future, so I let it go. "You can have all this, if you want it," I said.

Vivian looked in the bag, her mouth agape. "I do want it," she whispered. "Thank you."

"You're welcome."

She set the bag on the floor, reached into the folds of her cape, and pulled out a notebook. "Sit down," she said.

I sat.

"Now," she said, pulling out a pencil. "Tell me everything you know."

Readers' Guide for
After Life

Discussion Questions

1. What's the significance of the title? Why is it two words—After Life—rather than one—Afterlife? How would that change affect how you thought about the book?

2. Why do you think Ellis describes Train Line and its residents so meticulously? Could this story have taken place anywhere else?

3. How did you feel about Naomi? Is she an unreliable narrator of her own life? Do you think she felt remorse for what she did to Peter Morton? Is she a bad person? Or is she a good person who did a bad thing?

4. How do you think the spiritual elements tie in to the rest of the book?

5. What do you think this novel is about? Is it a mystery? A novel about relationships? Or about mothers and daughters? Is it about our society's fear of death and dying?

Suggestions for Further Reading

If you liked the whydunit aspect of Ellis's novel, try:

What Came Before He Shot Her by Elizabeth George. It's the second half of her mystery novel *With No One As Witness*; George explores the events leading up to the seemingly random murder of a young upper-class woman by a twelve-year-old boy.

If you liked the relationships aspect of *After Life*, try:

Gail Godwin's *A Mother and Two Daughters*, which focuses on the experiences of three richly described women—a mother and her grown daughters—as they try to navigate their lives and their relationships to one another after a traumatic event.

Amy and Isabelle is Elizabeth Strout's first novel, in which she brilliantly describes an often difficult relationship between Isabelle and her sixteen-year-old daughter, which is complicated by the guilt and shame Isabelle feels over her own dicey past.

Ann Patchett's *The Magician's Assistant*, in which she introduces us to Sabine, a woman who discovers after the death of her husband, Parsifal, a terribly talented magician, that he was also excellent at keeping secrets about his past well hidden.

Searching for Caleb by Anne Tyler. It's probably my favorite of all Tyler's novels, mainly because I adore the main character, Justine Peck, a fortune-teller who is much more successful unearthing the past and predicting the future for her clients than for herself.

If you liked the magic realist aspect of *After Life*, try:

Alice Hoffman's *Fortune's Daughter*, in which two women, both suffering from related but not identical losses, meet one another in Southern California during earthquake season, a time when reality can become more than a little bit elastic and anything might happen.

If you liked the psychological suspense aspect of *After Life*, try:

Paul Auster's *Invisible*, a beautifully written novel about the complex relationship between three characters (two men and a woman), in which the author examines the intricacies of memory and desire.

A Dark-Adapted Eye by Barbara Vine, the first of Vine's extremely unsettling psychological thrillers. Here she explores the darkness at the heart of the Hillyard family, a darkness that culminated with one of its members being hanged for murder. It won the 1986 Edgar Award for best mystery.

Rhian Ellis told me in an e-mail that anyone who enjoyed *After Life* will definitely also love Shirley Jackson's deliciously creepy novels. I completely agree. Here are the two with which I'd begin my reading of Jackson:

Jackson's third novel, *The Bird's Nest*, is likely to send a frisson of unease down the spine of any reader as she explores the life of Elizabeth Richmond, a young woman whose mind has broken into four very different personalities.

We Have Always Lived in the Castle, Jackson's final novel, describes the surreal and isolated existence of Merricat and her older sister Constance (who have always lived in the castle) and how their lives are shaken first by a series of murders in their family and then—more seriously—by the arrival of a fortune-hunting relative.

If you'd like to read about the real Train Line, try:

Lily Dale: The True Story of the Town That Talks to the Dead. Christine Wicker, who writes about religion for the *Dallas Morning News*, visited the town of Lily Dale, New York, to meet and talk with the people who made their home there and the tourists who visited it. Not only did Wicker get a sense of the town itself, but she also explored deeper issues such as the meaning of faith and the human need for comfort in the face of grief.

About the Author

Rhian Ellis grew up in Western New York State. She went to Oberlin College and the University of Montana, and she now lives in Ithaca, New York, with her husband, the writer J. Robert Lennon, their two sons, and many chickens.

About Nancy Pearl

 Nancy Pearl is a librarian and life-long reader. She regularly comments on books on National Public Radio's *Morning Edition.* Her books include 2003's *Book Lust: Recommended Reading for Every Mood, Moment and Reason;* 2005's *More Book Lust: 1,000 New Reading Recommendations for Every Mood, Moment and Reason; Book Crush: For Kids and Teens: Recommended Reading for Every Mood, Moment, and Interest,* published in 2007; and 2010's *Book Lust To Go: Recommended Reading for Travelers, Vagabonds, and Dreamers.*

Among her many awards and honors are the 2011 Librarian of the Year Award from *Library Journal;* the 2011 Lifetime Achievement Award from the Pacific Northwest Booksellers Association; the 2010 Margaret E. Monroe Award from the Reference and Users Services Association of the American Library Association; and the 2004 Women's National Book Association Award, given to "a living American woman who … has done meritorious work in the world of books beyond the duties or responsibilities of her profession or occupation."

About Book Lust Rediscoveries

Book Lust Rediscoveries is a series devoted to reprinting some of the best (and now out of print) novels originally published between 1960-2000. Each book is personally selected by Nancy Pearl and includes an introduction by her, as well as discussion questions for book groups and a list of recommended further reading.